VALENTINE HEARTS

JOSIE RIVIERA

Valentine Hearts

INTRODUCTION

To keep up on newly released ebooks, paperbacks, Large Print Paperbacks, audiobooks, as well as exclusive sales, I invite you to sign up for Josie's Newsletter today.

As a thank you, I'll send you a Free PDF ... The Beauty Of ...

Josie's Newsletter

5 STAR READER REVIEWS

Amazon Review by Teresa
5.0 out of 5 stars

"All the books in this set are wonderful. The characters face issues brought on by childhood distresses and adult tragedies. Whether dealing with abandonment issues, self-image issues, or life in general, the characters grow together in love and unity. Watching a couple fall in love and deal with the difficulties they face is heartwarming. To me, these books are a mix of Hallmark movies and the old Harlequin Presents books I read as a teenager. Those books started me on my journey of loving romance novels, and this set does not disappoint."

Amazon Review by A. Ferri
5.0 out of 5 stars

"I just finished reading 1-800-Cupid and this is a book that just makes you feel good when you get through reading it. The way it is written you can see it in your mind. This would make a great Hallmark movie. It has a great sounding recipe at the end."

Amazon Review by G. Johnson
5.0 out of 5 stars

"A Valentine to Cherish is a beautiful story of being accepted as you and finally finding a love you have been missing. Joseph, a handsome singer, just needs to convince Scarlett she is beautiful and worthy to be loved. That's what we all want a place to be accepted and Cherish,South Carolina just may be the place. All of the stories are inspirational and sweet."

Amazon Review by J. Tomalis

"A delightful short and sweet story just right for Valentines Day! The characters are well developed and the scenes are vividly described. Sally meets Oliver when she goes to pick up a specialty chocolate order at his diner where it is stranded. She quickly sees how he treats all of his customers and the joy he has in running his business. Can these two have a second chance for love?"

DEAR FRIENDS

A heartwarming story is the hallmark of a special Valentine's Day. Savor the magic with four joyful, sweet contemporary and inspirational romances in **Valentine Hearts**.

I Love You More

A billionaire and a single mother have more in common than they know.

1-800-CUPID

Can two broken hearts find a place to call home?

A Valentine To Cherish (Inspirational)

Valentine's Day is all about love. And God has a special plan for a small-town woman and a road-weary singer.

A CHOCOLATE-BOX VALENTINE

It's your last love who truly matters.

JOSIE RIVIERA

I Love You More

PRAISE AND AWARDS

USA TODAY bestselling author

CHAPTER 1

*A*nastasia grimaced at what her friend, Jaclyn, was saying as they walked to Jaclyn's car after a quick lunch.

"You needed to get away from the cold and come to Charleston," Jaclyn began. "After the cancer scare and your divorce ..."

Anastasia took a deep breath. "It was difficult leaving Soo-Min with my ex and his newest flame."

"I can't believe Justin actually married Eliza. She's one of his students and half his age."

Anastasia shrugged, hoping the gesture covered her sadness. Despite applying sunscreen, she adjusted the wide-brimmed straw hat to protect herself from the sun. Then she averted her face to hide her tears.

"Valentine's Day in Charleston means romance. February fourteenth will arrive in two weeks and the streets will be filled with love and chocolate-covered strawberries and horse-drawn carriages carrying good-looking men," Jaclyn said with a smile.

"Thanks for setting up a free lawyer consultation for me."

Anastasia lifted her travel bag over her shoulder and couldn't help a grin at her friend's matchmaking attempts. She'd need a city overflowing with fragrant red roses and Sea Salt caramels to distract her from her lack of romance back in Vermont. "You could hand out 'I Love Charleston' badges because you like it here so much."

"I love Carolina blue skies and cloudless days." Jaclyn shaded her eyes from the afternoon sun. "However, I think they're predicting rain for tonight."

"Then those good-looking men in their horse-drawn carriages will get drenched." Anastasia regarded a flower shop window overflowing with candy-red roses. Her grin faded as she reflected on her morning. Feigning a polite smile she hadn't felt, she'd handed over her precious four-year-old daughter to the man she'd once assumed she'd be married to forever. Now she believed his parenting skills were inadequate.

Although the textbook family she'd always wanted was gone, her priority was her daughter, and her determination to give Soo-Min a picture-perfect life remained firm.

"Your ex acts as if he's the next Shakespeare, but beneath that tweed blazer—"

"Is the father of my little girl," Anastasia said.

"He's the adoptive father."

Anastasia felt her face heat as she met Jaclyn's pale-blue gaze. "Whether a child is natural or adopted, the child is yours to love. In fact, you love that child more."

"I'm sorry. You're right. I've always considered my adoptive parents to be my true parents."

Anastasia gave her friend a quick hug. "Apology accepted. If Soo-Min wasn't mixed up in Justin's mid-life crisis, I wouldn't care what he did or whom he married."

Jaclyn tucked a strand of auburn hair behind her multipierced ear. "The custody dispute won't be easy. Justin is a community college professor and you're ..."

"A cancer survivor? Yes, and stronger because of the ordeal." *And fortunate to be alive.* "Is your bungalow far from here?"

"The house is in an oceanfront community a few miles across the bridge."

Anastasia easily kept up with her friend's pace. "Aren't you a struggling travel agent?"

Jaclyn laughed. "Yes." She pointed to a metallic-red smart car parked illegally and ducked into the driver's seat. "Get in. Oh, and I probably should've told you sooner, but it's not mine."

"Don't tell me you stole the car."

Jaclyn shook her head. "Not the car. The oceanfront house, and I didn't steal that, either. You remember my older brother, Luciano, don't you?"

An unexpected ache settled in Anastasia's throat. There wasn't a woman on the planet who wouldn't remember Luciano.

CHAPTER 2

*A*nastasia's ears burned remembering the embarrassing crush she'd had on Luciano when she was in her teens. He'd arrive home from his Ivy League college on long weekends all dark good looks and chiseled features and a different girl on each arm. His Italian name had only added to his broad-shouldered charisma. Anastasia had developed an obsession for him and had followed him around like a giddy schoolgirl. Which, in her defense, she had been. They'd spent many evenings on his back porch after his boxing matches, talking and joking, although she'd done most of the talking while he'd offered encouragement and good-natured jokes.

"What's he doing in Charleston?" Anastasia asked.

"He relocated his software company here because he wanted to be near family," Jaclyn said. "He'll be thirty-five on Valentine's Day. He didn't want to celebrate his birthday alone, although he'd never admit it."

"I'm surprised he never married."

Jaclyn turned the corner so quickly that Anastasia held tightly to her seat. "He did, but he lost his wife to lung cancer several years ago." Jaclyn stopped at the guard gate of an exclusive community and rolled down the window. "Jaclyn Donati," she said, then turned to Anastasia. "Fate and my adoptive parents must've been playing a joke on me. I'm the Irish girl with a strawberries and cream complexion and the last name Donati."

Anastasia smiled, then winced. Soo-Min was from South Korea, and she'd never look like either Anastasia nor Justin. Soo-Min was petite, her dark eyes perfect and slanted, her coal-black hair spiking wildly around her round face.

Anastasia pulled the car visor down and regarded her own pallid complexion, dotted with freckles, in the mirror. Gone were the days of slathering baby oil on her skin to achieve a golden-brown tan. She lifted her bangs to regard the small scar from the melanoma surgery on her forehead, then quickly pushed her bangs down to cover the scar.

"If you ever see a suspicious spot on your skin, call me," Dr. Leskin, her family doctor, had advised. "In the meantime, stay out of the sun for the rest of your life." She glanced at the small mole near her wrist and pulled down the sleeve of her cardigan to cover it. That mole didn't count. She'd had it for years.

Jaclyn started down a long driveway lined with hedges to a private courtyard. She parked and pointed to an imposing three-level mansion resembling an Italian villa. "Here we are, complete with maids' quarters. Luciano won't be back for hours. He gets so caught up in work that I need to remind him to take a breath and relax. That's why he's letting me stay with him while my bungalow is being refurbished. I'm his personal guru, and he can concentrate on being the math genius."

Jaclyn opened the large wooden double doors, and Anastasia stepped into the marble foyer. She set down her travel bag in the airy, circular hallway and drew an admiring breath. The living room floor-to-ceiling bay window provided a spectacular view of the Atlantic Ocean.

"The designer called this an open floor concept." Jaclyn flicked on an overhead shimmering crystal chandelier. "After all his work and sacrificing, this house is Luciano's reward. He loves beautiful things."

A tall, handsome man stepped into the living room and gave a lazy smile. "Are you speaking for me again, Jaclyn?"

Luciano. Anastasia tried not to react although her heart raced faster. His charcoal-gray polo shirt fit snugly around his muscular arms, his dress pants fit as if tailor-made. He was so tall he could've been a basketball star. In fact, she remembered he'd been offered a basketball scholarship but had turned it down. He'd preferred lifting weights and training at the boxing gym.

A golden retriever, whose muzzle was entirely gray, trotted beside Luciano.

Jaclyn stooped to pet the dog. "This is Lady."

Anastasia bent and stroked the dog's head. "She's sweet."

"And this is my brother." Jaclyn regarded Luciano. "You were supposed to be working at your office building in town."

"The weather service is calling for a storm so I decided to work from home this afternoon." He arched a dark brow. "Do we have company?"

Jaclyn stood. "You remember Anastasia, my good friend from high school?"

"He wouldn't remember—" Anastasia began. The dog nuzzled against her legs, gentle and welcoming. She stroked Lady's oversized floppy ears.

"*Si*, of course I remember you." Luciano's dark eyes warmed, intelligent and assessing. His rich chocolate-brown hair needed combing. "My sister's right. I love beautiful things." His admiring glance assessed Anastasia boldly.

She smoothed her skirt and stepped back. His slight Italian accent would forever make her weak in the knees. His handsome face sported the aristocratic features she'd remembered, and his nose listed slightly to the right as a result of the break he'd suffered from a boxing match.

"You always knew how to compliment a woman, whether you meant it or not," she said.

She waited for his rejoinder and was greeted with a broad grin instead. "Somewhere inside, I must've inherited the old Italian ways."

"Mom was Italian, too," Jaclyn reminded him.

Slight lines creased his forehead. "I'm referring to my real mother, not my adoptive one."

"Your real mother is the woman who raised you," Jaclyn said.

Anastasia sighed a little too loudly. She didn't want to be in the middle of an adoption dispute. "Where do you want me to put my things?"

"Will she be staying here?" Luciano asked no one in particular.

"If I'm a bother, I'll stay elsewhere." Anastasia bristled. "I don't need you to entertain me."

"Then you have changed." He smiled and the creases on his forehead disappeared.

There it was, that relaxed demeanor, the bald needling. Yet, simmering just below the surface, she knew he succeeded in keeping his true feelings carefully restrained.

Jaclyn glared at him. "Umm, a little rude, big brother, don't you think? I told you this morning before you rushed off that Anastasia would be spending the week with us in Charleston. She's meeting with Sam regarding a family court dispute because of her recent divorce."

"I apologize. I've had a lot on my mind and must've been preoccupied. Old friends are always welcome in my home."

"Or I can stay in Mount Pleasant," Anastasia offered. "Aunt Irina and Uncle Filipp retired there a few years ago, and they're expecting me to visit this week. They never had children and don't receive much company. I'll call them later to let them know I arrived safely."

"My bungalow is near Mount Pleasant so you can visit them when you check out my home renovations," Jaclyn said. "You don't need a week listening to your aunt extol the virtues of your wonderful mother, when we all know it wasn't true."

"If you remember, Anastasia's mother worked at the same hydraulic factory that I did," Luciano said. "We once compared notes on how much we disliked the harsh environment and hazardous working conditions."

Anastasia swallowed. Her mother's long hours. Factory work. She shook her head and held up a hand. Her lonesome childhood was a time she'd chosen to forget.

"I'll probably leave Charleston earlier than I planned, anyway," she said.

She was missing Soo-Min already, and she'd only been gone from Vermont a few hours. Perhaps she could catch an evening flight back and convince Justin to allow her to take Soo-Min for the night. Her daughter had seemed feverish when Anastasia had dropped her off. A bedtime snack of whole grain crackers and clear juice would help her sleep better. She could meet with Sam later in the week, when Soo-Min was feeling better.

Anastasia picked up her bag, intending to head for the door.

Before she took two steps, Luciano reached her and lightly touched her arm. "Please stay."

That deep voice. Guarded, but oh-so-smooth. Up close, she noticed dark circles under his eyes.

"Okay." She nodded and offered a brief smile.

She was here. She might as well stay.

Jaclyn pointed to an arched circular staircase. "The guest bedroom is upstairs on the right."

"Good. That's settled. You're staying and I'll retreat to my office." Luciano dropped his hand. "My investors are flying in from Europe tomorrow morning for the annual board meeting."

ANASTASIA'S BEDROOM was adjacent to a balcony overlooking the ocean. After she unpacked, she showered and chose a long, printed blue jersey sundress with matching sandals. The fabric hung loosely around her thin frame, reflecting the weight loss she'd suffered as a result of her cancer treatment. Dr. Leskin had assured her that muscle loss, exhaustion and lack of appetite was normal. She wore a maxi dress to cover the thick scar on her thigh from her excisional surgery. Pulling her shoulder length hair into a messy bun, she concealed the scar on her forehead with side-swept bangs.

She grabbed her phone, opened the sliding glass doors, and stepped onto the balcony. The sea air, tangy salt and seaweed, teased her nostrils. Stretching out her legs on the chaise lounge, she plugged her phone into the wall socket and punched in her ex-husband's number. Frowning, she scratched the small mole near her wrist. The mole had swollen.

Jaclyn knocked on the sliding glass doors. "I'm off to the market for fresh salmon and rosemary, and I'll pick up Liz. She and Sam are siblings and partners in their family's law firm. Luciano's offered to cook dinner because I think he's feeling guilty for his earlier rudeness. He needs a break from that software project, but he hopes to hit the Forbes list if he can convince the overseas investors to buy in. Can you believe there's a list for billionaires?"

Anastasia stopped in mid dial. "Luciano's a billionaire?"

Jaclyn shook her head. "Not yet, but give my ambitious brother time and he will be." She checked her watch. "It's four o'clock and I'll be back in two hours."

When the door closed, Anastasia slid off her sandals and redialed her ex.

Justin answered on the second ring. "How was your flight?"

"What a difference four hours makes," she said. "Ten inches of snow when I left Stowe and now I'm admiring the Atlantic Ocean." *Enough small talk.* "How's Soo-Min?"

"Eliza and Soo-Min are outside playing in the snow. Wait. Eliza just came in."

A loud kiss was heard through the phone line.

"Hello, Anastasia," Eliza said. "It's freezing here."

"Is Soo-Min outside by herself?"

"Yes. Don't worry, the yard is fenced in and I can see her from the window. She loves the snow, and we had the best snowball fight. I let her win, of course." Eliza giggled at her own remark.

Anastasia gripped the phone tighter. Eliza was the reason that Anastasia's marriage had failed. Although, if she were honest with herself, Eliza was the last of her ex's several affairs that had foretold an ended marriage years before.

"I told you this morning that Soo-Min felt feverish. She shouldn't be outside on such a cold day." Anastasia swallowed past the tightness in her throat.

"Don't be so uptight all the time." Eliza covered the mouthpiece of the phone for a moment and whispered something to Justin. "Can you call back? We're ordering Asian food."

"Asian food might upset her stomach. The pediatrician recommends chicken soup."

"We'll order egg drop soup," Eliza said. "It's Korean, and Soo-Min will like it."

Anastasia took a deep breath. Eliza's immaturity had shown itself in neglect for Soo-Min one too many times. Through family mediation after an initial dispute, Anastasia had agreed to amicable joint custody. Up until now she'd had no choice but to comply, but that agreement was soon to be modified. "FYI, egg drop soup is Chinese cuisine," she said.

"I'll make a note of it."

"I'll call back at six."

"Make it seven," Eliza said.

"Of course." Anastasia's voice choked as she hung up the phone. Wait. She pressed redial. She'd forgotten to tell Eliza that Soo-Min was allergic to eggs. Weren't there eggs in egg drop soup?

Firmly, she shook her head and let the cell phone slide to the balcony floor. Justin would accuse her of being a helicopter parent if she called back.

She collapsed on the chair, feeling broken. Just the thought of Soo-Min spending winter break with Justin and Eliza was bad enough. Physically leaving her daughter in their neglectful care was worse. A small sob escaped her and she put her head in her hands.

Sometimes she wanted to protect her daughter so much she could hardly breathe.

CHAPTER 3

*L*uciano strode up the stairs to the second-floor guest bedroom. He entered and crossed Anastasia's room to the balcony. Then he stared at the beautiful woman curled up and asleep on a chaise lounge. "Wake up. It's raining and you're getting soaked."

Anastasia jerked to a sitting position and stared up at him. He'd forgotten she had the most exquisite eyes, deep-set and round, a piercing, smoky blue-gray.

"Sorry, I must've dozed." She rubbed her eyes and shrugged apologetically. "I'm so tired lately that I fall asleep during the day without warning." Her pale-blue sundress had ridden up her legs, revealing a shapely calf and a thick scar along her thigh. She sprang from the lounge chair and smoothed her wrinkled dress. The hair from a disheveled bun framed honey-brown wisps of curls around her face.

"We both have sleep disorders," he said. "I don't sleep at night from insomnia, and you have narcolepsy."

She pressed her lips together. "It's fatigue, not narcolepsy."

"My mistake." He gestured to the heavy rain saturating

the beach. "Nothing like a restful vacation in a perfect climate to put things in perspective. At least, that's what my sister tells me."

"This isn't a vacation."

He rubbed his forehead. "Right. You're here on business. If you want a lawyer who'll win your case and wring the most money out of your ex, then Sam's the right person. Just ask him how many cases he's won and he'll talk for hours."

"I'm not seeking counsel for additional money." She stood straighter. "Sam's not ethical?"

Luciano hesitated and waved his hand as if it didn't matter. "He's supposed to be one of the best. He's certainly my sister's man of the hour."

An avalanche of sideways rain blew at them. He bent to retrieve her phone and unplugged it from the wall socket. Then he picked up her drenched leather sandals, handed them to her and grinned. "Let's go inside before we're electrocuted."

She grinned back at him. "You really get a charge out of your own humor."

"Clever response," he said. "Although you should've dissolved with laughter because my remark was funnier."

She reached for her phone. "What time is it?"

"Six o'clock."

"I need to call my ex at seven."

He frowned. "You have plenty of time."

"Jaclyn hasn't returned from the market?"

"Many people are getting off work and trying to drive over the bridge to the mainland, so traffic might be backed up." He closed the sliding door behind them and strode to her private bathroom. Returning, he handed her a plush towel. "Dry off your sandals before they're ruined. Your hair seems damp, too." He reached out a hand and patted her hair. "I like your hair pulled back."

A sociable pat. After all, she was an old friend.

"You're welcome to explore the house, as I'll be working on my project a couple of more hours," he added." I don't want to restrict you to only your bedroom while you're visiting me."

Brilliant, just brilliant. You haven't seen this woman in sixteen years and you're reverting to what you did back then. Shameless flirting.

She was always such a good sport. Even at sixteen, she'd had a freshness about her, an intelligence beyond her years, and he'd enjoyed their hours of endless bantering.

"Thanks for the towel." She dried off her hair and glanced toward the balcony. "I've never seen the ocean before and wanted to walk on the beach later. I've heard that the sound of waves is therapeutic."

"It's supposed to pour all night." He gave a short nod at the rain pounding against the balcony doors. "Wait until morning for your therapy."

A rueful smile lit her eyes. "I've waited all my life. I suppose I can wait another day."

A FEW MINUTES LATER, she padded barefoot into the kitchen.

"There's a threat of a thunderstorm," Luciano called from where he sat in his favorite leather chair in the living room. He'd clicked the radio to a classical station, and a Mozart piano sonata played softly from the home theater system. The golden retriever sat on the floor with her head cuddled in Luciano's lap.

Anastasia stopped in mid-step. "Do you make it a habit of appearing and disappearing? I thought you were working in your office."

"I was. I am. The dog kept barking and I assumed she needed a walk outside. Then I was distracted because I enjoy watching rainstorms." He glanced at the dog. "Lady doesn't like them, but she'll go wherever I go."

Anastasia regarded the floor-to-ceiling bay window and low gray clouds beyond. "Storms used to frighten me. When I was younger, I hid in a closet so I wouldn't see the lightning."

"You're not hiding in a closet now."

"There's no lightning." She offered a playful grin. Her luminous eyes gleamed as she stepped into the living room. "I realized that sitting in a dark closet by myself was more frightening than the actual storm." She rubbed the back of her neck, her grin wavered. "Now I've learned how to confront my fears, at least this fear, anyway."

She set her phone on the coffee table, then patted the dog. "I need to call my ex at seven."

"So you've mentioned," Luciano said dryly. "And Jaclyn phoned again. I told her to notify me when she arrived at Liz's house and then to stay indoors and wait out the rainstorm."

Anastasia nodded in that thoughtful way of hers. She'd always been so pensive. And charming. And affectionate. His adoptive parents had described her as "a hugger," whereas he was "standoffish and didn't allow anyone too close."

It's called personal space and people should respect it.

He lifted the beer he'd been holding. "Can I get you something to drink?"

She pressed her lips together and shook her head. "I'll see what you have, thanks." She padded to a corner cabinet stocked with beer and juices. She poured herself a glass of purple grape juice, then stepped back into the living room. Willowy thin, she moved with effortless grace.

She situated herself on the sofa and slanted a smile to him. His gaze dropped to her juice glass, then drifted to her face for a long moment. He wasn't surprised that she'd become an alluring, strikingly beautiful woman. She'd been an effortless beauty in her teens with her glossy honey-brown hair falling to her waist in a ponytail. And she'd never worn a drop of makeup.

She picked up a buttery-soft, red leather journal on his coffee table. "This is beautiful."

"It's from Italy."

"May I peek inside?"

He shrugged nonchalantly. "Suit yourself, it's empty."

She leafed through the blank journal and stopped at the last page. "Almost empty," she corrected. "There are some tiny words written in ... Italian? *Che Sara Sara.* What does it mean?"

"Whatever will be, will be."

She nodded. "From the song. 'The future's not ours ...,'" she sang.

"Che Sara Sara." Luciano chimed in for the ending.

"Who's it from?"

"My mother. This journal is the only memento I have from her. She told me to write in it every day."

She set the journal on the coffee table. "You obviously disobeyed your mother."

"There was nothing to write. I was a small child, and it was a scary time for me. When I arrived in America my adoptive parents tried ..." He turned to the window. The ocean, driven by a violent wind, seemed to connect with a bleak, leaden sky. Thunder rumbled from the distance. As if taking her cue from the storm, the dog huddled in a spot beneath the coffee table. The weatherman interrupted Mozart to upgrade the thunderstorm to a tropical depression.

Luciano turned back to her and raised his beer. "A toast to healthy living, Anastasia. At least for you."

"When you trained for your boxing matches, you ate lean meat, drank gallons of water and ate very healthy."

He shrugged. "I'm not a boxer anymore."

She took a sip of grape juice. Her smile was strained. "In response to your toast, Dr. Leskin advised me not to drink alcohol, and I'm following his orders."

His brows rose. *Why was she seeing a doctor*? She didn't offer an explanation. He didn't ask. He wanted to, but he didn't. He didn't know her that well. He knew her too well.

She tucked her dress discreetly around her model-perfect form, her gaze fixed on the ocean. "I imagine surfing the high waves would be fun."

"Surfing would certainly be an adventure." He leaned back in his chair. He'd always felt content when she was nearby. She exuded a cheerfulness he rarely felt.

"You were an excellent swimmer," he said. "I used to call you a mermaid."

She flicked him a glance and nodded. "College scouts from my dream university attended my last high school swim meet. They were offering a full scholarship."

He shifted. "I'd heard you waitressed after high school."

Her long black lashes swept up. "I'd worked to save for college. Then I studied to become a teacher because I love children." She avoided his gaze. "You'd graduated from Yale and had moved away by then."

He tapped his fingers together. "Were you ever offered that scholarship?"

But he knew. God help him, he already knew.

She shook her head. "My mother didn't arrive home on time to drive me to the swim meet that day. She said she was working, although she always said that. It doesn't matter anymore."

"It *does* matter." He wanted to cross the room and take her hands in his. He wanted to explain how he'd tried to take her mother's eighteen-hour shift at work that day so she could leave early, but their boss had taken a long smoke break. When the boss had returned, he'd refused Luciano's request.

"Congratulations on *your* success, though," Anastasia was saying. "I always thought of you as a Greek god who could accomplish anything."

He hesitated. "I'm not where I want to be yet. I'll let you know when I've arrived."

"I'd say you're already there. You definitely made the right choice pursuing math rather than boxing." She pointed to the wide screen television placed over the mantelpiece of the gas fireplace, then swept out her hand. "Now you own a three story oceanfront villa complete with maids' quarters."

"And no maids." He waved off the compliment. "I'm sure your place in Vermont is nice."

"It's quiet. If you remember, the town has fewer than five thousand people." She chewed her full lips, then smiled too quickly.

The weatherman interrupted Mozart again, this time to upgrade the storm to a tropical disturbance. As if on cue, a clap of thunder vibrated from the distance.

Luciano took a long pull of his beer. He should check to be sure that all the windows and doors were closed and rain wasn't getting inside. Instead, he leaned back in his chair and fingered the bottle, enjoying her presence.

"You really get a charge out of your own humor," she'd quipped. He smiled inwardly.

"Now all you need to complete your magnificent villa is an oversized crystal vase brimming with candy-red roses," she was saying. "I saw a wonderful display today in one of the shop windows in town."

"Do you like roses?"

Their gazes met and her eyes welled with tears. "All women like roses."

He hadn't expected her to cry because they were discussing roses. He set down his beer and looked away. He didn't deal well with weepy women.

"Our lives are made up of different chapters," he offered. Adeptly, he'd changed the subject.

She lifted a well-shaped brow.

"You seem to be in the middle of a rough one," he added solemnly.

"Very rough, actually." Thick black lashes framed her beautiful eyes. Her cheekbones were high, her porcelain skin had a dream-like quality. He'd always found her stunning and had been amused, then flattered, when he'd realized she'd had a crush on him when she was in her teens. She'd trailed him everywhere, laughing at his sardonic jokes, the banter between them refreshingly exhilarating. She'd always 'gotten' his humor; their personalities had connected.

However, she'd been a high school sophomore while he was a college sophomore. And he wouldn't permit himself to take the relationship any further.

Now he was a grown man and she was a grown woman, and his pulse stirred as he took in her perfect profile. Small, turned-up nose, and pale cheeks contrasted with the smokiness of her eyes. He'd never seen her that pale. She'd always sported a glowing-bronze tan because she'd spent hours in the pool during the summer. That span of freckles, which she'd always hated, was ever present on her cheeks, but now there was a slight scar along her hairline.

He rested his elbows on his knees and leaned forward. "Have you been ill?" Inwardly, he shook his head. He shouldn't have asked. *Too intrusive.*

But he knew her well.

He'd also learned to distance himself from others, especially sick others. The reflexive denial that a loved one could get sick and he couldn't do anything about it forever haunted him. He couldn't bear the thought of losing anyone else.

Anastasia granted him an amused look. "Luciano, where is your well-honed charisma? To ask a woman if she's been ill isn't flattering."

"I remember you as a vivacious, optimistic young woman with flushed cheeks who was never farther than a few feet away from me."

He expected her to smile, but her face remained impassive. "I experienced a cancer scare recently that ended up being melanoma in the early stages, and, thankfully, it was treatable."

"Perhaps you spent too many hours in the sun when you were a teenager. Your freckles used to turn red and burn."

Her eyes widened to defiance. "Do you think I'm some kind of idiot and should've known better?" She shook her head. "I remember when someone would get sick, you'd disappear from the room."

He returned her gaze and eyed her heated features. "Blame it on memories of an Italian hospital where I was forced to sit on a hard plastic chair and wait for news about my sick mother. I tried not to breathe in because the smell of urine and brown disinfectants was so strong I gagged. I waited hours before I was told she'd died the night before. Ever since, I've never liked feeling powerless."

His wife had also died unexpectedly. And there had been nothing he'd been able to do to prevent her death.

He sighed heavily, shrugged, then said aloud, "So there's your answer."

"I'm sorry," she said quietly. "I didn't know about your birth mother."

"No one else knows, not even Jaclyn." He motioned to the window. Tumultuous waves slammed the shoreline. "This storm has put me in a pensive mood. You were such a good friend and really listened to me when we were younger. Thanks for listening again."

"Perhaps this feeling of powerlessness is a fear you need to overcome, the way I overcame my fear of storms," she said.

"Perhaps." He gave her a meaningful look. "But you were a tanning goddess."

"Oh, for heaven's sake." She jerked to her feet. "I trained in the pool to shave seconds off my swimming times."

"I don't mean to offend you. In fact, I applaud your diligence."

"I see." She plunked her hands on her hips. "I was fifteen years old. Next time I'll know better and apply sunscreen." She went for her juice glass on the coffee table. It slipped from her grasp and spilled to the floor and the grape blush stained his pearl-white carpet.

"I'm sorry." She bent to pick up the glass. "I'll clean the mess."

"I'll hire a professional carpet cleaner tomorrow."

"No, I'll try to clean it," she said.

He raised a hand dismissively. "Don't bother."

She glared at him. "You know best." She grabbed her phone and whirled from the room.

CHAPTER 4

*S*he hadn't reached the kitchen when thunder and lightning sizzled together. The brightest light she'd ever seen flashed from the living room window, followed by a loud bang. Lady panted noisily. Luciano knelt on the plush carpet, whispering softly to the dog.

The house went dark.

Somewhere in the house, fire alarms shrieked. Anastasia sniffed. The air smelled odd.

She dropped her cell phone on the counter and raced into the living room.

"There's smoke coming from the hallway!" Luciano shouted. He bolted from the living room and Anastasia followed closely at his heels. As they raced into his office, sparks jumped from a laptop computer sitting on a richly carved mahogany desk. He grabbed a wet towel from an adjacent bathroom to smother the flame, then shook his computer and attempted to restart it. The computer didn't respond.

He brought a shaky hand to his forehead. "All my work," he mumbled.

She raised her eyebrows. "You didn't back up your computer files? Jaclyn mentioned you were working on some important project for weeks."

"Months."

Wind rattled the windows. He stared outside and didn't answer. The seconds ticked by before he turned to her. "My computer was connected to a power surger, but I didn't anticipate the house being struck by lightning. The weather service merely predicted a fast-moving thunderstorm."

"That was upgraded to a tropical disturbance, remember?" She whirled around. "I'd better get my cell phone." She rushed into the living room, attempting to switch on several lamps with a click. The air was flooded with the odor of charred wires. The sixty-inch-wide screen television whirred strangely, then blacked out.

Another bolt of ear-splitting lightning connected with the ocean. She raced to the kitchen, grabbed her cell phone and punched in Justin's number.

Luciano entered the living room holding his laptop. Lady whined beneath the coffee table.

Anastasia stared at the blank screen of her cell phone and set it on the counter as a cold shudder went through her. "The phone's dead."

"The cell towers must've been knocked out by the lightning." Luciano pulled on a canvas field jacket and slid open glass doors leading to the outdoor deck. "I'll check if there's any outside damage."

"I'll go with you."

"Okay. Leave the dog inside."

She scurried upstairs to her bedroom and grabbed a long cream-colored cardigan sweater and canvas slip-on shoes. She raced downstairs and slid the door shut behind her.

Luciano's lavish concrete deck sported a dangerously overflowing hot tub and magnificent concrete urns filled with drenched flowers. Storm sirens wailed, adding to the chaos of dogs barking and ear-piercing fire alarms. Weighty rain pelted her cheeks. Shivering, she rubbed her arms and glanced toward the sand.

Something was happening to the shoreline, as if the waves sought to engulf every expensive home lining the ocean. A wind-borne sign crashed into a neighbor's gazebo.

A strange whoosh, whoosh filled the air.

Luciano assessed the sky and grabbed her hand. "This community hasn't experienced coastal flooding in years, and there's no time to board the windows. I'll leash the dog. We're getting off this island."

Her stomach roiled. With cold fingers, she touched his arm. "My purse. All my belongings—"

"Anastasia, the wind is picking up. I have things I want to save, too, but there's no time. Soon we'll be in the middle of a hurricane, and your cell phone will be the least of your concerns." He dropped her hand, slid open the glass door and quickly leashed the dog.

Lightning splintered through ominous black clouds, followed by a rolling boom. The roar of the wind shook the house.

"What's happening?" Icy panic strangled her voice. She felt chilled. She was sweating. She needed to talk with Soo-Min, her precious child. There was so much to say. If anything happened, she'd never have the opportunity.

Luciano returned within seconds and squeezed her hand. "I'll keep you safe," he said in a disturbingly calm tone. "You can call your ex when we reach the mainland."

"It'll only take a few seconds to run back into your house and—" She yanked from his grip, whirled and slipped on the loose sand blowing across the deck, twisting her ankle, landing squarely on the concrete. Pain and nausea rushed through her.

Holding the dog's leash with one hand, Luciano bent and smoothed a strand of hair from her face, his gesture gentle and unexpected. "*Mia Cara*, are you all right?"

Mia Cara. My Dear. My Darling. He'd never called her that before. She looked up into his strong features, at the man she'd cherished when she was fifteen.

She suppressed a moan of pain. "I'm all right. It's just a sprain." Her dress had ridden up and she glanced down at the ugly scar on her thigh, prominent and bleeding.

He pulled a wet handkerchief from his pocket and dabbed at her scar, then ran his fingers over her ankle, his dark head bent over her. "Nothing seems broken." He looked up and gave a reassuring grin. "Welcome to sunny Charleston."

She returned a slight smile. Somewhere nearby a tree cracked in two. She could hardly see three feet in front of her because of the heavy rain and wind, and he'd made her smile.

He covered her cold hand in his warm one and pressed it against his chest. "Can you walk?"

She nodded. "I think so."

"Or I can carry you."

"I don't need any help." She stood too quickly. A surge of pain in her ankle forced her to collapse against him. She attempted to pull away, but his arms tightened. He watched her, apparently waiting for permission to lift her.

"What about the dog?" she asked. "You can't carry us both."

"I lifted weights all those years just for this moment. I can carry you with one arm and lead Lady with the other."

Anastasia attempted to put weight on her ankle, bit back a groan and leaned against him. Seawater sprayed against her back and saturated them both. "I'll take you up on your offer."

"Good decision."

She gripped his shoulders as he scooped her into his

arms. The storm shuddered as he sprinted to the side of the house where his Hummer was parked. He settled her into the passenger seat, clicked the seat belt around her, then unleashed Lady. The dog bounded into the back seat. Luciano belted the dog into a harness and tossed the leash on the floor.

"I'll start the Hummer after I check the road for potholes." He withdrew car keys from his pocket, then walked across the road, bending to check the depth of the rising muddy water. Muffled sirens sounded in the distance, although the island seemed deserted.

She rolled down the window and shouted, "Why is no one around?"

"February is the month to cruise the Caribbean, apparently." He turned back to the Hummer. Then he stilled, standing in knee-deep rushing water, staring at something behind her. He whispered something in Italian, then looked away.

Anastasia jerked around and met Lady's deep brown eyes, wide and panicked. She petted the dog's oversized paws, offering reassurances she didn't feel. When her gaze moved to Luciano's house, her breath stopped. One of the cement urns had become a twisted projectile and had crashed into the sliding doors. The terrifying sound of shattered glass filled the air, noisy and violent.

The wind twisted. Several hundreds of yards away on an empty stretch of beach, the force of ocean waves exploded the detached garage of Luciano's neighbor. Blowing faster, the wind lifted several roof shingles off Luciano's house. She blinked several times. *Impossible.* The roof was failing, the walls were collapsing. The hurricane was destroying Luciano's prized villa, carrying all his treasures away piece by piece.

CHAPTER 5

*L*uciano drove slowly through the flowing force of water, muscling the Hummer into the middle of the road, slipping the clutch and revving the engine. The wheels seemed to float.

"Open the door," he instructed.

"Why?" Anastasia's eyes widened. "We're trying to escape from the water."

"Trust me." He expelled his breath in frustration. "Letting the water flow into the Hummer will weigh it down."

Water poured in as soon as she opened the door.

"Now close the door. You can feel the tires gripping the road." He offered a reassuring smile and slipped one arm around her shoulder for a quick hug. "How's your ankle?"

"Much better."

"Once we're off this street, we'll be on the main road and take the bridge to Charleston."

She clasped her hands together and kept her gaze glued to the road. "Suppose the bridge is washed out and we're stranded?"

He couldn't trust himself to answer for the same thought had crossed his mind, although he wouldn't share that frightening possibility because it'd only worry her. He touched the brake lightly. The Hummer stopped.

He put the Hummer in neutral and attempted to restart. "The engine is flooded."

"What should we do?" she whispered.

He shook his head, more at himself than in answer to her question. As he stared through the windshield at the ensuing nightmare, he considered their options. None were promising. They could remain in the car or attempt to seek shelter in a building that might collapse on top of them.

Sweat dampened the back of his neck. Debris was windborne: garbage cans, market umbrellas, wicker chairs. Nothing and no one was safe from the torrential wind and incessant rain. He opened the door to assess the floodwater, and lightning lit the sky. Lady yanked from the harness and leapt out.

Luciano growled a curse and tore off his jacket. "Stay here. I'll go after the dog. The lightning must've terrified her." He grabbed the dog's leash, shoved himself from the seat and dove for the dog. Lady was swimming against the current toward the ocean, her head above the chop.

He waded toward the dog, then hesitated. His grip tightened on the leash until his knuckles whitened. The water was getting too deep.

He fired a curse at himself.

Behind him, the door slammed. A movement in his peripheral vision caught his eye and an uprooted tree trunk plowed directly into him. Anastasia screamed.

His body flew forward into fast-moving water and he let go of the leash. His side throbbed. He slowly regained his balance, touching a hand to his side, wiping the stickiness of blood from his soaked shirt.

He should've been prepared for these types of storms. He'd bought a home on the ocean and hadn't even backed up his computer files.

Somehow, Anastasia had limped quickly to his side and was lifting his shirt.

"Get back in!" he shouted.

Her hands stilled. "You can't catch Lady on your own." Her lips pursed, her gaze met his long enough for him to see the terror in her eyes. She cut past him and retrieved the leash from the floodwater, then cupped her hands to her mouth.

"Lady! We're here, girl!"

Luciano swiveled, intending to go after the dog, and lost his balance. He plunged into the water a second time. Time slowed to pounding rain and one loud heartbeat after another. Anastasia's panicked cries resounded in his brain as he hauled himself to his feet. She reached him within seconds. Soothingly, she touched his forehead, and her tormented blue-gray eyes locked on his.

"Are you okay?" she asked. "You keep falling and I can't always save you."

He mustered a half-smile, coughed and tried to pull his thoughts together. "I couldn't be better." He shook away the feeling of lightheadedness and felt his body sway.

She turned toward the ocean and screamed a warning. A rumbling wall of white seawater surged, seeming to eat her words. He followed her alarmed gaze and a chill went up his neck. His beloved dog was swimming toward a stretch of downed power lines. The gale wind was moving over the ocean carrying a dome of water with it toward land.

Anastasia held up the leash and shouted into the storm, "Lady, come back!"

His chest tightened. Lady wouldn't be able to hear Anastasia from that distance, and they wouldn't be able to reach the dog because she was nearing the ocean.

No, please no! Don't let me choose because I won't make it. He shook his head, knowing it was his duty to save his dog. Sure, he was scared, but he wouldn't admit defeat.

He took one heaving breath and headed toward the ocean.

"Lady, come back!" Anastasia shouted again.

Miraculously, the dog turned and paddled toward them, managing the currents with inborn ease.

Anastasia turned to Luciano. She raised her freckled arms, ready to dive into the water. "Lady will tire soon. Let's meet her halfway."

Luciano eyed the distance. "The dog seems to be out of danger. You go. I'll wait here." He grabbed the leash from her hands.

"C'mon, we'll go together. Lady will think it's an adventure."

Luciano drew a difficult breath and stared down at the floodwater lapping at his thighs. "I can't ... swim."

She dropped her arms and repeatedly shook her head. "You bought a home on the ocean and you can't swim? How did you plan on reaching Lady a minute go?"

He flinched. "Fear primed my body, not my brain."

Her expression softened. "You're very brave."

"Or very foolish."

She wiped droplets of rain from her face. "I'll get your dog, and you get us back to the Hummer. Deal?"

"Deal. My Hummer can plow through anything." *If it starts.*

Without glancing back, she dove into the water.

He willed himself to wade deeper, but his feet remained planted firmly in place. He hated the feeling of being powerless.

Anastasia reached Lady in several strokes, urging the dog to paddle, navigating them back. He'd forgotten her championship swimming style, her lean, perfect form. She was ever-confident in the water, her strokes fluid and sure.

She stooped over and gasped for breath when she reached him. He laid one hand on her shoulder to steady her while he leashed the dog with the other. When Anastasia stood, shivering, his arm went around her waist. Personal space didn't matter anymore.

He thought she'd shove him away, but she drew nearer.

He gathered her even closer. "I'm proud of you."

She grinned teasingly. "All that swimming was just for this moment," she echoed his earlier words. Guardedly, he scanned her beautiful face for a sign that she thought less of him.

Her blue eyes twinkled, answering his question. "You'll always remind me of a Greek god, just a non-swimming one."

"I lived in an orphanage, not a beach resort," he said with a wry, self-depreciating grin. He kissed her cheeks with a soft brush of his lips. "Notice anything different?"

Her brows came together. "You sprouted gills?"

He laughed out loud. "The rain and the wind are lessening." Leaning down, he kissed her, one more time. "Thank you for saving my dog."

She placed a trembling hand on his cheek. "It's the least I can do for an old friend."

He glanced at the sky. A slice of sunlight shone through the clouds. "Let's go back." He kept one arm around her waist, the other firmly holding the dog's leash as they slogged through knee-deep floodwater to where the Hummer had been parked.

A makeshift garage floated by. Some of the smaller buildings on the island had been turned into toothpicks. She ventured a glance up and down the deserted street. "Your Hummer ... disappeared?"

He fixed his gaze on the empty road.

The air grew still. His arm fell away as he turned to search the shoreline, just in time to see his five-thousand-pound Hummer being swept into the ocean.

CHAPTER 6

*T*hirty minutes had passed, and dusk descended at an alarming pace. Anastasia's sundress was dripping wet and she shivered, feeling cold and clammy. She threaded her hand through her hair, a soaked mass of tangles. Her gaze took in the devastation as they walked. The aftermath of the storm was as horrific as the storm itself. Sewer pipes were visible alongside downed telephone poles, and many luxurious homes were destroyed beyond repair. Strange, because some homes looked relatively untouched.

Her limbs felt heavier with each footstep, and her breath came slow and uneven. Her stomach growled, although she was more thirsty than hungry. She hadn't eaten since lunch.

Luciano offered numerous encouraging smiles that he'd obviously perfected and slid a hand under her elbow. "We're nearing the main road," he said.

Sure they were. He'd said that countless times. She couldn't meet his eyes, couldn't force a nod, trying to shake the dregs of exhaustion. Perhaps they could sink into the soaking wet grass and sit quietly. The world had gone mad. It could wait a few moments while they rested.

The dog stopped abruptly, stared straight ahead and barked.

"Anastasia! Luciano! I'm so relieved I found you!" a woman shouted.

Jaclyn's voice.

Anastasia's head jerked up as she spotted a bright yellow canoe paddling toward them. She covered her mouth as tears welled in her eyes. Her thoughts jumbled and she leaned on Luciano, his arm secure around her shoulders.

Jaclyn. Here. It couldn't be.

But Luciano was waving, greeting his sister with a string of relieved curses.

Jaclyn slewed through the flooded streets like a pro. "Are you okay?"

"Yes, yes!" Anastasia's throat was thick. She broke free from Luciano and raced through the floodwater. She'd never been so happy to hear her friend's voice in her entire life.

Finally, she'd be able to call Soo-Min. She needed to talk to her daughter, to reassure herself that the world was still spinning. She needed to hold her. She missed her so much.

Jaclyn slid the canoe near them. "Get in so we can get out of here."

Luciano lifted a brow. "Don't tell me you stole the canoe."

"Nope, just the paddles," Jaclyn said. "Why does everyone think I steal things? That one time ... that one pair of earrings when I was a teenager that I didn't need anyway—"

"That incident is water over the bridge." Luciano looked toward Anastasia for smiling approval of his joke, and she graciously complied. Then he planted his foot in the canoe's center, settling Anastasia and the golden retriever in the middle. Apparently mindful of the canoe tipping, he swung his other leg over, then sat at the other end opposite Jaclyn.

Jaclyn threw him a paddle. "First I needed a canoe rack. Then I needed two people to help me hoist the canoe onto the roof of my car, then I drove through really scary flood-waters. Consider all this a repayment for allowing me to stay in your house indefinitely."

He uttered a soft curse, his favorite epithet. "You said you were staying only until your bungalow was remodeled to your liking."

"I'm a perfectionist like you, and I'm not happy with the way the remodel is progressing. I'm adaptable, though, and I'll live in whatever million-dollar house you purchase next," Jaclyn said with a grin.

An hour later, the sky changed from dusk to darkness. They'd arrived at the bridge where Jaclyn ditched the canoe, then drove them in her smart car to her bungalow in a tidy residential area.

After everyone had remarked about the solitary toilet stationed in Jaclyn's foyer, they dried and changed. A few minutes afterward, Luciano lit a fire in the fireplace, then Anastasia and Luciano sat side by side on the living room couch.

Jaclyn had lent Anastasia a pair of lounge pants and a snug tunic top, and Luciano had changed into a spare tee shirt and jeans he'd kept in Jaclyn's closet. Several candles furnished flickering lights, and a battery-powered radio dispensed weather information. With a contented yawn, Lady found a comfortable corner by the hearth.

Soo-Min. Anastasia thought of little else, although she tried to concentrate on the conversation.

"I was driving to Liz's house when we lost phone connection," Jaclyn explained. "Who expected a hurricane to develop so fast?" She turned to Luciano, her tone tinged with amusement. "We penniless peasants weren't hit nearly as hard as you fancy island billionaires. Sorry you lost your villa, big brother. I know it meant a lot to you."

His expression turned impassive. "I didn't need an eight-thousand-square-foot home. I'll buy something smaller. Considering my lack of swimming abilities, perhaps I'm better suited to a place in the mountains," he finished with an apologetic shrug toward Anastasia.

She chuckled. "I can't box and you can't swim, so we're even."

"As long as your next mansion offers ample bedrooms and private baths, I'm good. " Jaclyn teased with a laugh. "Spectacular mountain views will be a nice change."

"I'll look for a house surrounded by acres of land at the top of a mountain." He gazed at Anastasia and wrapped one arm around her. A light came into his gaze, that powerful, unleashed determination. Nothing could stop him from reaching his goals.

She leaned into his comforting, masculine body. Despite her protests that her ankle wasn't swelled, he'd insisted on propping her leg up with several pillows and wrapping her ankle in a bag of ice.

She looked around. "Is there a cell phone working anywhere?"

"All the cell towers are down. Perhaps your aunt and uncle have a landline?" Jaclyn asked.

"Can you drive me to their townhouse? You'd mentioned they didn't live far from you, and I want to be sure they're safe. I'll make my call from there."

"Despite our ordeal, you're focusing on a phone call to your ex." Although Luciano shook his head in admonishment, his gaze held a gleam as if he were anticipating an enjoyable verbal sparring match to follow. "It's well past seven o'clock, so you missed *that* deadline. Does your ex know about your meeting with Sam, the lawyer extraordinaire?"

"I'm not meeting with Sam because of my divorce," she

explained. "It's a free consultation regarding my daughter's custody dispute."

Luciano dropped his arm. "You have a daughter?"

She flashed him a smile. "Yes, she's four years old and in preschool." She reached for her purse to show him a picture, then realized she didn't have a purse, or money, or credit cards. Everything she'd brought to Charleston had been lost in the hurricane.

She drew a long, quavering breath. "All Soo-Min's precious baby pictures in my wallet are gone." Shock was wearing off and reality was taking a firm hold.

"Anastasia adopted her daughter from South Korea," Jaclyn was saying. "You probably were immersed in some business deal, big brother, and weren't listening when I told you a few years ago." She swiveled to Anastasia. "He always wanted a large family. As I mentioned, his wife died."

Anastasia placed her hand on his sleeve. "I'm sorry for your loss. As a single father, you can always adopt."

He stared at the fire in the fireplace. "Never."

She dropped her hand. "Why not?"

"He believes our parents adopted him out of a sense of duty to society, which couldn't be more wrong. Although they led fulfilling lives, they wanted to share their home with children." Jaclyn arched a carrot-red brow in Luciano's direction. "He still grieves the loss of his birth parents."

"Enough, Jaclyn. I wasn't brought to America until I was four years old. I have good memories of my childhood home in Italy before being left in that neglectful orphanage." The smooth, impassive features were back in place. He focused his gaze on Anastasia. "So why *are* you meeting with Sam tomorrow?"

Anastasia flinched and briefly closed her eyes. She didn't care about Justin anymore, so that certainly wasn't the reason. Their final conversation before their divorce had sparked a wound that wouldn't heal. She replayed his harsh and condescending words in her mind.

She'd lain in a hospital bed after the excisional surgery. *"But why do you want Eliza and not me?"* she'd asked. *"I'm your wife. We adopted a beautiful child together."*

She cringed. She'd been pathetic. Blame her sorrow on the resultant weakness after her surgery, the feeling of defeat. Never again, she vowed to herself. She'd rely only on herself.

"It's not that I don't love you," Justin had explained. *"It's just that I love Eliza more."*

Then he'd walked out of the hospital room. Anastasia's mind had been numb for days.

She took a long breath and pushed the devastating exchange aside. Prompted by the awful memory, the idea that had consumed her when he'd married Eliza came tumbling out. "I want to be awarded sole custody of Soo-Min."

Luciano tapped his fingers on his thigh. "Your daughter's best interests will be better served if she's raised by two united parents."

Anastasia dug her nails into her palms. "After years of endless affairs, Justin married a woman who's immature and irresponsible." Her voice shook as she spoke. "At first I agreed to the court's decision regarding joint custody, but in hindsight, I know that neither Justin nor Eliza deserves parenting time with my sweet, impressionable daughter."

Luciano raised a cool, challenging brow. "Your unbiased opinion, I presume?"

She sank back into the couch. "My daughter's an adoptee. Who knows what type of life she experienced in her Korean foster home before arriving in America? Those first few months are crucial to a child's development. She deserves unconditional affection and constant protection. Justin and his latest love provide neither."

"I lived in an orphanage. I turned out okay," Luciano replied.

"You always said you felt like an underdog and didn't belong anywhere," Jaclyn piped in. Then, she slapped a hand to her forehead. "In all this excitement, I forgot to mention that Sam's office called earlier. His schedule changed and he's out of town until next week. He had to meet with some big-shot client in Las Vegas, a movie star." She fiddled with the sleeves of her sweatshirt, exposing matching butterfly tattoos on each wrist.

Luciano smirked. "Still sizing him up as an eligible bachelor?"

"So sometimes he's not that dependable," Jaclyn agreed. "Nonetheless, he's still rich. He might even be richer than you."

Anastasia put her face in her hands. "Meeting with Sam is one of the main reasons I came to Charleston."

"Why don't you set up counsel with Liz, instead?" Luciano asked. "She's probably available."

Jaclyn swung him a knowing look. "She's always available, especially for you."

"We're just friends," he countered.

"Does she specialize in child custody disputes?" Anastasia asked.

"Although she's practicing law part-time, she seems to be always seeking new clients." With that, Jaclyn stood. "I'll take the dog for a walk. When I return, I'll drive you to your aunt's house, then I'll stop at Liz's place and set up a consultation for you tomorrow. Sound like a plan?"

"You can drop me at my office in town," Luciano said. "One of my computer files might still have my project notes. Providing I can get the generator to work, I'll be able to power it on. I have a small apartment in my building, so I'll stay there for the night."

Jaclyn pulled on a bright-yellow raincoat, matching rain boots, and then leashed the dog. She flicked on a light switch in the hall and shook her head. "Why do I flick on light switches when I know there's no power?" Muttering to herself, she grabbed a flashlight. "The flights in and out of Charleston airport were canceled. Your meeting will definitely be delayed."

Anastasia's stomach rumbled. "Is there anything in the fridge?"

Jaclyn shrugged, gave an exaggerated leap over the toilet in the foyer, then stepped out the door.

Luciano took the bag of ice off Anastasia's ankle. "I'll go check. Knowing my sister, any food will be either extremely healthy or extremely unhealthy."

CHAPTER 7

A few minutes later, Luciano returned to the living room. "I found dry celery stalks and bottled water in the fridge, so unfortunately we caught the healthy week. I threw the celery in the bin."

Anastasia smiled and levered herself up to accept the water. "Water is good, thanks." She drank greedily, then placed the bottle on the coffee table. "Although a Sea Salt caramel would've been wonderful."

He loaded several small pieces of wood into the fireplace to keep the fire burning and settled beside her. She didn't acknowledge him, just stared at the flicks of curling flame. The firelight complemented her flawless complexion, the warm glow illuminating her exquisite features. He gazed at her silky, honey-brown hair fastened at the crown with one of Jaclyn's hair clips. The style accented her finely sculpted cheekbones.

"Are you missing your daughter?" he asked.

"Yes, very much. I should've never left Vermont."

His first impulse was to pull back in case she became too weepy.

"You came here to consult with Sam," he said. "You'll want to be armed with his extensive knowledge before opening a custody dispute."

"Yes, but there were other reasons why I came to Charleston, selfish ones. Do you want to know something?" She turned. Her magnificent eyes sparkled with tears. "I was afraid I would've bumped into Eliza bringing Soo-Min to the local art center or movie theater. Stowe's a small town," she whispered. "And I wouldn't have been able to bear the pain of seeing them together."

His arm slid around her, the instinct to comfort her coming naturally to him. He offered quiet encouragement and she accepted, pouring her tears into his chest. When her crying subsided, he tipped her chin up and smoothed the wetness from the corners of her eyes "Can I ask you something?"

She sniffed and nodded.

"Why did you pursue international adoption if your marriage was so troubled?"

Her gaze shadowed with hurt, and for a moment he chided himself. She was worn out and all the more sensitive to criticism. She needed rest and comfort, not condemnation.

She drew an unsteady breath and squarely met his gaze. "Because I desperately wanted a child and had exhausted all the other options. Justin and I were infertile as a couple. Thirty years old was a number that was nearing, and my biological clock ticked a little too loudly. I felt like a failure because I wasn't able to get pregnant."

"You're not a failure, and there's nothing shameful about infertility."

She looked away. "And if I'm completely honest with myself, some small part of me hoped that a child might save my marriage."

Luciano took her cold hands in his. "That admittance takes a great deal of courage."

"Thanks." She regarded him with a teary smile. "And then Soo-Min arrived at the New York airport, and you know what? Everything changed. All the heartache, the fighting with Justin, everything. I remember that day so well. She was ten months old and was escorted by an elderly Korean man, along with three other babies. She was adorable, dressed in a bright-pink Korean Hanbok, which is a traditional Korean dress. Immediately, I fell in love with her."

His brows drew together. "I love your story, I really do. But I don't agree with adopting internationally."

Her eyes narrowed. "You, of all people. Why, you're an international adoptee yourself!"

"I've researched and read countless studies. International adoptions aren't fair to the child because it displaces that child from a true home environment and culture."

"And there are many other articles proving otherwise," she countered. "Your adoptive parents were wonderful and caring. I was at your house many times hanging out with Jaclyn. Your childhood was filled with affection and couldn't have been more perfect."

He pressed a kiss on her forehead, hoping to take the sting from his words. She'd confided in him. The shared trust and understanding they'd begun to build again after all these years apart could easily crumble. "You're absolutely right. I loved my adoptive parents very much and miss them more each day."

"Your opinions are contrary to what I believe." Her gaze shimmered with understanding. "Although I know you miss your adoptive parents."

"They tried, you know? However, I've never recovered from the ache in my gut that my birth family abandoned me," he admitted, underlining his words. "The memory of living in a tiny apartment in Italy haunts me every day. I can still smell the meatballs in a tomato and garlic sauce simmering on the stove." He drew in a deep breath. "All my life I've been searching for something, although I don't know what I was looking for. Perhaps the answer lies in Italy, my birthplace."

He'd said too much, divulging a sadness he'd never shared. He focused on a hole in the ceiling.

"Everyone's curious about his or her heritage. Someday, you'll find information about your birth family and you're bound to be pleased, for their kind hearts will surely match yours."

He cleared his throat. "I've searched exhaustively and hired thirty investigators, but they haven't found any information. The adoption agency in Italy said that the records had been sealed."

"Keep trying."

He intended to, using all his money and resources. When he found his birth family, he'd buy them all a home and throw a celebration. In fact, he'd buy the entire Italian town.

"Meanwhile, I'll be the perfect mother for my daughter in the perfect little town."

He chuckled. "I lived in that snowy little town for many years, and it isn't my idea of perfect."

She granted him a sweet, genuine smile and rested her head against his chest. "When you and I were younger, we talked like this all the time, remember? I'd complain endlessly about my lonely home life, and you'd sit and listen and encourage me."

He stroked an errant fringe of side swept bangs away from her face. He noticed the small scar and didn't comment. "I admired your perseverance. You were fearless."

After a moment, she murmured, "I wasn't fearless. I wanted a happy family."

He gathered her in his arms. "Close your eyes."

She chuckled and complied.

He whispered close to her ear. "I enjoyed every one of our conversations, although I never would've admitted it back then."

She opened her eyes. "And now?"

"Nothing's changed," he recognized. She was still the provocative, exhilarating woman he'd admired sixteen years ago.

It was as if they'd resumed where they'd left off, conversing on his back porch after his boxing matches, her long hair pulled up in a damp ponytail, her cheeks flushed from the exertion of a hard swim practice.

She slanted an audacious smile at him. "Where were you sixteen years ago when I needed you?"

"I'm here for you now, *Mia Cara.* Never forget that."

Without his urging, she tipped her face up to his. He gathered her close and pressed his lips against her forehead, her hair. Ever so gently, his thumbs stroked the freckles on her cheeks.

Her lips parted and she sighed. Her arms glided around his neck and his mouth moved to capture hers. He caught her arms and pulled her onto his lap. "You'll be more comfortable." He offered a charming, teasing smile. Looping his arms around her, he drew her near and kissed her deeply. His blood hammered as she melted her provocative body against his.

The front door burst open.

"I'm home!" Jaclyn stopped short in the entryway and unleashed Lady. The dog, all sixty pounds of her, bounded through the foyer to jump on the couch.

Luciano expelled a long breath. Anastasia attempted to lurch to a sitting position, but he kept her on his lap.

Jaclyn strolled into the living room. "I doubt there's any hot water, although I'm showering anyway before I drive Anastasia to her aunt and uncle's house." She grinned. "Unless, of course, my big brother needs that cold shower first."

CHAPTER 8

*G*ripping a flashlight and overnight bag packed with a set of Jaclyn's clothes and toiletries, Anastasia stood at the doorway to her aunt and uncle's townhouse and knocked on the door. Although the rain had lessened, evidence of the storm shone from the burning candles flickering through the windows. Apparently, most of Charleston was still without power.

A short, stubby woman with salt-and-pepper hair flung open the door and ushered Anastasia inside the tiny foyer. Her plump face wreathed into a smile. "Thank goodness you're safe. I was so worried, I was driving your uncle crazy."

"I had no way to reach you. I know my visit tonight is unexpected but—"

"Why didn't you call when you arrived in Charleston?"

"Sorry, the afternoon went by so fast and then my cell phone lost power. In fact, it was swept away by the hurricane." Anastasia placed a kiss on her aunt's cheek and hugged her. "Do you have a working landline? I need to call my ex's house."

"The phone's in the kitchen," Uncle Filipp called from the

living room. "Grab some pasta salad and tea while you're in there."

"Thanks." Anastasia pointed to the smart car idling in the driveway. "Jaclyn dropped me off. Can I stay the night?"

"Of course. We have a spare bedroom. There's so much to catch up on," her aunt said.

Anastasia set her bag in the foyer, steeling herself for her aunt's interrogations sure to follow. She lingered at the doorway and waved to Jaclyn and Luciano as they backed out of the driveway. "See you tomorrow!"

Luciano rolled down the car window. "May I take you to lunch at one of my favorite restaurants in Charleston?" he asked in a deep, polite voice that brooked no dispute. She noted the guarded hope in his gaze along with his lazy smile, and her heart gave an unexpected lurch.

She returned his smile. "Yes, I'll look forward to it." She paused by the entry door as the car sped away, then closed the door and crossed the foyer into the living room.

"I swear if another storm comes through, I'll never recover from the fright. I told your uncle we should've moved to Florida," Aunt Irina was saying. "I was torn between screaming my head off or fainting dead away every time the wind roared through here."

"Believe me, when I saw a dome of ocean waves, I felt the same way," Anastasia replied.

Uncle Filipp came to his feet and peered at Anastasia above his reading glasses. "You look like you walked through a hurricane."

"I did, actually. And ran, and swam and screamed bloody terror." She pecked a kiss on her uncle's forehead and headed for the kitchen to call Soo-Min. Then, because she'd memorized the number, she'd call her bank to cancel her credit cards. She'd brave the long lines at the DMV for a new license when she returned to Stowe.

After five rings, Eliza answered groggily. "Your number came up on the caller ID. Why are you calling so late?"

"Haven't you heard? A hurricane came through Charleston."

A hesitation. "I didn't see anything on the news," Eliza said.

"Can I speak with my daughter?" Anastasia asked.

"It's midnight and I put her to bed hours ago. I must've read that book about the furry barnyard animals three times before she finally went to sleep. I'm certainly not waking her up."

"Eliza, please ..." Anastasia swallowed. "It's been a rough day. I want to hear my daughter's voice."

"Sorry," Eliza responded in a sharp tone. "Disrupting her from a deep sleep won't accomplish anything except make you feel better. Call back in the morning."

The phone clicked. Anastasia stared at the receiver and shook her head.

She stepped into the living room while balancing a tray containing a plate of pasta salad, a fork and two china cups brimming with hot tea. She offered one cup to her aunt, then sank into a shiny turquoise rocking chair. Anastasia placed her teacup and pasta on the coffee table.

Aunt Irina, comfortably ensconced on a worn plaid sofa, peered at Anastasia over the rim of her steaming cup. "By the look on your face, dear, I'm assuming your call to Justin didn't go well."

"I wanted to talk to my daughter. However, Eliza wouldn't allow it." Anastasia's vision blurred and she wiped hastily at her eyes. "I suppose it's my fault because I didn't realize how late it was."

Uncle Filipp shot her aunt an exasperated look. "Let your skinny niece eat. She looks terrible."

Anastasia bit back a grin and reached for the pasta. "Thanks for all the compliments, Uncle Filipp."

"Who was that man in the car?" her aunt asked. "He looked like Jaclyn's brother."

"Yes, that man was Luciano."

"I remember him. Wasn't he captain of the football team?"

"He was captain of the boxing club," Anastasia corrected. "Jaclyn lives with him while her home is being renovated. Except now, she has a home and he doesn't." Anastasia tightened her grip on her fork as the emotional stress of the day's events hurtled through her mind.

"Isn't their last name 'Donati'?" her uncle asked. "There's an impressive office complex downtown with that name emblazoned across the front. Some software company."

Anastasia nodded and took a bite of pasta. "That's probably Luciano's office. Jaclyn said he's on his way to becoming a billionaire."

Her heart swelled with pride as she spoke because he'd earned his success on his own. Of everyone she'd ever known, Luciano was the one person who could accomplish such a remarkable feat. He was sharp and witty, brilliant yet infuriating.

She sighed and shrugged that last thought aside. She believed in him, admired him. He always made her laugh, despite the circumstances. And he'd be the first to poke fun at himself.

"I lived in an orphanage, not a beach resort," he'd wryly observed.

Her cheeks heated, remembering his lips moving tenderly over hers.

"I always liked him." Aunt Irina proffered her broadest grin. "Whenever he came home from college, he'd attend your swim meets."

Anastasia shook her head. "You must be mixing him up with someone else. He never attended my meets."

Her aunt downed a generous gulp of tea, then set down her cup and pushed up the sleeves of her flowing housecoat. "He stood in the sidelines near the edge of the bleachers. Sometimes we talked about the back-breaking factory work and deafening conditions that he and your mother endured, although Luciano was determined to help his parents pay for his college. I'm surprised he never mentioned our conversations to you."

Anastasia smiled kindly at her elderly aunt and didn't argue with her reflections. She was obviously mistaken.

Her aunt bestowed an exaggerated wink. "What brings you to Charleston besides that good-looking billionaire? When you called me last week from Vermont, you said you'd explain when you got here."

Quickly, Anastasia recounted the circumstances of why she planned to petition the court for full custody of Soo-Min, explaining Jaclyn's recommendation to meet with Sam for a free consultation.

"Free or not, there's no reason to consult with a lawyer from another state, plus you want the home town advantage." Uncle Filipp held his fingers loosely behind his back. "Your parenting plan with Justin was approved by the court for joint custody."

Anastasia nodded. "I'm planning to request a modification. Besides—"

He checked her explanation in mid-sentence. "Your relationship with Justin is good and he pays child support?"

"Yes. However, his new wife is too young and immature to parent properly."

Aunt Irina sank her sturdy body farther down into the couch. Two spots of vibrant-pink appeared on her well-rounded cheeks. "We've all witnessed Justin's bad temper on several family occasions. Nevertheless, he's obviously a good father who's devoted to Soo-Min. Still, who can predict how a man will retaliate if he fears losing the privilege of seeing his child?"

Uncle Filipp lifted a bushy brow at his wife's outburst, then frowned at Anastasia. "You're no fool. However, what if you lose the custody hearing? You smoothly navigated the international adoption process, but Soo-Min may be caught in an angry dispute with your ex which may drag on for years."

"And what about your cancer, dear?" Aunt Irina's mouth took a grim twist. "Your mother would've been so concerned about your receiving the best possible treatment if she were still alive."

Anastasia jabbed at her pasta with a fork. "I'm cancer-free and doubt she would've noticed any signs of melanoma."

"She was a single mother struggling to make ends meet and working long hours. Your swim meets were very costly," her aunt countered. "She paid for all the expenses on her own."

Anastasia set her plate on the table and went for her cup of tea. "Aunt Irina, I appreciated that you attended my meets, but my mother wasn't there. I'd look up before I dove into the water for my freestyle swim event and never saw her. I was her only child and she never sat in the stands cheering for me. Family should've been more important than working in that awful factory or staying out late with her boyfriend. I sat alone in an empty house my entire childhood. Besides—"

Her aunt cut off Anastasia's next sentence with a sweep of her arms. "She tried her best and worked hard."

"Perhaps." Anastasia sat straighter. "Although you can be sure that my daughter's childhood will be different." She set her teacup clattering on the saucer and rubbed the back of her neck. "I intend to be an outstanding mother and provide a stable, nurturing home. I've read all the latest parenting books and scoured the websites. I'm prepared."

"Like your mother, you're a single parent," Uncle Filipp said in a sharp tone. "Without any support, you'll face financial challenges. And who'll help with the day-to-day responsibilities?"

Anastasia summoned a brave smile. "I plan to return to teaching. The elementary school where I worked several years ago offers an excellent after school day care. Soo-Min will enter Kindergarten in the fall, and she can attend school there. They assured me I could return whenever I wished."

"You're assuming there's a job opening waiting for you and not taking into account that there may not be any vacancies. But let's hope you're right, because you'll need money. The cost of all those court hearings and missed work days will cost thousands of dollars," Uncle Filipp said.

Anastasia opened her mouth to refute him, although Aunt Irina interrupted with a glare aimed at Uncle Filipp. "Our niece is obviously exhausted, and she's endured more than enough anxiety for one day." Aunt Irina stood, lifted her dainty teacup for another gulp that wasn't there, and scowled into the empty cup.

IN THE SPARE BEDROOM, Anastasia slid off the snug tunic and sweat pants borrowed from Jaclyn, took a quick shower and donned a night shirt. She'd placed one lit candle on the dresser, then covered a yawn with her hand, although she felt too wound up for sleep.

Absently, she scratched the mole near her wrist, then sat on the bed to inspect it. The mole was scaly and felt tender. Perhaps she'd scraped it when she'd slipped and fallen on Luciano's concrete deck, although she didn't remember hurting her wrist, only her ankle. Still, the day had brought fright and turmoil, so unexpected injuries were expected.

She stretched out her legs. The lilac-flowered comforter had been turned down, and the cozy bed beckoned. Sleep would restore her spirits and sweep away her fatigue. She slipped between the covers and closed her eyes, seeking comforting dreams.

Hours later, she lay awake on her stomach and listened to the sound of rain drumming against the windows.

She'd been convinced she was doing the right thing in pursuing a custody dispute, for a proper home situation was in Soo-Min's best interests, wasn't it? She mulled over the conversation with her aunt and uncle and couldn't fault their opinions because they offered logical advice. Could she, in fact, juggle the challenges of parenting while working full-time, without a husband or family support network to share the workload?

She rolled to her back. She'd planned it all—the white picket fence, two adorable children, a loving husband. However, life hadn't happened the way she'd planned. That perfect family she'd always wanted was an elusive dream.

She placed her hands behind her head and stared at the ceiling. What did a perfect family even look like, anyway? She bit her lip and sighed.

With a strong frown and stronger opinions, Luciano had voiced disapproval regarding adoption, although Anastasia reasoned that his opinions were spurred more from his own inner conflicts. His adoptive parents had been kind, encouraging and clearly loved their children. For a man so brilliant, didn't he realize that his experience as an adoptee contradicted his research?

She didn't fault his resolve to travel to Italy. In fact, she'd encouraged him to research his heritage. He'd once told her that he dreamed of someday having a loving wife and several children. Optimistically, his search would reunite him with many Italian aunts and uncles and boisterous cousins.

During the summer as a young man, he'd spent endless hours tutoring neighborhood children in math, his obvious forte. If a child needed extra help, Luciano would give up time at his beloved boxing gym. There was no doubt that he'd be a wonderful father.

And then there was Luciano, the man. Despite the terrifying day they'd shared, she'd felt safe with him. His calmness disarmed her, even when she was so frightened she could hardly string two thoughts together. And throughout their ordeal, she'd felt him watching her, protectively. She'd trust him with her life. Always had.

Sixteen years ago, he'd never given her reason to believe he was interested in her romantically. Nevertheless, there was no mistaking his expression tonight before he'd kissed her. He cared for her, and not just as an old friend anymore. And if she examined her feelings, she knew she'd always cared for him. The handsome college sophomore she'd had a mad crush on had become more sophisticated, more exasperating, and even more vital.

"Mia Cara," he'd whispered, his gaze dark with concern. He'd bent to check her ankle and rubbed the soreness away.

They'd enjoyed a comfortable friendship in their youth, and that friendship had deepened. The guarded hope in his expression when he'd invited her to lunch was unmistakable. She knew he was eager to see her again. And she was just as eager to see him.

CHAPTER 9

*L*uciano glanced at the enormous oak wall clock chiming noon in the lobby of the Fullman law offices. He shifted, unbuttoned his navy sports jacket and shoved his hands into the pockets of his gray flannel pants. For the third time in fifteen minutes, he'd peered out the large front window, waiting for Jaclyn to drive up in her smart car with Anastasia. He'd given his sister hundreds of dollars, insisting that she and Anastasia shop at several boutiques on King Street for new wardrobes. Anastasia had lost literally the clothes on her back, her purse, wallet, and personal belongings since arriving in Charleston. She hadn't seemed concerned about her material possessions, valuing only her daughter's baby pictures.

He smiled, outrageously pleased with the principled, honorable woman she'd become. Dauntingly fearless during the hurricane, she'd trusted his instructions to open the door and let in more water even though the Hummer was clearly sinking. She'd also bravely rescued his dog as the storm roared and a dome of water rushed toward them. Afterwards, she'd slogged through blocks of floodwater without a word of complaint, despite her sprained ankle and the weariness displayed on her pale features.

He yanked off his sports jacket, placed it on an expensive antique chair and strolled closer to the window. His frustration regarding the postponed board meeting with his investors was compounded by canceled plane flights and rescheduling conflicts. Fortunately, he'd been able to retrieve most of the project information from his office computer.

Earlier in the morning, he'd filed insurance claims for his home, possessions and Hummer. His lease on a new BMW was promised by late afternoon. He'd need to drive to the island with the insurance agent to assess the devastation to his home and property.

He rubbed his jaw. Sometimes he considered leaving all the meetings and schedules and tension behind and living a simpler lifestyle. Were his possessions and success truly bringing joy? Would peace, a cheery fireplace and an exhilarating woman by his side take away the wounds of being relinquished and abandoned as a child?

He kept his gaze fixed on the window. Where were they? He was eager to see Anastasia and show her Charleston. After her consultation with Liz, he'd take her to lunch at one of his favorite restaurants, perhaps taking a horse-drawn carriage ride afterward. Although the skies still growled with gray skies, the afternoon with Anastasia would be perfect.

Despite their ordeal yesterday, he couldn't stop gazing at her. Her beauty had matured to an unassuming grace, her face reflected the years in between with both resolve and heartache. It was no secret that her daughter was her primary concern and she'd soon be leaving Charleston behind.

He crossed his arms. Just why her leaving bothered him was something he couldn't explain. He told himself it was because they were old friends, recently reunited, and there was so much more to talk about because they never ran out of words when they were together.

But there was more, he knew there was more. Her teasing smile warmed his soul. Her light touch ignited his desire. She was unpretentious and sincere, unaffected by her good looks, gazing tenderly into his eyes when he'd kissed her. She loved life and laughter and his teasing jokes.

He stared out the window and ran a hand over his bristled jaw. Several palm trees swayed fitfully, a harsh reminder of the after-effects of a hurricane.

Anastasia's musical laughter from the day before paraded through his mind. *"You really get a charge out of your own humor."* His mind riveted to the way she'd looked as she lay on the chaise lounge on his balcony, the blue knit sundress clinging to her curves, her face flushed from sleep. The thought of never seeing her again left a pang of loneliness he couldn't shake. After sixteen years, how could he lose her a second time?

Liz walked into the lobby from another office and glanced at the bright overhead lights. "Well, at least the power was restored early this morning. Without it, I wouldn't have been able to see any clients today. I look a fright when I can't use a curling iron on my hair."

He bestowed an indulgent smile in her direction, taking in her lush blonde curls and the two carat diamond earrings gleaming from each ear.

"You realize I'm offering this free consultation as a favor to you and Jaclyn," Liz added.

Luciano grinned unapologetically. "And because your brother canceled. Anastasia flew in from Vermont specifically to speak with him."

"You're placing quite a priority on this woman. Who is she again?" Liz asked.

"An old friend," was all he said while he continued to peer

out the lobby window. With a smile, he noted the metallic-red smart car pulling up to the curb.

When Anastasia entered the lobby, laughing and chatting with Jaclyn, his heart stopped in his throat. She looked exquisite. He strode to her and took her hands in his. They were so close that his shirt brushed against her sweater. "You look like a Greek goddess," he said.

"Thank you, although it's embarrassing to compete with a handsome Greek god." She grinned. "Have you been waiting long for me?" She glanced around. Apparently suddenly aware of Jaclyn and Liz staring at them, Anastasia withdrew her hands and stepped back. She wore a breezy maxi sundress in smoky blue-gray to match her exquisite eyes, her slim waist accentuated by a leopard belt. A loosely knit cream sweater covered her trim arms, and black suede ankle-tie shoes and a patent-leather purse completed the outfit. As usual, she wore no jewelry.

Once, she'd explained that her high school swim coach forbade the swimmers to wear jewelry, even a hair band. Apparently, Anastasia had grown accustomed to the absence of jewelry. He wondered if she'd worn a wedding ring when she was married.

A knowing smile touched Jaclyn's lips as she extended a hand toward Anastasia, who blushed attractively. "Quite a transformation from the woman you saw last night, big brother. I've officially introduced Anastasia to designer fashion." Jaclyn twirled, calling attention to her poppy-colored floral sundress and white sneakers. "We happily spent all your money."

Luciano grinned at Anastasia. "My money was well spent."

"I'm not used to wearing such expensive clothes. Suppose I spill something on them?"

"Then my brother will buy you another outfit," Jaclyn provided.

Liz focused an icy look at Jaclyn. "Well, now that we've enjoyed your fashion commentary, we can get started." She stepped forward, extended a hand toward Anastasia, and said flatly, "I'm Liz Fullman."

Anastasia smiled and accepted the woman's handshake, apparently impervious to Liz's razor-edged gaze. "I'm Anastasia Markow."

She'd used her maiden name, he smiled inwardly. She had so much spirit, staying true to her convictions to create a better, independent life for herself and her daughter.

He picked up his sports jacket, brushing a kiss on Anastasia's forehead. "I'll walk to my office and return within the hour. My secretary is attempting to reschedule the board meeting for some time later this week." He gave a brief wave and headed out the door.

"And I'm off to my travel agency to book a cruise, then on to my canoeing lesson with my hunky new teacher. I thought I knew everything about canoeing, but he's teaching me new skills." Jaclyn turned to Anastasia and Liz. "Enjoy your expensive lunch at The Turning Rhinestone!"

Liz sighed. "My favorite restaurant, although I'm taking a train to Vegas tonight to assist Sam in a high profile case. He knows I can't resist movie stars. He's not famous yet. However, he's had a one-line part in a couple of big movies."

"You weren't invited to lunch, Liz," Jaclyn corrected with a teasing smirk. "My brother wants Anastasia all to himself."

ANASTASIA FOLLOWED Liz up the marble stairway to the second floor law offices. The woman was breathtaking, her lavish curves fitted in a pea-green silk dress, every inch the professional, accomplished woman.

Liz nodded to a secretary busily answering calls in one of the offices.

"Good afternoon, Ms. Fullman," the secretary said briskly, ignoring Anastasia.

At the end of the hall, Liz opened the door and flicked on the lights in a large conference room. One entire wall boasted a mural of the city of Charleston, and slightly curved chairs in chrome detailing surrounded a heavy oak table. Clearly, no expense had been spared to impress well-heeled clients.

Liz gestured toward a couple of wooden chairs and a desk in the corner. "Shut the door behind you," she instructed. She promenaded to the desk, seated herself and recovered a long sheet of paper from the bottom drawer. She requested Anastasia to sit across from her. Then she smiled and drawled, "I don't mind sharing him, you know."

Anastasia blinked. "I'm sorry, I don't understand."

"Of course you do. You're a beautiful divorcee with a small child appealing to him for help. Luciano would never refuse a sweet-talking-woman in distress."

Anastasia paused, settling her expensive patent leather purse on her lap, knowing Liz was waiting for an answer. "Luciano and I are old friends," she said cautiously.

"You can enjoy him for the afternoon. I enjoyed his company last night."

Anastasia's head jerked up. Luciano had said he was spending the night at his office. He'd never mentioned that he'd planned on seeing Liz.

She pressed herself into the chair. With rising annoyance, she studied this elegantly coiffed blonde woman sitting across from her.

Seeing Luciano standing in the lobby, Anastasia's heart had skipped a beat. He'd never looked so handsome, his creamy-white polo shirt hugging his muscular, tanned arms, his long legs fitted in gray flannel pants, a shadow of a dark beard on his strong jaw. His bold gaze had roamed appreciatively over her body, then had captured her gaze with an approving smile. He'd tossed a navy sports coat over one shoulder, looking completely at ease in the richly-decorated lobby. He was every inch the successful millionaire and she was beginning to realize that he was completely out of her league, just as he'd always been. To make matters worse, Liz oozed self-assurance. And, she was more gorgeous than any other woman Anastasia had ever met.

"I've been filled in on your case," Liz said crisply, retrieving two additional pieces of stapled paper from her desk drawer. Apparently, she could switch to her professional persona without blinking. "You'll need to submit your modification custody request in writing to the Superior Court in Vermont. Expect a fee for filing, of course. And I assume it's been at least one year since your initial custody agreement?"

Anastasia bit her lip and nodded. "My divorce decree stated that I could revert back to my maiden name, which I did. I'd like to petition the court to change Soo-Min's last name to my maiden name, also. Currently, her last name is Parker, which is my ex's name."

Liz jotted notes on the paper. "Any domestic violence or child abuse?"

"No."

"Good. Otherwise there'd be an investigation, although be prepared for the court to call in a social service agency to evaluate your ex-husband's home situation. Your child's physical or emotional health isn't endangered when she's with him?"

"Justin's home situation is good, it's just that his new wife is so young and—"

Liz checked another box and glanced at her watch. "Has Justin disobeyed the custody agreement in any way?"

"No. He's very dependable." Anastasia braced her hands on the desk for support. "Do I have a case?"

Liz pushed that question aside with a wave of her hands. "Maybe. The court has the authority to decide, and the case will be determined by the best interests of the child."

Anastasia flinched, then straightened her shoulders and met Liz's indifferent gaze directly. "Of course, I want what's best for her. I'm her mother."

Luciano opened the door of Liz's office and strode in without knocking. Apparently, he was very comfortable in her office. He propped a shoulder against the wall and crossed his arms. "Making headway?"

"We're finished. Perfect timing, as always." Liz gave a stunning white smile accompanied by a throaty laugh as she shoved the papers aside. She handed Anastasia her business card and stood abruptly in an obvious attempt to dismiss Anastasia.

"Can you assist Anastasia with her case?" he asked.

"You wanted me to offer her my free expertise and I did, although all the courts respond differently. When are you filing, Anastasia?" Liz asked.

"I'd like to file as soon as I return to Vermont." Anastasia pushed back her chair, dangled the gold chain of her purse over her shoulder and stood. "Although I understand the need to fill out the form correctly and would prefer a lawyer present."

Luciano ran a hand through his hair. "Is it possible for you to fly to Vermont, Liz?"

Liz hurled an unapologetic excuse. "I'm sorry, I can't. The Clerk in Vermont will record the file and set a date for the first hearing. Perhaps at that time I can clear my schedule."

"Would you consider going to Vermont earlier if I came, too?" Luciano gave Anastasia a conspiratorial wink.

Liz's face brightened. "Perhaps you and I can ski while we're there."

"Perhaps." He strode to Anastasia and offered his hand. "Shall we go to lunch?"

Anastasia took his hand. "I'll ... I'll call you?" she asked Liz over her shoulder as she and Luciano walked out of the office.

Liz clasped her hands together in hopeful, mock anticipation. "You do that."

With a nod to the brisk secretary, Luciano and Anastasia crossed the hallway, down the lobby stairs and out the front door. The air smelled fresh and clean, the sky slowly clearing. They strolled past sleeping formal gardens and lush green manicured lawns, as well as stately homes graced with pillars.

Despite what Liz had insinuated regarding her night with Luciano, Anastasia dismissed the conversation. He wanted to have lunch with her, not Liz. His warm hand was clasped firmly around hers, not Liz's. And he'd help ensure that the court petition would be filed correctly in Vermont, the first step before the initial court appearance.

"As long as your ankle isn't bothering you, we'll walk a couple of more blocks to one of my favorite restaurants located in the peninsula. I reserved a small private dining room for us." He grinned boyishly. "Do you like steak and salad along with Italian food?"

"I like all kinds of food and especially salad. Which reminds me, I know a great joke. Want to hear it?"

He grinned. "Absolutely."

"What did the bacon say to the tomato?"

She was rewarded by his deep chuckle. "That's an easy one. Lettuce get together."

A few minutes later they arrived at The Turning Rhinestone, a Charleston institution. Arched windows and the warm scent of wood-burning fireplaces greeted them.

"These heart-pine floors are one hundred years old," Luciano said as they were led to an exclusive private room in the back of the restaurant. He seemed unaware of the stir he was causing while several uniformed waiters whispered approvingly.

After they were seated and given menus, Luciano grinned at her with a gleam in his eye. "Is it too soon for hurricane jokes, or should we wait for everything to blow over?"

"Only if it's been downgraded to a tropical depression," she laughed.

His expression softened. "Are you recovered from yesterday's ordeal, *Mia Cara?*"

Mia Cara. Her breath came out ragged as she nodded.

"Good. Because I want to kiss you."

She looked around the fancy surroundings and shook her head. "Not here."

"I've never been one to listen to advice." He leaned over the table and cupped her chin, his lips moving firmly against hers.

A white-shirted waiter approached carrying a silver platter with menus and two fluted glasses, one filled with champagne, the other with ice water. He politely cleared his throat and set the glasses on the table.

Feeling her face flush, Anastasia smoothed her dress while attempting a gracious inclination of her head.

"The reservation stated this is a celebration luncheon, Mr. Donati?" the waiter asked.

"Yes." Luciano smiled and sat. "Ms. Markow and I survived yesterday's hurricane intact. We've been apart for sixteen years, so this lunch is a celebration of our reunion."

"Very good, sir." The waiter handed them menus.

Once the a la carte entrees were explained and orders placed, Luciano asked, "How is your daughter faring without you?"

Anastasia perched her chin on her hands. "I called her this morning from my aunt's house while Jaclyn took your dog for a walk. Soo-Min said she missed me, although she sounded happy. I'm anxious to return home and see her, then begin custody proceedings."

He reached for her hand and gave an encouraging squeeze. "Liz will offer legal expertise, and I'll come along for moral support." He lifted his glass and prompted her to do the same.

"A toast to spirited friendships and forever friends." A quiet smile kindled in his espresso-colored gaze as they clinked glasses. "May I have the good fortune to win a special woman's loyal heart, and the worthiness to deserve her love."

CHAPTER 10

*L*unch was an extravagant affair which began with jumbo shrimp cocktail appetizers and a chopped green salad, followed by crispy crab cakes seared to perfection, and creamy whipped potatoes.

Luciano's perfectly cooked steak arrived sizzling at the table. Carrots in a soy glaze and thick cut fries accompanied his meal. Hardly Italian cuisine, nonetheless, the meal was exquisitely satisfying and delicious.

A rich, creamy rice dish was offered for dessert, which they shared.

Full to bursting, Anastasia eagerly accepted Luciano's offer to walk and show her the streets of Charleston. They strolled aimlessly hand in hand while he pointed out important monuments and distinguished museums, his delight infectious. He glanced at his watch as they walked toward the historic district. "Would you like to take a carriage ride before dark?"

She stopped to admire an iron gate adorned with a flower box filled with purple pansies and couldn't help her smile, thinking of Jaclyn's romance comment regarding good-looking men in horse-drawn carriages. She hesitated, prolonging the moment. "I'd love a carriage ride with you."

They strode to the end of a cobbled street where horses with carriages were lined. Luciano assisted her into the leather seat of the carriage, then sat beside her. His arm possessively went around her shoulders, and she turned into his warm body and reassuring strength.

"I'm looking forward to visiting you in Vermont," he said. "I haven't been back there since I graduated from college."

"Will you arrive in time for your Valentine's Day birthday?" she asked.

He sat back and grinned. "How did you know about my birthday?"

"Jaclyn told me."

He shook his head. "I should've known."

"Soo-Min's a wonderful little helper in the kitchen and loves to lick the icing off the mixing spoon," Anastasia said. "I took a cake decorating course a few years ago, so be prepared for a fancy cake." Inwardly, she smiled. Years ago, she'd purchased a heart-shaped baking tin and never used it. She visualized a three-tiered cake adorned with chocolate curls and butter cream frosting.

"We bake a sour cream chocolate cake to die for," she added.

"I like vanilla."

She burst out laughing. "Do you like strawberry jam? I can spread it between the layers."

"Chocolate or vanilla layers?"

"I'm a versatile baker and can make an equally delicious vanilla layer cake."

"Perfect." He leaned over and his mouth slowly descended on hers. "Remember, I like anything sweet."

The carriage jolted forward, sweeping through a main iron gate, and the good-natured driver pointed out rows of rainbow-colored houses. Glimmering lights began to shine from the homes, signaling the approach of dusk. The flame from the coach lamps flickered rhythmically with each clip-clop of the horses' hooves.

"Before I forget, we should exchange cell phone numbers." Luciano dropped his arm and pulled out his cell phone. "I'll give you my office number, also."

She plugged his numbers into the new cell phone she'd purchased that morning. He plugged in hers.

Her wrist itched. Without thinking, she absently scratched through her sweater, surprised to feel a wetness. She pushed up her sleeves and gasped. The mole on her wrist was scaly and oozing blood.

Luciano's gaze collided with hers. "When did that happen?" His dark brows drew together as he lifted her wrist and examined the mole.

She yanked free from his grasp. "I've had the mole for years and noticed it was swollen shortly after arriving at your house yesterday. I'm sure it's nothing, although I'll call Dr. Leskin when I get back home. He's my family doctor."

Luciano withdrew a handkerchief from his sports jacket and pressed it against her wrist. "You're going home immediately to have this mole checked by a specialist." He rapped for the driver to stop the carriage. "We're taking a taxi back to your aunt and uncle's house. Then I'm putting you on the first and fastest train out of Charleston."

She looked down and pressed her hands to her temples. No. Not again. The surgical excision, the scarring, the talk of safety margins and healthy-looking skin tissue also removed. She couldn't face the terrifying prospect alone.

"Are you able to come with me?" Her voice choked, she was shaking. She sounded desperate. Pathetic. Again. She closed her eyes. *Rely on yourself.*

When she opened her eyes, Luciano was gazing intently

at her and shaking his head. "I can't. I want to .... but I can't. My secretary was able to move the board meeting to tomorrow. The investors rescheduled other appointments to accommodate me and I can't cancel."

No one had ever supported her when she was sick. Slowly, she shook her head and a heaviness filled her body. "I understand."

"I'll fly to Vermont as soon as my investors and I come to an agreement," Luciano was saying. He was offering false hope and a weak smile. He'd explained the reasons why he was uncomfortable around hospitals and doctors. He didn't like the feeling of being powerless, and the gut-wrenching memories.

So, in the end, despite his good intentions, his good reasons, his good excuses, he wouldn't come.

She swallowed hard. "I'll miss you."

CHAPTER 11

*W*ith a thin cover draped around her naked body, Anastasia sat shivering in the office examining room, waiting for Dr. Bon, the dermatologist, to scrape the top layer of the mole on her wrist after the anesthetic took hold. At Luciano's insistence, her family doctor, Dr. Leskin, had referred her to the specialist.

"As you know from your previous history, this is a minor biopsy which my office will send to the lab," Dr. Bon explained. "We should get results back in a week. If it's suspicious, we'll schedule an appointment to remove the rest of the mole."

She nodded and thanked him as he left room. Dr. Bon had inspected every inch of her body. Fortunately, he'd found no other suspicious moles.

She inched off the examining table and hurriedly dressed, anxious to pick up her daughter. The previous day, she'd gotten off the train in Vermont and arrived on Justin's doorstep soon afterward. He'd been surprised to see her several days earlier than planned, but Eliza had seemed relieved that her week entertaining a four-year-old child had ended.

Soo-Min had greeted Anastasia's return with a scream of delight. She'd broken into an enormous smile, then bombarded Anastasia with questions about Charleston.

Anastasia retrieved her phone from her purse. There were no calls from Justin, who'd agreed to watch Soo-Min for the appointment, although there were three text messages from Luciano:

'I'm thinking about you. Are you at your appointment? Text me.'

'These pompous board members insist on dragging these endless meetings one more day. Text me.'

And finally, 'Where are you? Text me.'

A few minutes later, she ducked into her car and texted him back: 'Dr. Bon scraped the mole and is sending it to the lab. He'll call when the results come back in a week.'

Immediately, Luciano responded: 'I've booked the first flight out of Charleston to Vermont the day after tomorrow and arrive at ten o'clock in the morning. Can you pick me up at the Burlington airport?'

'Yes,' her fingers typed quickly. "Soo-Min will be with me. She's still off from preschool because of winter break.'

She waited several minutes for his next reply and tapped her fingers on the steering wheel to pass the time. Finally, he texted: 'Looking forward to it.'

No words were added regarding when Liz was flying to Vermont to file the appeal.

Sighing, she eased her car out of the parking lot into traffic. A forty-five minute car ride from Burlington with Luciano and her chatty daughter should prove to be an adventure. She smiled at the thought.

· · ·

"HI, MR. LUCIANO, I'm Soo-Min. What's your favorite color? I like blue."

Luciano gazed at the adorable little girl sporting straight, shiny-black bangs and wild pigtails, hopping on one foot at the Burlington airport. She held up a sign pointing to thick letters scrawled in Crayola-blue, reading, 'Welcome to Vermont.'

Then he gazed at her gorgeous mother and brushed a light kiss on Anastasia's lips. "I missed you. Three days is a long time," he said.

Her alluring body moved closer to his. "I missed you, too."

He bent to the little girl's height. "Hello, Soo-Min. I've heard so much about you."

Soo-Min pushed oversized eyeglasses up her nose and stared at him. "Your eyes are different from mine."

"Your eyes are prettier," he assured.

"Mommy said you're nice and tell funny jokes. Can you tell me one?"

"Age appropriate," Anastasia prompted.

He grinned and put a finger to his chin, pretending to ponder. "What did one tomato say to the other tomato?"

Soo-Min stopped jumping and attempted to balance on one foot. "I don't know, what?" She grabbed his hand to steady herself.

"You go ahead and I'll ketchup."

Her gurgle of laughter echoed in the parking garage as Anastasia guided them to her old Ford. He ducked into the passenger seat while Anastasia buckled Soo-Min into the back car seat.

"I hope your flight went well." Anastasia slipped into the driver's seat. "Did the board come to a decision regarding your software project?"

"They're considering a couple of other projects in the U.S. They'll let me know in a few days."

"I'm sure your schedule is packed. We're glad you made time for us." She slanted him a grin.

"Lonely and missing me?" His gaze slid meaningfully to her lips. "There's no place I'd rather be than here with you."

She flushed and drove down the ramp. "How long are you staying?"

"A few days, or until the investors come to a decision. Then I'll fly back to Charleston and return, hopefully, with Liz. I reminded her last night that you're anxious to file the petition."

"I thought she was in Las Vegas."

"We spoke on the phone." He looked at the clock on her dashboard. "I arranged for a car and rented a house while I'm here. I'll come by your apartment later this evening."

She gave him her address which he plugged into his phone.

"Then we can plan some fun activities with Soo-Min for the rest of the week," he added.

She eased the Ford into the left lane and picked up speed. "You haven't lived here for many years. Let me remind you that Stowe's population is still around five thousand people. Weekend excitement is a trip to a village shop for a cup of coffee or a visit to Stacy's Chocolatiers for a box of Sea Salt caramels." She gave a quick thumbs-up with one hand. "Although the Winter Carnival starts soon and is kid-friendly."

"You and I competed in a snow volleyball game at the Winter Carnival, remember? Guys versus girls."

She laughed. "And the girls won."

The girls won. And Anastasia had been exuberant with glee. She'd goaded him throughout the game with impertinent sidewise glances whenever he missed a shot, her smoky eyes ablaze with laughter. She'd been full of life and breathtaking. He'd wanted to take her in his arms even then.

As they sped past picturesque, snowy fields, he admired tree branches bowing under the heavy weight of snow. He'd forgotten how beautiful a winter scene in Vermont was. He rolled down the window a couple of inches and sniffed. Cold air whistled through the car, the scent frosty and exhilarating. Lovingly designed snowmen complete with carrot noses, short and tall, sat poignantly in every yard, a misshapen stick propped nearby. The desire to leap out of the car and make a dozen snowballs was number one on his 'to-do' list when they stopped.

"Soo-Min and I are preparing dinner tonight," Anastasia was saying. "You can expect kid's fare, which means macaroni and cheese and chicken fingers."

"I'll bring dessert." He turned to the backseat. "Soo-Min, what's your favorite dessert?"

"Chocolate ice cream!" Soo-Min declared. Then, she added, "Do you know The Wheels on the Bus song? I know every word of it. Want me to sing it to you all the way home?"

CHAPTER 12

Soo-Min sat in the middle of Anastasia and Luciano on a park bench on Stowe's Main Street. Anastasia's cheeks tingled because of the freezing temperatures and her feet felt numb. She rubbed her gloved hands together and breathed into them, sending puffs of her warm breath into the air. Although she'd bundled her daughter in several layers of winter clothing, she still asked her, "Are you cold?"

Soo-Min licked traces of hot chocolate from her mouth and fanned at her face with mittened hands. "No, Mommy, I'm hot. And I'm squished because the zipper of my coat is choking my neck." She peered up at Luciano. "Can I sit on your lap?"

"No, honey," Anastasia began.

"That's all right. I like holding her." He lifted Soo-Min onto his lap. "As long as I can take her picture first. Lean in, Anastasia. We'll take a selfie." She complied as he pulled out his phone and began singing, "Twinkle, twinkle, little butterfly ..."

Soo-Min giggled and Anastasia burst out laughing as his camera clicked.

"Ice carving demonstrations on Main Street are one of my favorite Winter Carnival events," Anastasia said after she'd wiped the tears of hilarity from her face. "I'm fascinated by the skill involved."

"Mommy, what ice sculpture are you voting for? I like the butterfly because it's a song." Soo-Min wiggled on Luciano's lap and gazed up at him. "What about you, Mr. Luciano? Will the butterfly fly away before we vote?"

He laughed and put his cell phone back in his coat pocket. "I think the butterfly is happy right where he is, just waiting for our vote so he can win."

Soo-Min let out a joyful squeal. "It's a she!"

"I knew that," he corrected himself.

Anastasia sat back and let the feelings of optimism surge through her. She loved Vermont. Thick snowflakes fell softly from the afternoon sky, and the little town would soon be covered by a fat white blanket.

Five days had flown by since Luciano had arrived, and he'd planned to return to Charleston in the morning. His investors had come to a decision, they'd informed him. Disarmingly calm, although an impending multi-million-dollar deal would greatly affect his billionaire status, he'd finalized the call with a professional 'thank you.'

He pointed to a run-down building across the way. "Isn't that my old boxing gym?"

"Yes, they went out of business several years ago."

He frowned. "That's too bad. Boxing kept so many guys off the streets and out of trouble. Any self-discipline I learned was taught at that gym. After hitting some punching bags, I'd feel physically and mentally exhausted when I got home."

"And all sweaty." She stared at the building, trying to drag her thoughts away from him leaving before she'd gotten her test results back from the lab. She'd hoped he'd insist on staying, declaring that the investors could wait because she was more important.

She needed his calm reassurance, his solid arm wrapped around her shoulders.

His gaze caught hers and he nodded, seeming to read her thoughts. "If the negotiations with my investors move along quickly, I'll return in a couple of days."

"You just want your birthday cake." She kept her tone light and avoided his eyes.

"I just want you, *Mia Cara*." His head dipped to kiss her. He, wearing a navy-blue parka and worn denim jeans, was recklessly handsome. They sat on the corner of Main Street, kissing with a passion that soon had her daughter giggling and pushing their faces apart.

"What about me, don't you want me?" Soo-Min asked.

Luciano bounced her on his lap and pressed a kiss on her forehead. "Of course I want you. Who wouldn't? And did you know I own a dog and her name is Lady?"

Soo-Min giggled and looked around. "Where is she?"

"My sister, Jaclyn, is watching the dog."

"I want to see your dog. What does she look like?"

"Well, she's big and has golden brown fur. She's a Golden Retriever." He pulled his phone out of his pocket. "Here's a picture."

Soo-Min stared intently at the photo. "I love Gold Treaters!"

"I do, too. She's an older dog, though, so I didn't want to take her on an airplane."

Soo-Min folded her tiny arms together. "I love dogs, and Mommy won't buy me one."

"I promise I'll bring Lady with me soon so you can meet her. Is that okay?"

With a nod, Soo-Min snuggled against his chest.

"Have you booked your flight back here?" Anastasia

inquired.

"I'll book when I return to Charleston. Jaclyn considered flying back with me, but she's been canoeing with her new instructor every day and seems preoccupied. Besides, she usually watches my dog when I'm away. I talked with Liz a number of times, and as soon as this Las Vegas case is wrapped up, she'll be able to come. Then we can file that petition."

He spoke so confidently, yet all Anastasia could think about was that he'd talked with Liz a number of times.

She looked away. A boulder settled where her optimism had previously surged. He might be spending every waking hour with her and Soo-Min, ice-skating and sledding, attending Broomball and hockey events at the ice arena, but he'd been free to talk all night with Liz.

"So, should we hold off on your birthday celebration so we can celebrate with Liz?" she snapped. "I can't fit thirty-five candles on one cake, by the way."

He seemed visibly taken aback by her churlishness. "Who said I wanted to share my birthday cake with anyone except you and Soo-Min?"

She fixed her gaze on a florist shop across the street, pondering whether or not he was telling the truth or just humoring her.

And why the answer meant so much.

"Look. We can see the house I'm renting from here." Luciano pointed past the florist and candy shop to a distant hill. "It's that little speck of a house at the very top."

Anastasia shaded her eyes from the rays of the setting sun. "The old Cobbo mansion? I didn't realize that home was vacant. The Cobbos used to boast about their 'expansive views of the Worcester mountains.' Isn't that mansion over seven thousand square feet?"

With a nod and a smile, he said, "Complete with a wood-fired pizza oven, a nine car garage and a large barn for horses, none of which I've used. The property is vacant, and the realtor said I could rent month to month until it sells. The view from the outdoor balcony is truly breathtaking."

But all she focused on was the 'renting month to month' observation, meaning he'd given thought to staying in Vermont after his birthday and for the filing of the custody petition.

"I'd love to see the property when you return. Your visit went by so quickly." She viewed the row of houses at the bottom of the hill where the lights were beginning to flicker from tiny windows as night settled in. Her vision blurred because of the snow falling on her eyelashes and she wiped at her eyes. Or perhaps it was because he was leaving and she felt a void she couldn't explain. "We should head back to my apartment. Soo-Min's enjoyed a very exciting day."

Luciano put a finger to his lips. "She's sleeping. I'll carry her to the car."

Carefully, he lifted Soo-Min from his lap and bundled her into his arms.

Soo-Min's eyes flew open. "Mommy, did the butterfly win?"

"They haven't announced the winners yet," Anastasia replied.

Soo-Min's small mittened fingers pointed to the park behind Luciano. "Can I play with the other kids?"

Anastasia shook her head. "Not today. It's getting dark and time for dinner."

Soo-Min tugged at the collar of Luciano's coat. "Do you know how to make snow angels?"

"Snow angels," Anastasia corrected.

"That's what I said, Mommy, snow angles. It's easy, Mr. Luciano. I can show you in my backyard while Mommy's cooking dinner."

CHAPTER 13

*A*nastasia plunked her hands on her red-aproned hips and shook her head at the mess in her once neat kitchen. Now she knew why she'd given up cake decorating. Her gaze stopped at the mountainous heap of bowls and spatulas piled in the sink. Soo-Min stood on a chair at the kitchen table, a mixing bowl in one hand and large wooden spoon laden with butter cream frosting in the other.

"Mommy, this frosting is delicious!" She took another leisurely lick on the spoon. "Won't Mr. Luciano be happy when he sees our beautiful cake?"

Anastasia stood back from the table to admire their masterpiece. The heart-shaped, three-tiered vanilla cake sat proudly on a white pedestal stand. An empty jar of seedless strawberry jam sat on the table. Cherry-red decorative piping on the cake read, 'Happy Thirty-Fifth Birthday, Luciano.' As a garnish, Anastasia had added fresh strawberries and chocolate leaves on one side of the cake and dipped several strawberries in melted chocolate around the cake's border. On a whim, she'd added a pair of red boxing gloves, shaped like mittens, below the piping.

Her kitchen clock chimed four o'clock. Luciano had called the previous morning, assuring her that he'd arrive in plenty of time to celebrate his birthday. He'd sounded rushed and preoccupied, the same way he'd sounded every day on the phone since returning to Charleston, answering her inquiries regarding his meetings with clipped, short replies.

Suppose he was too busy and didn't show?

No. He'd never disappoint her and Soo-Min, especially on Valentine's Day.

Although, she thought wistfully, throughout the day she'd half-expected the florist to ring the doorbell of her apartment holding a bouquet of flowers from Luciano, along with a tender note written in his bold handwriting, assuring her that he was counting the minutes until he saw her again.

No flowers had arrived. Certainly, no note.

It was his birthday, not hers, she chided herself. She pulled off her apron and kissed her daughter's sticky chin, envisioning his lazy smile when he strode into the kitchen and viewed his birthday cake, ablaze with candles. She'd purchased a small red leather journal for his birthday gift. After nibbling on the end of her pen for several minutes while she'd considered what was in her heart, she'd written inside the front cover: 'Che Sara Sara.'

Whatever will be, will be, she mused, because the future wasn't theirs to see.

Below the Italian song lyrics she'd added, 'Your future will be magnificent. I hope you'll fill this journal with wonderful memories in the coming years.'

She paused, envisioning him as a brave little Italian boy with disheveled brown hair and a pensive, penetrating gaze, clutching his birth mother's journal, his only memento of her. What had been his thoughts, his fears when he traveled to America? How frightening it must've been for him to step onto a foreign country with so many different sights and smells assaulting him all at once. Her heart swelled with pride at the principled, successful man he'd become.

"Tonight's going to be perfect, honey," she declared to Soo-Min.

"Every day is perfect with you, Mommy!" Soo-Min giggled.

Anastasia dabbed at her eyes with her apron. Her daughter knew just what to say to chase away any doubts. Of course he'd arrive. He was a millionaire and had projects and employees and business ventures, all vying for his attention. *Be understanding.*

Anastasia lifted her daughter down from the kitchen chair. "Let's get you in the bathtub so you'll look beautiful for Luciano."

"I'm not wearing that lace dress you bought. It's too itchy."

Anastasia laughed. "You can pick out whatever you want to wear tonight, as long as it's red."

"Why?"

"It's Valentine's Day."

"Are you wearing red?"

"Yes." Anastasia had bought a lace dress. It was clingy and shorter than she usually wore, a crimson lace sheath lined in satin and with an open back. She'd splurged on a pair of black lace-up stilettos and planned on pulling her hair back in a messy bun. She grinned, thinking about his seductive perusal and approving smile when he arrived.

EXCEPT HE NEVER SHOWED.

Anastasia sat with her daughter on their worn living room couch. Between them, they'd eaten almost half the birthday cake, although Anastasia had eaten the most.

"Mommy, we never finished blowing up the balloons, and

there's a red and a white one left." Soo-Min sat on the couch swinging her legs, then somersaulted across the living room floor, her chubby legs clad in patterned tights, her feet facing upward as she attempted a head stand. She'd decided to wear a dress after all, adorned with sequins along the sleeves and a crinoline petticoat underneath.

"It's after eleven o'clock and well past your bedtime." Anastasia unlaced her stilettos and flung them off. "You've had way too much sugar." She changed her daughter into a pair of warm pajamas. After teeth-brushing, she tucked her into bed. The bath and hair wash could wait until morning.

Anastasia's inner voice chattered in her ear, reminding that she'd failed the perfect mother award today.

For the past several hours, she'd constantly checked her cell phone, waiting for a text message or phone call from Luciano. But he hadn't bothered to contact her.

More than once, she'd been tempted to call him. She'd even checked her email for his flight numbers, realizing that he'd never sent her that information. Usually he was so meticulous, with each day of his life completely planned.

But not today.

After reading the barnyard animals book to Soo-Min, her daughter imitated the sound of a bleating lamb for the tenth time, petted the soft fuzzy fur in the book and fell asleep.

The clock in the kitchen chimed midnight. Valentine's Day was officially over.

Anastasia padded to her bedroom and sat on the bed. Hesitating at first, she slowly punched in Jaclyn's phone number, mentally rehearsing what she'd say. She didn't want to alarm Jaclyn, but it was normal to be concerned about Luciano, right?

Jaclyn's phone rang several times, then went to voice mail. Her recorded voice declared, "Today's Valentine's Day and the best day to book a cruise. You may be here, but I'll take you there. Leave a message."

In the background of the recording, a dog barked, sounding suspiciously like Lady.

So where was Luciano?

Anastasia clicked the end button. She didn't leave a message.

CHAPTER 14

*a*nastasia jerked up from a jumbled dream to the sound of an insistently ringing cell phone. She stared at the time, astonished that she'd slept until eight o'clock in the morning. Even more surprising, her daughter's room was quiet and she was apparently still asleep.

"Hello?" Anastasia answered.

"Dr. Bon's office calling for Anastasia Markow," responded an efficient sounding nurse. "Your lab report came back and Dr. Bon would like to see you in his office today."

"Can ... Can you share the results with me?" Anastasia asked slowly.

"I'm sorry, that's not allowed. However, Dr. Bon will explain everything. The earliest appointment is eleven o'clock this morning."

"I see, and thank you. Eleven is fine." Anastasia clicked the end button.

Appointment. Dr. Bon. She stared at her bandaged wrist, the conversation hitting her hard. It was bad news, or the doctor's office wouldn't have scheduled an appointment so quickly. The thought was like a crushing weight on her chest, and she grabbed the bedpost as she stood, staggering to her feet. She'd be facing her doctor's appointment alone. Again.

She expelled a long, drawn-out breath. For the first time in her life, she'd half-believed that a man really had cared about her and that Luciano was more than a childhood friend and ally. Somehow, she'd believed he'd offered love and support, but those were the daydreams of a giddy, foolish schoolgirl. *Pathetic.*

She lifted her chin. *No. Not this time.*

She made a hasty call to Justin and Eliza, who both assured her that Soo-Min would be well taken care of and encouraged Anastasia to take all the time she needed.

She felt a twinge of guilt for what she did next, because she dialed Liz's office in Charleston.

The secretary with the brisk voice answered. "Fullman law offices."

Anastasia felt her hands start to sweat. "This is Anastasia Markow. Liz Fullman is arranging a trip to Vermont regarding a custody filing. Is she back in town from Las Vegas?"

The secretary hesitated. "Ms. Fullman is out of the country. Let me check your file." The secretary stepped away from the phone for several minutes. Returning, she said with polite indifference, "Ms. Fullman is sending Miss Debbie Porter, one of our junior associates, to Vermont. When the associate arrives in a few days, she'll contact you to arrange a time to meet at the Family Court Clerk's Office in Hyde Park."

With a 'thank you,' Anastasia walked to her daughter's bedroom. Soo-Min sat on her bed with a pillow propped behind her head. She was reading the barnyard animals book aloud, mimicking the sounds of the animals.

"You'll be going to your father's house today." Anastasia

opened the painstakingly neat dresser drawer to pull out a pair of corduroy pants and matching unicorn top for her daughter.

Soo-Min jumped off the bed and clapped her hands. "Yay! It's fun at Daddy's house. He throws a ball with me inside, Mommy, in the living room, and Eliza never gets mad about the mess."

"Oh," Anastasia answered quietly. Perhaps Justin and Eliza were better parents than she realized. Soo-Min seemed happy and content whenever she visited them. She came back clean and well-fed, filled with stories of her adventures. Sure, they allowed her to stay up late sometimes, although hadn't Anastasia done the same thing last night?

But Soo-Min ... Soo-Min was her daughter, the child she'd waited for all those endless years of infertility treatments. At thirty-two years old, she'd promised herself that Soo-Min deserved to have the best. The best mother, care, parenting. Nonetheless, that image of her daughter laughing and clapping her hands, excited to go to her father's house, played continuously in Anastasia's mind.

She let out a breath she hadn't realized she was holding as she dressed. Perhaps she was wrong. Perhaps Soo-Min needed her parents to work together.

SEVERAL HOURS LATER, Anastasia sat on a heavy wooden chair in Dr. Bon's office.

"The diagnosis of melanoma has been confirmed," Dr. Bon began, sitting across from her at his desk. "I suspected as much because the tumor was cracked and bleeding. However, it's in the early stages. I'll order blood work and, assuming the results show no traces of melanoma in any organs, I'll schedule surgery to remove the tumor and surrounding tissues."

She took a deep breath. "And then?"

He smiled reassuringly. "And then no other treatment is needed."

"Thank you." Her cell phone pinged and she reached inside her purse. "I'm sorry. I thought I'd left my phone on vibrate. I won't be long. The message might be about my daughter."

Dr. Bon pushed back his chair and readied himself to leave. "Take all the time you need. My office will call you with details of the surgery date." He left the office and kept the door ajar.

She opened her phone to a text and photo from Luciano:

'Buona Sera, Mia Cara, I'm in Italy! I found my Italian family and can't wait for you and Soo-Min to meet them. I'm in a little town in northwestern Sicily and staring out at the Egadi Islands as I type this, although it's getting dark because it's nearing six o'clock. My Nona, the woman with the white streak in her gray hair, is standing beside me. My great-aunt is the lady wearing the funny straw hat. And they said I have a birth sister and that she was adopted as a baby. Her name is Clara and she lives in Ireland. I have so much to tell you. I will call as soon as I get a good cell phone connection. I miss you and Soo-Min. *Arrivederci.'*

In the photo, Luciano sat at the bottom of a broad band of stone steps flanked by rugged mountains on one side and a distant, sandy seashore on the other. He was smiling broadly, holding a stem of fresh basil. He was surrounded by several dark-haired children and his Nona and great-aunt stood beside him. In the far corner, just beyond the steps, a breathtaking blonde woman was laughing into the camera.

Liz.

Anastasia's hands closed around the arm rails of the chair, a lump of sadness lodged in her throat. Luciano was in Italy. With Liz.

CHAPTER 15

*A*nastasia drove directly to the familiar school where she'd taught several years before. She walked to the office, surprised by the pert, new secretary with curly auburn hair sitting behind a computer with her hand on the mouse. The previous secretary must've retired. Anastasia noted that the auburn-haired secretary was surfing the internet and was about to purchase some new makeup.

"Is Mrs. Danner available?" Anastasia asked.

The secretary shook her head. "Mrs. Danner hasn't been the principal here for a couple of years."

"Can I speak to the new principal?

"Mr. Norr? Sorry. He won't be in until next week. Would you like to make an appointment to see him?"

"Yes, and I'd like to fill out an application for a teacher position. I'm certified in grades Kindergarten through sixth grade. I used to teach here."

The secretary took her hand off the mouse and mini-mized the computer screen. "All the applications are submitted online. There hasn't been any new hires for a couple of years, though, because of state cutbacks."

"Thank you."

There were other schools, Anastasia told herself encouragingly, as she walked back to her car. She could apply to every school in the district online, which was much more convenient.

Nevertheless, to return to her apartment in order to begin submitting, she'd need to drive. And she couldn't muster up the strength to put her key into the ignition. She sat in her old Ford in the parking lot, staring at a run-down school she hardly recognized.

Her cell phone vibrated. She recognized the Charleston area code, although the caller ID identified the number to 'Liz Fullman.'

"Yes?" Anastasia answered.

"*Mia Cara*, finally, I have decent cell phone service. Did you get my text and photo? You didn't respond."

She swallowed, feeling her heart beat triple time. "When did you arrive in Italy?"

"My investigators contacted me by email when I got back in Charleston. Then they called and said they'd found a solid lead and I needed to leave immediately for Italy. It happened very fast."

"Why didn't you call? I waited ... waited ..." Angrily, she swiped tears from her cheeks and covered the phone with her hand so he wouldn't hear her choking up.

"Did you get your lab results?"

"Yes." Her fingers trembled as she held the phone. "It's melanoma."

There was a hesitation on the line. "What's next?"

She leaned weakly against the car's seat. "The same procedure as last time."

"We will get through it together."

How? From Italy? She shook her head. She didn't state her reservations aloud.

"*Mia Cara*, are you there? Italy is exactly how I remembered— *bella,* the sky, the sunshine, the fig trees. You and Soo-Min will love it."

Except they'd never see it.

"We baked a cake for your birthday." *And Valentine's Day.* "Then we waited all night for you to arrive."

"I'm sorry. I spent my birthday in a jet-lagged haze. This flight takes over fifteen hours counting the layovers."

She inhaled, then spoke sharply. "So Liz flew to Italy with you?"

The silence of the next few moments was interrupted by static. "She dropped all her appointments to come with me. She's leaving Italy today and flying back to Vegas."

"How long are you staying?"

"Another week, perhaps. There are some cousins I haven't met who live in a neighboring town."

"I'm happy for you." She pressed the phone close to her ear, holding it so tightly her fingers cramped. Then she took a long, suffocated breath. "Please, Luciano, don't call me again."

"What? What did you say?" The phone crackled. Luciano's voice was a static blur and the connection ended.

CHAPTER 16

"Y̶ou're acting ridiculous," Jaclyn scolded over the speaker phone as Anastasia drove to the Family Court Clerk's Office in Hyde Park a few days afterward. Liz's junior associate, Debbie Porter, had arranged a ten o'clock meeting to assist Anastasia with the custody petition filing.

Anastasia's insides had cringed when she'd asked Justin and Eliza to take care of Soo-Min. Her explanation had been vague and she'd mumbled something about checking out neighboring counties for a teaching job. Although if she were honest with herself, she was being deceitful to a man who may not have loved her anymore, but who was proving to be a good father.

Anastasia huffed into the phone. "Luciano left without a word. No phone call, no text, nothing. Soo-Min and I baked the most beautiful cake for his Valentine birthday."

"So bake another cake."

"It's too late, his birthday's over. Valentine's Day is over. He could've called from the airport before he boarded the plane. This was such an important time in his life, finding and meeting his Italian relatives."

"And you wanted to share that moment with him."

"Is that so wrong?"

"Can't you be happy for him? There'll be other moments. He didn't have time," Jaclyn said. "His secretary said he received a phone call during the board meeting, answered the call, and then got up and left the meeting with no explanation. He asked her to call me to watch Lady with an abrupt explanation of where he was headed, and then he was gone."

Anastasia drew a ragged breath. If she said the words aloud, they'd become a fact. "Liz is with him in Italy, isn't she?" She wanted to add that it didn't matter in the least. Instead, she said nothing.

A brief beat ticked by. "They're friends, nothing more, although she'd certainly welcome his advances. His secretary said that Liz had just gotten back from Vegas and stopped in his office when he received the call from the investigator. She had her bags packed from Vegas and insisted on going with him."

'What about me?' Anastasia rubbed the back of her neck, remembering her daughter's adamant voice. She was starting to act exactly like Soo-Min, as if she were a four-year-old child.

He'd pressed a kiss on Soo-Min's forehead. *"Of course I want you. Who wouldn't?"*

But nobody wants you, Anastasia, an inner voice whispered. Not your mother, not your ex-husband. No one loves you. She squeezed her eyes shut for a second. *Luciano, I thought you were starting to love me.*

Jaclyn sighed impatiently. "The main reason I called was to ask about your mole. What did the lab results show? Did you call your aunt and uncle and let them know?"

"It's melanoma and no, not yet."

"Anastasia, I'm so sorry." A pause. "What's next?"

"Dr. Bonn said the surgery will be minimal, same as last time."

"Not so bad."

"Not so bad," Anastasia echoed, driving up to a large brick building. "I'm in Hyde Park and there's a very pretty young woman with long blonde hair waiting outside the Clerk's Office. She's probably Debbie, the junior associate."

"Call me when you're done filing that petition," Jaclyn said. "Although, honestly, this custody proceeding is going to be emotionally and physically draining for everyone. The more you told me about what your aunt and uncle had said, the more I'm agreeing with them. Okay, so Justin's a jerk, but it doesn't matter if he's a good father. And Soo-Min seems to enjoy Eliza. Do you really want to upset your daughter with home studies and arguments and disruptions?"

Anastasia parked the car. Her chest tightened with an aching lump of contrition. "I'm not so sure anymore."

"Well, it's your decision. And by the way, you haven't asked about my canoeing lessons with Bart."

"Apparently Sam isn't on your eligible bachelor radar anymore?" Anastasia looked in the mirror and gave her friend a long-distance grin. "I hope Bart's rich because you love a lavish lifestyle."

"He's as poor as a church mouse, as the saying goes. Although now I realize that love is all you need. Not money, not prestige, not a great job and expensive home. Just love and a canoe."

"I'm assuming your Valentine's Day went better than mine."

"Bart looks at me the way Luciano looks at you. I've watched my brother, and he's in love with you. And you love him, right? You always have."

"It's hard to get over being hurt."

"I'm the first person to let my brother know when he's done something wrong, but he'll make it up to you. I know him. He didn't mean to hurt you."

"I thought I knew him, too," Anastasia whispered, clicking off the phone. She ducked out of the car and walked toward the Family Court Clerk's Office.

She'd traveled to Charleston for information to file for sole custody of Soo-Min. Sure, it'd been wonderful to see Luciano again and renew their friendship. However, she hadn't been looking for romance.

Why then, couldn't she stop visualizing him laughing while making snow angels, 'snow angles' according to Soo-Min, in her tiny backyard? And why couldn't she forget his grinning rendition of 'Hark the Herald Angles Sing,' sung in his deep, baritone voice?

She'd joined in the chorus, laughing uproariously, so hard that tears had run down their cheeks. She remembered her daughter's endless giggles, and how the creases on Luciano's forehead had disappeared the entire time he'd been in Vermont.

Funny, she hadn't thought about that until now.

But now was too late. Because now it was over.

CHAPTER 17

"*Hi*, are you Anastasia Markow? I'm Debbie Porter, a junior associate at the Fullman Law Offices."

Anastasia extended her hand, surprised to feel the young woman's sweaty palm. "Yes, I'm pleased to meet you."

"Ms. Liz Fullman sent me, as you know." The associate looked around. "Where's your ex-husband? What's his name again?"

"Justin. I wasn't aware he was supposed to be here. No one told me."

The associate frowned and scratched her head. "I'm not really sure, either."

Anastasia dropped her hand and bristled. "Shouldn't that be something you'd know?"

"I was assigned this case a couple of days ago. Ms. Fullman mentioned being obligated to do a quick favor for someone. All the case files are backed up because of the Charleston storm and all the other lawyers in the Fullman offices are overloaded."

Anastasia struggled with her impatience and began

walking toward the doorway. "Shall we go inside, introduce ourselves and get started?"

The associate stared at Anastasia with a look resembling stage fright and stopped mid-step. "Actually, this is my first case, and I don't want to make a fool of myself. This could have devastating consequences on my career."

Second by second, Anastasia felt any confidence she'd had left filtering away, but she could do this on her own. She'd promised herself she wouldn't rely on anyone. She turned to the associate. "I don't need your help."

"Really? Are you sure?" The associate looked so relieved that Anastasia almost wanted to put her arms around her to offer reassurance.

Anastasia nodded. "I'm sure. Thanks for coming, and sorry that Liz sent you all this way for apparently nothing."

The young girl offered a hopeful smile. "I can make the one o'clock flight back to Charleston if I leave now."

"Then you should go." Anastasia stood in the doorway of the clerk's office and watched the associate hurry back to her car and drive off. She paused with her hand on the door handle and gazed inside the office without going inside.

A woman from the office came to the door and opened it. "May I help you?"

Anastasia hesitated, just for a moment, and shook her head. "No. I thought I needed something here. I was mistaken."

She walked to her car with her shoulders erect and drove to Justin's house. Eliza and Soo-Min were playing cards on the living room floor. Justin was in the kitchen, watching a TV Food channel, and the chef was explaining the proper way to make sticky rice.

"How's your day going?" Justin asked.

She met her ex's smile with an open nod. "Everything's better now. What about you?"

"I'm enjoying my week off from work. There are advantages to a professor's schedule."

"Mommy," Soo-Min called from the living room, "can I spend the night at Daddy's house? We're going to wrap seaweed around the rice Daddy's cooking. It sounds yucky, but it's really good. Eliza said it's from Korea."

Anastasia laughed. "Yes, of course you can spend the night, honey." She walked to the living room and sat on the floor. "Thanks for everything, Eliza. I know how much you care about Soo-Min. I'm sorry I've been so critical in the past."

"Apology accepted." Eliza pushed a pale blonde streak of hair from her face. "It isn't easy striving to meet your high standards, although I try my best. We hadn't expected you home for another few days, so if you need the time to prepare for your surgery or submit job applications, we're fine with that."

"We'll save some seaweed for you, Mommy. Eliza taught me how to do cartwheels. Wanna see?" Soo-Min pushed her cards aside and demonstrated two flawless cartwheels across the living room.

Anastasia, Justin, and Eliza clapped in unison.

"Thanks, I could use the next several days to submit teacher applications. I'll take Soo-Min to the last day of the Winter Carnival at the end of week," Anastasia said. "They'll be announcing the winners of the ice sculpting competition."

"No problem," Justin said.

And there it was. Parents talking with each other, without the courts involved, doing what was in the best interests of their child.

Anastasia smiled at Justin and Eliza and whispered, "Let's hope the butterfly sculpture wins or I'll be dashing off Main Street and straight back to your house with a very unhappy little girl."

CHAPTER 18

*W*inter in Vermont was a season that lasted for months, although every day in February seemed a little brighter and closer to spring.

Anastasia stood in the playground, pushing Soo-Min on a 'big girl' swing. The weather had warmed, and tiny blades of grass pushed through the thawing snow.

"Higher, Mommy, higher!" her daughter exclaimed. Soo-Min turned to another little girl swinging next to her. "I want to swing as high as Justine. She's my new friend and goes to my school."

Anastasia grinned at Justine's mother. They'd exchanged phone numbers to set up play dates for the girls.

"You don't need to stand here while the girls swing. I can handle both munchkins," Justine's mother said.

"Are you sure?" Anastasia asked. "I'd love a cup of coffee."

"Go ahead. I guarantee we'll still be here in twenty minutes."

Grabbing her hot coffee a few minutes later, Anastasia found a bench near the back of the park where she could see her daughter and new friend swinging.

She sipped and smiled, comfortable with her custody decision. She'd made peace with herself, and peace with Justin and Eliza. She'd been jealous and admittedly bitter of Justin's happiness with Eliza, and she wasn't proud to acknowledge those traits in herself.

She half-sighed. Her face burned with memories of how she'd spoken to Eliza on several occasions— judgmental and dismissive of the young woman's parenting skills. Her apology to Eliza had been long overdue and had been graciously accepted.

That morning, Anastasia's aunt and uncle had been encouraging and understanding during their phone exchange.

"If your prior school doesn't have any teaching vacancies, apply at others," Uncle Filipp had instructed. "You're a smart and determined young woman."

"Actually," she'd replied, "there's a job opening for a second grade teacher in a nearby district that I hadn't considered until I looked online. If I get the job, Soo-Min can attend Kindergarten there, so we'll both be at the same school."

"Sounds good, dear. And how is Luciano, your handsome billionaire friend?" her aunt had asked.

At the mention of his name, Anastasia's lips had quivered, and she'd closed her eyes for a moment to hold back the bleakness filling her chest.

"I believe he's in Italy," she'd answered vaguely.

"He'll be back," her aunt had assured.

Although he wouldn't be back, because he'd finally found what he'd been looking for in Italy. His heritage. His birth family. And with the elegant, successful Liz by his side.

With an audible sigh, Anastasia's gaze shifted restlessly to the crowd of people filling the park, apparently waiting for the ice competition's results. The weather was turning blustery, and she took a last sip of coffee, then folded up the collar of her scarlet wool jacket.

She'd lived in this little town her entire life. It was her home. But today, despite her daughter's laughing shouts coming from the nearby swings, the festive scents of outdoor barbecue and hot chocolate in the air, she felt lonely and forlorn.

She set her empty cup on the bench, opened her large purse and pulled out the small, red journal she'd bought for his birthday gift. She'd decided to keep it with her, keeping a log of her daily activities. So far, she hadn't written a word.

She fingered the smooth leather. '*Che Sara Sara*, whatever will be, will be,' she'd written. A special gift, a special Valentine. She'd assumed Luciano had been on a plane flying to Vermont while she and Soo-Min were baking his birthday cake, although in reality he'd been flying to Italy, his birthplace, with Liz.

Anastasia furiously swiped away the tears streaming down her cheeks and placed the journal back in her purse. Her grip on her feelings was apparently tenuous when it came to Luciano.

No more thinking, she told herself sternly. But her mind wasn't listening, continuing to batter her emotions with replays:

The first time they'd met, he'd returned home from a boxing match, his chin bruised, holding a bag of ice on his swollen, bloody nose. He'd shrugged off her worried teenage exclamations. Never had he looked more handsome, or more vulnerable. Her beat-up, non-swimming Greek god. As she'd predicted that day, his nose, indeed, had been broken.

And sixteen years later, sitting in his luxurious Charleston mansion:

"Our lives are made up of different chapters," he'd said solemnly. *"You seem to be in the middle of a rough one."*

Briefly, she squeezed her eyes closed and leaned back against the cold bench. She must bring her emotions in check. Sure, she'd once been a giddy schoolgirl with a mad crush on a man who's always been out of reach. But not anymore. Today was the conclusion of this rough chapter of her life.

"Mommy, you're not listening." Dimly, her mind registered that Soo-Min was tugging at her sleeve.

Anastasia bent her head. "I'm sorry, honey, what did you say?"

Soo-Min pointed toward Main Street, an impish smile glowing in her eyes. "I said that dog looks like Mr. Luciano's Gold Treater."

Anastasia slowly stood, staring at the tall, muscular man walking along Main Street, firmly holding a Golden Retriever's leash in one hand, and a large brown bag emblazoned with 'Stacy Chocolatiers' in the other. The man seemed to be searching for someone, his gaze drifting past the barbecue and hot chocolate stands, past the butterfly ice sculpture. Anastasia's heart pounded as his brown-eyed gaze looked directly into hers.

She blinked. Her feet seemed rooted in place. She wanted to tear her gaze away and look somewhere else, anywhere else, although his penetrating gaze wouldn't allow it.

He looked tanned, a black bristled beard along his strong jaw. He strode quickly toward her, jostling through the crowd, holding her gaze, remorse and desperation etched on his masculine face.

"Mr. Luciano. Mommy, that's him!" Soo-Min grabbed Anastasia's hand and yanked her forward, wending their way around groups of children and parents. "Hurry, Mommy, you're moving too slow!"

A moment later, they stood a few inches apart.

Anastasia found herself breathing heavily, trying to collect herself.

"Anastasia," he said in a beloved, familiar voice, "I've missed you so much." The sincerity in his tone sent a trembling up and down her body. He handed her the large brown bag. "These are for you."

Inside were a dozen red foil boxes of Sea Salt caramels.

"Thank ... thank you. How ... how did you know they're my favorite candy?"

"I know you as well as I know myself." He shrugged in that endearingly boyish way of his and drew her to him, gently sliding his arm around her. "I would've bought more but—"

She shook her head and moved closer to him. "It'll take me a year to eat these, and my daughter will never go to sleep from being on a sugar high."

"Good. We can stay awake at night and watch the Worcester mountains from the top of the hill."

"How will we be able to do that? You don't live—" She stopped in mid-sentence and moved back a step. "What hill?"

"Mr. Luciano!" Her daughter petted the dog. "I saw Gold Treater first. And I love candy!"

Luciano bent down. "I've missed you, Soo-Min."

"And I love your dog!" The dog wagged its tail and nuzzled against Soo-Min. "Can I hold his leash while you and Mommy kiss?"

Luciano grinned. "Lady's a she. And yes, you can hold her leash while your mother and I kiss." He stood and wrapped both arms around Anastasia. "We have your daughter's permission."

She hesitated. "How long have you been back from Italy?"

"Speaker phones are a brilliant invention." He pressed her tighter to his strong form. "How long does it take to fly eighteen hours with two layovers, buy a new Hummer, a house, a business, then drive to Stowe from Charleston?"

Her heart skipped a beat. "Twenty-four hours?"

"Give or take twelve hours, considering Lady needs walking every few hours during a car ride."

"You bought the Cobbo mansion?"

"It's the perfect house for a guy like me because there's no ocean in sight." He gave her one of his lazy smiles, and his hands slid possessively up her back. "Can I show you how much I missed you?" He didn't wait for permission. His lips came down on hers.

Sighing, she twined her hands around his neck and the kiss deepened.

Soo-Min jumped up and down. "Mommy, can you hold Lady's leash? I want to play with my friend by the monkey bars." She glanced at the dog. "Sorry, Mr. Luciano, but Lady rolled in the snow and got all muddy."

Anastasia broke the kiss and grabbed the leash from Soo-Min. "Go ahead, honey. We can see you from here."

"Your daughter has the opposite of perfect timing," Luciano wryly remarked. He rested his chin on her head. "Don't ever leave me again," he whispered.

She tilted her head up. "You left me."

"I'm sorry. I needed to act quickly. My heritage search has been so elusive with many false leads and dead ends. However, one of the thirty investigators I'd hired was certain he'd found my birth family."

She rubbed her hand against his bristled jaw. "You don't need to explain or apologize. I understand how much this search meant to you."

"Come to Italy with me this summer. You and Soo-Min?" He looked down, apparently to ensure that Anastasia had nodded. "I bought a villa in a tiny Italian mountain town, and you'll love my birth family. They're loud and funny and content with very little. I offered to buy them whatever they wanted, although they refused. They said that my returning to the town, and knowing I was okay, was the greatest gift ..." He cleared his throat.

"And you have a sister in Ireland?" she prompted.

He nodded. "My younger sister, Clara. I vaguely remember a baby in my family's apartment in Italy, before my mother got sick. Clara was placed in the Italian orphanage soon after I was, although I never knew it."

She smiled up into his beloved face. "Sounds like I better update my passport."

He laughed. "First, will you and your daughter come for a ride with me? I have a surprise for you."

A FEW MINUTES LATER, they retrieved Soo-Min from the monkey bars and piled into his Hummer, following a road leading to the Cobbo mansion. The sun was dipping lower in the sky as Luciano parked near the entrance of the sprawling estate. With the dog trotting by his side, he led them across the driveway. "I read a funny joke while I was on the plane," he said with a wink. "Want to hear it?"

Anastasia couldn't help a smirk of helpless amusement. "Go ahead."

"Why did the billionaire leave his oceanside mansion?" he asked.

"I'm sure you'll tell me."

He tried to keep a straight face and ended up grinning. "The mansion was too current."

"That is so *not* funny!" She gave a bark of laughter anyway and Soo-Min twirled and chuckled.

They crossed a wide front porch to a triple wooden door

fixed with double brass handles. "Remember I said this was a surprise?" He covered her and Soo-Min's eyes with his hands, clicked open the door and ushered them inside.

"Ready?"

She nodded. Soo-Min giggled.

He dropped his hands. The large living room overflowed with hundreds of candy-red roses, the light, fragrant scent filling the expansive living room. Crystal vases filled with white roses lined the expansive staircase.

She gasped. Soo-Min squealed with delight. The muddy dog barked and bounded for a pristine white couch.

"I wasn't sure if you liked red or white roses." he explained. "I wanted to send them to you for Valentine's Day, but because of the travel and time difference, I lost track of the days."

Tears filled her eyes. "They're beautiful!"

"Mommy, I'm going to sniff every single rose," Soo-Min declared, dipping her nose into each bouquet as she began circling the room.

Luciano drew Anastasia into his embrace. She looked away, uncertain of meeting his gaze.

"What is it?" he prodded.

"It's too much, the candy, the roses—"

"You wouldn't want to deprive me of giving you gifts?" He smiled and chucked her chin. "You know I love beautiful things."

She rubbed the back of her neck and her gaze swept downcast. "I know."

"Then what is it?" he prodded.

She didn't want to ask, although she needed to, because otherwise the hurt and jealousy she harbored would spread and put a wedge in their relationship.

"It's Liz," she said quietly.

"I heard her assistant wasn't much help filing the custody case."

"No help at all. However, in the end it was for the best because I've decided not to file. Justin and Eliza care about Soo-Min as much as I do, and everyone was right; it's in my daughter's best interests to have a good relationship with them."

He tightened his hold and lightly kissed her. "And Liz is a friend, only a friend, who didn't like Italy, by the way. Once we arrived, she didn't venture within five miles of my birth town, declaring the entire town decrepit, old, and utterly boring. She's pursuing that movie star nobody's heard of and happily headed back to Vegas."

Anastasia smiled with a mixture of relief and happiness.

"Mommy, Lady and I are gonna race up and down the stairs. Wanna watch us?" Soo-Min asked.

A vase filled with roses and water toppled as Soo-Min and Lady sped past.

"They'll make a mess of your beautiful home in no time," Anastasia predicted.

Luciano shrugged. "I hired a small staff, including a housecleaner, horse handler and stable keeper. Can Soo-Min help me select a couple of ponies tomorrow? I researched and Welsh ponies are a good choice for small children."

Laughter quivered on Anastasia's lips. "I'm sure she'll love lending her expertise."

HOURS LATER, they sat together on the living room floor. The sun had set and a warm fire burned in the fireplace. Luciano gazed down at his beautiful wife-to-be. She'd been quiet for several minutes, snuggled in his lap.

Soo-Min snored softly on the couch, an 'I Love Vermont'

blanket bundled around her. She kept one arm firmly around a devoted Lady stretched out beside her.

Luciano brushed a strand of hair from Anastasia's temple. "Are you sleeping?" he murmured.

She snuggled a laugh into his chest, then turned her face up to his. "Not anymore."

He pressed his lips to her forehead. "There is much I need to explain."

She leaned back. "Beginning with Italy? I understand if you feel your real home is there." Her voice shook slightly as she spoke.

"I believed that the only place I truly belonged was Italy, and discovered I was wrong. Sure, my ethnic identity was fractured, and I blamed everyone except myself, although any barriers I put up were within me. My adoptive parents gave me food, shelter, and most importantly, love. Without their support, I wouldn't have been able to accomplish everything I've done." He gazed into her smoky blue-gray eyes. "What I'm saying is that my home is here, and I want to live life with you and your beautiful daughter. That is, if you'll have an opinionated, dead-wrong guy for a husband."

Her eyes glistened with tears. The room filled with silence.

"Will you marry me?" he asked.

She nodded.

He framed her face in his hands. Her tousled hair tumbled over her shoulders. "Say it out loud. I've waited sixteen years."

"Yes, yes, of course!" She flung herself against him for an endless, breathless kiss. Then she drew back and stood quickly. "You've given me so much, and I also have a gift for you." She retrieved her purse and pulled out a small red journal. With an enchanting smile, she handed it to him. "Happy thirty-fifth birthday."

He leafed through the pages in a surreal sense of wonder. "How did you know what this would mean to me?"

Her voice was tender, yet serious. "I know you as well as I know myself." She echoed his earlier words.

He read the inside cover aloud. "*Che Sara Sara*," then changed the wording. "*Our* magnificent future is ours to see." He wanted to tell her how much she and Soo-Min meant to him. He was only able to whisper, "Thank you," before bending his head to kiss her.

A while later, he stood to light several candles and placed them on the mantel. Then they both stretched their legs out on the carpet, propping pillows against the couch so that they could lean against it.

"What about your business?" Anastasia asked, half to herself.

"I can run my business from here."

"But you're giving up so much. Your beautiful Charleston office, for one."

He shrugged and his lips twitched. "A billionaire can do whatever he wants."

She regarded him with a questioning expression. "Your negotiations went well?"

He smiled, confirming, "The investors liked my software project."

"What about Jaclyn?"

"She moved in with her canoe instructor while her bungalow is being renovated. I'm sure they'll visit us."

Tears came down Anastasia's cheeks. His arms automatically encircled her as she turned her body closer to his.

"I'll stop crying in a minute, I promise." She sniffed and regarded him with a rueful gaze. "It's just that I'm so happy and love you so much."

He shook his head and silenced her tears with a kiss. "But I love you more."

THE END

A NOTE FROM JOSIE

Dear Friends,

Thank you for reading I Love You More. This book is available in ebook, Paperback, Large Print Paperback, Hardcover, and Audiobook.

If you loved this sweet Valentine romance as much as I loved writing it, please help other people find *I Love You More* by posting your review.

I'd love to meet you in person someday, but in the meantime, all I can offer is a sincere and grateful thank you. Without your support, my books would not be possible.

As I write my next sweet or inspirational romance, remember this: Have you ever tried something you were afraid to try because it mattered so much to you? I did, when I started writing. Take the chance, and just do something you love.

My Spotify Play List for I Love You More is here.

With sincere appreciation for your support,

Josie Riviera

P.S. Thousands of families around the world have opened their homes and hearts through international adoption. Soo-Min is the embodiment of many, many fortunate adoptive children and parents who've together created forever families.

RECIPE FOR CHOCOLATE COVERED STRAWBERRIES

Ingredients:
    1 pint (2 cups) fresh strawberries
    1/2 cup semisweet good quality chocolate chips
    1 teaspoon vegetable oil

Rinse strawberries and dry completely on paper towels. Line a cookie sheet with waxed paper.

In saucepan, melt chocolate chips and oil over low heat and stir frequently. Remove from heat.

Dip the lower half of each strawberry into chocolate mixture; and drip excess back into saucepan. Place on waxed paper-lined cookie sheet.

Refrigerate uncovered for thirty minutes. Store covered in refrigerator.

USA TODAY BESTSELLING AUTHOR

JOSIE RIVIERA

1·800· CUPID

A SWEET CONTEMPORARY NOVELLA

CHAPTER 1

*T*wenty thousand dollars.
Click.

Candee Contando licked her dry lips. She'd done it. She'd placed an online bid on a home-auction website for the Victorian mansion on Thompson Lane. Her dream home, her dollhouse. Her dilapidated project.

Two years of savings. Gone.

No matter. Under her guidance, she'd transform the mansion to its former majestic state, painted a mustard-yellow offset by ornamental burnt-sienna "gingerbread" trim. The sounds of children's giggling and music and barking beagles—yes, beagles—would echo across all five acres of the property.

She surveyed her offer and beamed, savoring the moment.

Now if she only could ensure that no one else bid on the property and drove up the price.

She studied the ticking clock on the website. Stay optimistic, she told herself. Deteriorated by age and wear, the Victorian would scare off any prospective buyer.

She pushed away from her desk and surveyed her real estate office. Although only one room, she prided herself on the cheery décor. One wall featured photos of North Carolina—the majestic peaks of the Blue Ridge parkway and scenic waterfalls. Below the photos hung a map of the area with local real estate listings highlighted by pushpins.

She peered out the window into the street below. Since noon, a bright sun had been at odds with January's wind—a wind crazy in its intent to blow the streetlights off their wires.

For the umpteenth time, she checked her nonringing cell phone for messages. Surely the real estate market in Roses, North Carolina, would improve. Didn't prospective home buyers begin looking in January? And wouldn't these buyers call her rather than her competitors? Candee prided herself on her professionalism and up-to-date listings.

Then why hadn't she made a single sale since August?

On the heel of that depressing assessment came a cheerful one. In two hours, she and her older sister, Desiree, planned to enjoy dinner at Desiree's country club.

Candee stepped back to her desk and switched off the computer.

Two single women in their late twenties, she mused, spending Friday night alone and dateless, four weeks before Valentine's Day.

Her cell phone rang, most likely Desiree firming up dinner plans and reminding Candee not to be late. Regardless of what time Candee met her older sister anywhere, Desiree always arrived before her.

Candee clicked on her phone. "1-800-Cupid," she said with a laugh.

"Contando Realty?" a man asked.

"Yes, yes …" So much for professionalism. Candee felt her cheeks color. She hurried to her desk, dropping into the chair and switching her phone to speaker. "Are you looking to buy a home today, sir?"

"I am." The man hesitated. "Is this the correct number?"

She powered on her computer. "Absolutely."

"I'm new to the area and checked into the Roses Hotel last night," he said.

Envisioning the rundown hotel, Candy raised her eyebrows. Although in all fairness, the hotel was the only lodging open in the winter. Roses, North Carolina, was a summer tourist town known for bubbling hot springs and cool mountain temperatures.

Her fingers poised on the keyboard. "I'm more than happy to assist. Your name?"

"Teddy. Teddy Winchester." He had a deep voice, a slight southern drawl.

"What type of home are you searching for, Mr. Winchester?"

"The worst home in the best neighborhood."

Yup. It figured. No significant sales commission to pay the mortgage this month. Fortunately, her part-time job at the local hardware store was stable, although the pay was meager.

She scrolled through the listings. "For yourself, sir?"

"I'm an investor."

"How many bedrooms and baths?"

"Three bedrooms, two baths. Single family and one level."

"Budget?"

"Anything below $50,000."

She rubbed the back of her neck. *Who did he think she was, a miracle worker?*

"Mr. Winchester, the nicer neighborhoods in Roses are priced well above $100,000."

"Nope. Too high."

Certainly a man of few words.

"Perhaps—"

"I'll take another look on the Internet." He seemed to ignore her completely. "Thanks anyway."

She wouldn't lose a potential sale.

"Wait." She feigned checking a non-existent schedule. "I may have an opening this afternoon. I know the area well and I'll find properties to show you. Will three o'clock work?"

"In a half hour? Fine. I admire a realtor who works fast. Should I meet you at your office? The address is listed on the Internet."

Candee verified the street number and ended the phone call with a cheery, "See you at three."

She clicked off and checked her watch. Thirty minutes wasn't enough time to drive to her apartment and change. Her worn jeans and blue flannel shirt would have to suffice.

Immediately, she phoned Desiree. "I may be late for dinner."

"I'm so glad it's you," Desiree said. "Scott, a new lawyer at the firm, asked me out tonight. Barring the fact the invitation was last minute, I said yes. Desperation, right?" She paused. "Can we plan for dinner together tomorrow night instead?"

"Right, sure. The reason I called is because I have a client who's interested in seeing some properties."

"You have a real live client?" Desiree cut immediately to the question.

Candee envisioned her sister, thick blonde hair piled high, sitting behind a mahogany desk in her law firm. Proper, well-dressed, every inch the high-powered attorney. Desiree had proven that, with the right help, a disadvantaged childhood could lead to a successful adulthood. She worked late hours at her law firm advocating justice for low-income families and their children.

"He's an investor," Candee said.

"Maybe he's tall, dark, and handsome?" Desiree said with deceptive casualness. "And rich?"

"Investors are usually short bald men." Candee adjusted her shirt's wrinkled collar, then checked out the frayed hem of her jeans. She let out a frustrated groan and ran a hand through her unruly auburn waves.

"You'll need a rich man if you plan to go through with your insane idea to purchase that Victorian," Desiree said. "The place will eat up all the money you hope to earn in a lifetime."

"I'll handle most of the work myself. Remember, when we lived in foster care, I learned carpentry from the family who took us in."

"How will you offer a quality after-school environment to disadvantaged kids if you're busy driving nails into crumbling walls?"

"Watch me." Briefly, Candee squeezed her eyes shut. It was her turn to pay it forward.

"Well, don't discount short men. They prefer tall, willowy red-heads with green eyes," Desiree said. "Who knows? He might be struck by Cupid's golden arrow when he meets you. This guy might be the one."

Candee drew in a breath. "The one what, exactly?"

"Your partner, your love, your support system. The one who can help pay off the mountainous amount of debt you'll incur if you actually buy the biggest dilapidated disaster in the state."

"Someone supportive? For me? After what happened?"

Desiree's voice grew quieter. "Not every guy pretends to be something he's not."

A lump lodged in Candee's throat. No man was worth having her heart broken again, although she didn't vocalize her feelings. Desiree was an eternal romantic.

With a promise to meet her sister on Saturday evening,

Candee clicked off and bent to pick up a broken pencil lying on the floor. Not once since the ill-fated night two years ago when her long-time boyfriend had walked out had she broken the vow to herself and wept. Life went on, although a sadness she couldn't shake remained precariously close to the surface.

Some lessons were more difficult than others. Her ex had taught her the hardest—she wasn't interesting enough, pretty enough or vivacious enough.

Tears welled and she brushed them away. Standing, she tossed the pencil into a garbage can by the door. While she confirmed two house showings for Mr. Winchester, she cast a critical assessment of her reflection in the mirror by the office door. She pinched her pale cheeks and added a touch of rose lip balm to her lips. Then she gathered her hair into a ponytail, securing the thick curls with an elastic band. With a final glance in the mirror, she pulled on her cream-colored woolen jacket and wound an emerald-green paisley scarf around her neck.

Her suede purse under her arm, she pushed open the exit doors and stepped outside. The sun had buried itself under a formless cloud, and a swirl of wind blew her paisley scarf across her face. She tucked it securely beneath the collar of her jacket. The day was typical January weather for Roses, undecided if it was warm or cold.

CHAPTER 2

$\mathcal{T}$eddy Winchester pondered for the umpteenth time how he'd ended up in Roses, North Carolina. Certainly the town was charming, tucked along a backdrop of the Blue Ridge Mountains. He'd taken a ride around the region before he'd checked into the hotel. The shopping seemed adequate and the town center exuded storybook appeal, retaining a New England quaintness, complete with a bandstand.

Rob, his not-so-silent business partner in Florida, had assured Teddy the North Carolina weather was always cooperative, even pleasant for mid-January. And the area teemed with real estate bargains because Roses, population five thousand, had never fully recovered from the recession.

Rob was wrong on both counts. Relentless gusts battering under the drafty hotel's window had sent a chill through Teddy all morning while he'd sat in his room, and the inventory of low-priced homes on real-estate websites proved nonexistent.

Roses wasn't what he'd hoped for. He needed a quick turnaround investment to help pay for his nephew Joseph's physical therapy. A horrific car accident and the loss of his nephew's father had left Joseph traumatized and weak, and the extensive physical therapy included strength building and stretching.

Teddy took a deep breath, still reeling from his older brother's death. *Christian, we promised to never desert each other. And now you're gone.*

In an effort to keep busy, Teddy perused his email, then texted an abridged list of instructions to his secretary on how to proceed with the sale of his late brother's farm. He assumed Christian retained life insurance, which would help pay for the mountain of medical bills steadily piling up, as well as lawyers' fees. The papers declaring that Teddy was Joseph's legal guardian weren't finalized yet. The courts took their time, although the will guided the court's decision.

With a sigh, he tapped in Rob's business number.

Rob's gruff voice answered on the fifth ring. "Rob's Marvelous Muffins."

"Hi Rob. Is Joseph around?" Teddy asked.

"He's up to his elbows in Valentine muffin ingredients. A four-year-old's favorite activity is making a mess with a cupful of flour, right?" Rob chuckled. "I'll put him on speaker."

"Hi Uncle Teddy!" Joseph's high-pitched voice vibrated through the phone. "Mr. Rob and I are putting a surprise in our muffins and writing something special on each one. Wanna know what's inside?"

Teddy laughed. "Then it wouldn't be a surprise, right?"

The boy hesitated. "Right."

"Is there anything we can do about that?"

"I can save a muffin for you, Uncle Teddy."

"Great idea, buddy. I'll fly to Miami in a couple weeks, and we'll eat muffins together at Mr. Rob's bakery. Okay?"

Joseph giggled. "Okay."

It was the first time he'd heard the boy laugh since his father had died.

"I love you, Joseph," he said softly.

"Love you, too, Uncle Teddy."

Rob got back on the phone. "He's a good kid. You should see how he's mixing the butter and sugar together."

"Maybe he's a born baker like you, Rob."

"Or a farmer like you."

"I was never good at farming." Which was true. It wasn't until he'd met Rob and gone into real estate that he'd discovered his forte.

"Maybe you haven't discovered the right crop. Try tomatoes. Those plants grow regardless of—Hang on a sec." Rob turned away from the phone, but Teddy could still hear him directing one of his employees to be careful attaching the food grinder to the heavy-duty electric mixer he'd recently purchased. His voice returned to normal strength as he inquired how the house hunting was going.

"I'm meeting a local realtor this afternoon."

"Shouldn't take long. It's a buyer's market." He barked another order to one of his employees, then goaded, "You miss slaving over a hot oven?"

Teddy could easily visualize the twinkle in Rob's crystal-blue eyes. "I haven't baked so much as a boxed cake in years," he said, chuckling.

He and Rob had met years earlier at a cooking class for men. Teddy had soon discovered his speciality would never include burning another muffin, but Rob had gone on to build a successful chain of bakeries in the greater Miami area. Teddy could practically inhale the delectable, sugary aromas coming from Rob's spotless commercial kitchen.

"And I'll take Joseph to his equestrian session this weekend," Rob was saying. "The kid has really formed a connection with horses."

"Exactly the reason his therapist advised it," Teddy replied. "She said horseback riding would reduce Joseph's anxiety after the trauma of the accident."

"She's right," Rob said. "And she's such a pretty thing, isn't she?"

"Rob, she's Joseph's therapist."

"Yeah, yeah, I know. And she's a few years younger than me, anyway." Rob gave an exaggerated whistle. "Remember to keep me in the real estate loop."

"Do I have a choice?" Teddy grinned. He was impatient with lawyers and their endless legal jargon and talk of probate court. However, with the man and mentor he owed his real-estate start-up business to, Teddy's patience was limitless.

"Hey, thanks for watching Joseph for me," he added.

"What are oddball friends for? Your job is to snag the best buy in Roses." The usually brash Rob tempered his tone. "And Joseph's no bother, you know. When someone's down and out they need help, right?"

"These past few months ... Thank you. For everything." Teddy clicked off and stared at the phone. Sometimes, he didn't know what he would've done if Rob hadn't been there to pick up the pieces after Christian's death.

He checked his watch, then pulled on a gray T-shirt. He was still half-wet from his shower and the T-shirt stuck to his body. He shook his damp hair, threw on a Florida State baseball cap, stuck his wallet in his jeans pocket, and zipped up an olive-green vest. Out in the parking lot, he fired up the engine of his red truck, and at exactly three o'clock arrived at Candee Contando Realty. He needed someone experienced to help him get just the right property, and from the Internet reviews he'd read, Mrs. Contando had been in business over thirty years.

He walked to the entrance of an older brick building

housing various offices and stopped midstep, admiring the beautiful young woman waiting in the doorway. The collar of a cream-colored jacket framed her oval face, along with an absurdly colorful green scarf. A pair of tiny gold cross earrings dangled from her ears. Her features were all high cheekbones and generous lips.

He tipped his baseball hat. "Hello. I'm supposed to meet Mrs. Contando here."

"I'm *Miss* Contando, although please call me Candee." Her smile enhanced her fascinating emerald eyes.

His heartbeat slowed and he had to prompt himself to swallow. "This is *your* realty?"

"Actually, it was said to be my mother's company for a while." She pushed back a stray wisp of auburn hair, handed him a business card, and then extended her hand. "Are you Mr. Winchester?"

"Teddy." Tight jeans emphasized her shapely legs and rounded hips. This woman's stunning good looks could stop traffic.

"I expected someone older," he managed to say.

She let go of his hand, swept her gaze up his six-foot frame, and grinned. "I expected someone shorter."

He met her grin, debating where he should look next.

Her lovely face enhanced by a sprinkle of freckles? Nope, not at all professional to stare. Instead, he gazed at the weathered door behind her and cleared his throat. "Did you find any listings?"

Her mouth curved into a polite smile. "Yes. Ready to see your future house?"

Unexpectedly, he felt drawn to her. She wasn't at all what he'd expected, although his good sense warned him away. He was completely satisfied with being single, having made peace with that reality ever since his one serious relationship with a woman had ended badly. He'd lost his self-reliance once, and once was enough.

He gestured toward his truck. "Should we use my vehicle or yours?"

"Mine." She pointed to a rusted Honda Civic. "I'll drive. I know these roads well."

He opened the car door for her, then came around and settled in the passenger seat.

She buckled her seatbelt. He buckled his, then took in a quick breath. A faint whiff of her scent lingered in the air. Roses. He grinned. Why not?

"So, Candee, have you lived in Roses all your life?"

She glanced at him. "I've lived here and there."

She returned her attention to the road, and an overlong moment passed in silence.

He waited for her to continue. When she didn't elaborate, he asked if he could turn on the radio. The station was set to Classic Rock and "Unchained Melody" by the Righteous Brothers came on, the heartfelt lyrics about "Oh, my love, my darling," filling the little car.

Teddy was about to suggest they try for more upbeat music when she gushed, "I love this song."

Okay, he thought. She must be a romantic.

"How many showings did you schedule?" he asked.

"Two, both in Glenhaven." Flicking on her signal, she turned onto another road. "You want three bedrooms and two baths, correct?"

"The perfect flip house."

"You don't intend to live in the property?"

"Nope. I want an easy fixer-upper that won't take longer than six weeks to renovate. I'm working with another investor, and we intend to make a quick and substantial profit."

"Don't we all," she murmured.

Their gazes met and they shared a grin.

Soon, they were driving past neatly manicured lawns and one-story homes.

She stopped in front of a beige bungalow, parking on the street. "The previous owners relocated, and this house has been on the market over sixty days." They got out and walked toward the house. As you can see—" she gestured to the tidy neighborhood and matching mailboxes—"Glenhaven is lovely."

"The neighborhood is too cookie cutter." He stood on the front porch and studied mismatched shingle patches nailed to the roof. "Needs some work."

"Inside, the home is beautifully decorated."

"The bigger the mess, the bigger the profit." Automatically, he provided the investor's mantra. "What's the asking price?"

"One hundred thousand dollars, although the owners are willing to negotiate."

He shook his head. "Too expensive." *Why did realtors try to sell homes over the buyer's stated limit?*

Noting Candee's downcast expression, he lightened his tone. "Are there any other homes in this town under fifty thousand?"

"There is … one." She paused and pressed a finger to her lips, seeming to search for a reason not to answer.

He overlooked her lack of enthusiasm. "Price?"

"That particular house is listed on an internet auction site and meets none of your criteria." She paused. "It's a rambling Victorian and—"

"Where is this house?"

"On Thompson Lane at the edge of town. It's unoccupied."

"How much land comes with the property?"

"Five acres."

"Can the land be sold off in parcels? Is it zoned commercial or residential?"

"You can get on the website and download the report." She slid into the driver's seat and shut the door.

Had he heard a grunt of disapproval?

"Sorry I can't help you, Teddy," she continued, when he got into the passenger seat. "I'll drive you back to my office to get your truck, and I'll phone if anything in your price range becomes available."

Now he had to beg her to view a property? She might be gorgeous, but she was certainly the world's worst realtor.

"Do you have the lockbox code to this Victorian, Candee?"

She raised her delicate brows. "Yes, but—"

"I assume an appointment isn't necessary if no one lives there."

She inserted the key into the ignition. "My pleasure."

He didn't know why, although he'd bet she was being sarcastic.

A few minutes later she turned onto Thompson Lane. As they passed an elderly man with gray hair and glasses perched on his nose, she waved, explaining he was Mr. Dunworthy, a widower who owned a Queen-Anne-style home two doors away. He'd lived in the neighborhood forever and refused to give up his large home, although it was becoming more and more difficult for him to maintain.

She drove to the end of the road, sped up a circular driveway and parked in front of an imposing three-story house. An octagonal tower soared from the steep multigabled roof. Century-old trees flanked both sides of the property. On one corner of the overgrown front lawn, an oak tree boasted a tire swing. Teddy imagined himself pushing Joseph on that swing. Joseph needed to play more, needed fresh air. He'd been so pale since his father's death.

No, Teddy told himself. Quick and easy sale.

Of course, he could purchase the property for the land and build five new homes, more than tripling his profit. Or build low-income housing. Rob would agree with that decision.

He rounded the car to open the door for her, but she'd already gotten out. They stood side by side and stared at the house. For the first time in many years, he drank in the stillness of a cool winter afternoon, admiring a home he'd only imagined in his dreams—and was well aware of the insane impulse to hold Candee's hand as they walked to the front door.

He extended his hand to her.

She stared at him in surprise, but then she took his hand.

"The home is beautiful, isn't it?" she said as they walked to the front porch together.

It was, although the Victorian sat beneath layers of peeling yellow paint that marred its exterior and several of the windows were boarded up. A covered front porch curved around to the side, and there was also a side entrance. Teddy imagined white wooden rocking chairs, a row of lush Boston ferns, and ceiling fans spinning lazily on a warm summer afternoon.

The land, the land, he reminded himself.

Candee dropped her hand and tapped in the code for the lockbox. She tipped her head toward the purple front door. "In its former glory days, this home reflected the wealth of the owners—the Langrone family. They owned a prosperous knitting mill in Roses."

"And then?"

"And then the mill went out of business. Too much foreign competition. The Langrones declared bankruptcy and moved out shortly afterward. All the owners since then moved in with high expectations until they discovered they weren't able to maintain the upkeep."

What a waste of a beautiful home.

As if she'd read his thoughts she lingered on the porch, a wistfulness in her gaze. "This Victorian was built in 1889 and definitely requires TLC."

An absolute understatement, Teddy decided, when they walked in. The outside needed extensive work, and the hardwood floor of the grand foyer was badly gouged and scratched.

Candee flicked on a light switch. Nothing happened, and she offered an apologetic shrug. With lights not working, they were left in semidarkness. And although the odor in the entrance hall stopped him cold, she didn't miss a beat and continued walking.

"This is the kitchen," she was saying. "The cabinets are an olive color …"

"What's left of them." He eyed the traditional arched raised panel doors and a lone cabinet left on the floor. So much beauty amidst so much neglect.

He stepped onto rusty linoleum. Luxury vinyl it was not because the floor felt soft and spongy beneath his work boots. Water damage, and hopefully not too extensive and requiring a floor joist.

Candee caught the focus of his gaze. "Avocado was a popular color in the 70's when the owners updated the kitchen."

"Avocado is back in style," he replied.

Hadn't Rob uttered the same words when he'd designed his showy corporate office in Miami?

Teddy opened and closed a cabinet door and examined the hinges. "With lots of elbow grease and white paint, these cabinets might work. Better than tossing them in a landfill."

Candee shook her head. "Nothing in this kitchen is

salvageable." She opened the oven door. With a shriek, she slammed it shut.

He inspected the grease-encrusted stove burners. "I'd install stainless steel appliances. The stove can stay. Six burners are a good selling feature, and the microwave can be mounted above the stove. Granite countertops, travertine flooring, a dishwasher, disposal …" He swung around. "If I open this wall, there'd be an expansive view of the yard, which would be great for kids."

He didn't miss her speculative glance at his ring finger when he mentioned children.

"I'm not married," he said. "It's just me and my four-year-old nephew, Joseph."

She hesitated. "Where is he?"

"He's in Miami spending the next few weeks with my business partner, Rob. Rob's the one who got me started in real estate."

He'd said too much. How could he put into words the way his gut split every time he pondered Christian's death, or the pain Joseph had endured because of his numerous operations, or how Teddy had recently debated selling everything and starting over—somewhere quiet and peaceful—away from the high-pressure lifestyle of fast-paced Miami?

"Every home I take on, I treat as my own," he whispered.

Although this home wouldn't be here, because every bone in his practical body insisted it should be demolished.

He ran the faucet, and rusty water spewed into the chipped porcelain sink.

"City water and sewers," Candee said.

"Good. No septic issues or a dry well save money. What's this house going for?"

"No one knows the final price with an auction."

"Square footage?"

"Over 5500 square feet."

"This house is bigger than I thought." He pressed his lips together. "What's the current bid?"

She paused for a long while. "Twenty thousand dollars. You know you'll pour money into a house this size in order to get it back into shape."

"Did you know you're the exact opposite of a sales-woman, Candee?" With a grin, he stepped forward into what he presumed was the formal living room, appreciatively remarking on the marble fireplace with its updated gas fire-place and the twelve-foot ceilings.

"No use in traipsing through a ramshackle house—" Candee began.

"I noticed there's a dining room and parlor," he interrupted.

"Yes. And an adjacent library. And a music room."

That same wistfulness in her voice again.

He struggled to find the right words, debating whether to ask if she was upset about something. Hesitating, he changed direction. "Is the music room next?"

"You're the buyer." Had she silently inserted the adjective *foolish*?

He assessed the lengthening shadows signaling early nightfall. With no electricity, the house was growing darker by the minute.

As they headed into the music room, the toe of his boot caught on a torn piece of shag carpeting. He heard Candee call out a warning as he lost his footing and fell through the floor.

CHAPTER 3

*C*andee peered through the hole in the floor into the shadowy basement. Although she heard Teddy's footsteps, she couldn't see him.

"Are you all right?" she called.

"Sure. I wanted to examine the basement, anyway. It appears to be a walk-out."

She leaned over, her eyes adjusting to the darkness. "What's it like down there?"

"I'll let you know in a minute." He switched on his cell phone's flashlight and peeked up at her, waggling his dark eyebrows. "Care to join me?"

He couldn't possibly be flirting.

"Uh no. I'll wait here, thanks."

Teddy pulled himself back up into the music room. "Maybe next time?"

With one hand in his worn jeans pocket, the other wielding a tape measure, he was rugged and impossibly good-looking, his muscled arms straining against a thin gray T shirt. He brushed dirt from his vest and yanked off his baseball cap. His wealth of black hair was mussed, and the late afternoon sun gilded thin strips of golden highlights to the tips. Perhaps he'd stepped right off the cover of the latest men's home improvement magazine without telling her.

Although she'd walked through this house many times, she hadn't ventured into the basement. Desiree often called Candee the opposite of a realist, although what would the world be like, Candee rationalized, without dreamers?

Teddy carried the broken kitchen cabinet from the kitchen and placed it over the hole in the floor.

As they continued through the house, he snapped photos with his cell phone.

"After I see the upstairs, I'll send these pictures to my partner Rob," he said.

She gestured to the sweeping spindle staircase. "This home has five bedrooms, five baths, and five fireplaces. It's the opposite of a perfect flip house."

"Nevertheless, lead the way. There're two more floors to check out."

After he'd inspected the upstairs bathrooms and admired the worn brass hardware on the master suite's mahogany double doors, they made their way downstairs.

When they reached the foyer, he glanced up from his cell phone and said, "I want to make an offer."

She shuffled back two steps. "You're joking ... right?" Her gaze shifted to the entrance. She'd made a serious mistake in mentioning this house to him.

"I never joke about real estate."

"This home"—she swept out her hands—"is a money pit."

"Which is why Rob and I will buy the property for the land."

Candee's heart stopped beating.

"We'll demolish the house," he added.

Her house, she wanted to shout. *Her* land for disadvantaged children. She'd envisioned beagle puppies cavorting across the lawn, perhaps an acre set aside for a working farm. Children needed to connect with nature. It was time to get them away from technology and back to values that really mattered.

And music. The music room off the kitchen would reverberate with glorious sounds again.

Teddy faced her. "Anything the matter?"

There was kindness in his gaze, interest on his handsome features. Should she share her ideas with a man she'd known for less than two hours—a man who was bent on destroying those very same ideas? A man who'd held her hand in his strong grip and gazed at the Victorian with the same wonder and appreciation as she had?

Struggling to hold onto her composure, she reminded herself she was a professional. Besides, this house was nothing like what he was looking for.

She lifted her chin. "Not a thing."

Lightly, he touched her cheek, his gesture completely unexpected. "I understand how you feel about a house like this. It's very beautiful, but beyond repair."

Turning away, she quickly dabbed at her eyes. She settled into the tune she'd known the past two years: no matter how sincere, how charming, men couldn't be trusted. Better to hold him at a polite distance and keep her plans to herself. He'd soon be gone back to Miami.

"Are you sure you're okay?" he asked.

She feigned her brightest smile. "Of course."

He waited a beat, then silently followed her, standing on the porch while she locked the front door.

"Any idea what the current bid is? You mentioned under fifty thousand."

Candee rubbed her temples. A quick search on the Internet would spew all the information he'd need to place a bid.

"Twenty thousand dollars," she finally said. "And bidding ends in three weeks."

So many mistakes today, beginning by answering the phone. 1-800-CUPID. Hah!

"Then I'll offer thirty thousand dollars," he said.

An uneasy quiet descended. A cold breeze brushed across her cheeks.

"The auction accepts bids in twenty-thousand dollar-increments," she said.

"Then I'll bid forty thousand, which is still under my fifty-thousand-dollar budget."

"The bank may not accept a lowball offer." Her remark was nonsensical, since she was hoping the bank would accept her offer, because twenty thousand dollars was all she had. She glanced at Teddy's determined stance. Surely there was a way to convince him not to bid. However, thirty years of proper Southern behavior stopped her from saying more.

"I can offer all cash," he said. "Plus, my partner and I can close immediately. On a foreclosure, the bank will take everything into consideration."

"Don't you want to walk the property? If you're interested in the land, there are building requirements and permits—"

He reached into his pocket and handed her a business card. "I do this for a living, Candee. I know all about due diligence." He gave a lazy grin. "And there's another clause, which can either make or break the deal."

She fisted one hand on her hip. "The bank should just hand over the house to you?"

"A definite bonus." He laughed, rich and full. "I'm hoping my lovely realtor will grant me the pleasure of her company at dinner."

"I can't." Her refusal was quick, a knee-jerk reaction. She hadn't dated in two years and wouldn't start now, especially with a tycoon investor who assumed that by flaunting the cash in his pocket, he could take her castle in the air away from her.

"Not even for a slice of pizza? I don't know my way around Roses yet."

She retreated a step. "Tony's Pizza on Main Street is always open. You can spot the red and green awning a mile away."

"Are you saying no, Candee?"

"Is my refusal a deal breaker, Teddy?"

"Not if I can get this property for under fifty thousand dollars."

"If you decide to bid, you'll have to wait three weeks to find out if you've won."

His gaze lingered on her face. "Some things are worth waiting for."

CHAPTER 4

*T*eddy's cell phone buzzed on the nightstand in his hotel room. Awake anyway, he answered it and heard a recognizable woman's voice.

"Teddy?"

"Yvonne?" He peered at the clock on the nightstand. "You realize it's three a.m.?"

"Are you awake?"

He pushed a hand through his hair. "Should I be?"

"It's nine in the morning here in Madrid."

"I'm not in Spain," he countered.

"Such a shame you aren't with me." A long feminine sigh. "I'll never get used to the time difference. Look, my network in the States wants me in Madrid another few weeks to cover the recent drought. Water levels in the reservoirs are abnormally low, and they're aiming for a human-interest story to boost ratings and land a prime-time slot."

Teddy had met Yvonne—an attractive woman with honeyed skin, her thinly arched black brows offset by a pixie cut of platinum-blonde hair—when he'd been offered a weekly television segment featuring tidbits on flipping

146

homes. His fifteen minutes of fame had lasted, well, fifteen minutes. His relationship with Yvonne was going on five months, although he hardly ever saw her. Her job involved a great deal of travel, and he wasn't diligent about keeping in touch with her. He wasn't adaptable to the ever-changing elasticity of dating a woman he saw only twice a month.

He extended the expected congratulatory remarks. Compliments were a prerequisite when dating Yvonne Evette. She was a career woman bent on reaching the top, although what 'the top' was had yet to be determined. Currently, it meant an anchor position on a major American network.

After good-byes, he clicked off his phone and shifted restlessly on his narrow bed. The previous morning when he'd arrived at the Roses Hotel and realized the four-star rating wasn't accurate, he'd debated about sitting on the bed, much less lying on it. Still, he'd pulled back the bedspread, flopped down, and peered at a stain on the ceiling, trying not to ponder how it got there, for it certainly wasn't a water stain.

Now, in the darkened room, he punched a pillow and rolled onto his side.

Night after night since his brother's death, sleep had been elusive.

That's what happened when two brothers grew up together facing the shared futility of scarcity and endless beatings from their drug-addled father. Nothing was left of the Winchester heritage except the old Florida farm, the rundown homestead sitting on two acres of land at the end of a county road. And no matter how wealthy Teddy became, his roots were fixed in poverty.

Fortunately, his brother Christian had held onto the farm after Christian's wife died a year earlier, refurbishing the place and attempting to grow citrus fruit. The crops hadn't produced one grapefruit, as far as Teddy knew. Neither he nor Christian had the knack for farming, and Christian had always struggled when it came to financial success.

Lately, Teddy found himself talking to his late brother: *Christian, should I do this, should I do that? I'm a bachelor. Am I the best choice as Joseph's legal guardian?*

Christian had been an exemplary father. How was Teddy expected to fill those impressive shoes? Perhaps he should marry, he pondered, providing a stable home for Joseph as his brother had done.

Turning onto his back and linking his hands behind his head he thought about Yvonne—her suggestive words, her open invitations, her sultry voice. However, he didn't want Yvonne. His mind traveled instead to *Miss* Candee Contando, the beautiful realtor with the creamy complexion, a mass of red hair framing her face and long legs that went on forever.

Her realty skills were non-existent. When he'd pressed her for details about any property under fifty thousand, she'd hesitated for a lengthy spell before answering. When they'd stood together and stared at the Victorian, he'd had to fight down the impulse to kiss her while holding her hand. She was gorgeous and witty, with a cool no-nonsense façade. And somehow, he knew she'd require a sizable amount of convincing to date him.

He didn't know the reason for his next decision. He only knew he wanted to see her again.

He'd visit her office first thing Monday morning with some excuse, and then invite her to lunch. Perhaps he'd bid on the property with her assistance.

Envisioning Candee's beautiful face, he drifted off to sleep.

* * *

"PIZZA?" Desiree repeated. "The guy's taking you out for pizza?"

Candee smoothed the collar of her royal-blue silk blouse. She wore an outfit appropriate for dinner at the fancy country club her sister belonged to—the silk blouse and a black pencil skirt, and black stilettos.

"If you recall," she said, "I'm not going."

"Was he bald?"

Candee sipped her water. "No. His hair is dark and wavy."

"Short?"

"Wrong again. He's at least six feet tall. If anything, he's exceptionally handsome." Her heart gave a peculiar little pitch as she remembered his outrageous smile when he'd asked if she wanted to join him in the basement.

"Married?"

"No, although he talked about his nephew."

Desiree reached for her crystal wineglass filled with a local red wine. "Rich?"

"I checked his business listing on the Internet. R and T Realty in Miami is legit."

A teasing smile tilted Desiree's lips. "Then why would you refuse his offer to go out for pizza?"

Because all her energies were focused on the Victorian house, Candee wanted to say. Because she wasn't ready for a relationship.

"Because he's placing a bid on the Langrone mansion so he can tear it down," she responded aloud.

Desiree beckoned to a waiter who immediately splashed more water into the women's glasses. "Has he lost his mind like you have?"

Candee assessed her perfectly coiffed sister. Desiree was her usual stunning self, her blonde hair caught at the crown of her head with a glittering rhinestone fastener.

Forking a piece of lettuce, she replied, "Perhaps that's how these high-roller investor types go about flips."

"Once the house is torn down, what's he going to do with a vacant five-acre lot?"

"He didn't explain." Candee pushed her half-eaten meal of salad, grilled salmon and roasted red potatoes aside. "Who spends thousands of dollars to tear down a beautiful piece of property which should be preserved, not destroyed?"

Desiree finished her wine and set her glass to the side. "His reasons might be good ones."

"Well, he won't have the opportunity to tell me. I won't be seeing him again."

"Give him a chance. He sounds utterly gorgeous. Call him."

Candee leaned back and crossed her arms. "I've never called a guy in my life."

"Your life, your decision." Desiree's gaze traveled through the expansive dining room. "Did I mention the club is having a Valentine's Day silent auction and dinner dance? I remember how beautifully you helped me decorate the dining room two years ago. We filled champagne glasses with candy hearts—and the chocolate fondue was fabulous!"

Candee faked a glibness she didn't feel. "You're referring to the night my ex walked out on me for another woman."

"You'll be happier if you don't dwell on the past," Desiree said. "Besides, you'd discussed ending your relationship with George two months before the actual breakup. Focus on what's ahead and let the past stay where it belongs."

Before Candee could answer, Desiree trilled a giggle and waved. "Scott's here, the man who took me out last night."

Candee peered over her shoulder. "The guy with the blond crewcut sitting alone at a table near the bar?"

"Yes. I mentioned we were eating here tonight, and he said he might join us for dessert, and then we discussed he might bring a friend … umm … for you. The friend's name is Allen Allen."

"You planned to set me up on a blind date?" Candee half-stood. "Thanks, but no thanks."

"What's wrong with meeting a man for coffee and dessert? Maybe we can double date for the Valentine dance."

"The dance I'm not attending," Candee reminded.

Desiree peered in Scott's direction. "I don't see anyone with him." She frowned, then pulled her vibrating cell phone from her handbag. She flashed Scott a smile and read his text aloud. "Allen heard the weather might take a turn for the worse, so he decided not to come."

"The guy's name really is Allen Allen?"

"He practices law in a neighboring town. He and Scott went to school together."

Candee was no longer listening. She was peering out the nearest window, assessing the weather. The earlier light drizzle was turning to sleet, and she thought it prudent to leave sooner rather than later. Within a few minutes she was pulling on her jacket, a faux fur capelet, and Desiree was sharing Scott's table with him.

As Candee prepared to exit, she walked straight into a tall attractive man wearing navy pants, a striped polo shirt, and a gray sport coat.

"Candee? What are you doing here?" Teddy's gaze slid slowly up her, from her stilettos and slim-fitting skirt to her silk blouse, finally stopping at her face.

She fingered her gold cross earrings. "May I ask you the same question?"

"My partner has a reciprocal agreement with private clubs around the country. Since you refused my pizza offer last night …" He gave an appreciative male smile. "You know, you're a knockout when you're all dressed up."

Heat flushed her cheeks. "Thanks for the … compliment?"

"I mean, you're a beautiful woman whether you're wearing jeans or—"

Now the flush warmed her ears. "Well, thanks again. I was just leaving."

"Me too. I ordered takeout food and forgot forks." He flourished a bag with the country club's logo as proof, then glanced out the window by the front door. "Roses certainly has unpredictable weather."

"It's not usually like this." She attempted to brush past him. "Whereas Florida's weather is predictably hot and sunny."

"Especially Miami." He grinned. "Where are you parked?"

"I came with my sister, Desiree, who's ditched me. She prefers to drink coffee with her latest conquest, a new lawyer at her firm." Candee glanced over her shoulder at the bar area. Desiree was watching her, and she grinned and offered a thumbs-up.

Candee didn't respond, turning back to Teddy. "She and her newest conquest had planned a blind date for me, although Allen Allen, another lawyer, decided I wasn't worth the effort of driving in bad weather."

Teddy's dark eyebrows quirked. "This guy's first and last name are the same?"

"Yes." She surprised herself by adding, "It would have been my first date in two years, although I would've refused."

"His loss is my gain. I'll take you home."

Absolutely not.

"No, no." Candee shook her head while securing her capelet. "I planned to call a taxi."

Teddy gestured toward his pickup truck. "I'm parked at the curb. And your vocabulary might improve if you substituted yes for no once in a while."

"I can't. Really—"

"Say yes."

No use in arguing with him. His references had checked out and he wasn't a total stranger. She smiled. "All right. I don't live far from here."

"Much better."

With his hand on her elbow, he guided her outside to his truck, opening the passenger door and helping her up and in. Her tight skirt didn't allow for much climbing, and she shifted into the seat, hoping her skirt wouldn't ride up her thighs.

It did, and judging from his appreciative smile, he noticed.

"My address is 121 Juniper Street," she said, after she'd adjusted her skirt to a more proper length.

"I'll plug it into my cell phone."

She glanced at his profile as he slid into the driver's seat. Way too attractive, she thought, in a roguish way.

"What about your silverware for the takeout?" she asked.

He flashed a boyish grin, displaying even white teeth. "The club's signature hamburger can be eaten with human fingers, and there's a supply of paper napkins in my truck's glove compartment."

"You're well-equipped."

For a fleeting second, his gaze turned somber. "I try, although sometimes life throws some unexpected curves."

At close range, she noted a scar below his right eye. It certainly didn't affect his good looks, but she wondered if it indicated some of those unexpected curves life had thrown at him.

CHAPTER 5

*T*he sleet came faster, making visibility difficult. Still, Teddy seemed to recognize where they were as they neared the turn-off for Thompson Lane.

"You know the code for the lockbox, right?" Teddy asked.

"Yes, I have it memorized," she said.

"Mind if we stop there first? I'd meant to check the water heater yesterday. In the excitement of falling through the floor, I forgot."

She caught her lower lip with her teeth to stop from blurting out. He wanted to see *her* Victorian again?

"The weather—" She gestured theatrically to the icy roads.

"I have 4-wheel drive."

"Did you offer me a ride tonight in order to get into the house again?"

He slowed the truck, studying her for a couple heartbeats, and she attributed his silence to his interest in the Victorian. "I had no idea you were dining at the country club this evening," he said.

There was enough truth in his statement to make her cheeks burn. Still, she persisted. "But when you did, you seized the opportunity."

He offered a disarming chuckle. "Perhaps that was my second thought."

She couldn't help a reciprocal grin. Truly, the guy was impossible. "And what was your first thought?"

He glanced at her, and for a moment, she was caught in the spell of his irresistible dark eyes. "How lucky I was to see you twice in two days," he said softly.

A faint smile touched her mouth. She stared out the windshield at the falling sleet, trying to decide if he was harmlessly flirting with her or telling the truth.

"There's no electricity at the house, Teddy. It will be freezing and dark."

"There's a gas fireplace in the living room. I called the gas company this morning. The meter is running as the gas was never switched off." The truck slid on the slick road. He reduced his speed again, gripping the steering wheel and focusing on the taillights ahead of them. "And I keep extra flashlights and candles in my truck."

"Are you always prepared, regardless of the circumstances?"

His lips twitched. "I try to think of everything."

When they reached the circular driveway, he inched his truck along it and slid to a stop. At night, the Victorian loomed majestic and mammoth, set against the stormy winter sky. She imagined smoke curling from all five chimneys, the welcoming fireplaces blazing in the enormous hearths.

"This house is a proverbial jewel in the rough," she murmured.

"Yes, it is." Teddy's expression softened. He got out of the truck, hoisted a knapsack over his shoulders, and then opened the passenger door for her.

"I could get used to this," she said.

He assisted her out of the truck and took her hand. "Used to what?"

"Being treated like a lady."

He blinked. "Is there any other way to treat a woman?"

Unfortunately, yes, there were plenty of other ways.

She drew in a sharp breath, remembering the verbal abuse she'd suffered with George. How he'd yell to silence her when she didn't agree with him; his chiding, "Come on, can't you take a joke, Candee?" after he'd made fun of her cooking, or her clothes, or her mannerisms. Their relationship had sent her into a tailspin of self-doubt and self-preservation.

Teddy interrupted her musings. "Shall I carry you up the stairs and over the threshold?"

"I can walk perfectly fine on my own."

She took one step and skated forward.

He slipped an arm around her shoulders. "Just in case, I'll keep you steady."

"Stilettos weren't made for walking," she joked, accepting his embrace and leaning into his solid chest as her heels crunched along the crusty ice.

He chuckled. "I'm not complaining."

They walked to the house under an onslaught of bone-chilling, wind-blown sleet.

Teddy was proving to be a gentleman, she mused, holding her securely and concerned about her welfare, in a fast-paced era where common courtesies were oftentimes forgotten. Gratefully, she smiled up at him.

When they reached the porch, she punched the code into the lockbox, extracted the key and unlocked the door.

He flicked on his phone flashlight and steered them to the living room. "I'll get the gas fireplace running and then we'll have dinner." He pulled a blanket from his knapsack and set it on the floor, gesturing her to sit. Then he placed his gray sport coat beside her.

"You can't light the fireplace and you shouldn't eat in here. The bank owns the house—we don't." She removed her capelet and installed herself on the blanket with her legs straight out, her tight black skirt tucked securely around them. "There are laws, Teddy …"

"If anyone asks, you're my realtor and I'm the man buying the house."

"And as your realtor, may I remind you that you're making a mistake by even thinking about purchasing a home in such poor shape? This isn't a wise investment for a house-flipper."

"I'm tearing it down, remember?" He walked to the fireplace and held the pilot button down for a couple minutes. A flame flickered, and the fire soon glowed, warming the room.

She sighed. "What else is in your knapsack?"

"Soy candles." He brought out a tidy boxed candle set along with a book of matches. He lit the candles and placed them on the fireplace mantel. "The box described these candles as part of the 'jasmine and cedar wood atmosphere collection.'"

"Well then, they're perfect," she said, amused.

He sat beside her, opened his takeout box and held up a massive hamburger. "Ah, dinner by candlelight."

"No dessert? I love caramels coated in chocolate."

"I'll bring caramels next time. Dark or milk chocolate?"

"Dark." She chortled. "Bring those, and how could I refuse?"

"Hopefully, you can't refuse anything I offer." His teasing

laugh was potent, and his affectionate appraisal made her heart rate rise. Along with the aroma of the cedar candles, she inhaled Teddy's clean scent, all male, and the air around them heated.

They fell into companionable silence, as he shared his crispy fries and had a bite of his hamburger. On top of the dinner she'd already eaten, she was consuming more calories than she normally ate in two days.

When they were finished, Teddy picked up the napkins strewn beside them. "What do you do when you're not selling real estate?" he asked.

"I volunteer at the Roses no-kill animal shelter every Sunday." She wiped her fingers on a napkin. "And I work part-time at the hardware store in town, since I like making things out of wood. My foster family's business was working with wood."

His hands stilled. "Your foster family?"

"When we were teenagers, my sister and I were removed from our home and placed into the state welfare system as foster children."

Once she blurted out the words, Candee chided herself. What had compelled her to divulge so much information? If she'd blinked, she would have missed the kind interest clouding Teddy's face before he replaced his expression with a teasing grin.

"And what do you make out of wood? Should I book you a spot on the home improvement channel?" he asked.

"I'd wait about fifty years if I were you. I'm not ready for my own television show." She fixed her stare on the burning gas logs in the fireplace. "I made a detailed dollhouse once with my foster father, complete with a rocking chair measuring three inches." She paused as tears threatened. "I still have that chair."

He kept his gaze on her face. "Care to tell me about your foster family?"

"Which one?"

"There was more than one?"

"We were shuffled to five different families." Her throat tightened as the memories washed over her. "The agency urged each foster family to keep us, and then the family would decide not to adopt."

Two teenage girls with no parents hadn't been worthy of love or a stable home.

Teddy was watching her closely. "Go on," he said quietly.

She swallowed. "The last family Desiree and I were placed with ended up being our 'forever' family." Candee commended herself on her steady tone. "We attended church together, and in the evening we often sang hymns around their old upright piano while I attempted to plunk out the tunes."

"I'm impressed." He considered her with open admiration. "You make dollhouses and play the piano and volunteer at a no-kill animal shelter. That is, when you're not selling real estate."

He'd turned the conversation away from her past, and she was appreciative. Most days, she secured her childhood memories in a protected compartment in her mind. Sitting with Teddy, who seemed so attuned to her, she felt comfortable and safe.

She half smiled. "I don't do any of those things remarkably well, except volunteering at the animal shelter. Animals love you no matter who you are or your background."

He shook his head. "I've never had time for animals."

"Doesn't your four-year-old nephew live with you?"

"Yes, although it's only been for the past few months, and we're still getting used to each other. Rob's watching him now while I'm away. Joseph rides horses on weekends at an equestrian center near Miami, and now he wants a horse."

"He'll probably beg for a dog at some point, too."

Teddy chuckled. "He already has asked."

Get him a rescue dog, preferably a beagle, she wanted to encourage. Although, seeing the closed expression on Teddy's face, she didn't pursue the subject.

"Do you read music?" she asked.

"I'm no Beethoven, although I can keep a steady beat on a timpani drum." He stood and gathered their trash in the carryout bag. "I'd like to go with you to the animal shelter—if I'm properly invited. You volunteer every Sunday?"

"Immediately after church."

He paused, then winked. "I'm waiting for an invite."

She couldn't help laughing. "The shelter needs all the help it can get, although volunteers must first attend an orientation, give references and then commit to a certain length of time."

"Can you vouch for me? I'll be living in Roses for the next few weeks."

"All right."

"Flexible hours?" he asked with amusement.

She grinned. "Absolutely."

"Then I'll assist in any way I can." He pulled a battery-operated transistor radio out of his knapsack. Turning it on, he fiddled with the dial until he found a crackly station playing 80's music. "Would you like to dance, Candee?"

"You want to dance—now?"

"You're still shivering a little." He offered a playful smile. "It's better to move around when you're cold."

"I'm not shivering," she informed him. "And I haven't danced with a man in forever."

Any further protest died on her lips as he pulled her to her feet.

160

"I can't remember the last time I danced with a woman, either." He placed his arm around her back. "Although I remember I liked it."

Candee silenced another protest. *Why not dance? The entire evening had a one-of-a-kind, storybook quality to it.*

"Unchained Melody" came on.

"I love the Righteous Brothers," she announced.

Teddy smoothed his fingers across her shoulders and pulled her closer. "I noticed when we were riding in your car yesterday."

They swayed in step to the enchanting words of the ballad about lonely rivers flowing and sighing.

The glow of the fireplace, dancing slowly with this strikingly handsome man, made her forget the previous two years of heartache and aloneness and dateless evenings.

"This music is in twelve eight time," she said.

He kept his fingers joined with hers. "It's beautiful."

With a quiet sigh, she submerged herself in the melody of the timeless song. The minutes passed and she lost track of the following medley of classic songs. She simply relaxed against Teddy's chest and allowed herself to experience the reassuring presence of his solid body against hers. His heart thudded in a steady meter and her own heart felt strange, beating oh-so-fast.

"Candee?" He lifted her chin. "If I was that guy with the same first and last names, I'd have rented a snowplow to meet you at the country club tonight."

His deep brown eyes darkened. Her body warmed with anticipation as his hands drifted down her shoulders, pressing her nearer.

It was there, an invisible thread drawing them together.

Her mind warned: It couldn't be, not after knowing him for a day.

But it was.

She knew he was going to kiss her, and she met his insistent lips with an eagerness she'd never known. He kissed her slowly, thoroughly. The strength of his powerful body molded intimately to hers, bringing her to life. The longer the kiss went on, the more she responded, straining to be nearer him.

The doorbell rang.

Teddy broke the kiss. "Are you expecting dinner guests?" He tipped up her chin. Affection and desire smoldered in his gaze as his thumbs stroked her heated cheeks.

Her hands flattened against his polo shirt and she rested her head on his chest. "Not unless they brought chocolate."

He laughed. "It must be the wind."

The odd chime of the doorbell ringing a second time prompted her to pull from his arms.

A moment afterward, the front door opened sending a blast of cold air into the living room.

"Anyone home?" a gruff voice called out.

A pair of heavy footsteps tromped down the hallway, and an elderly man with gray hair appeared in the living room doorway. With one hand, he pushed up a pair of thick glasses. With the other, he raised a sizable wooden baseball bat.

"Who are you two?" he demanded.

Candee retreated a step. "Mr. Dunworthy?"

"Candee Contando? What are you doing here?" The aging man hobbled into the room, using the baseball bat as a cane. "I saw candles flickering and smoke coming from a chimney. I figured it was teenagers up to mischief and decided to walk down here to see for myself."

"Mr. Dunworthy." Teddy came forward. "Candee was showing me the house."

"At this hour?" Up close, the dark age spots on the man's

face showed prominently. He squinted and stared at Teddy. "You live around here?"

"No. I'm from Florida, actually. My name is Teddy Winchester. I live in Miami and I'm an investor." Teddy extended his hand.

Mr. Dunworthy placed the baseball bat on the floor and the men shook hands. "I'm Charles Dunworthy. I live two doors down and I'm your basic nosy neighbor.

CHAPTER 6

*T*he following day, Candee attended church services. Upon returning to her apartment for a quick lunch, she checked her cell phone. Teddy had texted her.

Happy Sunday, his text read. *Planning to volunteer at the animal shelter this afternoon?*

She glanced at her watch—half past noon. *Yes*, she texted back. *On my way now.*

Can I join u?

Teddy was persistent and apparently interested in her. He was so good-looking and not at all arrogant. His manner was compelling, gentle, yet with an aura of control. She so regretted that Mr. Dunworthy had interrupted their one kiss.

She suppressed a grin and texted back. *All hands are welcome.*

She sent him the address and then changed into a plaid flannel shirt, old faded jeans, black leather boots, and a light navy jacket. After pulling her hair into a casual pony tail, she tied the green paisley scarf around her neck. Despite the freezing weather the previous evening, the sky was a brilliant

Carolina blue, the sun efficiently melting any sleet left on the ground.

Candee recognized Teddy's pickup as soon as she drove into the shelter's parking lot. Lounging against his truck, he displayed an easy charm, looking exceedingly handsome wearing dark jeans, his olive-green vest zipped over a black T-shirt. He was ruggedly fit, his arm muscles taut and hard.

He strode to her car, his boots crunching on the graveled parking lot, and had her door open before she'd taken her key out of the ignition.

"Did you attend services this morning?" His slow, lazy smile made her shamelessly wonder how it would feel to kiss him again.

As she got out of the car, she drew a long breath to steady her fluttering pulse and focused on the simple wood-sided entrance door. "Yes, and the sermon was amazing. The pastor spoke about how grace is the way to heaven and faith is the route we choose to take. Do you attend a church?"

His nodded. "A contemporary church in Florida. They stream their services online and I watched on my computer early this morning before I called my nephew."

"How is he?"

"He sounded happy. I'll fly to Miami next weekend to see him. He's having a good time with Rob." He peered past her at the modern concrete and brick building. "How long is our shift?"

"Four hours. And an application is required."

"Done," he said. "I attended the orientation already and used your name as a reference. Was that okay?"

"Of course." She paused. "When you texted me, were you already at the shelter?"

He shifted. "I guess I was."

"You guess? You blithely did nothing while I texted directions?"

He raised a hand. "Guilty as charged. Last night you invited me to join you, remember?" Grinning, he took her hand. "Shall we go inside?"

She liked his easy-going sense of humor. In the spirt of friendly bantering, she teased, "Do you want to clean the crates, walk the dogs or stuff envelopes?"

"I have a choice?"

She chuckled. "It depends on whether you want to sit or stand. I prefer walking the dogs and love being outside."

He gazed down at her and squeezed her hand. "I'll go wherever you go." His words hung significantly in the crisp January breeze.

The next four hours passed amidst amiable sparring and chatter, with Candee teasing Teddy that he was supposed to be walking the dogs—the dogs weren't supposed to be walking him.

Dusk had fallen by the time Teddy was placing the last dog back in its enclosure as Candee explained the shelter's protocol and safety procedures to help limit the transfer of disease. For the next fifteen minutes, they assisted last-minute customers with animal visitations.

As they got ready to leave, Candee called out a jovial good-bye to Agnes, another volunteer.

"Will you and your boyfriend be back here next week?" Agnes asked.

Candee blinked.

She was coming to value Teddy's friendship … but *boyfriend*? No, no, no. She wasn't ready to open her heart to another relationship—because Teddy would leave, like her parents, like the foster families, like George. Absolutely, she wanted to build a social life for herself again, but not at the expense of another heartbreak.

She took a steadying breath, resolve firmly in control. "Teddy and I met three days ago, Agnes. I'm his … realtor."

"Oh." The woman studied them. "You two just look like you're together. I assumed you were a couple."

From the corner of her eye, Candee noted Teddy's quirked eyebrow, although he said nothing. She glanced at her hand in the crook of his arm. It felt natural, although she didn't remember placing her hand there.

As they walked away, Teddy whispered in her ear. "Well, that opens up a landslide of potential for us, doesn't it? Now will you join me for dinner?" Leaning over, he opened her car door.

"I'm at my realty office by eight o' clock on Monday morning." She bit her lip, debating his invitation. "In the afternoon, I work at the hardware store."

"I promise to get you home early." His grin was wide, his gaze glinted with merriment. "Say yes, because we're a couple now. Just ask Agnes."

"I never said—"

Lightly, he kissed her forehead. "We've been on our feet for hours. Don't you need nourishment? Eating a few slices of pizza won't take long."

Her hand hovered uncertainly above her car keys before she agreed. "I'm starved, actually."

The sun was descending as they arrived at Tony's pizzeria on Main Street. They parked their cars near the entrance, and Teddy came around to open her car door.

She smiled as he complimented her, citing how magnificent she was with animals and how much he prized her nurturing manner.

He gestured to the entrance of the pizzeria. "I made reservations. I didn't want us to sit around waiting for a pager to go off. Especially since you go to work early in the morning."

The soft tenderness in his deep voice took her breath away.

Was it wrong for her to enjoy being well-treated? she

questioned herself. Teddy made her feel special—listening attentively while she spoke, sensitive to her moods and attuned to her emotions. He obviously cared, showing initiative and planning ahead so she'd have a decent night's rest.

He took her hand as they walked into the pizzeria.

Mouth-watering scents of freshly cooked pasta, pizza, garlic, and oregano drifted through the darkly-lit restaurant. A portly woman, looking just like an Italian grandmother, escorted them to a table near a cheery fireplace. The woman was dressed in pressed black slacks and a turtleneck sweater, with "Tony's" stitched in red on the collar. A spiked-haired pizza maker stood in front of an open brick oven tossing pizza dough in the air and then covering the circle of dough with tomato sauce, pepperoni, and cheese.

Candee took in a deep breath. "Italian is my favorite food in all the world."

"MINE, TOO," Teddy agreed. As he pulled out a chair for Candee, he took in Tony's traditional decor—red and white checkered tablecloths, Italian statues and grapevines, the muted atmospheric lighting enhanced by votive candles at each table.

He took a seat, and they accepted menus from the waitress, a sandy-haired teen who seemed far more interested in the pizza tosser than in her customers.

Teddy perused the menu. "I love anything with the word pizza."

"Tossed salad is a nutritious alternative," she said.

After they were both served, Candee tucked into her salad while Teddy loaded up his plate with three slices of Margherita pizza.

"Do you have a favorite dog?"

He stopped in midchew to consider her unexpected question. "I came across many breeds today and it's hard to say. You?"

She smiled, but there was a hint of sadness to it. "I love beagles."

He was about to ask why when the waitress appeared. "More water? Coffee?"

"Black coffee for me," Candee said.

"Two cups, please," Teddy said.

A few minutes later the waitress set steaming cups of coffee on the table, cleared their empty plates, and encouraged them to order dessert.

"You haven't eaten any pizza yet," Teddy said. "There are two slices left."

"Box up what's left," Candee said to the waitress. "Teddy, you can have the leftovers for a midnight snack."

He laughed. "Since I professed my love for pizza earlier, I therefore have a good excuse for eating most of it." He gazed at Candee, who was twirling the ends of her thick red hair. He knew he was monopolizing her weekend, but she had been utterly enchanting while she'd handled the animals, treating every dog with respect and compassion, sensitive to the different breeds. She'd walked the dogs alongside him, hips swaying, her tall willowy figure provocative, laughing out loud at his knock-knock jokes.

Finally, he'd met someone who appreciated his sense of humor.

He loathed giving her up quite yet, and he planned to ask for a coffee refill when the waitress came back.

As the waitress went around the corner to box up the pizza and flirt with the pizza tosser, Teddy leaned forward. "Why do you love beagles, Candee?"

She broke eye contact and shrugged. "Long story."

"I'm a good listener." He scuffed his chair closer to the

table. "Last night you mentioned your 'forever' family. I'm assuming the two stories go together. Care to elaborate?"

She cupped her hands around her coffee cup as the waitress set the boxed pizza by Teddy. He waited while Candee sipped coffee and fixed her gaze on the crackling fire in the fireplace. Setting the cup down, she said, "The Johnsons encouraged Desiree and me to attend college."

"They sound like good people. Are you still in touch with them?"

"Six years ago, they moved to Chicago. I haven't seen them since I graduated from college. We still email, and I hope to visit them someday."

"What about your other foster families?" he asked gently. "You mentioned there were five families altogether."

She waved a hand dismissively. "Why would you be interested in hearing the sad story of my childhood?"

"Because I'm interested in you and everything about you."

She blushed and slowly exhaled. "Desiree and I encouraged each other every time we moved, assuring each other everything was fine, but it wasn't, you know? Between the ages of twelve and seventeen, we'd lived in four foster homes. New parents were complete strangers to us, and every house had its own set of rules—where to sleep, how to dress, what to eat, chores that had to be done."

Reaching out, he traced his finger along the curve of her cheek. "Those must have been very hard and scary years for two teenage girls."

The smile she offered quickly faded. "I always felt like a misfit. We didn't do anything normal teenagers did. No sleepovers, no driver's licenses—only a continuous series of knowing we were outsiders wherever we went."

She paused and stared down at her coffee. She'd hardly drunk any.

He took her silence as consent that she'd continue, and waited.

She gazed out the window at a cluster of clouds sitting low in the sky, then shifted her gaze to his. "Looking back, the hardest part was the beginning. I can still visualize my sister and me packing all our belongings into green trash bags the day we were taken from our home. I was twelve at the time. Desiree was fourteen."

"May I ask why you were put in foster care?"

She stared past him. "Our parents were declared unfit, and the state deemed it necessary for my sister and me to live in a safer place." She fidgeted with her gold earrings. "Although I didn't understand at the time, in hindsight I see there was no other choice. Our parents died soon after we were removed, and the doctors blamed their deaths on substance abuse."

"I'm sorry." He took her cold, fidgeting hands in his. "And now you've grown into a beautiful young woman. From my brief glimpse of your sister, she seems to be doing well. She's a lawyer?"

"And a good one, advocating for children's rights," Candee responded brightly. "I'm committed to making a difference in children's lives too. I have a plan that includes a rambling property with five acres, where children can safely go after school and learn music and play with dogs and finish their homework and eat healthy snacks ..." Her voice trailed off.

"I applaud you." He grinned approvingly and glided his thumbs over her hands. "What's your plan?"

It was just like her to want to help others, he thought. He imagined her as a kind and caring mother—a perfect mother for Joseph.

Perfect for Joseph and perfect for him. He scowled at himself, surprised the idea had drifted into his mind of its own accord. With a long sigh, he acknowledged the truth. Candee was an extraordinary woman, compassionate and warm-hearted. At thirty-two years old, he'd never felt such an instant attraction to a woman. After knowing her for only a few days, he was already half in love with her.

Perhaps fate had brought them together.

"You might as well know all the facts, Teddy," she was saying.

His thumbs froze on her hands in midstroke. He made himself resume, collecting his thoughts before asking, "What facts?"

She pulled her hands from his. "I should have addressed the situation and told you everything on Friday." Her voice was so low, he strained to hear her.

"Tell me what?" He leaned in closer, promising himself that whatever these facts were, it didn't matter.

For a fleeting moment, she closed her eyes, but then she pushed her shoulders back and squarely met his gaze. "The twenty-thousand dollar bid on the Victorian? It's my bid. I'm planning to live there and renovate the downstairs space, making it an after-school day care for disadvantaged children." Her voice caught. She paused before her words rushed out. "Therefore, I'd appreciate if you took your money elsewhere, preferably Miami, because the Victorian is taken."

CHAPTER 7

*T*aken? The Victorian was taken?

Teddy jerked off his vest and threw it on the worn oak chair in his hotel room. He approached the window and gazed out at a thick black sky. In the distance, the twinkling lights of shops in the town square beckoned. Somewhere near, a church bell tolled the hour.

He tapped his hands together and spoke softly to his brother. "Really, Christian? Candee bid on the irreparable property in Roses that I'm interested in?"

With a heavy sigh, Teddy shoved his hands into his jean pockets. There were few moments in his life when he recalled being at a loss for words, but he definitely hadn't known what to say when Candee announced her plans. He'd mumbled something about having no idea she'd wanted the property, paid the restaurant bill while acknowledging her 'thank you,' then matched her swift steps as he walked her to her car.

At first, he'd been angry. Why hadn't she simply told him? True, he'd been insistent about seeing the property. However, if the Victorian meant that much to her—which it apparently did—she should have never taken him to see it.

His anger had evaporated on his drive back to the hotel. In retrospect, her intentions explained her hesitancy, her efforts to talk him out of buying it himself. And if he hadn't been so intent on purchasing a bargain, he would have spotted what was clear in hindsight—she loved the house. He'd clearly seen her wistful gaze when she'd held his hand and stared at the property with him.

He shook his head, berating himself. Here he thought she was the world's worst realtor. Instead, she was trying to protect her investment, and perhaps her heart. Her life had been filled with trauma and transience, yet in what he recognized already as true Candee style, her aspiration was to transform the house into a safe environment for disadvantaged children.

His head-strong, courageous Candee.

He recalled the night before, the candlelight living room and her amused, "You want to dance—now?" After the music started, she'd snuggled close, her soft curves pressed against him. She'd felt warm and responsive, and the mere touch of her hands on his shoulders had heated his pulse. Just thinking about the tumultuous highs of the past three days made the short time they'd spent together all the more significant.

He sensed she was beginning to care for him too. Nonetheless, common sense warned that love had no place in his life. He owned a thriving real estate business in Florida and had a nephew who needed him there.

There was no reason he couldn't continue seeing her, though, his heart encouraged. All that stood between them was the house and a distance of over seven hundred miles. Both easily remedied, he assured himself, between phone calls and Skype, although his conscience nagged about how he didn't do well in long-distance relationships.

With a low exhale, he turned away from the window.

Before they'd departed, he'd pressed a kiss to her forehead and informed her he intended to talk further in the morning. She hadn't agreed, although she hadn't disagreed either. Nonetheless, he'd seen the resistance in her green eyes. It had taken the last grain of his self-control not to bring her to his chest and placate that resistance with soft assurances and numerous kisses.

First thing in the morning, he'd arrive at her realty office and check off the first part of what was keeping them apart. He had decided to visit her office on Monday anyway, although now his reasons were different.

He glanced at the clock, dreading the lengthy night awaiting him. At least there were leftovers, he mused.

He uttered a soft curse as he looked around his room. In their quick departure, he'd forgotten the leftover pizza at the restaurant.

More importantly, he'd forgotten to ask Candee why she loved beagles.

Tomorrow. There was always tomorrow. For her sake and for his, he intended to straighten out everything. Tomorrow.

* * *

AFTER CALLING his nephew and speaking briefly to Rob, Teddy arrived at Candee's realty office at nine a.m. His arms were laden with four boxes of chocolate-covered caramels he'd bought at a local supermarket and a carryout bag from the trendy coffee house in town: two espressos topped with steamed milk, a dusting of cinnamon, and dark chocolate curls. A peace offering.

He rapped on Candee's realty door and walked in, smiling his approval at the tastefully decorated sun-lit office.

Candee sat behind an uncluttered desk with her laptop open, clicking rapidly on the keys. It appeared she'd taken extra care with her appearance, wearing a light-pink blouse and tailored black slacks. Her luxurious red hair was pulled back from her face and fastened with a floral-colored barrette, the rest of it falling to curl naturally around her shoulders.

His heart stopped. She was so beautiful.

She didn't seem quite as enraptured to see him. Her greeting consisted of a curt nod.

He held the candy toward her. "These are for you. I realize it's a little early in the morning for chocolate."

"It's never too early for chocolate." A slow smile came across her face as she stood. She accepted the candy and placed the boxes beside her laptop. "Thank you, although I can't eat all this candy."

"I can help you." Encouraged by his success, he pulled up a chair and set the coffees on her desk. "I assume you expected me, and I have four reasons for coming."

She sat back down in her chair. "Teddy, I … The Victorian …If you knew how much the home means to me."

"That's the main reason I'm here." An odd lump formed in his throat at her vulnerable yet unwavering expression. "I have no intention of bidding on the property anymore."

She pressed a palm to her heart. "You don't?"

"Absolutely not. Prompted by the right incentive, of course." He paused. When she didn't respond, he continued, "Besides, I certainly wouldn't want to go against you in a bidding war."

A determined glint shone in her gaze. "Considering you know I'd do anything to win?"

"Considering that fact and everything else, I won't even

try. When you're bent on a course of action, I believe nothing can stop you."

"You've come to know me well in four days." She leaned back in her chair and grinned. "Besides, my twenty-thousand-dollar bid is all the money to my name, and I wouldn't have the funds to bid against you." Without warning, her grin turned into a sob.

He went around her desk and knelt, sliding his arms around her. Turning into his embrace she cried harder, murmuring between sobs about how relieved she was, and how she knew the house could be salvaged with hard work and diligence, and she planned to use the acreage for a small working farm.

When her tears waned, she stayed where she was, her head resting against his chest.

He offered a napkin from the coffee bag. "Everything better?"

Self-consciously, she dabbed at her eyes and composed her features. "I haven't allowed myself to cry in years."

"I haven't cried in a long time either," he admitted. Rising, he skimmed a kiss across her temple.

She offered a rueful grin. "What are the other reasons you're here?'

"Well, the first was to bring you coffee and chocolates, and the second was to inform you I won't be bidding on the Victorian."

"But you mentioned a 'right' incentive. What might that be?"

"I'd like a thank-you kiss in return for preferring to be your ally, not your adversary."

She smiled.

He lifted her from her chair and pulled her into his arms. Gently, he brushed his lips over hers. Her tongue swept across his lips, and he welcomed her, his body shamelessly hungry in its response. His fingers tightened possessively to draw her closer, and an eternity passed before he lifted his mouth.

"The reason you came to Roses was to find a property and now you're giving it up," she murmured. "You would do this for me?"

He gazed into her glistening eyes, brimming with happiness.

"I would do anything for you," he answered thickly, surprised he'd spoken his thoughts aloud. "Although I truly believe the Victorian is beyond renovation."

She pulled out of his arms. "I'm a fairly good carpenter."

His gaze narrowed, although he didn't want to spoil the moment by informing her the house needed at least a dozen carpenters working around the clock—not to mention plumbers, electricians and roofers.

The silence lengthened. His heart gave a lurch at the resolve in her gaze.

"And do you know what I've learned from being a carpenter?" she asked. "Good old-fashioned perseverance and staying power. Even my simple three-inch rocking chair demanded endless hours and a lot of care."

"Making a rocking chair for a dollhouse is a lot different from tackling a five thousand square foot house that's been abandoned for years," he said.

"I'm not impatient. I'll focus on the process and—"

"I'll support you." His quiet tone stopped her from continuing. "However, from my knowledge as a contractor, sometimes you need to move on. Bringing the house up to par with city and code requirements will take a lot of capital."

Adamantly, she shook her head. "I'll never give up my dream."

He noted the guarded hope in her voice and carefully chose his words. "I have an offer for you. Your plan for after-school care is a good one, and I'd like to invest in it. Make me part of your equation." He lifted the coffees from the bag and handed her a cup. "Will you consent to viewing other properties in Roses that might also suit your dream?"

She opened her mouth, presumably to argue.

"Keep an open mind," he reminded.

"I can't accept any money from you, Teddy."

"Consider it a loan, then. I'll even throw in my free expert advice."

She managed a wan smile before sinking into her chair and thoughtfully savoring her coffee.

He glanced around the room. "Your mother owned this business?" He congratulated himself on changing their conversation's direction.

"Those were the days when my mother wasn't drinking. By the time I graduated from college, this office had been boarded up, so I earned my real estate license and opened using her name."

"Which is the reason I called you and not your competitors," he said. "I assumed you'd been in business for many years and knew the area well." Fate again, he thought.

"I wanted to continue my mother's legacy in some way. She wasn't a terrible parent, just terribly misguided." Candee absently touched her gold earrings. "And of course, the drinking and the drugs ..."

"I've noticed you wear those earrings every day. Are they from your mother?"

Sadness flickered across her beautiful face. "It's all I have left as a remembrance. She bought them at a consignment shop for my twelfth birthday. It wasn't long afterward that Desiree and I were moved to our first foster home." A hint of a smile wavered. "Now you've given me three reasons."

He grinned. She didn't miss a thing.

"I'm flying to Miami in a couple weeks to consult with

Rob and see Joseph," he explained. "Joseph's a wonderful kid. I think I mentioned that on weekends, he goes to a horse training therapy facility."

"Do you have custody of your nephew?"

"Hopefully soon." Teddy exhaled a deep breath. "My brother was killed in an automobile accident a few months ago, and I should be granted guardianship of Joseph fairly soon. It's so hard for him right now ... For us ..." Teddy glanced out the window and knuckled an unexpected tear. She waited in silence while he cleared his throat before turning back to her. "I'd like you to fly down to Florida with me to meet Rob and Joseph. You alluded to a working farm for disadvantaged children and you might want to expand the concept and include animals as therapy."

"It sounds like a wonderful idea, although I can't go. I have too many commitments in Roses."

"We'll be gone from Friday afternoon until Sunday evening and you'd have almost two weeks to prepare for the trip."

"What about my real estate business?"

"Your one client is sitting across from you."

She hesitated. "I've never seen Miami."

"Bring shorts and flip-flops. You can stay at one of Rob's places. He owns apartments above several of his businesses, and one is a five-minute walk from my condo."

"I'd never impose."

"Believe me, Rob owns more properties than he knows what to do with. And didn't you advise me last evening to fly back to Miami? Well, I'm following your advice, except that I want you to join me."

CHAPTER 8

*T*he next two weeks flew by in a pleasant flurry for Candee, as she and Teddy viewed prospective houses and stopped daily at the Victorian home. He'd offered advice on cost-effective strategies to modernize, while staying true to the house's character. Though they'd viewed numerous modest properties more in sync with her nonexistent budget, none came close to matching the Victorian's architectural design, aesthetics, or sheer grandeur.

Together, she and Teddy researched adding a horse farm to the property; and she'd discovered that horses, with their unique nature, were considered mirrors of a person and an excellent choice for therapy. Furthermore, being around horses bolstered a person's self-confidence, as horses were believed to relieve stress.

"You have the acreage," Teddy had encouraged her after they'd exhausted her property search.

On the last afternoon before their departure to Miami, they volunteered at the shelter. When they were about to leave, a pregnant whimpering beagle was brought in. After the veterinarian examination, it was determined the dog was approximately fifty days pregnant and due to give birth to six puppies within the week.

"Where was the dog found?" Teddy asked.

"This poor beagle was left on the side of the road." Candee gazed at the hound-dog look the beagle gave her, and her heart melted. "I may not be able to travel to Miami with you, Teddy, considering how large the beagle's stomach is. I want to be here with her when she gives birth."

He'd assured her they'd technically be gone for one day—traveling to Miami on Friday and returning to Roses on Sunday.

As he knelt beside her, she whispered, "After the beagle has her puppies, I want to keep her."

He raised his eyebrows. "Do you mean her or the puppies?"

"Both. A dog with puppies is costly for a shelter." Lightly, she caressed the dog's black and tan coat, and the dog didn't try to bite. "I'll be a foster mom until the pups can be adopted. All they need is a warm home."

"And food and nursing and a loving caregiver," he murmured, recovering admirably from his shock.

He carefully carried the compact hound dog to her own enclosure with food and water, and Candee placed a worn blanket beneath the dog.

"Try to eat, girl." She offered the beagle a piece of fruit. The dog sniffed and slowly inched toward Candee's outstretched hand.

"Beagles are known to be loving, gentle, and extremely sociable," Candee told Teddy.

Seeing his expression as he brushed a sprinkling of dog hair, which resembled black pepper, from his vest, she assured, "And beagles don't shed, except in the spring when they're ridding themselves of their winter coats."

"You know a lot about these dogs." At the sound of

Teddy's deep voice, the dog keenly watched him and wagged her tail. "Why do you love beagles so much?"

"We owned a dog once, a sweet beagle, and Desiree and I were forced to leave her behind." She hesitated, not trusting her voice to continue. "We called her 'Kisses.'"

The pregnant dog stared up at them with wide-set pleading hazel eyes.

"'Kisses.' Your dog's name was Kisses." Apparently weighing his words, Teddy carefully replied, "You're taking on a tremendous amount of work with a monstrous house filled with rubble and weeds and all these dogs."

"I cannot abandon her. And in eight weeks her pups will be adoptable. And yes, I'm naming the beagle Kisses."

She'd been ready to puff up with indignation if he'd tried to discourage her. He didn't. Instead, he smiled and offered his assistance, agreeing that Kisses was a perfect name for a beagle. Stating he wanted to "seal the Kisses decision," he pulled her close, his arms cradling her body as his lips passionately explored hers.

Hours later, Desiree joined them for a festive dinner at a new farm-to-table restaurant in downtown Roses. Although their table had ample room to accommodate the threesome comfortably, his muscled leg had touched Candee's throughout the meal. It seemed like he always made a point to keep her close to him.

Teddy had laughingly concurred with Desiree as she waved a forkful of miniature crab cake and declared, "No one in their right mind places a bid on a property that looks like a tumbledown haunted house. And now my sister is stepping up to take on a pregnant beagle about to give birth to a bunch of puppies?"

"'Kisses needs a home," Candee said staunchly. "And the children at the daycare can teach her and the puppies how to sit and stay and fetch."

"And you'll need to hire a full-time staff," Teddy said while aiming a subtle nod at Desiree. "Although knowing you, Candee, you'll attempt to juggle everything yourself."

"You've offered to help, right?"

He studied her face and replied, "Yes, and I never go back on my word."

She stared up at him, his smiling features, the firm line of his jaw, enveloped by his commanding presence. His gaze locked with hers. Both of them completely disregarded her sister's presence as he lowered his head, his lips hovering close before he kissed her lightly. Her breath caught as his bracing outdoor scent tingled her senses.

When she returned to her apartment that night, she fell into bed, pleasantly exhausted. As she did every night before retiring, she checked the bidding on the Victorian, relieved her twenty-thousand-dollar offer remained the highest.

She courted sleep, although it didn't come. She was too excited, her thoughts humming with elated expectation. Soon she would own her dream house, and she'd be building that dream with Teddy. Yes, he lived in Miami and she lived in Roses, but with Internet and phone calls and airplane travel, their relationship could continue to grow.

Her mood had lightened with each hour she'd spent with him, and life was definitely taking a turn she'd never expected. Perhaps Desiree was right and Cupid's arrow had been aimed directly at Candee and Teddy.

Sighing contentedly, she rolled onto her stomach and drifted to sleep.

CHAPTER 9

he following afternoon, Candee made sure every employee at the shelter knew to call her if Kisses went into labor. Then she and Teddy boarded the plane from Asheville, North Carolina, to Miami, Florida. The trip to the airport took less than an hour, and Teddy did the driving. Their flight was under three hours, and sudden air pockets and strong winds prompted gasps from the passengers in the cabin.

Candee was still recovering from the rough flight when an impish boy, echoing Teddy's good looks, raced to greet her and Teddy while they were retrieving their luggage at baggage claim.

"Uncle Teddy!" the boy called.

"Hey, Joseph!" Teddy squatted, fiercely hugging the boy. As he stood, he hoisted his nephew onto his shoulders.

Pivoting, he motioned to Candee. "Joseph, meet my new friend, Miss Candee Contando."

She extended her hand. "I've heard a lot about you, Joseph."

"Hi." The boy leaned over Teddy's head. "Mr. Rob said Uncle Teddy mentions you every time he calls."

"And I'm Mr. Rob." A short, heavy-set, balding man bent at the waist in an exaggerated bow. Along with a good-natured smile, his blue-eyed gaze was welcoming. He stole Candee's luggage from her and thoughtfully cocked his head. "You're too ravishing to be anyone else. Welcome to Miami, Candee."

Teddy swung Joseph back down to the floor as he offered introductions. He kept one hand possessively around her waist, and as she glanced up at him, he was staring down at her with heartfelt pride.

"No wonder she was one of your main topics when we spoke," Rob said, clapping Teddy on the back. "Everything's certainly coming up Roses, eh?"

The group dissolved into good-natured chuckling.

As they stepped out of the airport, the air of the Miami evening was balmy and inviting. Candee pulled off her paisley scarf and tucked it into her carry-on bag. Teddy walked between her and Joseph, holding their hands. As they walked to Rob's car, they passed an outdoor kiosk brimming with Valentine candy.

"No candy for me," Rob said. "I'm on a diet."

"Again?" Teddy teased.

"I haven't cheated in twenty-four hours. I'm on a roll." He kept his gaze fixed on the sidewalk and whistled an out-of-tune melody.

"We're not dieting." Teddy turned to Candee. "Carmel dark chocolate sound good?"

"I can't. My stomach is reeling from the turbulent airplane ride."

"Dark chocolate helps." He picked up two decorative gold boxes filled with candy, along with a red-foil rose and a jumbo heart swirl lollipop for Joseph.

"Chocolate and more chocolate?" she joked as he handed her the rose and boxed candy.

"Sugar and chocolate is the cure for most maladies."

"Yeah," Rob interjected. "That's been my bakery mantra for years."

She chuckled and eyed the lollipop. "You realize, Teddy, that your nephew will be on a sugar high tonight and you'll only have yourself to blame?"

"Guilty as charged." Teddy held up a hand, then swept a kiss on her lips. "I'll pick you up at Rob's apartment tomorrow at eleven."

He was so wonderfully generous, and when he kissed her, she heartily kissed him back. At least until Rob's raucous throat-clearing broke her and Teddy apart.

* * *

FOLLOWING a leisurely shower in Rob's high-end penthouse Saturday morning, Candee checked her appearance in the bedroom's full-length mirror. The weather was a comfortable seventy degrees, and she was pleased she'd brought a soft royal-blue crepe dress accented by gathered cropped sleeves. She rubbed a drop of her favorite rose fragrance to her wrists, and pulled on black leather ballet flats for walking ease.

She had just knotted the gold tie belt around her waist when she heard a light rap on the penthouse door. Teddy had arrived exactly at eleven a.m.

She smiled as she opened the door. Yes, he was devastatingly handsome, standing in the doorway wearing cotton khaki pants and a slim-fitting gray polo shirt that accented his strong physique. However, it was the little things that drew her to him—his kind actions, how he was true to his

187

word, and the way his eyes lit with boyish enthusiasm whenever he described the Victorian's renovations.

"Good morning." He took her hands in his and gazed at her with bold dark eyes. "Your beauty lights up this place."

Self-consciously, she laughed. "You must be focusing on the view behind me. You know, the sixteen-foot floor-to-ceiling windows looking out onto Miami beach and 'millionaire's row.'"

He drew her to him. "No, it's you," he whispered. "Only you." His mouth came down on hers for a long passionate kiss, and her heart thumped hard in her chest.

She placed her cell phone in her handbag and slung the bag over her shoulder. Down in the lobby, they encountered a pacing Rob and an exuberant Joseph demonstrating a cartwheel across the marbled floor.

"About time, you two." Rob pointedly stared at his watch. "What normally takes me five minutes took you ten."

"We were detained," Teddy said, reclaiming Candee's hand. "Shall we all walk to your bakery?"

"Absolutely." Rob patted his round stomach. "Some of us can use the exercise."

In the glittering daylight of the promising morning, Candee tucked her fingers in the crook of Teddy's strong arm. A welcoming breeze lifted her loose hair from her shoulders like a whirlpool.

As the foursome approached Sixty-Fifth Street, Rob's body language punctuated his proud tone. "What's not to like about America's favorite vacation city?" He gestured to the glass skyscrapers on both sides of the street. "Miami boasts a trendy nightlife, boat shows, auto racing, golf, tennis, cruises and deep-sea fishing."

"And we've never done any of those activities," Teddy said dryly.

"We had a lively time on the two-night party cruise a few years back, remember?"

"Lively time?" A knowing grin crossed Teddy's face. "You were seasick the entire forty-eight hours."

They crossed an intersection, and the enticing scent from Rob's bakery beckoned them into the store like a warm embrace. Glazed donuts, masterfully iced rainbow-colored cupcakes, and towering, three-tiered layer cakes frosted with buttercream sat proudly in a row of glass cases.

"I saved your Valentine cupcake for you, Uncle Teddy," Joseph said. And I made one for Miss Candee too. We froze them, and Mr. Rob took them out of the freezer yesterday." Joseph tugged on Teddy's hand. "They're in the kitchen. Come on, I'll show you."

"Save us a table," Teddy said to Candee. "We'll be back shortly."

When half of their group had disbanded, Rob examined a display case for fingerprints while a white-aproned employee boxed an order of cinnamon buns.

Candee hung back, standing behind a parade of customers.

When Rob returned carrying two mugs of coffee and a bag of donuts, he guided her to an inviting seating area adjoining the bakery.

"Freshly baked donuts!" He exclaimed. "Twenty-four hours on a diet is long enough." He set a white bakery bag emblazoned with his Rob's Marvelous Muffins logo and the two mugs on the small round table. "Black coffee, right?"

"Thank you." She inhaled the mouth-watering scent of chocolate iced donuts rolled in sprinkles and the aroma of rich dark coffee. "Your hospitality is generous, and both your places—the penthouse and this bakery—are amazing."

"I don't have any complaints about flattery." He took a large swallow of his coffee. "Keep it coming."

"I'd gain ten pounds in a week if I worked here." She grinned. "A bakery like yours in my hometown would be well-received."

He flashed a smile. "I own a half dozen bakeries in Miami. I haven't considered opening out-of-state, although you never know."

Rob went on to describe the process of running a bakery, embroidering his account of the time he'd changed a hit recipe and used confectioners' sugar instead of granulated, which had resulted in a string of complaints.

Her turquoise and silver bracelets cheerfully clinked against her coffee mug as she drank and listened. He was such a genial man and so talkative, she could imagine him having a conversation without her, chatting non-stop to an empty chair.

"Enough about me." His telescope gaze gave her a measured look. "Let's talk about your grand plans for the Victorian, Candee."

"Hasn't Teddy told you?"

He nodded confirmation. "Now I want to hear it from you."

She blew out an audible breath. "To begin with, every bathroom requires a complete gut job, and the carpeting in each room needs to be pulled up." She paused. "The wood floors are trashed, and Teddy recommended restoring them using four-inch red-oak planks."

"Do you have funds to pay for all these renovations?" Rob flatly asked.

His tone didn't intimidate her in the least. "No. I'll take out loans."

"And how do you intend to pay back these loans? All these restorations will take endless capital."

She let the reality of his words hang in the air between them. She'd learned to stay quiet when she wasn't certain how to answer, and she needed to think before replying. Her foster background, dealing with different people's expectations, had taught her that.

"I'll work extra hours at the hardware store," she said. "And I can wield tools and ladders. There's nothing like carpentry to test a person's patience."

Mentally, she thanked her "forever" foster father for permitting her to work with him in his woodshop.

She met Rob's piercing blue gaze and waved a dismissive hand at herself. "Who knows? Maybe I'll even sell a house or two in the meantime."

"Teddy said your perseverance and goals are admirable."

"I'm going to be the type of caregiver who attends every child's basketball game, every concert …" She forced herself to keep her tone calm and unemotional. "These disadvantaged kids need support."

"I've invested in Teddy's ventures for years, and he's never let me down. He approves of your project and he oversees numerous home-improvement crews."

"We'll give it our best shot."

"The hallmark of a successful baker is self-discipline, and the same goes for real estate." Rob gave a big throaty laugh. "At first, Teddy wanted to raze the house and build low-income housing on the five-acre lot. Our business ethos is to give to those less fortunate."

In the space of seconds, Teddy's ideas collided with hers, and she could see the merit in his plans for the property.

"He never told me," she softly replied.

"You're the best thing that's happened to him in a long time. Has he mentioned his childhood to you?"

She swallowed a deep drink of the exquisitely brewed coffee. "Hardly anything."

"I encouraged him to show you his old homestead," Rob said. "He said he's too embarrassed."

"It can't be any worse than my childhood homes."

Instantly, she was ambushed by scenes from her adolescence. Whenever her birthday had come around, she had waited, hoping for a birthday cake. The cake never came. Neither did the candles, or the balloons, or the birthday gifts.

"Teddy came from nothing," Rob said, "and he and his brother were constantly beaten by his drunken father. When life gets punched out of you, only the outstanding persevere. Unfortunately, after a hard childhood, a person's trust no longer comes easy."

She confirmed his words with a sad smile. Despite his outward bravado, Rob had an astute understanding of people.

"And what about your foster families?" he asked.

She shrugged. "Nothing to say."

He propped his elbows on the table, the gleam in his eyes matching his shiny round face. "Up until now, Teddy's been a confirmed bachelor like me. I'm the furthest a person can get from being a wedding expert, but he genuinely cares about you. He can't stop looking at you whenever you're together."

She stifled a denial as a giggling four-year-old boy raced to the table with Teddy close behind.

"We're back, Miss Candee," Joseph announced. "And we brought your Valentine surprise cupcake." He held up a basket, revealing a red muffin set on a red doily. Piped white icing gel on the muffin read, "Life is butter with you."

Her lips twitched with a grin. Impulsively, she hugged the adorable boy. "Thank you." She turned to Rob. "Clever sentiment, Rob."

Rob laughed. "They're all different. Took me weeks to come up with appropriate Valentine adages that wouldn't offend any customers."

"Taste the muffin and tell me what the surprise is, Miss

Candee," Joseph said. "I'll give you a hint. It has something do with kisses."

"Joseph, you're not supposed to give any hints to Candee, remember?" Teddy hooked his hands in his front pockets. His slow, devastating smile eclipsed all the busyness of the bustling bakery. "It's a taste test and she's supposed to discover the surprise by herself."

Candee bit into the muffin and briefly closed her eyes. The combination of strawberries and butter was delicious. She washed down the muffin with coffee, then took another bite. "There's chocolate inside. Wait …" she continued around a mouthful of cupcake. "A candy kiss is in the middle?"

"You guessed the surprise!" Joseph jumped up and down. "Like it?"

She laughed. "I love it."

"Me too." Teddy kissed her forehead, then pulled up a wing chair and sat facing her.

"Where's *your* Valentine muffin?" she teased.

"Gone in three bites."

"What was on yours?"

"The Browning quote." He kept his gaze on hers. "'Grow old along with me. The best is yet to be.'"

Positively emanating good cheer, Rob said, "And they all lived long and happily ever after. Long because it was for forty years, and happy for … two months."

Teddy grinned, glanced at his watch, then back at Candee. "Later today I want to take you to Joseph's horse ranch so you can see him ride his pony."

"I'm looking forward to it."

The cell phone in her purse rang. She pulled out her phone and checked the caller ID. "Please excuse me." She held up an index finger and answered the call.

When she clicked off, she took several quick breaths. Her

gaze flitted to the threesome staring at her before settling on Teddy. "It was one of the volunteers at the shelter. My beagle has gone into labor."

"Kisses?" Teddy's eyebrows drew together. "Don't labors take a long time?"

"For a beagle, anywhere from six to eighteen hours." She matched his stare with a firm one of her own. "I'm sorry. I have to leave this afternoon."

Teddy pressed his lips together and offered a weak smile. "I know how much this beagle means to you." He took his phone from his pocket and began checking the Internet. "There's a direct fight to Asheville leaving at four o'clock and one seat is available."

"Will you book it for me? I'll text Desiree and ask her if she can pick me up at the airport."

After the reservation was made, Teddy set his phone on the table. "Done. I'll keep my return flight to Roses on Sunday night so I can spend more time with Joseph."

"Yes, of course." Looking at the boy, she said, "I'm sorry I can't see you ride your pony."

"That's okay, Miss Candee," Joseph replied. "I ride him every weekend. I love horses! I love every animal in the world!"

She laughed. "Animals and children are very special."

Teddy stroked the auburn curls falling about her shoulders. "You're not even gone yet, and I miss you."

"Okay you two flames, save it for later." Rob cut his gaze to Teddy. Giving him a meaningful look, he lowered his tone. "Your lawyer called this morning. He couldn't reach you and left a message with me. It's about a court date to finalize your guardianship." Rob raised his tone, apparently for Joseph's benefit, who'd been intently watching them. "Hey Teddy, can I talk to you in the back?"

"Sure." Teddy quickly stood. "I wanted to behold the new commercial mixer you purchased for the kitchen, anyway."

"The heavy-duty one? It broke. The grinder lasted a week."

Teddy gave a sharp laugh. "Aren't you glad you came to Miami to meet the special people in my life?" he asked Candee.

She smiled. "Very glad."

He glided his knuckles down her cheek. "Is it all right if I leave Joseph with you for a few minutes?"

"My absolute pleasure."

Teddy grabbed an activity sheet and crayons at the counter and placed them on the table for his nephew. "How about sketching me a horse, buddy?"

"I want to draw the pony I ride at the ranch. His name is Blackjack because he's black."

Candee swallowed a chuckle as the men headed to the kitchen.

"What an excellent name for a pony," she said to Joseph. "I'm sure Blackjack is a beauty." She sat back in her chair, sipping her coffee and watching Joseph color. When Teddy's phone vibrated, she automatically picked it up and scanned the displayed number.

"You can answer it," Joseph said. "Uncle Teddy doesn't mind. I answer his phone all the time."

She debated. The phone number was identified by two initials—YE. A business call, she wondered? Assuming the call might be important, she answered. "Hello?"

"Who's this?" a woman asked.

Candee frowned into the phone. "Candee Contando. And you?"

"Yvonne Evette. Is this Teddy's phone?"

"Yes. May I take a message?"

"Put Teddy on the line," the woman said.

"He's not here."

"Tell him I'll be in Madrid another week and to phone me as soon as he gets this message. That means immediately." The woman hung up.

Candee stared at his phone as she set it on the table. "Who's Yvonne Evette?" she asked aloud, not expecting an answer.

"You mean Miss Yvonne?" Joseph made a face. "She's Uncle Teddy's other girlfriend and she's famous. We watch her on TV."

The shock of Teddy's betrayal knocked the air from Candee's lungs. She swallowed hard.

Unfortunately, Teddy and Rob chose that moment to emerge from the kitchen. They were obviously enjoying themselves, laughing and talking. Rob veered off to speak with an employee. Teddy was still grinning when he approached Candee's table.

He stopped, his probing gaze fixing on her. "What's wrong? You've gone pale."

She pushed back her chair. "Your cell phone rang and I answered it. I shouldn't have—I thought it might be important."

"Who was it?"

"A call from Spain."

Teddy stiffened. "Yvonne?"

"Yes, and she said to call her immediately."

Unnoticed, Rob strolled to the table. "Anything wrong?"

Heartsick from sadness and fury and defeat, Candee shivered and rubbed her arms. "Rob, where's the restroom?"

He pointed to a sign, and she shot past him.

"Candee, wait." Teddy strode purposefully after her. "I can explain."

She inhaled a tortured breath. She'd heard enough explanations from her ex to last a lifetime. And she'd never allow Teddy to see how much his duplicity had hurt her.

"It's not what it seems." He caught her wrist, and she snapped around. "Look," he said, "I've been seeing Yvonne for several months. She travels a lot and I ... I don't do long-distance relationships well."

Tears sprang to Candee's eyes. Firmly, determinedly, she held them back. "You don't do any relationship well."

"Please let me explain."

She deliberately stared down at his hand until he released her.

"I'll walk back to the penthouse and call a taxi to the airport," she said. "Please don't follow me. And tell Rob thank you for everything. Kiss Joseph good-bye for me and tell him I love animals too." She pivoted and entered the restroom. Inside, she splashed cold water on her face and peered at her reflection in the mirror above the sink. Her pallid complexion emphasized her emerald-green eyes, giving her a much-too-vulnerable appearance.

Again she was a fool, and she only had herself to blame. How could she have believed it was possible to fall in love with a man after knowing him a few short weeks?

Love. Love happened to other people, not to her. The sooner she came to grips with reality, the simpler her life would become. No more broken hearts, she vowed. Not ever again.

Two hours later she stood alone in the Miami airport, waiting for the boarding to begin.

To pass the time while waiting in line, she checked the foreclosure website. She gasped, almost dropping her phone when the house came on the screen. Her bid was no longer the highest.

She refreshed her phone. Surely, there must be a mistake.

No. The new bid was $40,000, driving the next bid to $60,000—money she didn't have.

This couldn't be happening. Her stomach felt heavy, her heartbeat raced.

Quickly, she texted Desiree. *I logged online at the airport, and the Victorian is now at 40K. Who bid on MY house?*

Online means the Internet, came Desiree's reply. *So that means anyone on the world-wide web. No use worrying. Whatever happened, we'll sort it when u get home. Have a safe flight and see u in Asheville.*

Candee attempted to pull her mind away from one looming fear. She might lose the house.

Another text floated across her screen, this one from Teddy. *Have u boarded the plane?*

He'd texted numerous times since she'd abruptly left Rob's bakery, and she'd ignored him.

However, he'd made and paid for her plane reservation and she knew she should text him.

Soon, she replied.

Can I call you tomorrow?

She hesitated. Her cold, clammy hands clutched the phone tighter.

Something prompted her to ask, although surely his answer would be no.

Did you place a bid on the Victorian house? she texted.

Air stopped entering her lungs as she waited for his response. Time seemed to be slowing down until a single word appeared on her phone.

Yes.

CHAPTER 10

*A*s usual, Desiree had arrived at the country club before Candee. Candee hung her fur capelet by the door and greeted her sister with a hug.

Desiree looked gorgeous in a red velvet figure-hugging pant suit. She went back to arranging a plate of chocolate-covered strawberries on a silver serving tray. The club was empty, save for black-suited waiters setting glass vases of red tulips and rose peonies on every table.

Candee appraised her own outfit—a sleeveless petal-pink lace dress. Unlined along the hem, the dress allowed a peek-aboo of her long legs. She'd parted her hair on the side and let the thick curls flow down the opposite shoulder.

Satisfied with the strawberry arrangement, Desiree turned to her. "Finally, I was able to talk you into attending the dinner dance. You can leave those puppies alone for a few hours. Valentine's Day is one of the biggest events at the club. Thanks for coming early to help me finish decorating."

"You insisted you needed help, although there's so much to admire." Candee looked around the room. "The lace ribbons and pom-pom wreaths are glittery and sophisticated, and those smooch balloons are gorgeous."

"White balloons with a stamp of my red lipstick." Desiree puckered her glistening red lips.

Candee smiled and fingered an arrow-toting Cupid on the banquet table. "No use in me sitting in my apartment with Kisses and her six puppies, watching television and hoping that Meg Ryan and Tom Hanks will get me through the evening."

"Her puppies are adorable. So firm and plump."

"And active," Candee replied. "Plus, they've doubled their weight in less than two weeks. Kisses is the best mom in the world. I supply high-quality puppy food and a vitamin mineral tablet, and she does the rest."

Desiree popped a chocolate-covered strawberry into her mouth and smiled. "All is well then."

Was it? The lump in Candee's throat threatened to choke her, and tears burned her eyelids. She swallowed and poured herself a glass of water. She wouldn't cry. She was strong and had made a vow to herself.

Desiree was watching her closely. "Have you heard from Teddy?"

"He's texted me every day and apologized numerous times about Yvonne, although it doesn't matter anymore." Candee forced herself to sound calm and detached. "As far as I know, he hasn't returned to Roses. He said something about being tied up in Miami court because of Joseph's guardianship."

"Did you text him back?"

"Only to tell him I landed safely." She missed him intensely, especially on a night like tonight, Valentine's Day. She squeezed her eyes shut, remembering the feel of his strong calloused hand around her waist while they'd danced, his lips capturing hers.

"If I was that guy with the same first and last names," he'd said. *"I'd have rented a snowplow to meet you at the country club tonight."*

How could he have become so important to her in the short time they'd known each other? Each day that passed, she felt more and more empty without him. She'd even been tempted to answer his texts with an invitation to join her for dinner at Tony's. That night they'd gone there, he'd said that, like her, Italian food was his favorite in all the world.

But Teddy lived in Miami with Yvonne, and Candee lived in Roses with Kisses and her puppies.

Once she allowed them in, her tormenting memories took over. She'd loved listening to his remodeling ideas, the quiet decisiveness in his voice when they'd agreed that horse therapy suited her project perfectly. And then there'd been the comforting reassurance of knowing they were venturing into these daunting tasks side by side.

Hah! Had he played her for a fool the entire time, planning to take her house right out from under her? The auction had just closed, and most likely demolition would begin any day. Candee promised herself she'd never drive down Thompson Lane again. Idly, she wondered if Teddy would manage the project himself, or send one of his many home-improvement crews to demolish the house.

Desiree had advised her to set her sights elsewhere. Perhaps a five-hundred-foot Cape Cod made more sense, considering her budget. Smaller dreams were more realistic.

She opened her eyes.

Her sister's gaze clouded with concern and she clasped Candee's hands. "You know, we tried to raise the funds, but neither Scott nor I had an extra $40,000 hidden under our pillowcases."

"Thank you." Not only was Desiree her sister, but she was also a true friend.

After that, Desiree adeptly changed the subject, resulting in a half hour of setting red candles around the room. But Candee's fragile composure began to slip. Other guests would be arriving soon, and she wasn't sure she could make conversation with anyone. She attempted to bolster herself by remembering she'd agreed to attend the event for only two hours. She eyed an ornate grandfather clock on the opposite wall. An hour and a half left.

Desiree jumped to her feet as two men entered the room. "Scott is here, and he brought ... Allen Allen?" she shrieked. Desiree turned so pale, Candee feared the many chocolate-covered strawberries Desiree had eaten had made her ill.

"You're joking, right?" Candee said to her sister. "You invited him?"

Desiree seemed rooted to the floor. "No, actually, I didn't."

Candee threw up her hands. "I'm leaving by seven o'clock," she reminded Desiree.

"Dinner is served at six, leaving you plenty of time." Desiree's gaze narrowed on Scott. Then she grabbed Candee's hand and started toward the two well-dressed men for introductions.

Dusk was streaking pomegranate colors in the darkening sky when Allen seated Candee to his right for dinner. A waiter set glasses of sparkling apple and pear cider at each place setting.

Teddy preferred coffee, she thought, reminding herself that she should be indifferent to his choice of beverage. She frowned. She didn't feel indifferent to anything about him. She missed the bantering they'd shared, the warm strength of his strong muscled body close to hers.

"The first course is a cheese and hazelnut green salad," Desiree declared to the others at the table, rousing Candee from her thoughts of Teddy. "For the entrée, the club is serving chicken in champagne sauce."

"I'm certain the meal will be delicious," Candee replied graciously. She took a long swallow of cider and lapsed into a reflective silence.

* * *

HOLDING HIS NEPHEW'S HAND, Teddy strode into the Roses country club exactly at six o'clock. The flight from Miami to Asheville had been bumpy, and getting his truck from the long-term rental parking lot had taken longer than he'd planned. The Valentine's Day festivities were well underway. A quick assessment of his worn jeans, polo shirt, and vest assured him he was underdressed for the formal occasion.

"Uncle Teddy, where is Miss Candee?" Joseph hopped on one foot. "Look—they have candy hearts in those little glasses by the window. Can I get some?"

Before Teddy could reply, the boy had scurried off. He gazed at him—a bundle of boundless energy and perfection, his dark eyes framed by thick black lashes. His adorable nephew, now his son to raise to the best of his ability.

I can do this, Christian, Teddy thought. Two weeks of endless paperwork had resulted in Teddy being awarded legal guardianship of Joseph.

It had been a difficult two weeks. After Candee had left Miami so abruptly, Teddy had tasted a painful defeat. No matter how much he plunged into his work, or cared for Joseph, or signed papers in the courtroom, he couldn't fully concentrate.

And then he'd made his decision.

His mind told him to stay in Miami. His heart told him otherwise.

"Are you expecting dinner guests?" he'd asked her that night when they'd danced.

Her beautiful green eyes had stared into his. "Not unless they're bringing chocolate," she'd quipped.

She possessed such enthusiasm, such spirit. And he'd hurt her by not being upfront about his relationship with Yvonne. Although in all fairness, he hadn't considered Yvonne a part of his life after he'd met Candee.

"Uncle Teddy! There she is!" Joseph shouted around a mouthful of pink candy hearts.

Teddy's gaze riveted on Candee. She sat at an elegantly decorated table with Desiree and two men. Teddy recognized Scott from the night he'd seen him at the country club. But the other man? He'd better not be that guy with two first names.

He grabbed Joseph's hand and stalked past a group of waiters serving champagne in fluted glasses to the guests.

He stopped Joseph from grabbing a white balloon, and he let a waiter show Joseph where the balloons were stored in an adjoining room.

When he looked at Candee again, she was out of her chair walking toward him.

"Teddy?"

She was exquisite, a glamorous, stunning goddess. Her glossy auburn hair hung to the side, a rosy tint creeping up her flawless cheeks. Her lacy pink dress displayed her alluring figure to full advantage. He was so relieved. Desiree had responded to his texts and told him that she'd finally persuaded Candee to attend this dinner.

He took her hands in his. "You are gorgeous."

She grinned shyly. "Thank you."

His gaze wandered across the crowded dining room, and he was annoyed at their lack of privacy, for all he wanted to do was kiss her inviting lips. Already, the hum of conversation was fading, and several diners were staring at them.

He slipped his arm around her shoulders and guided her into the hallway.

"Why are you here?" she asked.

"Because I missed you."

Her green eyes were soft and tender. "I missed you too."

"Can you leave?" He gestured impatiently around the corner, indicating the threesome at Candee's table.

"Yes, of course. I'll get my capelet."

"Hi, Miss Candee!" Joseph skipped over to them holding three white balloons. "Did you know Uncle Teddy and I flew all the way from Miami today?"

"Joseph, I'm thrilled you're here." Candee affectionately embraced the little boy.

"Uncle Teddy said today is Valentine's Day. I like balloons," Joseph said.

"We've noticed." Chuckling, Teddy put an arm around Candee's waist and held Joseph's hand in the other. He glanced toward the dining room, grinning when he noted Desiree's thumbs-up and conspiratorial smile.

"Where are we going?" Candee asked as they exited the club. Teddy buckled Joseph into the child car seat, then came around and opened the door for her.

"I want to show you the Valentine's gift I bought you." He started the car, and they covered the miles to Thompson Lane in under fifteen minutes.

"I'm still eating the chocolate from two weeks ago," Candee said. She tackled a white balloon that had floated into the front seat and turned to give it back to Joseph. When she turned to face front again, she paled, "Please, Teddy, don't drive down this road."

"How else can you see your Valentine's gift?"

He parked in front of the Victorian, then went around to

unbuckle Joseph. The boy raced to the tire swing, leaving three forgotten white balloons in the car.

Coming swiftly to the passenger side, Teddy opened Candee's door.

In the deepening dusk, she followed his gaze to the large red SOLD sign posted on the front door.

"Congratulations," she said softly.

"The Victorian isn't mine. It's yours."

She flashed him a dubious look, then gazed blindly ahead. "I don't understand."

"Some men buy roses for Valentine's Day, some buy candy. I prefer to buy houses." He paused, continuing in a solemn voice. "And this particular house is for you."

"Me?" She sucked in a breath and her eyes widened. She stared at the house with the same wistfulness he'd seen on her face the first day they'd met.

"Teddy—I … I can't possibly accept such a gift."

"Yes, you can, under one condition."

"And that is?"

"You allow me to help you renovate."

"How? You're in Miami."

He heard the pain in her voice, and his heart squeezed.

"Not anymore. I'm selling my apartment and moving to Roses, although my realty business will require that I fly to Miami a couple of times a month." He framed her lovely face between his hands and gazed into her shining green eyes. "I'm assuming you'll let Joseph and me adopt one of the beagle pups."

"You can adopt all six," she gladly agreed. Leaning back, she stared lovingly at him. "Will you please tell me the reason you bid against me?"

"I'd intended to bid all along, and your sister knew my plan. Somehow along the way, I managed to mess things up. I never meant to hurt you, and I'm sorry."

She glided her fingers through his hair. "You texted your apology a great many times and you're forgiven." She paused, glancing at the tumbledown Victorian and Joseph skipping up and down the porch steps. "Where will you and your nephew live?"

"I didn't want to stop at one house when I could buy two." Chuckling, Teddy gestured to Mr. Dunworthy's home. "He was more than happy to sell, and he'll be moving into a retirement community so he can be closer to his son."

"You're doing all this for me? Why?"

He hugged her close, breathing in her shiny hair, the scent of sweet and spicy roses.

"Because building a new life often begins with tearing down a few walls." He smiled at the stunning woman nestled in his arms. "Candee Contando, I love you."

"I love you too," she whispered.

And then he kissed her, sealing the most important deal of his life.

THE END

A NOTE FROM JOSIE

Dear Friends,

Thank you for reading *1-800-CUPID*, the first book in my contemporary sweet romance series: *Flipping for You.*

If you loved this sweet romance as much as I loved writing it, please help other people find *1-800-CUPID* by posting your review.

House flipping is a subject I've always been fascinated with. In my spare time I enjoy watching home-improvement television shows, and several were an inspiration for my story.

1-800-CUPID is available in ebook, Paperback, Large Print Paperback, Hardcover, and Audiobook.

My Spotify Play List for 1-800-CUPID is here.

Want more of the 1-800-Series, Flipping For You?

Click here.

RECIPE FOR ROB'S SURPRISE MUFFINS

Makes: 12 muffins

Ingredients:
  6 tablespoons butter
  3/4 cup sugar
  2 eggs
  1/2 cup milk
  14 strawberries, fresh or defrosted frozen
  red food coloring
  2 cups all-purpose flour
  1/4 teaspoon salt
  1 tablespoon baking powder
  Hershey's Kisses, Hugs or strawberry jam

Directions:

Preheat the oven to 350 degrees Fahrenheit.

In a large bowl, cream butter and sugar. Mix eggs one at a time and add milk. Rinse strawberries and mash. Stir berries into the butter and milk mixture, adding a few drops of red liquid food coloring.

In separate bowl, sift flour, salt and baking powder, and stir. Add flour mixture to the berry mixture and stir with a wooden spoon to stir until the white disappears.

Line muffin tins with paper liners. Drop the batter from a tablespoon to fill the cups halfway. If you are adding the "surprise", place an unwrapped Kiss, Hug or 1/2 teaspoon of jam in the middle of each muffin. Then spoon batter to fill almost to the top.

Bake until muffins begin to brown and a toothpick inserted near the center comes out clean, 20 to 25 minutes. Remove muffins. Cool. Serve warm in a basket lined with red doilies.

JOSIE RIVIERA

a Valentine to Cherish

A SWEET AND WHOLESOME NOVELLA

PRAISE AND AWARDS

USA TODAY bestselling author
#1 Bestseller Women's Religious Fiction
#1 Bestseller Contemporary Religious Fiction
#1 Bestseller Inspirational Religious Fiction

CHAPTER 1

*S*carlett Evans eyed Joanna, the skinny girl sitting beside her on the wooden park bench. The girl's legs were drawn up to her chest, her limp brown hair parted to the side and pulled into a ponytail. As always, her hair was tangled, as if she'd forgotten about the process of grooming in the middle of the activity.

Scarlett gathered her face into a sunny smile. "Good thing the rain stopped, Joanna."

"Are we going to Dr. Troutman's alpaca farm?" the girl asked.

"He put his farm up for sale last month, remember? There's someone else taking care of the property now, one of his former employees." Scarlett sighed, preferring to forget the slim sandy-haired man who had stolen her heart and then moved away. They'd been in love, or so she'd assumed. Sure, he'd been twice her age and she'd been warned about having a boyfriend twenty years her senior. But he was self-assured and successful, a noteworthy departure from the insecure twenty-something men she had previously dated.

In the end, though, Judson Troutman didn't want to get

married again after losing his first wife, nor did he want to be raising a child in his sixties. At least, that's what he'd divulged the day before his departure when he'd broken their engagement.

Children. A family. That resounding black hole between them.

And, he'd admitted, he'd grown tired of Scarlett's loud, boisterous manner.

Since then, she'd attempted to be quieter, more subdued. Messy and spontaneous? These were fixable traits. Disorganized and overweight? Well, she was working on it.

"I thought you liked alpacas," Joanna said.

"The farm wasn't mine, and it was his choice. I love animals, but truthfully, an entire pasture full of alpacas was more than I could handle by myself. My new job learning how to train service dogs at Canine Helpers is wonderfully rewarding, so at least I'm still working with animals." Scarlett heard the hollow emptiness eddying between her excuses. The alpaca farm would have been perfect and she'd counted on it.

Restlessly, she fiddled with her bright-red shoulder bag.

How foolish to believe that a well-educated veterinarian could fall for a woman like her. A woman who wasn't polished. A woman who was too brash and flamboyant for his refined taste.

Joanna worried the sleeves of her worn pink hoodie. No matter the weather, rain or shine, the hoodie was a staple in her limited wardrobe. "Is he coming back to Cherish?"

"No." Scarlett shook her head as the familiar desolation crept in. All these years she'd dreamed of a man who would truly love her, a man who wanted to share her life.

How had she missed the most important part? She couldn't have a real relationship, because she was afraid to trust and had put up a protective shield.

With good reason. People always left, oftentimes without saying goodbye. She couldn't count on anyone except herself. In the end, she had probably pushed Judson away with her brash manner—an attempt to hide her insecurities.

"Dr. Troutman moved back to his family home in Arizona," she said. "His father fell ill, so he's helping his elderly mother. His parents also own a vet business, and he felt obligated to take it over. That's why he sold his practice here in Cherish."

There it was. More reasons why she had not only lost her fiancé, but also her job as his receptionist when the practice closed.

Quiet enveloped Scarlett and Joanna for a beat, broken by the chirping of a cherry-red cardinal frequenting a bird feeder, designed for the birds as well as the bird watchers. Not far away, a forgotten Christmas ornament hung on a branch of a tall pine tree, the shiny silver bulb catching the sunlight.

Joanna reached for her dog-eared copy of *Fifteen* by Beverly Cleary. At ten years old, the girl was already an incurable romantic. "What about you? Dr. Troutman should've asked you to go with him."

Scarlett hung an arm around Joanna's thin shoulders. "He did. I refused."

He'd asked half-heartedly, but she didn't insert that part. Besides, she was too loyal to Joanna, her Little Sister, to leave her. For Joanna's sake, Scarlett needed to be dependable. The girl had experienced constant disappointment in her young life when her father had abandoned her and her family, and her childhood reminded Scarlett of her own unhappy past.

"Long ago," Scarlett said, "I made a decision to stay rooted in one spot for the rest of my life. I just didn't know where that spot was."

"So you decided on Cherish, South Carolina?" Joanna

gave a horrified burst of laughter. "This town is way too small for me. I want to have an apartment in a big city when I'm eighteen."

"I lived in Chicago my entire childhood and tried to establish roots there as an adult. All I found were flashing neon signs, traffic lights at every corner, and car horns forever honking." Scarlett scooted closer to Joanna. "I landed here after I applied for the job as a receptionist for Dr. Troutman. And now I intend to stay because I love southern towns."

Certainly, people described Cherish as an *if you blink when you pass through, you'll miss it kind of place*, but the picturesque charm appealed to her. As soon as she'd arrived, she'd known she had finally found a hometown.

She reached into the pocket of her bright-yellow raincoat and pulled out a slim chocolate candy bar. With a snap, she offered Joanna half, then glanced at her watch. "Hey, it's almost three o'clock. Wouldn't you rather hang out with your friends on the weekend than with me? It's not too late to text them."

"What friends?" The girl pushed out a dramatic sigh. "You know what I would give to have a real friend right now? Besides you, of course." With those wisely chosen last words, Joanna added an impish chuckle.

"Thanks," Scarlett joked sarcastically before her tone sobered. "Just remember I'm always here for you."

"I know." Pausing, Joanna took a breath. "Although it's just that … as usual, I'm the new girl in town."

"You came to Cherish in September, and it's January."

Before Scarlett could say more, Joanna frowned. Lately, she smiled often, so the frown was unexpected. "I'm uncomfortable when all the students in my class stare at me."

"Then stare back at them."

"I can't." The girl studied her hands. "I'm not friendly and loud like you."

Friendly was a good thing. Loud—not so good. Demure, polite, and ladylike were never traits Scarlett had mastered, but this was a new year. January, the season for fresh beginnings and resolutions.

Soothingly, she tucked a strand of Joanna's brown hair behind her ear. "Remember you're not the new girl anymore, although you're definitely the sweetest."

Scarlett had been matched with Joanna to be her mentor and Big Sister after she'd attended a recruitment asking for volunteers to give of their time. The Big Brothers Big Sisters program was community based, and it focused on low-income families.

Joanna's homelife consisted of her mother, Tania, a slight, ebony-haired woman who incessantly smoked; a scattering of younger siblings; and never enough money to get the family through the month.

"No, you're the sweetest," Joanna said, looking up at Scarlett. "And the prettiest. I wish I had red hair and green eyes and a gigantic smile."

Scarlett grinned, positioning herself so that she and Joanna could hold hands. Here in this park bordered by a hill, they could breathe in trees and fresh air and solitude. The past few months, the park bench had become their place to sit quietly together. Lately, the air smelled of spring—damp soil and grass and new birth.

God promised new beginnings in the normal trappings of daily life. He gave purpose to common situations. Surely, He would help Scarlett not only survive her heartbreak, but be strengthened by enjoying nature and this precious little girl.

Joanna eyed a clump of low-growing pansies, the deep-violet and eye-catching yellow adding vibrancy to the glistening green grass. "Not that I don't appreciate your candy, but I'd love for a boy to give me chocolate for Valentine's Day."

A boy? Stiffly, Scarlett drew back her head. Joanna was certainly growing up fast. She was only in fifth grade, although with today's social media and television programs, kids grew up faster than when Scarlett was young. Still, the idea was disconcerting. Shouldn't Joanna be more interested in roller skating or board games?

Still, she was tempted to say, *Me too*. She kept the contemplation to herself because a candy delivery wasn't coming her way anytime soon. She squeezed Joanna's hand. "But we have each other, right?"

"Right."

That morning had brought rain, a quick storm rattling trees and sweeping across tidy lawns in Scarlett's working-class neighborhood. Now the clouds had parted, and an afternoon sun emerged in a brilliant blue sky, a typical winter day in the Carolinas, where the weather changed from cold to warm within hours. Nearby, dogs barked and teenagers tossed Frisbees to each other.

Scarlett sat against the park bench while Joanna munched her chocolate bar.

"Aren't you going to eat your candy?" Joanna asked between mouthfuls.

"No. You can have mine too." Scarlett handed Joanna her half. She loved candy and crunchy peanut butter ice cream and all kinds of junk food, and deliberated for a half second before giving the candy bar up.

No, no, no. She pushed out a breath. She couldn't count the number of times she'd attempted to diet unsuccessfully. The lead balloon feeling of failure never left, nor its silent counterpart, shame.

Solid looking, people described her. Or, *She has such a pretty face*. Or her favorite, *She's big-boned*. All subtle reminders she should shed thirty pounds.

This time she would lose the weight, she vowed.

She'd heard the cabbage diet worked well, although she'd never liked cabbage.

Tomorrow. She'd begin a new diet tomorrow.

"C'mon, let's head back into town." Scarlett came to her feet and took Joanna's sticky hand in hers. "We can stop for a slice of pizza at Frank's Pizzeria."

At the end of the street, guitar music wafted toward them. People in the park reacted, drifting toward the music, bobbing their heads to the beat of a Christian contemporary song.

"'And we sing, you are our God …'" The tenor male voice resonated through the air.

"Look, Scarlett." Joanna slowed and pointed to a poster mounted to a streetlamp. The poster advertised a Valentine-themed benefit concert sponsored by Musically Yours, the local music store and conservatory. The event would be held outdoors in the park, rain or shine.

The concert was being held to raise money for Cherish Elementary School's music program. Accompanying the poster was a picture of a good-looking man with dark wavy hair, stubble on his chin, and piercing blue eyes.

Joseph Slater, a Christian recording artist, was headlining the event.

"Isn't he handsome?" Joanna had eaten the entire candy bar, evidenced by smears of chocolate on her chin.

"Yes, but he's a musician," Scarlett said.

"Is that good?"

"It means he's busy recording and performing, so handsome doesn't count because he's unavailable." Scarlett read the poster listing his recent tours and managed a *wow*. Was he ever successful.

"A few months ago, I listened to one of his hits on the Christian station," Scarlett continued. "The DJ went on for five minutes about Joseph Slater because he writes all his own music, as well as songs for various Christian artists. And he was nominated for a Grammy award."

"I knew he was famous." Joanna tented her hands over her eyes and read aloud, "'An international recording phenomenon who recently returned from Australia and is touring the U.S.'" She had a breathless, excited look about her. "We should totally go to the show and meet him. Then you can fall in love again."

At the idea of it—love, dreaming new dreams—a shiver of longing quickened Scarlett's pulse. She believed in the possibility of happily ever after. Just not for her, and certainly not with a touring musician who was here today and gone tomorrow.

"They're selling tickets to the concert at Musically Yours." Joanna tugged on Scarlett's hand. "Don't you know the people who own that music store?"

"Ryan and Dorothy Edwards are dear friends."

"Then you wouldn't want to disappoint your friends, right?"

The joy on Joanna's pale, freckled face had Scarlett fishing for her wallet and hoping she had enough money to cover the ticket prices.

"No disappointments allowed," she declared, counting out a wad of one-dollar bills.

"C'mon." Joanna was off like a rocket, her thin legs moving rapidly toward the music store.

Scarlett couldn't help her smile and quickened her pace. She wanted to attend the concert anyway because she appreciated all kinds of music.

As they rounded the corner, Joanna skidded to a stop.

"That's him! I recognize his picture! Joseph Slater. Playing the guitar."

He sat on a stool in front of Musically Yours, his sharp profile outlined against a sunlit sky. In person, he was even more handsome than his photo. His wavy hair curled at the nape, framing a strong face, straight nose and chiseled jawline. Thoughtfully, he strummed his guitar and sang an inspirational melody to a small enchanted audience. They stood around him and listened intently.

He looked up after he sang his final number, the lyrics about love and peace particularly moving, the deep, rich timbre of his voice striking an unexpected chord in Scarlett's chest.

His clear blue eyes met her gaze.

She sucked in a breath, attempted to wave or applaud, but shelved the idea. Instead, she murmured, "I love that song," to no one in particular. For once, she'd really stopped and listened. The melody was beautiful, and the heartfelt lyrics about trusting God hit her emotionally.

Tears rose in her eyes and she brushed a hand across her lashes.

Silly. She was being silly. Usually, she didn't listen to Christian music, preferring top 40 hits. Besides, she didn't feel comfortable around men who were too good-looking, and this guy lifted drop-dead gorgeous to a whole new level. Attractive guys made her self-conscious about her weight. Besides, in her slick yellow raincoat, she probably resembled a chubby lemon.

She had no idea how many albums Joseph Slater had recorded, but made a mental note to Google him as soon as she returned to her apartment. He'd just topped the number-one spot on her hit list, edging out her favorite rock singer.

"He's staring at you," Joanna whispered.

No. Scarlett was staring at *him* like a gape-mouthed schoolgirl.

He set down his guitar, thanked the audience, and placed the guitar into its case. Smiling an acknowledgement to the cluster of fans, he shrugged on his worn leather jacket, picked up the case, and strode toward her.

Oh my. Now? She was coming face-to-face with him? Now? She must look the size of a house with her wrinkled cotton pants and red boots. And her sweater. She indulged in good cashmere sweaters, although this fitted charcoal-gray one sported a hot fudge sundae graphic on the front. Not exactly a motivation, but the idea of wearing a piece of celery made her inwardly chuckle.

A crisp breeze snapped through the air, and a loose strand of her curly hair fluttered across her forehead. The dampness of the earlier rain had caused her hair to frizz, and she probably looked like she'd been electrified.

As he approached, she felt a jolt of expectation. She and Joanna exchanged glances, and Joanna gave a thumbs up. That is, until he angled past them with a polite smile and entered the music store.

CHAPTER 2

A few minutes later, Scarlett and Joanna greeted Dorothy Edwards inside Musically Yours.

"You're just in time." Dorothy crossed to them and gave Scarlett a teasing, wicked grin. "Joseph Slater is one of Ryan's former classmates. Isn't he all that? And he's a bachelor."

Scarlett paused, at a loss for words. Joseph Slater was well-known for his Christian music, as was Ryan Edwards for his operatic voice.

"I didn't realize Ryan knew him," Scarlett said.

Ryan Edwards, Dorothy's husband, had settled in Cherish when he married Dorothy. They were high school sweethearts, although ten years had passed before they'd met again.

"This way to meet Joseph." Dorothy tugged on the sleeve of Scarlett's raincoat.

Dorothy always looked so polished, her dark hair pinned into a classic chignon, her perfect figure accentuated by a black pencil skirt and burgundy silk blouse.

"There's no need." Scarlett stayed where she was, at the

entry of the music store. She hadn't started her diet yet. Maybe in a year or so.

"Of course there is, because we're all good friends," Dorothy said.

Scarlett twisted her fingers together and eyed the exit. "Joanna and I are here to buy tickets for the Valentine show, but we can come back tomorrow."

"And miss meeting him? You're here now." Ignoring Scarlett's hesitation, Dorothy gaily recited Joseph's numerous awards.

"So your husband went to college with Mr. Slater?" Scarlett asked.

"Mr. Slater?" Dorothy giggled. "That sounds so formal for a casual guy like him. They both received music scholarships to Juilliard. Joseph was only there for a year, though. Then he went on to study worship music in Australia." Dorothy promptly brought Scarlett to the end of a long line. She chuckled at Scarlett's protesting head shake and strolled away with Joanna, showing the girl a stack of musical bracelets—pianos, flutes, and a harp—and encouraging her to pick a favorite.

"I don't play any instrument," Scarlett overheard Joanna saying. "It's hard to choose."

"I think harp lessons will suit you perfectly, so pick a harp bracelet," came Dorothy's reply. "And I know the ideal teacher. Her name is Emmanuelle and she teaches on Monday evenings. I'll tell Scarlett to bring you back to the store then."

Emmanuelle was Dorothy's sister-in-law who married Dorothy's brother, Nicholas.

Harp lessons? Scarlett mouthed as Dorothy caught Scarlett's gaze. Dorothy nodded. Obviously, the lessons would be free of charge, and a generous opportunity for Joanna to explore the arts.

Scarlett shifted in line. Mr. Slater sat in a corner behind a desk, autographing CDs.

His leather jacket was slung over a chair. He looked exactly how she imagined a recording artist—the black leather jacket, faded jeans, a white T-shirt that hugged his wide shoulders. The shirt read *Just Have Faith*, and was embellished with a tiny cross.

Have faith? She'd tried that, attempting to lean on her father, praying he'd reciprocate her love for him. She believed in God and attended church. It was just that God had been absent from her life lately.

"Credit your father for doing the best that he can," her mother had encouraged. "Beneath his bad temper, he's a good man."

So Scarlett had tried, while seeking his attention. When she'd been in elementary school her father had propped her up, complimenting her fiery red hair and lively manner. Later in life, when she was an overweight teen, he'd paralyzed her with his indifference.

She blamed her low self-esteem on her upbringing. Beneath her bravado she was almost shy, especially when the man she stood in line to meet was male-model perfect.

Self-consciously, she took a slight step backward when it was her turn.

"Hello, Mr. Slater," she said softly.

There went that handsome-man effect again.

"Hello. Did you purchase one of my CDs that you want me to sign?" Glancing up, he smiled at her guarded retreat, although he didn't remark on it.

"I don't own any. Are they for sale?" Brilliant. Of course they were, which was the main reason he was here. An artist, even an inspirational artist, was probably contracted by his agent to promote, promote, promote.

He nodded toward a stack of CDs placed on a shelf

nearby. "Indeed they are. This CD is a few years old, but the single was nominated for a Grammy."

"Indeed," she echoed blankly. Coupled with her low self-confidence, she was actually starstruck. She began to chuckle at the absurdity of her nervousness. She was a grown woman, not a starry-eyed adolescent.

Surprisingly, his laugh joined hers. "So ... did you want to purchase one?" His gaze drifted over her, his astute blue eyes warmly affirming.

"A CD?"

"Yup."

"No. Well, rather, yes." Her hands stilled as she reached inside her shoulder bag. "Unfortunately, I don't have the money. You see, I'm buying two tickets to the Valentine concert, and I only stuck one-dollar bills in my wallet. We had planned on going out for pizza tonight, and then—"

"We? Is that an invitation?"

"No. I mean ... Joanna and I." Scarlett could feel the flush of heat on her cheeks. "The little girl—" She was babbling and closed her mouth.

He regarded her for a beat, then reached for a CD on the shelf. He had to duck when he stood. He was tall—probably six feet—and the music store's ceiling sloped at the corners.

"Here." He handed the CD to her. "My treat."

"Your treat for what?"

"For standing in line to meet me. For your preferences. Pizza should always come first, although music and pizza together are perfection. And thanks for the un-invitation."

She laughed.

He grinned, settled in the chair, and uncapped his Sharpie. "What would you like me to write on your CD?"

"Whatever you want," she said. "Best of luck ... warm wishes ..."

His face lightened with humor. "Do you want me to personalize the message?"

"Sure."

"Should I sign this to you?"

She noted the line lengthening behind her. "Sure. My name is Scarlett. Scarlett Evans."

She peered down while he autographed and recognized her name, although his handwriting was so poor she could hardly decipher it. "That's two *t*'s in Scarlett," she instructed.

"Here you go, two *t*'s Scarlett." He wrote his name and then slid the CD across the table. "My pleasure."

Across the space, their gazes held.

"Thank you." She tucked the CD inside her shoulder bag. "Well, I'm off to buy those tickets."

"I thought you were buying pizza?"

"Oh, right." She was surprised he'd remembered her offhand remark. She shrugged. "Guess not."

"I'll take care of your tickets and leave them with Dorothy. I'm staying at the Cherish Hills Inn for the next few weeks until the concert, so I'll be out and about." He gestured toward the cash register where Joanna sat with Dorothy, swinging her legs on a stool. "Do you need two?"

"Yes, one for me, and one for my—"

"Daughter?"

She cast aside a couple responses. "I don't have any children. I'm Joanna's Big Sister."

The little girl waved gaily at Scarlett and shook her wrist to show off her new harp bracelet.

"Although, wait, please don't buy tickets for us," Scarlett said. "I know the owners and I'll come back to purchase them."

"I know the owners too, and I insist. There's only one catch."

Her head cocked to the side. Was he one of those musicians who assumed no woman could resist him? Would he possibly want to ask her out?

No. She was fairly certain a man of his status wouldn't be interested in a heavy-set small-town woman like her. Unless he was looking for … a fling?

Umm, she wasn't good at flings. And she certainly wasn't about to get hurt again.

"What's the catch?" She tried to keep the wariness from her voice.

He was quiet for several beats. She felt awkward, fingering her shoulder bag.

"Do you sing?" he finally asked. His voice was quiet, deep, velvety.

Taken aback, she chuckled. "Why? Do you need backup singers for your next CD?"

He shook his head. "I'm a soloist."

"Well, then, yes, I sing. That is, if singing in the shower counts?"

"Absolutely." He pressed his hands together. His hands looked strong, his fingertips callused, most likely from endless hours strumming his guitar.

"Should I add the verbs *barely tolerable* to my singing in the shower?" she asked.

"Barely is an adverb."

"Thanks for the English lesson, Mr. Musician." She burst into a wide smile. "What about a tolerable singer?"

"Tolerable is an adjective."

She kept her smile. For a guy who didn't write legibly, he certainly knew his grammar.

Behind her, a man cleared his throat impatiently, which startled her and seemed to visibly annoy Mr. Slater.

"So we've established I'm not a singer," she said.

He rested his hands on the desk and studied her. "You're a good person, being a Big Sister. That's what counts."

She was so disconcerted at the quiet caress in his tone, she blurted, "Although I don't sing well, I love to listen to music."

"Then I'll award you bonus points."

More customers filed into the store. He didn't seem to notice, keeping his gaze fixed on her. It seemed as if he didn't want their conversation to end. Neither did she.

She knew the flush on her cheeks had heightened to a bright pink.

"As long as you love music and promise to attend the concert," he continued, "then the tickets are yours."

No, she thought. He'd done enough, given her a free CD.

"I can't," she said.

"Please, it would mean a lot to me. I pray that my songs will continue to spread God's good word, so I need an audience."

"You're a modern-day writer of hymns, you know that?" She flashed him a smile.

"I used to be." It showed in his eyes, the quick glimpse of frustration before it vanished. He scanned the crowded store, the line behind her. "Not so much anymore."

She didn't know how to answer, eventually murmuring, "I've heard some of the songs you've written and they're amazing."

"Thanks." He signaled to the throat-clearing man to move forward. "I guess some people have been more than patient."

"Guess they are. Sorry," she mumbled to the impatient man as she curved around him.

"Don't forget to come back for your tickets," Joseph Slater said. "I'll leave them at the counter."

She glimpsed Dorothy's attentive expression as she avidly

watched the exchange. Dorothy's interest would soon become an inquisition, then slide into a matchmaking frenzy. She'd been bent on finding Scarlett a man ever since Judson Troutman had left town.

Scarlett couldn't help an inward grin before turning to smile brilliantly at Mr. Slater.

By now, she knew Cherish was different from Chicago, and a person couldn't go far without seeing someone you knew. He'd be in town for several weeks, and she was almost certain to run into him. The thought filled her with unexpected delight.

"Thanks. I won't forget," she said. "Joanna and I will look forward to the concert, Mr. Slater."

"Joseph." He extended his hand, their fingers touching as they shook. A warmth surged through her. She didn't want to let go. His strength was sure and solid.

She sent him an audacious smile and let go of his hand. She began walking away, then called over her shoulder. "Thanks again for your generosity, Joseph."

"That's Joseph with a J," he said.

Beaming, Scarlett expressed her gratitude to Dorothy, and told her friend she'd visit the following day to pick up her tickets. She took Joanna's hand, and the two left the music store and headed for the pizzeria, with Joanna chatting happily about her upcoming harp lesson.

* * *

AN HOUR AFTERWARD, Joseph shrugged on his leather jacket and collected his music as he prepared to leave Musically Yours. The trickle of last-minute customers had cleared out after Dorothy's announcement that the store closed at six o'clock.

"Owning this place is both my business and my passion,"

Dorothy said. She stood behind the counter and clicked her tablet screen while she balanced the money in the cash register. Every inch of space in the store looked inviting, a music lover's haven. Glancing over her shoulder, she added, "But I wouldn't have it any other way."

Joseph looked up. "What did you say?"

"Sorry to interrupt your dreamy-eyed musings." Dorothy's teasing voice roused him from his reflections. "Are you smitten by someone?"

"I'm sure I don't know what you mean." Vaguely, he was aware that Dorothy was watching him. He'd been thinking about Scarlett.

My singing is barely tolerable.

He'd accepted her pleasant jibe at herself with a chuckle. She was quick-witted and good-natured and he'd felt an unexpected pull. He knew it was crazy because of his foot-loose lifestyle. He was never in one city long enough for more than a casual dinner date. He'd nearly forgotten the names of all of them.

The cities. And the women.

Nevertheless, there'd been a spin of warmth, a raw attraction between them. She was enchanting, with lovely sea-green eyes and creamy fair skin. Unconsciously, she'd swayed back and forth while they'd spoken. She didn't seem the type to sit still for long.

Although other fans had been milling impatiently behind her, he'd wanted their conversation to continue, to get to know her a little better. It was unlike him. After finishing the gig in Cherish, he'd head to Raleigh and then New York City. Scarlett obviously lived in Cherish and their paths wouldn't cross again.

He gathered his Sharpies, song list, and business cards and packed them into his duffel bag. His outdoor concert had gone well. Judging by the enthusiastic crowd, promotion for the Valentine event was a success.

He'd arrived in Cherish that morning lethargic and slightly disoriented, jet lagged because of the long flight from Australia. His noise-canceling headphones, combined with the low whirring of the airplane engine, had lulled him into a deep sleep for much of the flight.

In the midst of a dream he couldn't remember, he'd woken at the airport feeling groggy, and the feeling continued on the train ride from Atlanta to Cherish. After he'd called a taxi at the train station, he'd ridden through the center of town. He'd let down the window and smelled pine trees and greenery and a whiff of spring. A magical morning light enveloped the neighborhood park.

For a moment, he'd been enchanted—until reality and his hectic concert schedule crowded his enchantment.

He shook his head. Admittedly, it would take more hours than he'd anticipated for his body clock to adjust to East Coast time. For the past few years, being on the road brought a weariness he couldn't explain. There was no silence, no peace in his life anymore. He hadn't felt at home anywhere in the world, not even his beloved Australia.

"On the contrary, Joseph, I'm sure you know exactly what I mean." Dorothy went to the door and posted a *We're Closed* sign. "And it's a wonderful idea."

He forced himself to listen to what she was saying. "What is?"

"Dating Scarlett while you're in Cherish." Dorothy walked over to him, pausing to organize some misplaced items on a shelf. "I saw how you looked at her, how you watched her leave the store. You didn't hear the next fan in line speak to you for a solid minute."

"You're right, but there's another word for smitten. It's called jet lag."

Dorothy grinned and handed him a box of CDs. "These are yours."

"Keep them in the store for giveaways. Or better yet, donate them."

"Happily." Chuckling, she arranged them on a display rack. He regarded his photo on the front of the CD, a black and white sketch of him improvising in a recording studio. He'd sat on a stool wearing headphones, playing his guitar, and singing into a microphone.

He hadn't worked in a recording studio for several years, because he had nothing new to record. Sheets of blank manuscript paper crowded his suitcase, waiting like expectant fans.

The last rays of daylight filtered through the shop's front window. How long had he been awake? Australia was sixteen hours ahead of South Carolina time. Did dozing on the plane count?

"In case you're wondering," Dorothy said, "Scarlett and Joanna went to Frank's Pizzeria for dinner. It's a short walk from here."

"She mentioned they were going for pizza." Briefly, Joseph toyed with the idea of joining them. Perhaps after they shared a pizza and chatted for a while, he could walk Scarlett and the little girl home.

"I'm not used to all this walking," he said. "In a big city, I'm either driving on a freeway or in a taxi."

"Living in a small town with sidewalks is better than any fitness center membership."

He chuckled. "Point taken." He made certain to find a gym everyplace he'd visited, knowing exercise kept him fit mentally and physically.

Dorothy went to the counter and shut her tablet. "Cherish is a town of warmth and light."

"You're a poet now?" he teased. "Or am I dreaming about Oscar Wilde because I'm so jet lagged?"

"You're the one who writes beautiful worship music."

"Once upon a time," he said quietly.

"I'd be happy to help you write the lyrics to your next song. That is, if you need any help."

He managed a smile. "I'll keep that in mind."

She went over to a drawer of sheet music and began to file the pieces alphabetically. "Cherish boasts a number of churches too. Ryan and I attend Memorial Street Church," she said. "Pastor Steven and his wife Christina welcome everyone. And Mrs. Marge Addyson, the associate pastor, was speaking just the other day about adding a contemporary worship service to Saturday evening."

He'd wondered where this was leading. Now he knew.

"And this contemporary worship service would be led by … your husband, Ryan?" he asked.

"Unfortunately, he's too busy. He's turned down at least a half-dozen opera roles, and refuses to travel farther than a few hours away from Cherish. Consequently, you're a good first choice." She passed her hand over the music almost lovingly before closing the drawer. "And don't forget, Cherish boasts an equally fine music store and conservatory run by yours truly. Ta-da!"

He grinned and applauded. He couldn't help surveying the tidy store in awe. Every square foot of space had been carefully planned and painstakingly categorized by instrument—piano, harp, guitar, as well as a host of others.

He gazed at a sign prominently hung at the entrance: *Proverbs 19:21: Many are the plans in the mind of a man, but it is the purpose of the Lord that will stand.*

Ryan and Dorothy had built their business on faith, and their diligence and hard work equaled success. Plus, they'd opened a professional music school.

"You and your husband have created a welcoming environment for music lovers of all ages," he said.

"Thanks." Dorothy took an exaggerated bow. "Therefore, you'll get the best of both worlds here. Music and a close-knit, faith-filled town. People in this community are proud to serve the Lord."

"Are you trying to get me to move here?" he half joked.

She grinned. "Maybe."

A track from one of his CDs supplied background music. "My God Is an Awesome God." He'd been inspired to write the song when flying over the ocean, high in a sea of white clouds. For him, every piece of music started with the melody.

"You know my lifestyle," he said. "I don't stay in one place long. Traveling to different locations, hearing my music played at a variety of churches, keeps my muse creative."

He frowned. Did it? Certainly not lately. He hadn't written a new piece in over two years.

He shifted, focused on the stack of unsold CDs.

"Maybe traveling is a season of your life that's over, Joseph," Dorothy said. "Maybe it's time to settle down. Haven't you been on the road at least five years?"

"Ten."

"Is that what you want?"

"It's all I know. Performing music. And writing ..." He focused on the floor, then her. "*Attempting* to write."

She paused, examining his expression. He attempted an easygoing smile, hoping she didn't catch the frustration beneath.

"Care to talk about it?" she asked.

"No."

"What if God is withholding what you want to direct you to what you need?"

He didn't answer, scarcely noticing the concern in her

voice. She was echoing a question that continuously nagged at him.

Resting for a week or two in one place between gigs wasn't enough anymore. For a while now, he'd been disheartened when he picked up his pencil to write music that wouldn't come. The door of his first love seemed to have been locked to him. Now it was the door of disappointment.

He believed in being honest. And he was, with everyone but himself. He just couldn't believe God wouldn't let him through that door anymore.

Is that asking too much, God—unlocking my creative muse so that I can compose worship songs again?

An image of Scarlett sparked through his mind. Why did his attention keep drifting to her?

"Do you want me to give you directions to the pizzeria?" Dorothy asked. Before he answered, she grabbed paper and a pen, and jotted down the address. "Scarlett and Joanna should still be there. Besides, you haven't eaten, correct?"

He stuffed the paper into his jacket pocket. "I'll grab something at the inn."

"I know Tom, the innkeeper, and he doesn't do dinner for his patrons. It's a bed and breakfast." Dorothy shut off the music and the lights, a clear sign she was ready to leave. "I'd invite you to our house, but I'm eating leftovers. Ryan is performing in Atlanta tonight, and I don't expect him home until much later. He's taken quite an interest in cooking and I'm encouraging him—mostly because my claim to fame is only pecan pies."

"You can't eat pie every day."

"A sad fact." She grinned. "Although Ryan could and would never gain a pound."

A loving expression came over her face. She and Ryan were so much in love. Joseph had been traveling when they'd married, but he'd spoken to Ryan a number of times and knew the guy was enamored by all things Dorothy.

When Joseph didn't reply, Dorothy asked, "So, you'll be off to Frank's for pizza?"

He hesitated. He shouldn't go. He should rest and listen to what his body was demanding. Get some sleep.

But he was hungry, he rationalized.

And when had weariness ever stopped him before?

CHAPTER 3

$\mathcal{I}$n his beautifully appointed room at the inn, Joseph unpacked and showered.

Although dog-tired, he'd then walked to Frank's Pizzeria. There, he'd been informed by the waitress that Scarlett and her young friend, Joanna, had ordered takeout pizza and left shortly before he'd arrived.

That's what he got for waiting so long.

He ordered a slice of pizza and a soft drink, brought both back to the inn, and then got a decent night's sleep in a luxurious king-sized bed. The linens were top-quality, and the wood plank floor and fireplace exuded homeyness and comfort.

The following morning, Tom, the white-haired innkeeper, prepared a mouth-watering breakfast, setting up tables by a stacked-rock fireplace. After a prayer of thanks, Joseph ate heartily—fresh fruit, homemade corn muffins, a cheese omelet with thick slices of bacon, and hot coffee with heaping teaspoons of sugar.

So now it was noon. Well-rested, overfed, and alert, Joseph zipped up his leather jacket and ventured outdoors.

The weather was brisk and bright, with not so much of a whisper of snow. Ryan had mentioned that Cherish's weather was mild, which proved true on this January day.

After a short walk, Joseph came to Memorial Street Church.

He paused, admiring the picturesque white church, its splendid steeple topped by a cross. He bounded up the church stairs and strode through the open double doors. Kneeling, he clasped his hands and bowed his head.

When would a breakthrough occur so he'd be able to write music again? he asked a silent God. Where was the Lord's blessing on Joseph's life?

True, Joseph had enjoyed the accolades when his songs were well received, the social media explosion of compliments. But he didn't write worship songs for awards and compliments. Did he?

Sometimes he felt like he was fighting a war with the outside world. If he wrote beautiful songs, then people would respect his writing abilities and subsequently, him. And they'd like him. Because it was important to be liked? Wasn't it?

But it was more important to be honorable, to do the right thing for the right reasons. And there was the battle— not with the world and social media. He was fighting a battle within himself.

He shifted on the kneeler. This was his prayer? *This*? Whining and demanding?

He shook his head, closed his eyes, tightened his clasped hands.

None of his failures were God's fault. God wasn't to blame. Any lack of creativity was Joseph's fault. If he got right with God, with himself, then things would fall into place.

As a Christian, he knew this. And if he was more honest,

he'd recognize that his immeasurable pride was in the way of his own blessing. The Lord knew Joseph was far from perfect, yet loved him anyway. Couldn't Joseph do the same, love and respect himself whether or not he was a successful songwriter?

"Through your grace, I will be healed," he prayed.

When he finished and stood, he couldn't determine if his problem had been solved. But he certainly felt more peaceful within himself.

He left the church, retracing his steps, then stopped at a sign mounted on a street corner.

Cherish—one of the most charming towns in the Carolinas.

They'd been spot-on with that description. His breath caught as he crossed to the sun-drenched park and strode around the village green. The town was more peaceful than any he'd seen. Surrounded by budding trees and homespun warmth, Cherish was a special, tranquil place.

He crossed Evergreen Street and discovered a gurgling stream behind an old railway line. Sunbeams glinted off the water's surface, and a scent of moss permeated the air.

"You should see the bluebonnets growing here in the spring," came a familiar voice.

Joseph turned as Ryan Edwards slapped him on the back.

"How are you, my friend?" Ryan asked as the men shook hands. They were the same height. In college, they'd borrowed each other's clothes, which often lay in a dirty heap on their dorm room's floor. None of that mattered then. They were young and carefree.

"Very well," Joseph replied. "You?"

"Couldn't be better." Ryan looked fit and happy, his dark gaze gleaming with contentment. He nodded toward the stream. "When we were teens, Dorothy and I held slingshot contests to see who could snap the most petals off the flowers."

"Who won?"

"Who do you think?' Ryan pulled a hand through his dark-brown hair. "She did."

Joseph chuckled. "Marrying the love of your life obviously agrees with you."

"That's because I married the most beautiful woman in the world."

Tiny specks of snow swirled around them. Here and there, tree branches swayed in a cool breeze. Ryan stuck his hands into his wool jacket and circled toward town. Joseph followed.

"Where are you headed?" Ryan asked.

"Nowhere in particular. Merely exploring the town," Joseph said. "And from what I've experienced in other areas, this weather is almost balmy for winter."

"It's typical South Carolina," Ryan said.

The men fell in step together.

"How was your concert last night?" Joseph asked.

"I sang the role of Gurnemanz in Wagner's *Parsifal* to a sold-out crowd. Are you familiar with the opera?"

"I am. Impressive."

"Thanks. I'm still able to perform in big cities like Atlanta, come home to my lovely wife at the end of the day, and join her at church services on Sunday."

"Therefore, you'll get the best of both your worlds here," Dorothy had said, voicing her not-so-subtle opinion. *"Music, and a close-knit, faith-filled town."*

"Is your life as easy as all that?" Joseph asked.

"No one said it was easy," Ryan said. "But I'm discovering a joy I once believed was elusive."

"Traveling is hard, though?"

"Yes. Although it's worth it when you're doing something you love." Ryan blew out a breath. "Admittedly, Atlanta is a long drive and I didn't arrive home until well after midnight.

Fortunately, Dorothy insisted on hiring an Uber for me, so I slept in the car all the way back."

When they reached the middle of town, Ryan gestured to a restaurant across the street from them. "Hey, if you haven't eaten lunch yet, I highly recommend The Garden Terrace."

Joseph patted his stomach. "I'm still full from breakfast, although I'd love a glass of something cold."

"We're in the south, so order sweet iced tea and a slice of sugar-free lemon cake. You'll never taste anything better." Ryan glanced at his watch. "I'd join you, but I promised Dorothy I'd take over at the music store this afternoon so she can have a break. We'll catch up later, okay?"

Joseph could think of nothing more inviting than finding a discreet corner in the restaurant where he could unwind. "Sounds good. Although my sweet tooth will demand regular lemon cake, not sugar free."

"The restaurant serves both. Enjoy." With a quick *later,* Ryan spun toward the music store.

The wooden door to the restaurant creaked as Joseph opened it. He slid into a booth at the rear and glanced around. Dimly lit, the place had a sense of timelessness, boasting thick wooden beams on the ceiling and deer antlers mounted on the walls. An appetizing array of grilled meats and homemade barbecue wafted in the mesquite-filled air.

Intending to peruse a menu for a light appetizer to go along with the lemon cake and iced tea, he noticed Scarlett sitting at a booth near the front. She dined with an older man who faced her. Although her back was to Joseph, he'd recognize her anywhere. Her red hair fell in curls over her shoulders. Deep in conversation, she bobbed back and forth. Her shoulder bag was set beside her.

Joseph studied the man, who resembled Scarlett in so many ways, he assumed he was her father. The man had the same strong facial features and wisps of red hair as Scarlett, although he was as thin as a popsicle stick, and his eyes, even from a distance, were watery and bloodshot.

Joseph ordered a sweet iced tea, then thanked the young waitress with spiked black hair as she set the glass in front of him. He grabbed three sugar packets to doctor up his tea to a sugar max.

"It's already sweet," the waitress reminded him.

"Not sweet enough."

She shrugged. "Anything else? We're known for our sugar-free lemon cake."

"So I've heard. I was going to order an appetizer too, but tea is good for now." He shut the menu and handed it to her. He'd changed his mind, preferring to watch Scarlett and her father. "Maybe next time."

"Thanks." She smiled and left the bill on the table.

He took in every detail of the bustling restaurant and soaked in the ambiance—the older couple to his left, sitting side by side, silently concentrating on their meals. The collapse of giggles from two teenage girls.

Joseph took out a notebook and pen he always carried in his pocket and swung his gaze toward Scarlett's table. As a songwriter, he liked to watch people and considered himself intuitive for analyzing what went on with them.

He waited for lyrics to come. Closed his eyes. Waited some more. Nothing flowed. Pinching his lips together, he stuffed the notebook back into his pocket.

As he glanced up, he noticed that the conversation at Scarlett's table had quieted.

She pushed her plate full of salad to the side. Shaking her head, she toyed with a straw in her tall glass of lemonade.

The older man's face reddened. Unexpectedly, he slapped his hand on the table.

Scarlett jumped and the patrons around them paused to stare, then averted their gazes.

Immediately, Joseph sensed the constraint between father and daughter. Although Scarlett froze in place, she attempted conversation again. In response, the man's gaze wandered, and he answered in monosyllables.

On his feet five minutes later, the older man briefly clenched his fingers, followed by words that Joseph couldn't make out.

Another beat, and Scarlett and her father left the restaurant. Outside, the man kept his hands in his pockets while she gave him a quick, awkward hug. As the two departed, they walked in opposite directions. He climbed into a big rig parked to the side.

On impulse, Joseph bolted up, threw money on the table for his iced tea plus a tip, and rushed through the exit.

"Scarlett!" he hailed as he sprinted toward her.

She paused, then whirled. "Mr. Slater?"

"Joseph with a J, remember?"

"Of course." Her voice was strained. She lifted her chin, a sheen of tears in her glorious green eyes. She wore a pink paisley scarf that complemented her peaches-and-cream complexion. Her wool coat was forest-green with a high shawl collar. A navy sweater peeked from beneath, offering a glimpse of a sequin-embossed butterfly. He liked her colorful style and openly admired her shapely figure.

"Umm." She pulled at the front of her coat. "Why are you staring at me?"

Whoops. He swung his gaze to the sidewalk, although it drifted appreciatively back to her face. "I noticed you and that man in the restaurant."

Who was he? Joseph wanted to ask, but stopped himself. He waited to see if she would explain.

She didn't.

"Was he your father?" he couldn't help asking.

"Yes."

"And?"

Ignoring the question entirely, she hooked her shoulder bag on her arm and looked around the street.

Alrighty then.

"A coincidence we were both leaving at the same time," he said into the silence. "I was wondering if you could recommend ..." He thought fast, pulling a hand through his hair. "Recommend a good place for a haircut. I wasn't able to schedule a trim before I left Australia."

"Cherish Styles and Clips is a short walk from here. They offer a full-service hair salon for both men and women, and I know the owner, Phyllis. I helped her move into her new place a few months ago." Scarlett pointed to an intersection diagonally from them. "Take a left on that corner, then a right. A couple more blocks and you're there."

"Can you walk with me? I've been known to get lost on a one-way dead-end street."

Not at all true, but he couldn't make himself be concerned with details. He wanted to spend time with her. His conscience tapped him on the shoulder. He'd just seen her the day before, remember?

He stiffened. And? Couldn't he see a woman twice in two days? Nevertheless, his excuse to spend time with her was anything but brilliant. A haircut. Really? So much for being a well-known lyricist. No wonder he couldn't write a noteworthy song anymore.

"Sure," she agreed. "I'll walk with you."

He could scarcely take his eyes off her as she guided him to the corner. They kept their pace slow as she pointed out local landmarks, then gestured to the streetlamps.

"Soon, the town will hang baskets of yellow petunias all along the main streets," she said. "On a sunny afternoon in May, the colors are amazing."

He wouldn't be here in May. For the first time, he understood what that meant and felt a twinge of regret. He'd seen streetlamps and flowers before, but with Scarlett, everything took on a fresh perspective. The whisper of snow, the comfortable strolling, the rays of a wintry sun, felt different.

"Cherish is even prettier than a postcard," he said.

They lingered to admire a shop window featuring a male and female mannequin dressed in red, standing in front of a white background. *Follow Your Heart*, the exhibit stated in bold red letters, with a string of rosy Valentine hearts taped to the window.

"Cherish celebrates every holiday," Scarlett said. "Some are more important than others." A softness came over her expression, making her look younger and somehow vulnerable.

"Where does Valentine's Day rank in holiday importance?"

"For the town?"

"For you."

"Near the top," she said quietly. A gust of wind ruffled her shiny hair. He wanted to stroke his hands through her curls. He wanted to hold her, right here in the middle of this appealing town. He wanted—

No. What was he thinking?

He cleared his throat. "Anything else?"

"Anything else about what? The town?"

"About you." He knew the difference between talking and listening, so he steered the conversation toward her. He wanted to listen. "For example, tell me about your Little Sister. You mentioned her name was Joanna."

"Where do I start?"

"How about at the beginning?"

"Well, I enrolled at the Big Brothers Big Sisters organization, then went through an extensive interview process to become a mentor."

"What are the requirements?" he asked.

"Applicants need to be eighteen years old. At the age of thirty, I was welcomed."

He laughed. "I'm thirty-five."

"You'd be approved too. You seem stable and would probably be a positive role model."

He couldn't contain his grin. "Probably?"

"Dorothy and Ryan speak highly of you, so I'll amend that probably to a definitely." She shared his grin. "The goal of mentoring is faith, and for the child to have confidence in you. They need to know you won't let them down."

Faith again.

"A mentor doesn't need to be rich or famous," she added, throwing him a meaningful look.

He was certainly not wealthy, as he donated half of the proceeds from his CD sales to charities. Famous? He shook his head. Hardly, although Scarlett might refute him.

Farther along the sidewalk, she stopped to study the ice-cream flavors on a sign posted outside Whitney's Ice Cream. Wistfully, she sighed and pointed to peanut butter crunch ice cream, describing it as creamy, decadent, and, well, crunchy.

"The crunch is the rice cereal," she explained. "And it's delicious."

The outdoor dining space beside the restaurant hosted an array of tangerine-colored, wrought-iron tables.

"Want to buy a cone?" Joseph stepped forward, examining the long list of flavors. "Do they carry candy?"

He could get a haircut anytime, he rationalized.

"Candy? Ice cream? You're joking, right?" With her corkscrew curls bouncing around her shoulders and a mischievous gleam in her eyes, Scarlett presented a delightful picture. "I'm staying far away from peanut butter crunch ice cream. It's one of my red-light foods."

"Which means?"

"If I have it around, I'll eat the entire container."

He was torn between drawing her closer for a kiss, or the similarly pleasant notion of feasting his gaze on her. For now, he decided to gaze at her.

"You'll need to go down the street to Charlie's Chocolatiers for your candy," she said. "Just don't ask me to taste anything because I'm on my ten-thousandth diet." A strand of hair fell across her eyes. She didn't push it away. "Which started today."

"Why?"

"Really?" She gave a small smile. "Look at me."

She was beautiful and full of life, and his heart skipped several beats as he studied her from head to foot.

"You don't need to diet. You look great."

"You've been traveling too long," she said. "Particularly in Western culture, women are encouraged to be as skinny as possible."

"I don't agree." He couldn't get his compliments out fast enough. "Truly, you're absolutely lovely."

A rosy flush crept across her high cheekbones, and her chin trembled.

"Hardly," she said, so quietly, he barely heard her.

So there were definite chinks in the armor beneath her smile.

And he wanted to get past the armor.

Nope, don't go there. No long-distance romances. He was leaving Cherish in a few weeks. Moreover, he'd closed himself off from emotional attachments and his barricade was firm. Two disastrous relationships in two different cities had been enough.

But the way Scarlett had brightened when he'd asked about Joanna, her cupid-shaped mouth and her eyes shining like polished emeralds, chiseled away at his barricade's unguarded cracks.

They resumed their walk.

"You were asking me about the Big Brothers Big Sisters program," Scarlett said. "Still interested?"

He gazed at her. "More than ever."

"The organization matched Joanna and me up. She comes from a single-parent home and faces difficult obstacles. This particular transition has been tough. The poor kid moved five times in three years, and she hasn't seen her father in ages." Scarlett took a handkerchief from her shoulder bag and dabbed at her eyes. "As she matures, it's my job to steer her away from risky behaviors."

"You fix things for her. You protect her. Bravo."

"As best I can, although that's not my role." Reaching into her bag again, she lifted out a small album with photos of Joanna—at the library, at the park, at the movies. Through the progression of time, Joanna's transformation from a sullen girl to a young lady bearing a proud posture was remarkable. In the last photo, dressed in a pink polka-dotted sweater dress, Joanna smiled broadly and gave a thumbs-up. She stood outside Memorial Street Church with an older woman and looked directly into the camera.

He nodded approvingly. "Who's the lady with the bright-red rouge?"

"Mrs. Marge Addyson, the associate pastor. A lovely woman, widowed, and she views everything in a Christian, down-home way. If you get a chance to meet her, you'll know what I mean. She's wonderful to Joanna, and is a mentor too."

"Every minute I'm in Cherish, I find more people to admire. You all follow the Lord's example of giving. Dorothy, Ryan, Mrs. Addyson, you …"

"We try our best. I'm here for Joanna to lean on and to share opportunities," Scarlett said. "Such as the Valentine tickets you bought for us, and the harp lessons Dorothy graciously offered."

"I bet you're a remarkable influence."

"I hope so." She indicated the harp bracelet on her wrist. "Joanna insisted that she and I wear matching bracelets, although I'm no harpist. It was a surprise and so considerate, along with Dorothy's big-heartedness, of course." Scarlett puffed a deep breath. "Soon Joanna will enter middle school. She'll face difficult choices—drugs, alcohol, peer pressure. I'll be there to steer her on a positive, Godly path."

"Joanna got lucky when her family moved to Cherish."

"Millions of kids need an adult role model. And I'm the lucky one. Joanna is smart and funny and has a heart of gold. I'm in and fully committed."

"How long is the program?"

"The organization asks mentors for a yearly commitment, which is no problem." Scarlett's entire face lit up. "It's understandable, because it takes time for a child to build up trust."

"Are you involved in any other worthy causes?" In the spirit of their comfortable rapport, he took her hand as they rounded the last corner to the hair salon.

She didn't pull away.

"Well, I love animals, although that's not really a cause. It's more like my passion. I was the receptionist at a veterinarian practice in town before it shut down." Her expression closed, briefly unreadable. "Currently, I'm learning how to train service dogs at Canine Helpers. It's part-time, Monday through Friday, and Thursday I work a half day."

"Service dogs for …"

"Any person with a disability who can benefit from the service. These dogs help disabled people lead a more independent life."

"Define disability."

"Any physical or mental impairment that limits a person."

"Fascinating." He squeezed her hand, and they continued in silence. It seemed like they could have a conversation without ever having to say anything. That was how in tune he felt with her. "I'd like to hear more about it."

A tap on the shoulder again from his annoying conscience.

In tune with her? How? You've only known her a short time.

"Anytime," Scarlett said. "Oh, and did you know dogs are the only species recognized as service animals?"

"Not horses?"

"Good question." Approvingly, she nodded. "No, not horses. Although miniature horses are regulated and sometimes used."

He smiled as they reached the entrance to Cherish Style and Clips. Purple pansies accented the shop's window boxes. "Any other worthy causes you'd like to share with me, Scarlett?"

"I like to call them passions, remember?"

"Passions, then. Even better." They were still holding hands. Beneath his fingertips, her skin was smooth and delicate.

"Cooking is my specialty," she said. "No shock there, I'm sure." Another deprecating laugh. She did that often, and there was no need. Didn't she realize how perfect she was?

"Any special recipe?" he asked.

"I've prepared a tasty meatloaf and mashed potatoes recipe my friend, Cathie, gave me. She works with me at Canine Helpers. The meatloaf is comfort-food delicious, and uses a homemade barbecue sauce with brown sugar and spicy brown mustard and tomato sauce."

"I'd like to try that sometime." Yes, dinner at her place sounded just the thing.

He knew he was staring at her mouth, and forced himself to look away.

Overhead, the sun was high. An abrupt gust of cold wind reminded that spring was still a couple months away. Notwithstanding, a young couple strolled past arm and arm, swinging a picnic basket.

Probably on route to the park, Joseph surmised. Already, he was getting to know the layout of the town.

Scarlett's gaze flicked to the hair salon, then back to him. "Are you asking me to cook dinner for you?"

"Is that too bold?" He took a step closer. He couldn't help himself. Everything about her intrigued him.

"No. I love to cook."

Lightly, his fingers grazed her cheekbone. "And I won't need dessert," he said softly. "You're sweet enough."

She retreated a step and pulled her hand from his. "This isn't a good idea."

"What? Cooking meatloaf?"

"This." She moistened her lips. "Us."

"Why?"

"Because you're in Cherish for a few short weeks. And I'm here ..."

"For the long haul." He finished her sentence. His gaze focused on her mouth again. Without thinking, he bent down and his lips brushed against hers. She tasted like fresh-squeezed lemonade—refreshingly tart, yet sweet.

She didn't stir, although she inhaled slightly. He hoped it was a sigh of pleasure.

"So we can date while I'm in Cherish," he murmured against her lips.

"You are so not listening." She shifted another step back. "You're a world traveler who has undoubtedly dated scores of women and then gone on to the next big city. I will not be one of those women." She pivoted, then seemed to change her mind as she curved back to him. "Thank you for the tickets, though."

He was still reeling from her refusal. He covered his disappointment with the lazy grin he'd adapted over the years. "You're welcome, Scarlett. Enjoy the concert. Thanks for showing me the way to my first haircut in weeks."

"Anytime. And say hi to Phyllis." A hint of a smile crossed her face. "Don't let her talk you into dyeing your hair purple or anything like that."

His gaze slid meaningfully to her hair. "I won't, as long as you stay a redhead."

"You never know." Her smile widened. "I always liked green."

"In your hair?"

"A few green highlights will complement the red. And the color green symbolizes nature."

"And red symbolizes a fiery personality."

"But not everybody can pull off both colors at once."

"You can, because you're amazing." He grinned, admiring her spirit, and said good-bye.

Goodbye for now, he amended.

As he entered the busy hair salon and took a seat, he was informed that Phyllis had the day off. Furthermore, as a walk-in customer, he would need to wait at least thirty minutes before a hairdresser could fit him in.

"No worries," he replied. The half hour gave him the opportunity to think about Scarlett. Her laughter, her optimism, her obvious passion about the things she cared about were utterly appealing. And they all revolved around three themes.

Faith. Service to others. Home.

Faith. He got that. He prayed that he could harness her faith, as his was elusive lately, and he was fast becoming a sorry excuse for a worship songwriter. How could he feel good about himself when he wanted God's guidance, but wasn't willing to make any sacrifices that went along with it?

Lately, his songwriting attempts had been half-hearted, and many times he'd given up before he began.

Service to others. Sorely lacking on that front too, he reflected. He'd visit the Big Brothers Big Sisters organization in Cherish to see if he could mentor in some way while he was here.

Home. For him, that was wherever he happened to be. He was on a never-ending trek to see the world.

With Scarlett, however, things were different. She was an obvious homebody.

Usually, he'd be looking right about now for the fastest way out of town if he had so much of an inkling that he was attracted to a woman like her.

But he couldn't, because he couldn't deny her desirability. Everything about her intrigued him. However, his reluctance to settle down in one place weighed equally as strong.

CHAPTER 4

*T*he next morning, Scarlett awoke to the incessant ringing of her cell phone. Blinking in bewilderment, she checked the time and glanced at the caller ID.

"Hi, Dorothy," she answered groggily.

"I didn't wake you, did I?" came Dorothy's reply.

Sluggishly, Scarlett opened her eyes to a peek of morning sun filtering through her bedroom's sheer white draperies.

"Nope. I'm always awake by seven a.m."

"Joseph came by our house last night with an idea," Dorothy said. "In fact, he and Ryan talked about it for hours. We wanted to run it by you."

"What is it?"

"Joseph wants a kids chorus from the Big Brothers Big Sisters organization to sing back-up for two of his songs at the Valentine concert, and he's hoping you'll help."

Well, whoa. Scarlett placed the phone in her lap and regarded her freckled hands, her clenched fingers. He hadn't mentioned anything of the sort the day before. And why was her stomach doing a somersault at the thought of seeing him again?

She had to think, reviewing the facts she'd gathered about him. She shouldn't be nervous. He'd been kind and pleasant the entire time they'd been together. And he was extraordinarily well-liked, evidenced by the excitement at the music store when she'd waited in line. That radio DJ had carried on and on about him too. And her dear friends, Ryan and Dorothy, spoke well of him.

So what was Joseph's motive? More advertising?

Unlikely. She couldn't imagine he'd seek more publicity, especially for a benefit concert. He seemed like he wanted to spread the word of the Gospel, a genuinely good Christian man.

And a handsome one at that.

Her heart fluttered at the image of his chiseled features and sparkling blue eyes. Did he know how good-looking he was? Did he know those good looks were intensified by his quiet charm, his apparent unawareness of his appeal?

Scarlett brought the phone to her ear. "What about my ticket? And Joanna's?"

"Joseph said to donate them. Perhaps a couple people from Canine Helpers might want to go."

Scarlett's mind scrambled for another excuse. "But Joseph is a professional solo artist. He wouldn't want a kids' chorus accompanying him."

"He's requesting something different. His pieces are beautiful and timely and the audience can sing along too," Dorothy said. "Did you know his songs are sung all over the world?"

"Yes. I checked his biography on the internet last night." Scarlett's cheeks warmed at her admission. The previous evening, she'd spent hours indulging her interest in him while she watched him sing and perform on YouTube. No matter how many times she'd scolded herself not to, she'd been too enthralled by his concerts to do anything except watch in admiration. He'd also been interviewed by a famous Christian pastor in Australia, and had responded to the pastor's questions with effortless grace. The clip had received numerous hits on YouTube.

"His biography stated that he hasn't written a new single in a while," Scarlett noted.

"He said he's been inspired to write a couple new songs. We'll record at least one at the concert, and it will get first-hand coverage by the local TV and radio stations."

"Record it where?"

"Ryan installed a recording studio in the conservatory's rehearsal room, complete with a computer, microphones, headphones, studio monitors—you name it. Now when he's recording music for opera auditions, he won't need to leave home."

"Your expansion efforts are nothing short of remarkable."

"Thanks. The Lord has truly blessed us." Dorothy hesitated. "So you will help us, won't you?"

Hauling herself up to a sitting position, Scarlett fluffed the pillows behind her and then collapsed against them. With more curiosity than enthusiasm, she asked, "How?"

"Well, you're involved in Big Brothers Big Sisters. Joseph suggested you be in charge of enlisting five kids to sing with him."

"I don't sing, so I'm no expert. Will I need to audition the children?"

"Of course not. He doesn't want perfection. And I assume you'll include Joanna because she'll love it."

Scarlett took a sip from the water bottle on her night-stand. Dorothy was right, of course. The kids would be thrilled. Joanna would be thrilled. The community would be thrilled.

But what about Scarlett? Her heartbeat accelerated at just

the thought of seeing Joseph again, working side by side with him.

Be rational, she told herself. This wasn't about her.

Okay.

Then she could admit she was ridiculously nervous about the entire undertaking. Joseph made her feel like a girl with her first crush, and she couldn't tamp down her attraction to him.

"Scarlett?" Dorothy asked. "Are you still there?"

"Of course." Scarlett studied the beams of sunlight creeping across her beige carpet.

"Without your assistance, his idea might not fly," Dorothy said. "He said you'll need to be at every rehearsal."

"Okay."

"What does that mean? Is that all you can say?"

Scarlett shoved a hand through her hair. "What do you want me to say? Somehow, I think this was all decided without me."

Dorothy laughed. "Just say *yes* with an exclamation point. What's stopping you?"

Joseph, she thought. Being close to Joseph.

But how could she share these reservations with Dorothy, or the fact that Scarlett had been thinking of little else but him since they'd walked to the hair salon the day before?

"Nothing's stopping me," she replied, tempering her voice. She didn't want to sound too enthusiastic. She didn't want Dorothy's matchmaking antenna to go up any higher than it already had.

"Consequently, you're good with this then, right?" Dorothy pressed. "We all assumed you would jump at the chance."

Aha. "Really? You all assumed?"

"Well, yes."

"Even Joseph?"

262

"It was his idea. He said you can be his assistant director."

Scarlett gave an exasperated shake of her head. She had informed him she didn't want to get personal while he was in Cherish. Apparently, he followed his own agenda.

Once more, she set the phone in her lap. With a sigh, she looked around the empty bedroom. So why would he assume she'd jump at the chance?

Reason one: Because he suspected she was already interested in him. She hoped her feelings weren't that obvious.

Reason two: He knew she'd never disappoint Joanna. A practical explanation.

Her heart, however, chose a different reason. Perhaps *he* wanted to spend time with *her*, thus using her involvement with Big Brothers Big Sisters as an excuse.

She couldn't contain her smile. She couldn't contain her hope, either. That is, until she quickly shoved aside that notion.

She refused to live in a fantasy world. He was a famous musician who had visited more countries than she could count on two hands. She was an overweight woman living in a small town. A woman whose fiancé had left her flat. A woman who, beneath her bright outward appearance, was self-doubting.

"You can't control your emotions," she'd once heard a pastor say, "but you can control your focus." And her focus should be about others, not herself.

"Scarlett? Where did you go now?" Dorothy asked through the muffled phone receiver.

"I'm here." Quickly, Scarlett pushed out a breath and drew the phone to her ear. "And I'd love to help."

"Great. I assume you'll stop at Big Brothers Big Sisters after work? I'll drop Joseph's music off there, so the kids can take a peek."

"As soon as my shift at the service-dog facility is over at

three o'clock," Scarlett replied. "And Dorothy, thank you. The idea sounds beneficial for the entire community."

"Yay! I agree."

The happiness and relief in her friend's voice almost reduced Scarlett to tears.

Sternly, she reminded herself she hadn't agreed because she'd have the opportunity to work with Joseph. She'd agreed because it was an amazing break for the children. Plus, not only would the concert provide delightful worship music for the town, but it also supported things that mattered—money for the elementary school's music program, and a one-of-a-kind experience.

A few minutes later, Scarlett sat at her chrome kitchen table eating a healthy breakfast—fat-free Greek yogurt, a banana, and black coffee. Today was the first day of her diet, and she felt excited and motivated. As she sipped her coffee, she went about convincing herself that this new undertaking with Joseph could also be healthy for her in a personal way.

Often in the past, she'd run away from anything that scared her.

In this case, working with a man who made her heart go into overdrive would be good therapy. This time, she wouldn't avoid the situation. She'd have to get over the fact that this tall, handsome musician brought up unresolved sadness from her childhood just by standing next to her.

These were feelings she preferred to keep under a protective bubble, but she wouldn't disappoint her friends and Joanna for anything in the world.

Would she?

Drop by drop, she felt her self-assurance draining away and swallowed hard.

Wasn't this how difficult things worked? A person faced challenges directly in order to move on.

She leaned back in her chair, placed her hands behind her

head, and glanced out the window. Already, the sky promised a gloriously sunny day.

She relaxed her muscles and stood. Her steps to her bedroom were swift and purposeful.

* * *

At three thirty in the afternoon, Scarlett arrived at the brick building on Main Street that housed Big Brothers Big Sisters. She'd successfully finished her work at the service-dog facility, training a German Shepherd to switch on the lights inside a home for a man suffering from PTSD. The man, Mark, had recently returned from combat duty over-seas and was feeling wary about his safety. The dog gave Mark a sense of security and also served as a physical barrier between him and the outside environment. Plus, the shep-herd forced Mark to exercise—going outdoors to walk the dog. A win-win on all counts.

Pausing at the entrance to Big Brothers with her hand on the brass door handle, Scarlett cleared her thoughts and swept inside.

Isaac Albertson, the director, was in his office. He stood with his back to her, studying the large bulletin board that listed the week's activities for the children and their mentors. He stepped out of his office to greet her with an enthusiastic hand slap.

"Are you here to see Joanna and your new chorus?" He reached for a leather briefcase and handed it to her. "Dorothy dropped this off for you." He grinned, and his silver-white mustache lifted. His balding head shone in the overhead fluorescent lights.

"Thanks. You heard about the children's chorus, then?" Scarlett unzipped the briefcase and peered inside. Five copies of Joseph Slater's sheet music entitled, "And We Sing,

You Are Our God" were neatly filed, the lyrics clearly typed.

"Dorothy briefed me, and the idea is excellent," Isaac said. "I asked all the elementary kids. Five are ready and willing. One is Joanna, and there are two other girls and two boys. I've checked with their parents, and permission slips are all signed."

"Wow, you are efficient."

"Shh." He pressed a finger to his lips. "Don't let word get out. Someone at the state level may want to cut my hours."

Scarlett grinned and couldn't help thinking that without Isaac's tireless work and enthusiasm, the organization in their little town would never have grown to the proportions it had. This brick building was just one small haven in a big, dangerous world, but it meant so much to these precious children.

Isaac followed her to a large gymnasium full of noise and confusion and laughter. Some children read books aloud with their mentors, others played board games, while a group of middle-school boys shot baskets.

"Here's your charges." Isaac gestured to a group of children sitting at one table. "Two are third-grade girls, and the other two are fourth-grade boys."

"And me," Joanna reminded as she stood. "I'm in fifth grade."

Scarlett grinned at the youngsters as they gathered around her.

"You're a great bunch," she said. "Can anyone sing?"

They all raised their hands. That is, every child except one of the fourth-grade boys. With a defeated slump of his shoulders, he said, "I don't want to be in the concert after all."

"Why not?" she asked.

"My older brother will call me a sissy." He jutted out his chin. "Besides, I can't sing."

"Do you want to be in the concert"

He shuffled his feet and looked down. "Yes," he mumbled.

"Remember, different people are good at different things. And I know if you work hard, you'll do great." She offered her most encouraging smile. "It will be fun, and I promise lots of great men are artists."

"Promise?"

"Promise. So will you sing with the other children?"

He peered up at her through a curtain of black bangs and nodded.

Isaac led the children into a rousing rendition of "Row, Row, Row Your Boat," then handed out the music to Joseph's song and read through the lyrics with them. When they finished, Scarlett applauded and shouted, "Bravo!"

The dark-haired fourth-grade boy peered up at her. "I'm Russell."

"I'm Scarlett."

He held a half-eaten chocolate cupcake in his hand and offered it to her.

She scooped him up. "Thank you, but I'm on a—" She was cut short when the boy threw his arms around her neck and gave her a chocolate-frosting-laden kiss.

"I really want to be in the concert," he whispered.

"Hurray!" She took a bite of his cupcake and smiled while her heart melted. What would she do without these kids? They'd enriched her life in more ways than she'd ever imagined.

After using the restroom, the children retrieved their coats, then Scarlett and Isaac herded them out of the building. They had so much energy, passersby chuckled at their boisterousness. They walked two blocks and took a right down Evergreen Street to Musically Yours. Isaac marched the children in single file through the music store, reminding them to be on their best behavior. As always, the store looked bright and hospitable, welcoming musicians and music lovers alike.

Emmanuelle Thompson, a lovely woman with silky blond hair, huge blue eyes, and a face that seemed carved out of bone china, smiled a greeting at Scarlett while assisting a customer. Scarlett paused to stop and say hello.

Emmanuelle was Dorothy's sister-in-law, having married Dorothy's brother Nicholas, the deputy in town.

"No children yet," Emmanuelle had once said to Scarlett with a laugh. "Nicholas and I are content with our dog, Molly Belle. Believe me, she keeps us extremely busy."

Emmanuelle had once been principal harpist in a prestigious orchestra. Nowadays, she taught harp lessons, performed locally, and worked in Musically Yours.

When Scarlett reached the large rehearsal room at the back of the store, she stopped to talk with Ryan, who was setting up a row of five chairs. While they chatted, the children bounded for the chairs like a shot.

After Isaac seated everyone, he took the opportunity to leave, explaining he needed to stop back at Big Brothers Big Sisters. He'd been asked to expand the mentoring program to a neighboring county, was meeting with a group of interested volunteers, and was sorry he couldn't stay. He didn't look the least bit sorry, Scarlett thought with an inner smile. Isaac was dedicated to the organization, but preferred his quiet office rather than a group of rambunctious children.

Dorothy sat at the upright piano, her fingers poised on the keys, ready to accompany the songs in a supporting role for the rehearsals. Joseph had claimed one of the two empty stools beside her. Despite Dorothy's pointed stares, he ignored her. He plucked the strings of his guitar with his long fingers, sang softly, and then hastily scribbled notes on a sheet of manuscript paper. The melody was lovely and one that Scarlett didn't recognize.

Even in this concentrated pose, with his brow furrowed in utter concentration and his full lips pressed together, she needed to assure herself that he was real. This handsome, famous man, wearing worn jeans and a long-sleeved navy T-shirt, was rehearsing for a concert in a town so small, it had only one elementary school.

He didn't belong here. He belonged on a concert stage performing for thousands of avid fans, as he'd performed at the Grammy awards on national television.

No, she corrected herself. He looked completely comfortable and in his element—singing in an environment with other professional musicians.

She was the one who didn't belong. She didn't know anything about music. She only knew about children and animals, cooking and volunteer work. She couldn't even sing on pitch in the shower.

She glanced down at her clothing, hastily picking the dog hairs off the sleeves of her green coat. Beneath the coat, she'd worn a color-block sweater in a flashy pink and purple, fitted blue jeans that were admittedly a tad too tight, and gray leather ankle boots. Any stylish effect was ruined by her unkempt hair piled in a side bun, and the chocolate frosting stain on the sleeve of her coat. The makeup she'd applied that morning had faded, and she hadn't had time to reapply lipstick.

Keeping her position in the doorway and feeling utterly self-conscious, she watched Ryan walk away and grab a bottled water from a cooler. While her insecurities tumbled in her mind and she considered retreating, she stole another surreptitious glance at Joseph.

She had vowed not to run from the situation, she reminded herself. She would be here for the rehearsals leading up to the Valentine concert. She was a Big Sister, a mentor. A woman Joanna could depend on. Without Scarlett's friendship, Joanna's precarious security and self-worth issues could be turned inside out.

Managing to look a million more times confident than she felt, Scarlett stepped into the room.

A couple of employees from the music store conversed amiably with Ryan. She overheard Ryan telling them that the audio interface connected to the computer was an integral piece of recording equipment.

From what she could hear above their conversation and the children's playful giggling, Joseph continued to pick out notes on his guitar while half-singing lyrics that were hard to make out. She paused, listening, counting the number of times he used the word *love*.

Yes, he loved the Lord. But this song seemed different. The lyrics sounded like a love song between a man and a woman. The melody was slow, reminding her of a long-ago ballad by Elvis Presley, "Can't Help Falling In Love."

As if sensing her presence, Joseph looked up, and his blue eyes caught her stare. Setting down his guitar, he strode to her.

"Hello, Scarlett." He studied her for a long moment. So long that the familiar flush of hot pink crossed her cheeks.

"Hi, Joseph."

"I'm happy to see you again."

She studied his face for a sign that he was teasing her.

"Not for my singing ability, I assume," she replied. "I don't want to ruin your concerts."

"I bet your voice is lovely." He stepped closer. "As are you."

She glanced down at her disheveled clothes. This close to him, she inhaled his scent of fresh air and a hint of leather.

"Hardly." Self-conscious again, she looked away. "Although I haven't dyed my hair green yet." Her gaze traveled to the ever-present dark stubble on his chin, his thick, wavy hair. Despite the haircut, his hair still curled at the nape.

"I've been reading up on hair dyeing," he said, "and a drastic hair change sometimes means a woman is looking for a transformation in her life."

She lifted her eyebrows. "All that? Can't it just be for a fun change?"

He turned her to face him squarely, placing his hands on her shoulders. "You look great either way."

"Suppose I dyed my hair blue?"

He grinned. "Surprise me." Taking her hand, he led her to the stool next to his.

CHAPTER 5

The next two weeks stretched in front of Joseph in a delightful routine.

Scarlett's part-time schedule at Canine Helpers allowed her to rehearse with him and the children after school. Because Valentine's Day was fast approaching, they spent an hour every weekday practicing.

On Thursday, he met Scarlett at noon and walked with her to the Goodwill store. Winter had tightened its hold on the town, and she was diligent in her efforts to keep every child warmly dressed.

Once inside Goodwill, he insisted on footing the bill for children's coats, scarves, and an array of woolen mittens. He knew Scarlett struggled with finances, as she'd recently lost her full-time job as the receptionist at a veterinary clinic in town.

As they exited the store, he took her gloved hand in his.

Notwithstanding the cold, a pale sun shone overhead, prodding jewel-colored violets to bloom. He snatched a delicate bunch from the ground and handed the flowers to her.

"An early Valentine's gift," he said.

She paused in midstep and sniffed them. "Thank you. They're beautiful." A radiant smile lit her expression.

Her green coat hugged her voluptuous curves, and leopard ear muffs partially covered her lustrous hair. She looked gorgeous, with the brisk air adding a healthy tint to her cheeks.

As he continued to gaze at her lively eyes, her pert nose, her cupid lips, he felt an unexpected melancholy. He would be leaving soon. And he would miss her.

She had such a likable personality, animated and earnest, especially when she smiled. He liked the optimism surrounding her and her patient love for the children.

She exhibited, he thought with an inward sigh of sadness, all the traits he'd been looking for in a woman.

"No one has ever given me flowers before," she said.

"Really? I'm surprised."

She dismissed his comments with a wave. "Your compliments are far too generous."

"On the contrary," he started to say, before she bit her bottom lip and turned away.

He'd pondered what to get her for Valentine's Day, the final day of his concerts. Flowers? Candy? A parting gift? He drew a long, ragged breath. His chest tightened. He couldn't imagine never seeing her again.

"When violets begin to bud," she said, "spring can't be far behind."

Her words carried the realization that a new season was upon them. Spring—rebirth and light, the promise that God's will in nature, and in life, would be done.

Shoulder to shoulder, they continued walking through the park carrying two bags of children's clothing.

"Why did the veterinarian practice close?" he asked.

She kept her gaze straight ahead. Nearby, a young family flew a kite, their toddler racing across the grass and giggling.

"The vet moved away," she finally said.

"And consequently, you were out of a job."

She flinched, but he wasn't sorry for bringing up the subject. "Dorothy mentioned that you and the vet were dating." Actually, Dorothy had told him about Scarlett's broken engagement, but he wanted Scarlett to explain.

She gazed at the kite billowing in the air. "I don't want to burden you with my problems."

"Try me." He beckoned her to sit on a park bench, then slid beside her.

"Judson and I were engaged." With a sigh, she tucked the bags beneath the bench, then fanned the violets carefully beside her. "And then Judson broke the engagement."

"He's a foolish man to let you go," Joseph said.

"He didn't like my personality." She blinked, then shaded her eyes, watching the toddler tumble in the grass. "Rest assured, I'm well over the good doctor," she hastily added.

"Good."

"Why?"

"Because I really like your personality." Joseph slid an arm around her. "And I like *you* a lot."

"Don't go there." Her shoulders stiffened. "My heart is out of reach."

"That's not what I see when we're together." He tipped her face up to him. She was so attractive, although her expression was full of wariness.

"Joseph, I—"

He lowered his head. "Kiss me," he murmured against her lips.

She didn't fight him. Instead, she pressed nearer to him, her mouth meeting his for a long sweet kiss.

When the kiss ended, he rested his chin on her head. She stirred, and his arms tightened. "Don't move yet," he whispered. "Let's stay like this for a while."

He longed to kiss her again, to have her drive away the ache that filled his chest. As the days had passed, he'd come to realize that his life was now fuller than it had ever been. And his muse had been restored, inspiring him to compose again.

She shifted. "We don't want to be late for your rehearsal."

"I have it on good authority that the rehearsal is being run by an extremely good-natured musician."

She laughed. "Do you happen to know his name?"

They gathered their bags and continued their walk to the Big Brothers building hand in hand. A light dusting of snow began to fall, a wintry reminder, transforming the landscape to a powdery white.

"There go the violets," he said.

"The flowers are hardier than you think. And, besides, this snow won't last. By tomorrow, the sun will come out and melt everything."

SHE'D BEEN CORRECT. The following day, the icicles on the eaves of the shops had melted and the sidewalks were clear.

Daily practices were even better than their walks, Joseph decided. He'd earmarked the stool beside him for Scarlett, encouraging her and the children to belt out the chorus of his worship song in their loudest voices. Admittedly, throughout the rehearsals, he only had eyes for Scarlett.

The following week, Joseph didn't know what to expect when he sprinted into the rehearsal room at exactly 4:00. Normally, he'd meet Scarlett beforehand at Canine Helpers, but he'd accepted a long-distance call from Australia and had texted her to go ahead without him. He hoped she'd managed okay—walking the children to rehearsal, getting them settled and handing out lyrics took a great deal of effort, and she'd admitted to him that she was disorganized.

He rushed into the rehearsal room with his guitar in hand. He'd made record time, dashing from The Cherish Hills Inn to Musically Yours in under fifteen minutes. He'd been in a hurry to finish the phone call so he could see Scarlett. "A pastor in Australia is requesting a new worship song for the grand opening of their church," he explained. He didn't add that he'd ended the conversation by saying he couldn't commit.

Joseph glanced around the rehearsal room at the children. "Hi everyone."

They giggled, waved, and held up their music.

"We're ready!" Joanna said.

"Joseph, you're out of breath," Scarlett said. "I'll get you a bottle of water."

She had been sitting on a chair next to Joanna and fixing the girl's ponytail. When she got up, he did a double take. Oh, boy. He could gaze at her forever. Her luxurious mane spilled over her shoulders, and her hips swayed as she walked over to the cooler for a water bottle and then brought it to him. She wore a magnificent peach-colored sweater, embellished with a sparkling daisy pin, and a pair of black slacks that outlined her stunning, curvy figure.

He met her halfway. Defying propriety, he placed an arm around her shoulders.

"You look gorgeous," he said.

That figure. Those sea-green eyes. He'd be thinking about her the rest of the evening.

"We are being closely watched by five children," she murmured.

"And I'm merely leading my lovely assistant director to her rightful place beside me." He kissed her lightly on the forehead, prompting cheers from the children.

Thirty minutes later, they'd reviewed the chorus of his song, "And We Sing, You Are Our God," several times.

"Can I show you something new I've been composing?" he asked.

Encouraged by the chorus of yeses, he plucked the melody on his guitar and then handed the lyrics to Scarlett.

"'The Kingdom Of Heaven Never Stops.'" She glanced at him. "Will you sing it for us?"

He obliged, playing the opening chords. "'No fear. The kingdom of heaven never stops.'" He sang straight through to the final chorus: "'We sing your praise on earth as in heaven.'"

He looked up. The room had stilled and Ryan and Dorothy stood in the doorway. Silently, they applauded before returning to the music store.

"My new favorite song," Scarlett breathed as the children clapped.

"Do you like it?" He grinned.

"I love it."

"Thanks. We'll sing this, and 'You Are Our God' for the concert finale," Joseph said. "Okay?"

"You're only giving us a few days to learn a new song."

"I just finished the melody last night. But I bet if the kids rehearse a few more times, they'll get it. They're professionals. They don't even need musical directors."

"Alright." Scarlett paused. "Dorothy mentioned you were writing two songs. Are you finished with the second one?"

"We won't need that one for the concert. It's … personal." He took a long drink from his water bottle. The song meant too much to him. He wanted to sing it to Scarlett when it was finished. When it was flawless. Like her. "So let's call this rehearsal a wrap and play cards."

"Cards? Play cards? During a children's music rehearsal when you've just given us a new song?"

"A couple more practices and they'll be top-notch." With that, he sat on the floor. Extracting a deck of cards from his duffel bag, he beckoned the children and Scarlett to sit around him.

"Who wants to play Crazy Eights?" he asked, laughing as Joanna raised her hand. He dealt out cards to each child and indicated a brightly wrapped box in his duffel bag to Scarlett. "I found Charlie's Chocolatiers," he whispered.

"Do you just follow around your sweet tooth?"

He winked. "Mostly I just follow around you like it's my profession."

A half hour later, he'd purposely allowed a different child to win each card game, and indulged them by giving out chocolates as prizes.

Scarlett chuckled. "Remember, we are the adults in the room."

"Adults play cards," he replied.

"That's not what I meant. Adults don't make funny faces after each play, or sing silly songs, or stuff three pieces of chocolate in their mouth every five minutes. The kids need to respect you so they'll cooperate with your requests."

"Aren't they cooperating?" he asked.

She shook her head. "Not if you keep acting like a kid."

"Lately, I'd forgotten the sheer joy of just having fun. Some of these children have serious home matters," Joseph said quietly. "Let's keep laughter in their lives."

He'd spoken with Isaac about becoming a mentor, and Isaac had explained that it was a commitment to one child for a year. Joseph's heart grappled with what that meant—a promise, staying in one place. And he'd prayed, waiting for God's answer.

Although what if his prayers weren't about God's response, but more about his own convictions?

"Time's up, kids," Scarlett announced, nudging Joseph and tapping at her watch.

As they stood, Russell raised his hand. "Mr. Slater, where are you from?" he asked.

"A small town in Pennsylvania," Joseph replied.

"Do your mom and dad still live there?"

"No, but my sister does." Joseph held the deck by its sides, and with a light touch, shuffled the cards before stowing them into the case.

"I didn't know you had siblings," Scarlett said.

"Yes. My sister Samantha." Joseph was silent for a moment. "She's a couple years older than me. She's not married, either."

"Where are your parents?" Joanna spoke up, twisting and untwisting the ties of her pink hoodie.

"They're in heaven." Briefly, Joseph smiled. "They passed away when I was a teen."

"Where do you live now?" Joanna again.

"Nowhere." He hesitated, reflecting. "Everywhere."

"You mean you don't have a house?" Russell asked.

"Nope."

With a defeated slump of his shoulders, Russell muttered, "Neither do I." He refused to join Joanna and the other children, now cavorting around the room.

"See what I mean?" Scarlett murmured to Joseph. "No discipline and we'll have chaos on our hands."

Joseph hardly heard her. He was paying particular attention to Russell. Striding over, he took a seat beside him and they chatted quietly for a while.

When Joseph rejoined Scarlett a few minutes later, she asked, "What was that about?"

"Russell is a good kid. I wanted to see if I could help in any way. It's obvious he's been wounded. I don't know if something happened at home, or at school …"

"That's a roadblock you'll encounter many times," she

said. "Home life, lack of two stable parental figures, limited finances. These kids have experienced many hard knocks."

Joseph drew in a quiet breath. Between him and Scarlett, the silence was broken only by the sounds of giggling children, and the heartbreaking sight of one small boy with slumped shoulders and straight black hair sitting alone.

Music blared from the music store, as Dorothy apparently had switched the background recording to a Mozart piano sonata.

"You don't have a home, then?" Scarlett asked.

"I haven't found a place to settle down."

Until now. The thought came to the fore, unbidden.

But didn't he consider himself a Nowhere Man? the name from one of his favorite songs by the Beatles. *He was a real nowhere man.* He glanced at Scarlett, who openly stared at him. As usual, she was in tune with him, although she hadn't said a word.

But was "he making all his nowhere plans for nobody"?

"I want to travel and see the world like you," Joanna declared as she raced by, with the other children happily in pursuit. "I want an exciting, fun life and I want to meet lots of cool people."

Cool people.

Joseph grinned. Scarlett grinned. "She's growing up too fast," they said in unison.

"I never met a stranger," he said to Joanna as she raced past him again. "Just remember no matter how far you travel, keep your family and friends close. And God is most important."

Joanna put her hands on her knees and leaned over to catch her breath. "You say that because you write worship music."

"God is the center of my heart, and my experiences figure

into my songs. What I see, what's occurred in my life, is all part of the song."

As Joanna scampered away, Scarlett asked, "Do you think she got any of that?"

"I hope so."

"Your songs bring tears to my eyes, you know that?" Scarlett said.

"Thank you. That means a great deal coming from you."

"Why? I'm no music critic."

"You're a million times better than any critic because you speak from the heart." He sealed his words with a light kiss on her lips.

At exactly five thirty, Isaac and another mentor arrived to escort the children back to Big Brothers. Scarlett helped with their coats and boots, then bid them goodbye.

"Can I walk you home?" Joseph asked as Scarlett grabbed her coat.

"Sure." She shook back her hair and tied her paisley scarf into a graceful knot at her throat. "I'd like that."

THEY STROLLED HAND IN HAND, covering the easy walk in thirty minutes. At the doorway to her apartment, she wavered. "Would you like to come in?"

"You said you cooked, right?"

"Yes."

"And it's dinnertime."

She regarded her watch. "Yes, it is."

"Then do you remember telling me about a meatloaf recipe your friend, Cathie, gave you, using homemade barbecue sauce?"

"You have an impressive memory." Quickly, Scarlett went over in her mind the food in her refrigerator and pantry.

Ground beef and potatoes, lettuce for a salad. "Are you up for mashed potatoes, as long as you peel?"

"Comfort food on a cold February night? Are you kidding? I'll peel a five pound bag."

"You'll only need to peel two pounds for us." She tried to tamp down the little thrill of elation that ran up her spine. After all these days, they'd be sharing their first meal together. Anxiety battled with elation.

They entered her apartment, and she switched on the lamps in the living room. She'd decorated the interior with care, opting for sunny yellow and turquoise throw pillows to offset her orange-checkered sofa and side chair. The coffee table was a miniature wine barrel she'd found at a flea market, and a fluted bowl of fresh oranges sat on the table.

"I love orange," she explained.

"And green hair," he reminded.

"Did you know orange is the color of enthusiasm and joy?"

"I do now," he said with a grin. "And the color fits your personality perfectly."

Her curtains were a pressed gray silk. She'd painted the walls greige, a combination of beige and gray, and a cream-colored carpet completed the airy design.

"Nice place." He took her coat, then shrugged off his own and hung them in her foyer closet. "Your creativity and sense of design is amazing."

It showed in his gaze, his sincere admiration and interest in her, and she smiled as she led him to her tidy, efficient kitchen.

He washed his hands at the sink, then pulled up a stool at the island. "Bring it on. I'm ready to peel."

"After the potatoes are cooked and drained, the recipe calls for sour cream."

He rolled up his sleeves. "I'm liking this dinner better and better."

After handing him a peeler, knife, and empty pan, she set to work making the meatloaf—washing her hands, dicing an onion, and including a loaf of Italian bread to the mix.

"Can I add something for Valentine's Day?" He rose to stand beside her as she spooned the meat into a baking pan.

"Valentine's Day isn't for a while yet," she reminded.

"But we're together now." He shaped the meat mixture into a heart and stepped back.

"Where did you learn how to cook?" she asked.

"Here and there. I've lived alone ever since I went on the road. A guy can't eat take-out every night of the week." He offered a devastating smile.

He was all male. His shoulders seemed strong enough to carry the heaviest burden. He was witty, talented, and generous. And his scent—sweat and brisk air—made her wish he would always be near, that this evening would last forever.

She knew it couldn't. He'd be leaving the day after the concert.

"Plus," he said, "my father always made meatloaf on Valentine's Day for my mother. I remember them laughing in the kitchen while he cooked. My sister and I would peek around the corner of the living room and watch them."

Scarlett set the timer on the oven for one hour. "Your father must have been very romantic. Most men think of just buying flowers and chocolates, or taking a woman to a fancy restaurant."

"Looking back, my father was a romantic. And do you know what happened next?"

She chuckled. "What? Your father burned the meatloaf?"

"Nope. It came out perfect every time."

Joseph brought her into his arms and pressed his lips to hers. "This happened." His hands slid across her shoulders and down her back, pressing her to him. Helpless, she surrendered as he kissed her thoroughly and repeatedly.

Please, don't ever stop, she thought, as she wound her hands around his neck.

Sixty minutes passed, and the meatloaf came out of the oven. She allowed it to cool, then set it on a white stoneware platter.

"Watch this." Grinning, Joseph carefully arranged mashed potatoes around the heart-shaped meatloaf.

They sat at her chrome table in her tiny kitchen, and he offered a prayer of thanks.

One hour later, they'd eaten dinner and cleared the table. Joseph insisted on helping her load the dishwasher, pausing between dishes to nuzzle her neck with a kiss.

She couldn't think beyond the gentle touch of his lips. The sweet tone of his voice as he sang—the Beatles, traditional hymns, a recent pop hit. His tenor voice filled her with optimism. She wanted this, wanted him, every day of her life.

Afterwards, in her cozy living room, he sat beside her on the sofa, legs touching, his arm circled around her.

"I was surprised this afternoon at rehearsal," she began.

"About how well the kids sang?" He pressed a kiss on her temple. He did that often. "Thanks to my excellent assistant director, they're well-rehearsed."

"It's not me. It's you. You have a way with them—a rapport that's innate. They worship you."

"I don't want them to worship me. I want them to worship God."

"I didn't mean it in that way. They look up to you. You're a good role model."

"As are you."

"Joseph." Unwilling to let anything dampen the marvelous evening, she gave him a reassuring smile before she spoke. "I learned something new about you today. Your tours take you far and wide, but you've managed to keep the relationships that really matter—with your sister Samantha, and with Ryan and Dorothy—close."

"Isn't that the way it's supposed to be?"

"I've always believed that relationships are more grounded if a person stays in one place." She sighed. "I suppose it's because of my father. He's a roamer. And still, after all these years, I can't accept that."

"Are you an only child?"

"Yes." She closed her eyes for an instant. "Unlike you, my father can't be depended on to stay in touch, especially after my mother passed a few years ago. Sometimes it's a few days, sometimes weeks or months go by without a word from him. I get so angry, so frustrated, when he goes dark and won't return my calls."

"You can't change him, Scarlett."

"I know, and I'm sorry."

A puzzled smile touched Joseph's lips. "For what?"

"When I first met you, I compared you to my father."

He frowned. "And that isn't a compliment."

"Sadly, no." She replayed the scenes of her childhood in her mind. "When I was young, I lived in Chicago with my parents. Every time my father was ready to leave, I would tug at his coat and beg him to stay. And then, after he left, I'd count the days until his homecoming." She closed her eyes, could hardly inhale. "The fat girl, staring out the window waiting for her father's return. Pathetic." She glanced at Joseph for his reaction, but his face remained impassive. Still, fearful he might feel sorry for her, she waved her hand airily. "It doesn't matter, of course."

"Did he travel on business?"

"He was a salesman, but he gambled his money. We always struggled financially. Now he drives a rig."

Joseph's arm around her tightened. "And your mother?"

"She never reacted, just always agreed with him." Scarlett's smile was grim. "My mom and I were exact opposites. I questioned him, whereas she stayed silent. 'Why couldn't he stay in one place?' I'd ask her. In my opinion, that's what made a person dependable and trustworthy."

"Strong roots. Staying in one place."

She nodded. "Yes."

"And you shared your opinions with him, also?"

Her gaze clouded as she recalled the distressing scenes—her crying, him walking out the door. "Many, many times."

"So when I saw you with him in the restaurant, he was just passing through Cherish?"

"My father's patented remark—*Just passing through*. He managed to have lunch with me, but when I asked him to stay longer … Well, he just couldn't, I guess." She blew out a breath. "What causes people to wander?"

"Travel sometimes ignites a hunger for more."

"More what?"

"I'm not sure. Maybe God placed wanderlust in some of us to carry the Gospel." he paused, silently reflective. "Many times at the end of a concert, I'd walk outside and find a quiet place, preferably at the top of a hill. I'd look out over the city, sparkling with lights, and sing a favorite psalm. I'd praise Him. I refused to allow myself to forget that God created everything."

"Joseph, your faith is truly inspiring." She realized she was staring at him with love in her eyes. This exquisite Christian man.

He looked down at her, and his expression of interest, of sincere caring, touched every nerve in her pulse. "Or sometimes," he said, "we wander because we haven't arrived yet."

"Arrived where?"

"Home." He traced his finger along the curve of her cheekbone. "Home at last."

Softly, she laughed, feeling outrageously elated. With him, she felt safe and loved. Sharing his faith, he'd explained that his sights were set on heaven, but his feet were firmly planted on the ground.

"Cherish is my home," she said.

"And as each day passes, I believe that God brought me here for a reason." He tipped up her chin, looked deeply into her eyes. "I'm a man who strives to tell the truth."

"And the truth is?"

"I believe I am falling in love with you."

Her heart felt like it was beating in triple-time. "It's too soon," she murmured. Her words said one thing, the right thing, but her emotions felt another.

"Not if it's meant to be. I'm hoping you're feeling what I'm feeling."

She was, but she couldn't tell him, for soon he'd be gone. She stroked her fingers against the ever-present stubble on his chin. "I care for you, but we don't know each other well."

He smiled. "So you've said." He seemed to accept her explanation, although he cocked a dark eyebrow as he spoke.

How could he believe her protests, when she didn't believe them herself?

His lips brushed against hers. "Can you admit you're as happy as I am?"

"Yes. Extremely happy." She attempted to smile, but tears blurred her vision.

Gently, he cupped her face between his fingers, and his thumb stroked an errant tear from her cheek. "So why are you crying?"

"Because you're a good man and—"

She left it at that as he kissed her.

He was a man who deserved a confident, slim woman by his side. And she deserved someone who would be there for her, not on some Skype screen halfway around the world.

Still, she snuggled into his embrace as she dashed the tears from her eyes and pondered his words.

Effectively, he had spun a new meaning to the term *wanderlust*. He'd proved there could be positive aspects to a life lived lightly rather than deeply grounded.

His path had taken him one way, hers another.

And perhaps either way was good.

CHAPTER 6

*A*s she did every morning, Scarlett walked to her job at Canine Helpers. The days with Joseph had delightfully blended together, and there was a decided spring to her step.

Her cell phone chirped, and she recognized the caller ID.

"Good morning, Dorothy," she answered.

"All three Valentine performances are sellouts," Dorothy said. "Friday and Saturday nights, and the Sunday matinee. Isn't that remarkable for such a small town? Ryan and I discussed a Sunday evening performance, but it is Valentine's Day and all."

"And all what?" Scarlett asked. "You and Ryan want to celebrate the holiday?"

"Not us. We're newlyweds and know we'll be together."

"Uh-huh." Scarlett expelled a long breath. "And?"

"And, well, you might want to spend the evening with a certain famous musician. Maybe dinner at a fancy restaurant, discussing your future, holding hands … Whatever two people in love might do."

"Two people in love?" Scarlett parroted. She blinked, massaged her temple.

Dorothy sniffed, an all-knowing sniff. "Your attraction to Joseph is written all over your face. On his too."

"Is it that obvious?" Scarlett blurted, and then quickly closed her mouth. But really, what did Dorothy see?

Love.

"The entire town is buzzing about how you two are so good together. In church this past Sunday, you held hands during most of the service. And word is that Joseph met with Isaac about becoming a mentor."

"He did?" Scarlett had reached the center of town. She paused to eye the shop windows, the traditional red and white Valentine designs festive and eye-catching.

"Didn't he tell you?" Dorothy asked. "I assumed that by now you two were sharing everything."

"No, as a matter of fact, he didn't mention meeting with Isaac."

This was completely new territory, and Scarlett wondered why Joseph hadn't spoken about it, especially because mentoring meant so much to her. But then, since he'd arrived, everything had happened so rapidly, coupled with the powerful feelings he ignited in her, that she'd barely had time to comprehend their chemistry. She just reveled in it.

"You're reading too many romance novels," she said. "Life doesn't work that way and Joseph is committed to perform in several major cities. He's leaving on Monday for Raleigh, and I'm sure he'll have a list of things to do before he checks out of the inn."

And he was checking out of her life. Any hope she'd clung to that he might stay had promptly disappeared with the passing days when he hadn't mentioned a future they might have together.

"You know him, but I know him too," Dorothy said. With that, she clicked off before Scarlett could ask, "What's that supposed to mean?"

Before she could harbor any false expectations, she dismissed fanciful dreams from her mind. There were Big Brothers Big Sisters organizations in numerous major cities, and Joseph could mentor a different child in each.

No. No he couldn't. The organization wanted a one-year commitment. So there went that idea.

Still, Joseph had hinted that he'd like their relationship to continue, although he hadn't come out and made a specific plan. Sure, they talked constantly—about nothing and everything, like what time of year bluebonnets were in full bloom, their favorite ice cream flavors at Whitney's, (hers was peanut butter crunch, his butter pecan although he preferred the candy store), and the benefits of eating dark chocolate versus milk chocolate.

And always the conversation swerved to encompass his music and songs, her passion for animals, her love for Joanna and how proud she was of her accomplishments. Much to everyone's delight, Joanna was excelling in her harp lessons —already reading music and practicing a measure at a time (as Emmanuelle had instructed) on a small harp Dorothy had lent her for home use.

In the evenings after rehearsals, Scarlett and Joseph would walk to her apartment, stopping at the grocer to buy fresh, nutritional ingredients for dinner. He'd insist on buying a bouquet of flowers—cheerful daisies with a button center, or rainbow-colored carnations, or an array of large golden sunflowers—and he'd arrange them in a large glass vase in the middle of her kitchen table.

After dinner, their non-stop talks went on until late in the evening. For a midnight snack, she'd brew a pot of herbal tea, along with toasted slices of whole grain bread topped with local honey.

He spoke of his travels, embellishing his descriptions about the lush greenery of Ireland, or the high-rises in New York City, or the natural beauty of an Australian beach. And his stories of those places made her yearn to travel, which surprised her.

Her. The homebody, who had vowed she'd never leave the safe, stable confines of Cherish.

This is risky, I'm endangering my heart, she'd think, as he strummed melodies on his guitar—some old, some new, some happy, some sad. She knew that no matter where he journeyed, after he left he would take a piece of her heart with him.

On his cell phone, he'd shot various selfies of them at Musically Yours, in front of Canine Helpers, and loads of photos with Joanna. He had developed many of the shots into large colorful photos and hung them on Scarlett's living room walls. In one particular photo of Joseph and Russell, taken in front of Isaac's office, Russell held a blue balloon proclaiming "Happy Birthday," as it had been Isaac's birthday that day. Joseph, dressed as usual in jeans and a T-shirt that proclaimed *God is Love*, had his arm firmly around Russell's shoulders. Both smiled into the camera.

"I care so much about these kids," Joseph had said when he'd hung that picture. He took Scarlett into his arms. "Almost as much as I care about you."

A shiver went through her as he held her close. She tried to make light of his remark by giving her standard answer: "We don't know each other well enough yet."

"I know all I need to know about you," he refuted.

"It's necessary to date a person a certain length of time before anything serious can develop," she said.

"How long?"

"Obviously, longer than a few weeks. There are certain rules, Joseph."

He shrugged. "I've never been a follower of rules."

She smiled, liking the sound of that. She'd wanted to press her cheek against the soft cotton of his shirt and declare that she'd never cared for rules, either.

Please stay. But she said nothing.

Hopefulness was a funny thing. It could break your heart quicker than anything else. Tear a person apart. And she couldn't hinge her dreams on a man who was here today, gone tomorrow.

He'd also made sizable donations to both Canine Helpers and Big Brothers, and word had spread quickly throughout the town of Joseph's generosity.

Therefore, the weeks since he'd first set foot in Cherish had been the best weeks of Scarlett's life. So much, that on the Thursday morning before the concert weekend, she grappled with surges of despondency and the stark realization that time was passing much too quickly.

At noon, Joseph met her on the steps of Canine Helpers. Neatly dressed in his favorite pair of dark-washed jeans, a graphic T-shirt that said *God Is with Us*, and his black leather jacket, he was impossibly handsome. She felt exhilarated, and smiled at the utter delight of seeing him.

He set down his duffel bag and enveloped her in his arms. "Today," he said, "we are going out to lunch."

"We can't." She patted her waistline. "I'm on a—"

He put a finger to her lips, opened his duffel, and extracted a brown bag. "I figured you'd say that. So I bought a salad at The Garden Terrace for you, and two slices of lemon cake for me."

"Two slices? Do you know how many calories are in a slice of lemon cake? If the second piece is for me—"

"The choice is yours. If you don't eat it, I will." He shook the bag. "The restaurant gave us plastic forks and bottles of water too."

"We were going back to the Goodwill store this afternoon, remember?"

He made a show of shading his eyes and staring at the vibrant Carolina sky. "You predicted the snow would melt. It did. And the kids now own so many gloves and hats that they could trek across the Arctic Circle and never be cold."

"It's February. More snow could easily be coming."

"We'll take our chances." With a flash of white teeth, he favored her with a charming grin. "At the restaurant I asked which salad is your favorite, and the waitress with spiked hair said that last time you ordered a Cobb salad and didn't finish it."

Scarlett laughed. "Now why would you go through all that trouble?"

He gazed at her for a long moment, drew her into his arms, and said in a velvety voice, "Surely you know why."

Her heart hammered wildly while caution screamed in her ears. *Don't risk it. A few more days and he'll be gone.*

She stepped away and whispered frantically, "Please don't look at me like that."

He stepped an inch forward and kept his hands at his side. "Also, I wanted to thank you for your help," he said softly. "Without you, I never would have been able to pull this concert off."

"I highly doubt it, but I'll accept your compliment." Considering, she stared at Canine Helpers—the covered walkway, the squat wooden exterior, the small forested area in the back. "The waitress remembered I didn't finish the salad?" she asked.

"Small towns. Everybody knows everything about everyone."

She burst out laughing. "You're 100 percent correct."

"I'm starting to like small-town life." He kissed her hair. "So we can play hooky today."

"What does liking a small town have to do with playing hooky?"

"Absolutely nothing." He stated it with such conviction, she didn't know how to dispute his reasoning. Shaking the bag again, he asked, "Lunch it is?"

"We can't." So much for not disputing him. "The kids will be disappointed."

"They won't arrive at Big Brothers until after school." This close, the warmth of his body made her feel like nothing could ever go wrong in their world. The faint scent of his leather jacket tingled her nostrils, causing her pulse to quicken. "And just in case, I phoned Isaac and informed him we might be a little late."

"As usual, you took care of everything."

He gestured toward a hill past the park. "You look gorgeous in that fuchsia blouse, by the way. I like you in the red family."

"Red family?"

"You know, red, pink, rose."

"The colors are a family?"

He grinned boyishly. "Why not?"

She laughed at his logic and studied him as they walked.

When the time comes, accept that he'll leave and don't cling to him. Be grateful for the affection you've received.

In the midst of sunshine and breezes full of expectation, he took her hand. His grip was strong and reassuring, bringing her comfort.

She tossed him a light-hearted smile. "Did you know I've lost five pounds?"

"I do, because you've mentioned it a half dozen times. And I always respond the same way— you don't need to diet. You're perfect."

"Skinny is considered the epitome of attractiveness."

"That's ridiculous."

"You're being very kind. But thanks." Despite her shrug, she smiled, his compliment warming her insides.

* * *

As THEY KEPT WALKING, Joseph couldn't stop himself from openly admiring Scarlett. The vivacious smile he'd come to appreciate, the freckles on her cheeks, the bright colors she wore—which today was that fuchsia blouse and matching slacks beneath her green coat. Shimmery green earrings dangled from her delicate ears, the color of emeralds, faultlessly matching her glorious eyes.

Everything about her was exceptional. Her appearance always eye-catching and somewhat outrageous, his Scarlett.

His Scarlett?

He couldn't help grinning as they walked hand in hand.

He opened his mouth to begin a conversation, then closed it. The Lord had taught him that it mattered where he started a conversation and where he ended it. Although he'd positioned his life around God, he'd also targeted his life around, well, himself. And *self* was a small focus to center on in such a big world. The realization that he needed more, needed her, was beginning to make absolute sense.

And so he'd planned this excursion for several reasons. Of course he wanted to spend as much time as possible with her before he departed. But there was another reason. He wanted to test his feelings about bringing their relationship to a deeper level—without the babble of pudgy-faced children, or in the midst of peeling potatoes, or within the confines of a noisy rehearsal room.

Wind plucked at the ever-present paisley scarf tucked around her throat. A flame of red hair, the whisper of her laughter, a jangle of shiny silver bangles on her wrist. Everything reminded him of Scarlett, because she had pervaded his senses until he could think of little else.

Did he want to develop their relationship on a deeper level?

Most definitely.

Because lately he could only focus on one thing. He wanted her. He wanted to spend every day, every night, with her.

In this scenic town, they'd embrace a simpler lifestyle, joining close friends at church, as they had every Sunday since he'd arrived. He'd grown to love the pastors, particularly Marge Addyson. Marge was also a mentor at Big Brothers and spent several days a week with Savannah, a troubled teenage girl from a broken family.

Marge was a knowledgeable woman with a rollicking laugh, often showering Joseph and Scarlett with shrewd observations.

"Seeing you two holding hands makes me as happy as a bouquet of bluebonnets in the spring," she had teased them after church last Sunday. "You belong together." As Scarlett had blushed gorgeously, Marge had fixed him with a laser-sharp gaze. "If you don't stay in Cherish, you'll never forgive yourself."

He'd laughed. On the church steps, they had all laughed.

But Marge Addyson had known.

He was in love with Scarlett. And he had told her in a thousand subtle ways, hadn't he?

He squeezed his eyes shut, sending up a silent prayer. *God, what should I do when second thoughts invade my happiness?*

Would he truly be content in a town this size? He knew Scarlett wouldn't be happy moving from one city to another. She wanted permanency and sameness, the security of building a family and living in one place.

They strolled through town, remarking on the shop windows exquisitely decorated for Valentine's Day. He guided her into the local florist and admired the artfully arranged designs—pink azaleas and long-stemmed roses in crystal vases, lavender daisies and white lilies with intense, fragrant blooms.

"Do you have a favorite flower?" he asked. He planned on surprising her with a festive bouquet after the final concert on Sunday.

"The roses are beautiful," she replied, complimenting the shop owner, who was dressed in jeans and a white blouse, an embossed apron draped over her slim body. "But I prefer handpicked flowers, and gifts that come from the heart."

He got it and knew better than to say anything, fearful he would spoil the Valentine surprise he had in store for her.

They exited and continued their stroll.

They discovered a broad winding path and wandered to a sun-dappled gazebo. Setting down his duffel bag, he steered her inside. The gazebo allowed them a limited amount of privacy.

He braced his hands on her shoulders and turned her to face him. Slowly, his head descended, his lips brushing against hers.

"Joseph—" Her voice was unsteady. "Here?"

"Kissing you on this beautiful day is perfectly acceptable. I have it on good authority the townspeople would approve."

Softly, she laughed. "Which townspeople, exactly?"

"Dorothy and Ryan," he said agreeably. "And Isaac and Marge Addyson. And Joanna. You mentioned she was a romantic."

Scarlett chuckled. "That awesome memory of yours again."

He drew her into his arms, and she tipped her head up for

a kiss. Moments later, without warning, she broke the kiss and stepped back.

He took her hands in his and regarded her. "Anything the matter?"

She glanced at the hill beyond, her expression solemn. "We should get going."

Quietness punctuated a lengthy moment.

"Okay." He tried to reply as impersonally as she had. He picked up his duffel bag and they continued at a quicker pace.

However odd her response, it was heaven to clasp his hand around hers, to be in a comfortable, Godly place without the barriers of travel and suitcases and exhaustion.

So what if she was quieter than normal? Women were quiet sometimes, weren't they?

When they arrived at the top of the hill, the view provided a picturesque expanse of the town. The sky provided a celebration of brilliant sunshine, and birdsong drifted from the trees. Beside him, Scarlett amiably responded to his questions about becoming a mentor.

He was surprised she didn't pry him for more details, but she didn't. Instead, she inserted stories about Joanna and Joanna's mother and siblings.

As Scarlett spoke with animation, he pictured her as a little girl growing up in big-city Chicago, her hair in red pigtails, carrying a pink lunchbox, skipping to school. And then going home, filled with confidence and its counterpart, uncertainty, wondering if her father would be there.

"I've packed everything for our picnic," he said. "Right down to …" He pulled out a blanket he'd stuffed in his duffel bag and spread it on the cool grass. They sat and ate the feast he'd provided, her salad and his lemon cake, and washed the food down with bottles of water.

When they'd finished, he pulled his gaze from the familiar scene of the town park.

"Let's go behind the railroad tracks," he suggested.

She sent him a wry look. "Excuse me?"

"Ryan showed me where he and Dorothy used to sling-shot when they were kids. Apparently, Dorothy was exceptionally good."

Scarlett laughed. "If you're gauging my abilities with a slingshot against Dorothy's, you'll be sorely disappointed."

"I don't carry one myself, so you're in luck. And I doubt I could ever beat Ryan, anyway."

She smiled, then eyed her wristwatch and stood. "High time we get to Big Brothers. It's almost three o'clock."

"I told Isaac—"

"Yes, but we don't want to be late. This afternoon is the final rehearsal before the concert tomorrow evening."

"Don't you want to spend our last hours alone together?" He attempted to keep his feelings in check—annoyance, disappointment, wanting her to explain why she didn't want to prolong the moment of being alone in this exquisite place.

"Joseph, we've spent the past three hours together. Isn't that enough?" She pursed her lips. The sharp tang of her remark cut through him.

He stiffened. "Sorry to waste your time."

She grabbed their belongings and began walking. "Don't be ridiculous."

"I'm leaving Monday morning." He hastened to keep up with her. "Shouldn't we talk about it?"

She slowed and gazed at him. Her beautiful eyes darkened with an emotion he couldn't read.

"Why? What is there to say?" she asked softly. He was surprised when the shrug she offered seemed somewhat indifferent. He'd expected a warmer response—a fervent *Yes, how can we arrange a long-distance relationship?* Or, *Have you considered staying in Cherish?*

"I'm thinking about becoming a mentor," he said.

"So I heard. I wondered why you didn't say anything when I was going on and on about Joanna."

It took a Herculean effort not to ask her why she hadn't mentioned anything to him. Of course, he hadn't mentioned anything to her, either, but that was because it was an idea—one based on prayer and faith and love—but still only an idea.

He shot her a quizzical glance. "I assumed you would be excited."

"I am. Good luck with it. I'm sure you'll find mentoring rewarding."

He waited for her to ask where he planned to mentor—in Cherish, in New York, in Atlanta …

"That's it?" he asked.

"I wished you luck. Should I add *safe travels?*"

"I'm not flying off to the moon." Slowly, he reached for her hand.

She pulled back. "Australia is almost as far."

"Our time together has just begun, Scarlett."

He wanted her to agree. *Assumed* she would agree.

She hesitated, tightening her green coat around her. "You and I must be on a different time frame. Our time together is ending."

Right.

Wrong.

His mind stopped working. He couldn't counter with a snappy comeback. He could feel her withdrawing further and further away and he didn't know how to bring her back.

"Is that what you want?" He stopped short. "We've continuously had fun together."

"Yes, it's been fun."

It's been fun but ... The word hung silently in the air between them.

And she hadn't answered his question.

"I think it's better," she said slowly, "if I don't join you for tonight's rehearsal."

"Why? What about the concert?"

"You said yourself the kids are so good they don't need a musical director, so they certainly don't need an assistant musical director."

"Now you're the one being ridiculous because you refuse to talk about it."

She winced and met his gaze straight on. "Talk about what?"

"You don't get what I've been trying to tell you all afternoon?"

"Apparently I don't." She took a deep breath and swung her gaze to the florist shop's window. All this time, they'd been walking toward town. He'd hardly noticed.

"And you know what else?" he challenged. "Perhaps that's what you've wanted all along. Me to leave. Perhaps that's what has made me so appealing to you."

"Well, you should know, because you've become such an expert about me in a short amount of time," she lashed out.

"Scarlett." He put his hands on her forearms. "Let's face it. This isn't about me, or even us. It's about you and your absentee father. And your absurd notion that a home has to be in one place or else it doesn't count."

He was spot on. He could see it from the wounded expression on her face—just before she spun from him and stormed away.

CHAPTER 7

*O*n Friday afternoon, Scarlett phoned Dorothy to explain that she wouldn't be able to help with the concerts after all. She added a sincere apology.

"Are you sick?" Dorothy questioned.

Frantically attempting to think of an excuse, Scarlett mumbled through a *not exactly*.

"Okay. Hope you feel better soon."

Dorothy was so caught up in the concert preparations, eager to discuss erecting a tent at the park in case of rain, the chair set-up for the audience, the recording gear and portable outdoor heaters, that their conversation was brief.

"Ryan is saying the sound equipment just arrived," Dorothy said. "And we hired two catering vans to serve refreshments. And security. I'd better tell Nicholas to get on that."

"It's good to have connections with the town deputy," Scarlett murmured. With a final *Good luck*, she clicked off.

Next, she reviewed her conversation with Joanna before she telephoned. As Scarlett expected, Joanna's mother answered. When Joanna insisted on talking, Scarlett offered up a brief apology, saying she wasn't able to attend the Valentine concerts.

Nonetheless, she told Joanna she and the other children would be great. "Break a leg," she added.

"Huh?" Joanna asked.

"That's show-biz talk for good luck."

"Breaking a leg is good luck?"

"It's a theater superstition. If you wish a person good luck, it really means bad luck."

"Huh?" Joanna asked again.

"Don't worry about it. Just have fun."

"Then you aren't coming to any of the concerts?"

Scarlett swallowed, knowing her voice was heavy with unshed tears. "No."

"Why not? Are you sick?"

"I'm okay."

"Are you faking because you're avoiding Mr. Slater? He was great at rehearsal yesterday, but seemed, I don't know, kinda sad somehow. Did you guys have an argument?" In her usual straightforward way, Joanna had zeroed in on the fact.

"Some things are better a certain way, and I know the concerts will be a huge success." Scarlett struggled for composure—to be the adult Joanna knew and respected. But as hard as she tried, she'd let the girl down this time and there was no hope for it. "I'll see you after school on Monday at Big Brothers, okay? I love you."

"I love you too. And Mr. and Mrs. Edwards are taping the concert to make into DVDs, so don't forget to buy one, okay?"

"I won't." Scarlett fidgeted with the tie on her terry cloth robe. "Sing well."

"Sure." With a resigned huff, Joanna clicked off.

Scarlett reassured herself that there were other people to

help with the children—Dorothy and Ryan, Emmanuelle and Nicholas. And of course, Isaac.

Now it was Saturday. Forty-four hours had passed since her argument with Joseph, and those days had been a blur. Her life had lingered in another place, another time, and refused to move forward. Every thought led back to one man.

Joseph. The first time he sang about love and peace in front of Musically Yours, expertly thrumming his guitar. And signing his autograph. *Here you go, two t's, Scarlett.*

Joseph, after finishing his new song, boyishly, expectantly watching for her reaction.

Joseph, waiting patiently for her in front of Canine Helpers. *Today, we are going out to lunch.* He'd respected her diet, asking the waitress which salad Scarlett preferred.

He'd phoned several times in those forty-four hours. He'd texted too. And she hadn't responded because, really, what would she say?

Goodbye? They'd already traveled that road.

Come Friday he'd repeated his calls and texts. She'd vacillated, staring at her cell phone and asking herself: Should I answer?

On the one hand, she knew she should. She wasn't the type of person to leave someone hanging. An argument could only be settled when two people talked openly and agreed to disagree.

On the other hand, what good would it do? He traveled all over the globe and she wouldn't accompany him, although his descriptions of exciting locales had called up a sense of adventure in her.

All good, although the truth was she couldn't handle living on the road. Her life in Cherish had been carefully built, and she wouldn't tear it down to follow a musician who never settled in one place longer than a few weeks. Of course, he also hadn't asked her to come with him. Nor had he said that he would stay.

Don't think about his handsome face, his kind eyes, his full lips.

Sadly, that was all she wanted to do.

Twice, she had reached for her cell phone to call him. Then she reminded herself that she couldn't endanger her heart again. Not even for him. If they did continue their relationship and she chose not to accompany him, she'd share her life with a man who was hardly ever around.

Never again would she be forced to stare out an apartment window, waiting for a man's return.

I yearn for you like crazy, although I refuse to wear rose-colored glasses. You're here, there, and everywhere. I'm in one place, where I intend to stay.

Still, she missed him more than anything, and compulsively replayed all the good things that had occurred between them.

In many ways, her weeks with him had been transformative. He'd forced her to face her feelings about loneliness and loss, about people leaving her life for purely selfish reasons and through no fault of her own, and to accept and forgive them anyway for being who they were. She'd been upset and incensed at Joseph's parting remark, but his words had niggled at her.

This isn't about me, or even us. It's about you and your absentee father. And your absurd notion that a home has to be in one place or else it doesn't count.

Blowing out a sharp sigh, she opened the living room window and let in a waft of air scented with evergreens. The February weather had been undecided, but today was a lovely spring-like day. The sunshine brought a glow, the grass a sparkling green, and new warmth promised wildflowers and tiny buds appearing on the trees.

She padded into her small kitchen and set a kettle on the stove for tea.

A cardinal hopped onto her windowsill, its feathers the color of crimson.

"Hi, little fella," she cooed.

The cardinal nervously flicked its eyes toward her and flew away.

Not once in the last two days had she cried, knowing that crying about a successful musician whom she'd never see again would turn her into an emotional faucet. However, in doing so, she had stored up a horrendous weight of emotion. A sweet bird who preferred to fly away rather than look at her was the final straw.

Tears welled, and she dabbed at her eyes. "Joseph Slater, don't you dare turn me into a blubbering fool." As tears streamed down her cheeks anyway, she poured her tea and went into the living room. Settling on the sofa, she drew her knees up to her chest and wept.

When there were no tears left, she wiped her eyes, perched her chin on her hands, and glanced at her watch. The hours had dragged; showing only midafternoon. Would it always be like this without him? The days long and desolate?

She did what any fat girl would do. She got dressed, went to town, and purchased a quart of peanut butter crunch ice cream at Whitney's, adding a slice of chocolate fudge from Charlie's Chocolatiers. Swinging the bags, she went back to her apartment.

Since Joseph had arrived in Cherish, she'd lost several pounds and was at a weight she hadn't seen since high school. Their nightly dinners included healthy entrées and nutritious appetizers. She'd stuck to her diet and eaten no desserts, save for local honey on toasted bread at midnight.

That was then. This was now.

She'd always used food to tide her over when she'd had a particularly trying day—after the breakup with her fiancé, when she'd felt anxious about her new job at Canine Helpers, pretty much whenever she needed comfort. Stress eating. Emotional eating. Because comfort food, which unfortunately was mostly sugary and processed, made her feel better.

She sat on the sofa and opened the ice cream container.

With the first spoonful halfway to her mouth, she caught the glimmer of sunshine outside her window, the sky dotted with fluffy white clouds.

She paused.

What was she doing, about to gorge on ice cream on this fine Saturday afternoon? After all the weeks of dieting, did she really want to sabotage her weight loss with ice cream and candy?

She fell back against the sofa and closed her eyes.

No, not this time. Making smart, daily choices was the way to wellness. She could banish the word *diet* from her vocabulary, because no magic diet would help her reach her goals. The entire process was solely up to her.

It was big, this change in her mindset, and she realized it. Had she always looked to food for consolation?

Certainly.

But no more.

She placed the ice cream container back in the freezer, the spoon in the dishwasher, the candy in the cupboard, and decided to check out the Saturday service at Memorial Street Church. Normally, she attended on Sunday morning, but there were two excellent reasons why Saturday evening was better.

First, Joseph, Dorothy and Ryan wouldn't be there, as they would be preparing for the concert. So there'd be no awkwardness, no avoiding people, no uncomfortable questions.

Second, Saturday offered a new contemporary service. Chances were good she wouldn't run into anyone except groups of teenagers.

When early evening approached, dusk washed across the sidewalks as Scarlett walked to church. The service proved inspiring and energetic, the pastor's words adding layers of meaning about forgiveness and obedience to God.

When it ended at seven, she slipped from the pew and headed to the exit at the back of the church.

"Scarlett? Is that you?" Marge Addyson's cultured southern voice stopped her. "What are you doing in church tonight?"

Scarlett swiveled, "Hi, Mrs. Addyson. Umm, right. I usually attend on Sunday morning."

Marge's proper pumps clattered across the aisle. For an older woman, she was spry and well-kept. As usual, her gray hair was perfectly coiffed. "What I mean is, I heard you weren't present for last night's concert because you were so sick you needed three beds."

"Is that what you heard?" Scarlett grinned and pressed a greeting kiss to Marge's rouged cheek.

The woman smiled back and tugged on the jacket of her powder-blue wool suit. "I missed you. We all did."

"I'm sure the music was lovely," Scarlett said, congratulating herself on how well she had sidestepped Marge's questions.

"The children were delightful. And that musician of yours has a dreamy, raspy voice that could melt butter. The last worship song—that new one—had everyone on their feet weeping during the finale."

"Yes, I've heard it and it's beautiful." The remembrance brought a well of emotion bubbling to the surface, and Scarlett dashed tears from her eyes, hoping Marge wouldn't notice. "We're not together anymore."

"You were the ideal couple. What happened?" Marge extended her arms, and Scarlett moved into the bear-hug embrace. Something within her wanted to burst open, to tell the elderly woman everything.

"It's a long story."

"The church is empty." Marge gestured to a pew in the back.

They sat in silence for several beats. Scarlett focused on an arched stained-glass window highlighting a full-length angel, the muted colors glowing as pure silver.

Never quiet for long, Marge nudged Scarlett's shoulder. "I'm a good listener, as well as a good talker, you know. Give me a try."

Scarlett wiped her hands on her pencil skirt. Firmly, determinedly, she fought to control the thickness in her throat as she explained Joseph's kindness, how good he was to her, his rolling-stone lifestyle. All the highs, all the lows. She spoke until there was nothing left to say.

"Dorothy's told me and half the town that you and Joseph are in love," Marge said.

"Has she now?" Scarlett felt a warm blush stain her cheeks as she recalled Joseph's lips moving tenderly on hers.

Don't move yet, he'd whispered. *Let's stay like this for a while.*

"And cute little Joanna told me the same thing when I mentored Savannah a few days ago."

"Joanna is a romantic." Scarlett shook her head. "And Dorothy. Well, Dorothy—"

"Knows you and Joseph well. So your stories about how kind Joseph is, how he opens doors for you and stands when you enter a room, leave out the most important part." Marge took Scarlett's cold hands in her own. "He loves you, and you love him. Everyone else realizes it. Now it's time for you to realize and do something about it."

Scarlett's stomach gave a funny lurch. "Like what?"

"Show up at the concert. There's still an hour left before it starts at eight." Marge tapped at her watch. For the first time, Scarlett noticed the dirt beneath Marge's fingernails. She'd taken up indoor gardening, planting a few tender seedlings. Knowing Marge, she would have the most beautiful garden in Cherish come summer.

"I can't. Not tonight," Scarlett said. "There's something I … Well, I'm making an appointment to go somewhere tomorrow morning."

"After your appointment, then. I'll be there because Ryan invited me to say the blessing before the concert." Marge placed an age-spotted hand on Scarlett's cheek. "You're a vivacious beautiful woman and full of life. Joseph is lucky to have you."

"Hardly." Self-doubt poked through. "He can have anyone. A sweet skinny woman would be able to—"

"He wants you just the way you are. You're foolish if you let a good Christian man leave your life without fighting for him. Go. And be sure to sit in the first row where he can see you. Be a blessing and an encouragement."

And there was the challenge. Hastily, Scarlett nodded, promising Marge before she lost courage. Only her hurt pride had prevented her from making the first move. And if she didn't reach out, Joseph would leave Cherish believing she didn't care about him, and nothing was further from the truth.

"Scarlett, one more thing, and it's the most important." Marge stood and pulled on a pair of tan leather gloves. "Ask God to lead your heart and mind. The Lord wants you to be happy."

A smile touched Scarlett's lips. She had come to church.

She had met Marge. Surely the Lord's hand was in this. With His blessing and her friends' support, she could do this. Besides, she couldn't imagine her future without Joseph.

On Sunday morning, Scarlett rose early although she hadn't fallen asleep until dawn. When the alarm rang, she sprang to a sitting position, hurtling from a bottomless dream to full wakefulness in five seconds.

"I can't do it," she whispered to the empty room. Marge had given the worst advice ever.

Of course you can. Just swing your legs over the side of the bed, shower, and get dressed.

Bundled in her terry cloth robe, she deliberated on her wardrobe choices. Cute clothes had always been a problem because of her size, although Joseph had complimented her on everything she'd worn.

She dressed with great care in a pink silk blouse that tied at the waist, black slacks, and animal print pumps sporting a kitten heel. It was Valentine's Day, after all. A bright rosy lipstick, red crystal drop earrings, and Joanna's harp bracelet completed the ensemble. Although the weather promised temperatures in the high fifties, she donned her green wool coat for extra warmth.

Then she texted her hairdresser, Phyllis, convincing her friend to pay back the favor from when Scarlett had helped her move into her new apartment. She made an appointment for eleven o'clock.

With a fluttery feeling in her stomach, she pushed back her shoulders and began a fast-paced stride to Cherish Styles and Clips. First the hairdresser, then the concert. The important thing was that she and Joseph would meet again, face to face. It was so simple, and all she had to do was look him in the eye and tell him how much she loved him.

At one o'clock, Scarlett emerged from the hair salon. The sky was a soft blue, the clouds drifting across it in slow motion. Chirping birds circled in languid arcs, while Scarlett joined the throngs of people headed for the 2:00 matinee. Outside the white canvas tent where the concert would be held, Emmanuelle chatted with Nicholas, holding their golden retriever, Molly Belle, by her leash.

The couple waved gaily to Scarlett and she grinned a hello. She'd reached the park in record time.

She went straight for the back-stage area and placed her coat on a chair.

"You made it!" Joanna exclaimed. "My mom came to the performance last night, and now you're here." She wore a pleated black skirt and white shirt, her hair pulled back in a neat ponytail, and her almond-shaped eyes shone with excitement. "And I love your hair! And your bracelet is awesome, just like mine." She jingled her harp bracelet, prompting Scarlett to do the same, and then nudged Russell. "I told you she wouldn't disappoint us. You owe me a dollar."

The boy elbowed her back. "No, I don't. Anyway, I don't have a dollar." He looked young and vulnerable, an oversized pair of black dress pants and freshly pressed white shirt overpowering his slight frame.

The moment Dorothy came around the corner, her gaze riveted on Scarlett. "Thank goodness you're here. Isaac is running late—some crisis at Big Brothers—and Ryan needs my help with the microphones. Can you watch the children backstage?" She indicated a row of chairs.

"I'm more than happy to help," Scarlett replied.

"Oh, and for the finale, the children are singing twice, the final number being Joseph's new worship song. Do you remember it?"

Scarlett drew a quiet sigh. How could she forget? "His lyrics are so inspirational, I hardly took a breath while he sang."

Ryan came backstage with Marge Addyson. "Are we

ready to begin?" he asked Dorothy, giving her a quick hug. "Thanks for organizing all this, my love."

Dorothy grinned. "Happy Valentine's Day."

What would it be like to have a man love a woman so much that he put her before any other goals in his life? Scarlett wondered. Seeing their interaction caused a flash of longing in her heart. She was truly happy for them, as their romance hadn't come about without trials. At the same time, their joy only expanded her own aloneness.

Marge patted Scarlett's arm. "I'm glad you're here."

Scarlett took a deep breath. "Me too." She paused, then turned. Joseph's voice came from the stage as he spoke with one of the sound technicians, followed by the familiar strum of his guitar as he warmed up. Tenderness flooded her heart. She couldn't wait to talk with him again.

She waded into the middle of another disagreement between Joanna and Russell, separated them, and sat them in a row with the other children. Then she peeked around the curtain to catch a glimpse of Joseph.

At 2:00, Marge and Ryan took the stage. Joseph stood in one corner as Ryan invited Marge to offer the opening prayer.

"Thank you, Ryan, for the privilege of praying with all of you." The epitome of poise and elegance, Marge bowed her head and clasped her hands together, requesting the audience to do the same. "Dear Lord, thank you for this fine February day. We are grateful that every seat for this concert has been filled. Bless all those present, and may the uplifting music fill our hearts and ears as we worship you in song. Amen."

After Dorothy seated Marge in the front row, Ryan continued. Engaging and relaxed, he spoke to the crowd with enthusiasm, wished everyone a happy Valentine's Day and thanked them for their support. He then expounded on the benefits of expanding the elementary school's music program.

"Music allows children to build self-confidence, as well as listening and math skills," he explained. "Studies conclude that music fosters creativity and relieves stress." He ended when Marge shouted from the front row, "Ryan, there's so much music and so little time. Let's get on with the concert."

With a broad grin, Ryan introduced Joseph to a deafening round of applause.

Scarlett watched as Joseph claimed his stool and took command of the stage. He studied the audience, his gaze drifting up and down the rows as if he were searching for someone. He looked breathtakingly handsome in his concert attire—black pants and a white dress shirt, and his broad shoulders filled out the shirt to perfection. He acknowledged Dorothy in the front row next to Marge with a tip of his head.

He played the instantly recognizable chord from his Grammy-award-nominated hit, "Sing Glory Forever." When the audience cheered, he smiled and encouraged everyone to sing along.

As she peeked from the curtain, tears blurred Scarlett's view of him. She'd listened to his songs countless times on his CD, and she loved them all.

As the one hour concert sped to its finale, Joanna whispered to Russell, "Are you nervous?" The children would go on stage for the final numbers.

When it was time, Scarlett encouraged each child with a quick hug, and sent them in single file on stage. As Joanna passed Joseph, she beckoned him to bend down and whispered something in his ear.

He looked around, expressions of hope, surprise, and happiness dancing across his handsome face.

Then he smiled at the children. "Ready?" he asked.

"'And we sing, you are our God …'" His familiar tenor voice resonated throughout the crowd, throughout the tent, and Joanna and the others joined him on the refrain.

After his second song ended, silence reigned for a beat. Then Joseph and the children bowed to a standing ovation.

Scarlett high-fived each child as they marched offstage, congratulating them on an outstanding performance.

"I'll take you all out for ice cream." She laughed. "Or salad."

"Ice cream!" they shouted in unison.

Isaac appeared. "I got here just in time. And I'll take you up on your offer for ice cream."

"You're on." She pulled back the curtain in time to see Dorothy gesture to the audience.

"Ladies and gentlemen," Dorothy said, "let's thank Joseph Slater and the children from Big Brothers and Big Sisters once more." Amidst another standing ovation, she started for the stage, but stopped as Joseph held up a hand.

"I have one more song I'd like to sing," he said. "I've been writing it ever since I came to Cherish." He cleared his throat, seeming nervous as he thumbed his guitar strings. "She's someone I think about all the time, and I want to wish her a happy Valentine's Day. And to tell her that she's the love of my life."

He hesitated, strummed a chord. "The name of the song is, 'I Need to Learn.'"

Scarlett stepped back, her hand pressed to her mouth. Was she breathing?

At first, he sang the lyrics softly. "'I need to learn that I don't got to travel anymore. / You're small town, I'm big city / but we both look at the same sky, both love the same God. / Oh, Scarlett, Scarlett, you've taught me how to dream.'"

Somewhere behind her, Scarlett heard Isaac ask in a whisper, "Scarlett, should I get your coat?"

She couldn't answer. She forgot about her coat. She forgot about everything in the world around her.

When Joseph sang her name again, sang about love, she touched her hand to her heart, the tears flowing freely. Everything around her seemed to quiet.

Somehow, Dorothy's hand had linked to her arm.

"He wants you to come on stage," Dorothy said.

"How?" Scarlett asked.

"By walking with me."

On legs like rubber, she followed as Dorothy guided her. "He's been writing this song for weeks," Dorothy went on, whispering in Scarlett's ear. "At first, I asked if he wanted my help with the lyrics. He said he didn't need my help, because the lyrics just flowed. He asked me to give the song to you this evening, but then Joanna told him you were here when she went out to sing."

Now they were on stage. Scarlett stepped into the spotlight, and Dorothy moved to the side.

Joseph set down his guitar, pushed back the microphone. He stood and came to her.

Her heart took a leap. He stood straight and tall, aching tenderness in his blue eyes. Up close, he looked a bit scruffy, hardly put together, like a man who had been pacing for days. His wavy hair was tousled, as if he'd incessantly run a hand through it. And he'd skipped a button on his shirt.

Still reeling, she gazed up at him as he fingered the highlighted strands of green hair around her face. He grinned and whispered, "No blue?"

"Just green."

He took her hands in his. "'I don't got to travel anymore," he sang softly, "'because I'm home.'" Certainty shone in his eyes. "'And we're both going to love each other right here in Cherish.'" The softness of his breath brushed against her cheek as he bent to kiss her.

He was professing his love in front of the entire town, hundreds of people. And wasn't all this being recorded?

She swallowed. "You're flying to Raleigh tomorrow." The risk of tears had passed, the lump in her throat disappearing. A stubble covered his jaw, shadows beneath his eyes, but his gaze radiated expectation and hope.

"I canceled it."

"Joseph, you shouldn't. Not for me."

He pressed his finger to her lips. "I did it for us. I'd much rather be here with you."

The moment Scarlett stirred, Dorothy and Ryan rushed over, and Dorothy jostled Scarlett and Joseph away from the spotlight.

"Quite the encore, you two lovebirds." Dorothy's lips trembled with laughter.

"How's that for a real Valentine's Day surprise?" Ryan joked to the audience with a wry smile. "A true happily ever after." He thanked everyone as murmurings grew to a fever-pitch, then asked the technicians to play one of Joseph's songs and turn up the volume.

* * *

Two hours later, as a light gentle wind teased the air, Scarlett and Joseph walked to the inn holding hands.

"The children enjoyed their ice cream," he said.

"Originally, Joanna had wanted candy for Valentine's Day, but she was okay with ice cream after all."

"And you ordered low-fat frozen yogurt."

She smiled. "My new favorite dessert."

"And now they're safely back at Big Brothers with Isaac."

"They deserved the applause, the ice cream, everything," Scarlett said. "They were awesome."

"And I'm going to be mentoring Russell personally."

Personally. A commitment. She laid her hand against his cheek. "You're a good man."

"I try."

They settled on the inn's porch on an old-fashioned love seat, until only a sliver of moonlight lit the sky. Once again, they held hands.

"I'm going to spend the next few weeks here at the inn. The owner, Tom, okayed it," Joseph said. "I told him my booking was temporary, just until we got married."

"You and Tom?"

He laughed softly. "You and I." He brushed a strand of hair from her temple. "Will you marry me?"

The flutter in her heart went straight to her belly. "Joseph, are you sure you've thought this through? Your fans are waiting for you all across the country."

"Other excellent worship artists will cover for me. While you were sorting ice cream flavors, I made a few phone calls."

"What about Australia?"

"I guess you'll have to come with me."

"I'm not sure. I might …"

"If and when the time comes, we'll discuss it." He kissed her forehead, her nose, her cheeks.

She chuckled. "Do you need glasses?"

"I don't think so. Why?"

"Because your aim needs to improve." She lifted her lips for a kiss.

After the kiss, he held her. "In the meantime, I'm a concert artist without a concert. Guess I'll be settling in Cherish with a certain green-haired redhead."

In the flicker of moonlight, she leaned back and gazed up at him. "Are you sure you like it here?"

"I love it. I'm even planning to lead the contemporary worship service at church. That is, if they'll have me."

"Suppose all this doesn't work out? What about your

wanderlust?"

"Together, we'll pray." He threaded his fingers through her hair. The curls were well beyond unmanageable by now. "God will show us the way."

"Us?"

"You and me. Husband and wife. Trust me, we can do it all."

She stared at him. "I didn't expect this."

"What *did* you expect?"

Truly, it was all a wonderful dream, with his arms securely around her.

"I assumed we would talk after the concert and hoped we would reconcile," she said.

"We did."

Absurdly happy, she laughed.

He framed her face between his fingers. "So, will you marry me?"

"Yes, yes." She nodded, nestled closer.

"I want children. I want a family." He brushed kisses on her cheeks.

"So do I." He wanted the same things she did—love and family—the things that mattered.

"I have something for you for Valentine's Day," he said.

"You wrote me a love song." She pressed her face against his broad chest, heard the solid beating of his heart. "Isn't that romantic enough?"

"Not on Valentine's Day." He stood and strode into the inn's lobby, emerging with a bouquet of hand-picked violets, a nearly illegibly written card attached to them.

She read the note aloud. "'Scarlett with two t's, you taught me that dreams can come true. Don't give up on me.'"

"I never did," she said quietly.

"Thank you." Joseph swallowed, always in tune with her, knowing the moment was poignant for both of them. "Tom's a good guy, keeping these flowers in water since I picked them this morning."

"He's the best."

Tenderly, Joseph stared at her. "Scarlett Evans, I love you. And when I didn't see you for a couple days, I realized if I left, I would have missed the most important person in my life. God brought me to Cherish for a reason."

"God's plan is perfect." She held the flowers close as Joseph's lips captured hers.

His kisses were sweet, his closeness warm and inviting. She planned to stay with him, here in Cherish, or wherever he traveled, forever.

As evening air touched her cheeks, she watched the twinkle of stars overhead, the landscape of Cherish ever changing, yet eternally the same. Like life itself. Strong, faithful, and always good.

What a perfect Valentine's Day. A wonderful sweet journey.

"I will always love you, Joseph Slater. Always." For the rest of her life when she remembered this special day, she knew she would cry tears of joy.

For God had given her a Valentine's Day to cherish.

THE END

A NOTE FROM JOSIE

Thank you for reading *A Valentine To Cherish*. I hope you enjoyed your visit to the scenic town of Cherish, South Carolina, the music store, Musically Yours, and all of the wonderful characters, including Scarlett and Joseph.

If you loved this inspirational romance as much as I loved writing it, please help other people find *A Valentine To Cherish* by posting your review.

A Valentine To Cherish is available in ebook, paperback, Large Print paperback, Hardcover, and audiobook.

My Spotify Play List for A Valentine To Cherish is here.

Want more of the Inspirational Cherish series?

Click here.

VALENTINE-SHAPED MEATLOAF RECIPE

Meatloaf (preheat oven to 350 degrees F)

2 pounds meatloaf mix (beef/pork/veal)
   1 medium onion, diced fine
   1 loaf of Italian bread or French baguette, stale
   1/4 cup of milk
   2 eggs
   1/2 cup Parmesan cheese
   1 tablespoon garlic powder
   1 teaspoon salt
   1/4 teaspoon pepper
   1 teaspoon Italian seasoning

1. Cut loaf of bread in half the night before you are going to make the meatloaf and cover it with paper towels.

2. When you are ready to start your meatloaf, remove all of the bread from the crust. Use the crust for something else.

3. Put the bread in a large bowl, and add the milk. Stir it to get the bread saturated.

4. Once the bread is saturated, squeeze out some of the milk. You want it wet, but not dripping. Pour out the excess milk and put the bread back into the large bowl. Add the onion, eggs, cheese, garlic powder, salt, pepper, and Italian seasoning. Mix well.

5. Add the meat to the bowl and with your hands mix everything thoroughly. Shape the meatloaf into a heart shape.

6. Place the meatloaf into a 1-inch deep pan.

7. Place in oven and cook for about 1 hour. Check to make sure the internal temperature is 165 degrees F.

Barbecue Sauce

1 can tomato sauce
1 tablespoon spicy brown mustard
1/4 to 1/2 cup brown sugar (to taste)

1. Mix in bowl and set aside until the meatloaf has cooked for 1 hour. Carefully drain fat from the meatloaf pan. Pour barbecue sauce over meatloaf and put it back in the oven for 15 minutes. Remove from oven. Tent with foil until ready to assemble.

Mashed Potatoes:

2 pounds russet potatoes
4 tablespoons butter (I prefer unsalted butter)
1/2 cup sour cream
Salt & pepper to taste

Milk for thinning out the potatoes, as necessary

1. Peel potatoes, cut into 1-inch cubes, then rinse. Place in a 2-quart saucepan with enough water to cover the potatoes and add 1 teaspoon of salt to the water. Bring the potatoes to a boil and after 20 minutes, check them for tenderness. If not quite done, check every 2 minutes until done.
2. Drain potatoes in a colander, and put back in the pot. Put the pot back on the stove on high. Shake the pan to dry the potatoes. When dry, move the potatoes to a bowl, add the butter, and using a mixer mix the potatoes until there are no lumps. (Using a potato masher will not add air to the potatoes to make them fluffy.) Mix in the sour cream. Add milk to lighten the potatoes, but still allow them to stay in peaks when you pull the mixer out. Add salt and pepper to taste.

JOSIE RIVIERA

a Chocolate-Box Valentine

This book is dedicated to all my wonderful readers who have supported me every inch of the way.
THANK YOU!

CHAPTER 1

*I*t was raining. Again. Hard and relentless.

Sally Elliot gazed out the window of Bloomingfield Candy Shop, the shop that she'd owned for nearly a decade.

From high school onward, she'd become passionate about candy making and dedicated all her efforts into turning her dream into a reality. She'd prided herself on her strong work ethic, because surely success would follow. And her shop wasn't a franchise. The shop was her *own* business, started from scratch.

However, as in the case of many newbie business owners, she'd overestimated her sales and underestimated her costs.

Yet, her perseverance had eventually paid off.

Or rather, her perseverance *usually* paid off, except that … Well, except that if today was any indication of candy sales for the month of February, she was skating directly toward a patch of thin ice. If she plunged through, she'd be out of funds within six months.

With a nervous sigh, she glanced out the front window of her shop.

Anxious thoughts clustered in her mind, as they invariably did when sales were slow, and she did her best to banish them. It was a gray, rainy and steely afternoon. Therefore, she attributed the lack of sales to the bad weather.

Okay, fine. She turned away from the window. She could deal with bad weather.

However, she couldn't deal with the fact that the delivery of the specialty chocolate she'd ordered, in fact, *needed*, was late. Not thirty minutes late, or an hour, but an entire half day. And this was a rush supply, because she had underestimated the amount of candy that customers would pre-order for Valentine's Day.

She'd read in a business magazine that fifty-eight billion pounds of chocolate were purchased during Valentine's week. Well, she was nowhere near selling that amount.

Still, her store sold a lot of candy.

Ben, her older brother, stood beside a white display case in the middle of the store, holding his cellphone to his ear. He offered a trace of a smile, then sobered. His gaze flicked from her to the free foil-wrapped candy kisses they offered to customers near the cash register. Gift cards were also conveniently stacked for last-minute buyers, who were mostly men.

Sally shook her head. Surely there was some psychology behind that. Perhaps men didn't embrace the shopping experience like women did. Or perhaps they were procrastinators, because they didn't have the right mindset to shop.

She wouldn't know. She hadn't been part of the dating scene for many years. In fact, because she'd married so young, had she ever been part of the scene?

Ben muttered into his cellphone, glanced at her, and then away again. She blinked in confusion at his somber expression, pressing away the prickle of awareness that something might be wrong.

No. This day couldn't possibly get any worse.

She walked to the front of the store. The vibrant red lollipops, balloons and gaily packaged gifts she'd added to the entryway brought a grin to her face. Several displays enhanced the different types of chocolate in the shiny cases lining the walls, and all reflected the upcoming Valentine celebration. As a savvy businesswoman, she recognized that placing beautiful and enticingly wrapped candy boxes where they would easily be seen resulted in impulse buys.

She'd been pleased with the result, though now she wasn't so sure.

Was the staging too white? Too red? Too cutesy? Had the displays put buyers off from entering the store today?

Thoughtfully, she nibbled on her lower lip as she second-guessed herself.

Ben ended his conversation, then jammed his cellphone into his pocket.

She turned to him. "Are you finally finished with your conversation?"

"Yep." His voice was quiet, his gaze probing. "And can you do anything else besides look worried?"

Her seasoned eyes took in his uneasy expression. "Can you do something besides acting so secretive?"

"Okay, that's a fair question," he said, "but I expect an answer from you first."

"Why?"

"Because I asked you first."

"Alright." She shifted. "Does my nervousness show because of our lack of customers today?"

"A little. Actually, more than a little." His unswerving stare unnerved her. "You don't seem to enjoy anything fun anymore. Often, Maise and I have invited you to dinner, and you consistently refuse."

"What does that have to do with my looking nervous?"

"Everything. Your business shouldn't be the focus of your entire life."

"It isn't," she answered with a self-conscious laugh. "My daughter is."

"Along with your business."

"This conversation isn't fair, Ben. The biggest candy holiday of the year is looming and I can't deal with any more guilt. I'm extremely busy right now."

"You're always busy because you're a workaholic."

"Please, Ben, not again, although I realize you mean well." Sally stood straight in open rebellion, using the cool business tone she usually reserved for her suppliers when she haggled over snagging the best prices. "You and Maise can invite me when Valentine's Day is over. I guarantee I'll say yes."

"We'll see."

Despite the five-year age difference between them, their features were similar—both blue eyed, tall and lean. However, that was where the similarities ended, because Sally had been a tangle-haired blond adventurer in her youth, whereas dark-haired Ben was a stickler for following rules.

Nonetheless, Ben was her financial as well as emotional support. When her daughter, Clarissa, had been born prematurely, so tiny and swaddled in pink chenille blankets in a hospital isolette, her husband, Leon, had deserted them. At the tender age of twenty, Sally had become a single mother and consequently depended on Ben and her two sisters, because Leon had disappeared from her life. Several years later, nothing had changed except for her hasty divorce.

Once, as a teenage girl harboring romantic fantasies, she'd assumed that she and Leon shared a love that endured forever. After all, they'd dated since high school.

She'd been wrong.

For better or for worse. She shook her head in mock disgust at her naïve illusions.

"So on February fifteenth," Ben said, "you'll revert back to the optimistic sister I formally knew?"

"You've known me all your life."

"I mean the fun-loving adventurous girl before you became an entrepreneur." At her frown, he hastily explained, "Which will be great, because I've never seen you this jumpy and anxious, not even during the Christmas holiday candy season."

Sally stooped to rearrange the trail of pink and lavender paper hearts she'd secured to the front window. With dismay, she realized that one of the hearts had torn. Did she have any extra hearts left? She scrambled to her feet, intending to rummage through the back storage room.

"I'm jumpy and anxious," she clarified, "because I need that case of specialty chocolate for my newest candy-making project. And you still haven't answered *my* question, Ben. You're looking so ... secretive." Ben's gaze was downcast as she rushed past him. He didn't reply, but her mind was already racing toward the next task. "Moonglow Chocolatiers supplies the finest chocolate and I'm depending on them to come through with my rush order."

"You don't *need* specialty chocolate," Ben said. "You *want* specialty chocolate."

She swung around. "I've advertised my new chocolate creations since January, and there are outstanding orders. Not to mention our walk-in customers between now and February fourteenth. I can't produce dark shells for salted caramel infusion candy without bittersweet chocolate."

"What is infusion candy, anyway?"

"I explained to you yesterday. It's—"

"I remember."

"Do you, truly?"

"Well, I remember the candy part." He threw up his hands. "I admit my knowledge of candy would fit into—"

"A peanut butter cup."

"Right." He smirked. "But as co-owner of your shop, I have permission to be concerned about you. You're spending excessive time and energy focusing on your latest product and you're exhausted and overwhelmed."

"Once I hire the two additional new employees—"

"Both of whom you haven't found yet."

She pushed out a breath. "Then I'll be able to relax."

He quirked a dark eyebrow. "You're a go-getter, but lately you've taken on too much of the workload yourself."

"We own a candy shop, Ben. Valentine's Day is a significant holiday in our world."

"Why not promote our signature chocolate coffee fudge, instead?" He scanned the row of sugar-coated candy apples and the popcorn machine she'd recently placed next to the fudge presentation. "Our fudge won first place at the women's shelter candy-making contest in December, and since then sales have doubled."

Sally eyed the red and white bento boxes chock-full of their number one selling fudge positioned at the entrance. "Thanks to your fiancée, Maise."

"I attribute our success to your candy-making skills. Maise simply wrote an outstanding newspaper article that helped bring in customers."

"She also awarded our fudge first place."

"Maise wasn't the only judge at the women's shelter contest. The other two judges voted for our chocolate too."

Ben's cellphone rang, and he fished in his pocket.

"Again?" Sally asked.

With a quick nod, Ben flipped open the phone and swiveled from her.

When he finished speaking, he fidgeted, placed his phone on the counter next to the cash register, then unwrapped a candy kiss.

Sally's gaze shifted from the candy kiss to Ben. "Who called this time?"

"The same person as last time."

"And that same person is—?"

He popped the candy kiss into his mouth. "Do you want to sit down first?"

Her response was an exasperated glance. "I'd rather stand."

"Your specialty chocolate shipment is delayed. That was Joe, the delivery man. He phoned earlier too."

"Joe? Why? What happened?"

"We were trying to work out a plan, unfortunately without success." Ben chewed the candy, swallowed, then displayed a bright smile. "No use in fretting, though. Our store has plenty of chocolate to carry us through Valentine's Day."

Fretting? *Fretting*? Ben never used words like that. This was his way of avoiding, then softening the news she didn't want to hear. She stepped to the counter and concealed her distress by taking a brisk swallow of coffee that had turned cold. She grimaced. "Exactly how late is the shipment?"

"Joe's truck broke down in Evanville and he's grounded at a diner called Olive's. More significant is an update that the major highways are flooding."

She frowned and drew her cellphone from the pocket of her black slacks, scrutinizing the weather map. "Heavy rain is in the forecast, but the storm is west of here."

Her brother's penetrating blue eyes leveled on her. "Which means?"

"I'll get the order myself. That way, I can return to the shop tonight and begin making infusion candy." As he shook his head she reminded, "Outstanding orders to fill, remember?"

He didn't bother to assure her that she was right. He merely blew out a sigh.

"Will you pick up Clarissa?" Sally grabbed her pink water-repellent jacket from the coat rack and slid on a pair of yellow rain boots. "School dismisses at three o'clock."

"Certainly." Ben nodded. "Provided you give Maise and me permission to take her to dinner. We may head to The Pasta Junction and see Julie. Lorenzo will be there after he gets off work at the television station."

Julie, their sister, owned The Pasta Junction. Lorenzo Rossi was the local weatherman, and they'd been dating for a few weeks. They'd met when he booked her restaurant for a first wedding anniversary dinner, a surprise for his mother and new husband. Over the excuse of baking the perfect Italian cassata cheesecake, Lorenzo had seen Julie several times, and they'd dated ever since.

They both shared a variety of commonalties—their appreciation for fine food, all things Italian, and film noir, which Sally had never watched, although Julie and Lorenzo raved about the stylistic black-and-white films.

Someday, perhaps, when she had more time, Sally promised herself.

Pulling her attention to the present, she said, "Dinner for my daughter is mac and cheese. Nothing fancy. Believe it or not, Clarissa also likes steamed broccoli."

"Can you repeat where you're headed?" Ben asked.

"Olive's Diner." Sally caught her brother's concerned stare. "I'll return by eight o'clock tonight."

"Stick to the main route, 29A. And check Lorenzo's weather forecasts."

"I will. And stop worrying, big brother. I'll call Joe and

meet him at the diner." Sally schooled her features into a reassuring smile, waved her cellphone in the air, and scurried out the door.

CHAPTER 2

*I*f there was one thing Sally loved about Valentine's Day, it was chocolate. She sold the idea, the rich, velvety taste, to her customers—celebrating romance by gifting exquisite candy to a spouse or partner, or any loved one.

The entire holiday was appealing, although a man's love was something she hadn't experienced in ages. If ever, if she was honest with herself. The holiday had lost all significance when her ex-husband had bailed on her and their daughter. He'd gotten a preview of the responsibility of caring for a premature infant, which meant little sleep and a selfless attitude, and he'd wanted no part of it.

So much for a dedicated partner and lifelong commitment.

She sighed as she surveyed the wet roads ahead.

Lorenzo had predicted rough weather, the message flashing across her cellphone screen. Sometimes he was right, other times wrong. This time, unfortunately, he was right.

The lengthy day was taking its toll, and six o'clock showed on her car's dashboard by the time she neared the diner. Joe, the delivery driver, had acknowledged her phone call with gratefulness, and assured he'd meet her in the parking lot.

Dusk fell early on a chilly, rainy day in California, and the evening had darkened sooner than Sally anticipated. A slow-moving thunderstorm had followed her, and there had been no break in the icy-gray clouds. Mercilessly, rain pounded her windshield, and the concrete highway became slick, then muddied. As she drove, her gaze flicked repeatedly to the edge of the road as she dodged sizable tree branches.

She gripped the steering wheel tight against the blustery wind swaying her car, tuned her car radio to a traffic station and was immediately bombarded by a series of flash-flood warnings.

"Travelers on route 29A are advised to choose another route." The announcer issued the advisory in a somber tone.

Her car crested the last hill. A neon sign back-lit in green blinked *Olive's Diner*, and soft light beckoned from the large paneled windows. The exterior walls in reflective silver reminded her of a favorite 1950s diner she'd frequented as a child, and she anticipated a blue plate special of savory meat loaf and creamy mashed potatoes, topped with homemade brown gravy.

She drove into the parking lot, relieved to spot the Moonglow Chocolatiers truck. The driver's door snapped open and a short, stocky man slid out. Wearing eyeglasses and a jovial expression, he hailed her. "Sally Elliot?"

She zippered up her raincoat, secured the hood, and stepped from her car. Several other vehicles, including an outdated pickup truck, were parked nearby.

"I'm here!" she called as he darted toward her. Horizontal, icy pellets of rain whirled around them.

"I'm Joe." He gestured upward. "The tree branches are

swinging like crazy. I heard on the radio that the wind gusts could reach forty miles per hour."

She brushed away the cold raindrops hitting her cheeks, tightened the raincoat's hood sheltering her head, then jammed her hands into her pockets. "Yes, I heard the same."

"I'll hurry and load the chocolate into your car, ma'am. Thanks for driving here."

"You're welcome." *Really, she'd had no choice, because she needed the chocolate now.* "I didn't want this shipment delayed another day." She peered toward the road. Here in the blinding rainstorm, everything blurred.

"As soon as you're finished, I'll be on my way back to Bloomingfield," she said. "If it's okay, I'll stay in my car to avoid the rain."

A cracking sound, then a creak, prompted them both to spin. A gigantic tree fell across the highway with a crash resembling a thunderous roar. It was so close that, for several seconds, Sally feared the diner had been hit.

Fortunately it hadn't.

However, the tree blocked her way home.

In the ensuing seconds of stunned silence, she heard herself gasp, scarcely audible above the whistling wind. A chill shivered up her spine as noise and chaos erupted around her.

A young couple rushed out of the diner. They gaped in disbelief at the fallen tree, shouting in shrill voices that they were phoning the police while signaling to Sally and Joe to hurry inside.

Joe's eyes widened as he gaped at the wide tree limbs spread across the road. "Wow, that's a huge tree. You won't be returning to Bloomingfield tonight," he said. "Let's get inside with the other stranded folks."

For a few seconds, Sally lacked the ability to utter a

coherent sentence. Absently, she rubbed her arms, then reached inside her car to retrieve her tote bag.

The only word she'd heard was *stranded.* With an unfocused stare, she darted a gaze toward the tree, then Joe, then the diner. The neon green sign was still blinking, so the diner hadn't lost power.

"You'll like the cook," Joe was saying. "We chatted before you arrived, and he's a good guy."

No, no, no. Good guy or not, this tree had to fall now? The same question raced over and over in her mind.

"The cook. Right," she tonelessly replied, realizing her voice shook. "Where is he? Didn't he hear the noise?" She dragged her thoughts from a situation she couldn't control and sprinted with Joe across the parking lot.

"Okay, Olive," she muttered to herself as they entered and stamped their wet boots in the entryway. "I hope you serve meat loaf." She envisioned a burly cook sporting a straggly white beard, a dirty apron tied around his protruding belly.

Joe shrugged off his jacket and swung it over a coat rack. He beamed at a well-dressed woman and slid into her booth. Eagerly, his voice raised above Elvis Presley crooning from the wall-mounted juke box, as Joe embellished the events that had taken place. The young couple that had raced outside were already snuggled in a corner booth. They bid Sally a quick wave.

"Are you all right?" the young woman asked. Her midlength chestnut-colored hair was damp from the rain. On her porcelain cheeks was a hint of red blusher.

"Yes, yes, I'm fine." Sally offered a nervous laugh, then raised her voice for the benefit of the man who had emerged from the kitchen and had begun brewing coffee behind the counter. "Oh, hello."

He curved around. "Hi. Glad you were able to get out of the rain."

Rain? His calm statement snapped the last thread of her reserve. "Are you aware a tree fell in front of the diner?"

"Yes. I was in the back room when it happened. The police have been called. You're safe here."

"Safe?" she parroted, surveying the oversized booths with seats covered in green plastic. The pink lights shining over each booth was casting the diners in rose-colored puddles of light. "This diner could blow … all the way to Kansas."

"No wicked witches here, and I assure you that you're not in Oz," the man countered. "This building has been standing here for a hundred years, and will be here long after we're gone."

"Now that's reassuring."

"No worries." His tone was composed, his manner amiable.

The first thing she noticed about him was his eyes. They were a wonderful hazelnut brown, shining and welcoming. He wore a smile which he freely extended. He was tall, muscular, and well-toned.

"I assume you're the cook?" she asked.

"Yes."

"Is the owner here?"

He sent her a brief grin. "You're looking at him."

Her lips parted. He looked too young to own a restaurant. She guessed him to be in his midthirties. But then again, she was young too, approaching thirty, having opened her shop several years earlier.

She tugged off her raincoat and draped it over a stool, apologizing for the puddle pooling on the black-and-white square tile flooring beneath her feet.

"It's all right. Tile is easy to clean." He gestured outside to the incessant rain. "I'm surprised anyone is out driving on a night like this."

"Well, I had no choice." She again glanced about the diner,

at the youthful couple nestled close together in their booth and the smartly dressed older woman wearing camel wool slacks and a cream-colored cardigan. She'd been sitting alone before Joe took a seat across from her. Now they were thoroughly engaged in conversation and didn't seem to notice anyone else.

"I don't know about the others," Sally continued. "I'm sure they have their reasons for being here."

"It's probably because of my food." The owner's lips quirked into a smile. "Why else would anyone venture out in a severe storm?"

"Chocolate," Sally murmured. "If they desperately needed a shipment of chocolate."

"Ah, chocolate, the ideal sweet treat." Amusement laced his deep voice. She noted that he didn't remark on her use of the word *desperately*. "But you can't beat a diner for a plentiful, wholesome American meal."

"Oh, but you can," she said.

"Excuse me?"

"I beg to differ. My sister, Julie, owns a fine dining establishment called The Pasta Junction. She serves homemade fettuccini."

"The restaurant is located in Bloomingfield, correct?"

"Yes, have you ever visited?"

"This diner keeps me in Evanville most days."

"My sister's latest addition is a brick pizza oven."

The result had been pizzas with a smoky wood flavor and charred crust that had quickly become a town favorite. Certainly, authentic Italian food beat a greasy diner any day.

When her gaze flew to his, she could tell by his smile that, to her intense relief, he hadn't read her thoughts.

"Emily comes here every evening and eats dinner." He gestured toward the booth where Joe and Emily sat.

"Rain or shine, apparently," Sally said.

"Apparently." He chuckled. "The kissing couple are on their honeymoon and were passing through town when the storm hit. They said they wanted to drive across America and discover new places—wherever their travels took them."

"They obviously aren't planners," Sally said.

"They told me they love being spontaneous."

"I prefer an organized agenda. I'm more productive and efficient that way." Sally turned toward the couple, then back to him. He was studying her with a concerned frown.

"Spontaneous individuals have more fun," he said.

"But planning ahead yields better results."

"Like encountering fallen trees, for instance?" he asked. "The best laid plans of mice and men often …"

"Often go astray," she finished.

"Awry."

"Yes, well, I'm familiar with that saying." To avoid the debate, she shifted. "Do you have many steady customers?"

"Thankfully, yes."

"So it gets busy here at times?"

"At times." That smile again. For a long moment he studied her, a warm look in his eyes.

Without warning, her heart began beating uncontrollably.

"A calm and deliberate pace wins the race," he continued.

"Another saying?"

"One of my own. And, a well-fed, contented customer will return."

"That's two sayings."

He shrugged. "I suppose, but they're both important."

She started to contradict him. A quick pace wins the race, she wanted to inform him. Instead, she toyed with the leather tote bag slung over her shoulder.

"Do you agree?" he inquired.

"No, sorry, I don't. At least, not with your first saying.

Calm and deliberate won't fly in our fast-paced world where customers are constantly in a hurry."

"We'll just have to agree to disagree, then."

This time she didn't respond immediately, her attention captivated by his tousled rich-brown hair and the shadow of a dark beard. High cheekbones and an angular jaw brought one thought to mind: he was beyond handsome, and because of her preoccupation with the fallen tree and her plans going off-center, she hadn't noticed his athletic good looks until now.

She flushed as they locked gazes. "If the saying applies to your diner, that's all that matters."

For you. Not for me.

She squinted at her watch, then at the bakery case filled with a selection of breads, including sourdough and whole wheat; a coconut layered cake and cherry pie; and a dozen chocolate chip cookies. She surveyed the fake potted lilacs adorning each booth, the thick tan-colored curtains hanging from the windows. An antique cash register was situated at the far end of the counter. Coins from the young couple jingled into the juke box as they picked out songs, and Dolly Parton replaced Elvis, singing about working nine to five.

"This is a nice highway for a diner," Sally remarked. Again, she shifted. Brilliant, Sally, just brilliant. Who used the word *nice* to describe a highway? She put on a smile. "Did you decorate the place yourself?"

"Hardly. My sister helped me." With an easy grace, he collected her coat and hung it on the rack by the door. "Please forgive my manners. I should have taken your coat sooner."

That wasn't his job, which she voiced aloud.

"My pleasure," he responded.

She trailed him and stole a glance in the mirror near the doorway, critically appraising her hair, which always curled when wet. She was forced to wait and see how it behaved when it dried and hoped that tonight it wouldn't spin into a super frizzy mess. Scrutinizing her reflection, she knew that the endless nights she'd worked late had deprived her of much-needed sleep, subsequently leaving shadows beneath her eyes.

The man turned, his smile ever-present.

She felt her cheeks heat.

"Is your name … Olive?" she asked. *Another stroke of brilliant conversation, Sally. Surely he'd named the diner after his sister.*

"Nope. I'm Oliver Menroe."

"And your sister?"

"Her name is Amy." Those brown eyes of his, so cordial and reassuring. She couldn't drag her gaze away. "And you are …?"

"Sally. Sally Elliot."

"*Miss* Sally Elliott?"

"Yes."

"I'm glad to hear that."

She paused, surprised by his remark, but decided it was nothing more than courteous flirtation with a potential customer. Still, her mind scrambled for a subject change. "So the name Olive is …?"

"The name from the previous owners. They were Italian and thought *Olive* had a nice ring to it."

"Didn't you want to add the *r* to the end of the word when you bought the place? There's a big difference between Olive and Oliver."

"The customers don't mind. It's a standing joke around here." Oliver wiped his hands on his clean white apron. *Clean,* completely shattering her preconceived notions of a short-order cook working at a diner in the middle of nowhere.

She pulled her cellphone from her bag and dashed off a text to Ben, explaining she was detained because of a fallen tree, had met Joe, the delivery man, and that they were both safely inside Olive's Diner.

Give Clarissa my love, she finished. *Is she having fun?*

A blast, Ben replied. *She's devouring a box of specialty infusion chocolates. (Kidding, kidding.) Let me know when you get back on the road. Maise and I will take care of Clarissa tonight and put her to bed. I have a key to your apartment, so don't fret.*

Fret again. Sally grinned and thanked him.

She snapped the phone shut and excused herself to freshen up in the restroom, then reentered the dining room. Although the diner was somewhat rundown and the fan above her didn't appear to spin, none of this took away from the inviting interior. Enticing whiffs of freshly ground coffee and buttery yeast rolls made her mouth water. She hadn't eaten since noon, an eggplant parmigiana takeout sandwich from her sister Julie's restaurant, and a cup of cold coffee.

Oliver strode into the open adjoining kitchen and stirred an enormous pot on the stove. Then he returned to stand behind the counter.

Sally indicated the display case, because she loved sweets. "Do you bake, Oliver?"

"I outsource to a woman in town because I realized my limitations early on. Would you like a chocolate chip cookie?"

"Certainly." She settled on a stool. "Thank you."

"I have a Greek salad in the cooler that's all made up."

"Perfect." Gratefully, she accepted the cookie while he arranged and garnished the salad, then set it, a glass of water, and a white paper napkin from the dispenser in front of her.

She flattened the napkin on her lap and bowed her head to offer a prayer of thanks to God. "How long have you been in business?" she asked.

"Five years." He shifted and switched on the grill. "Do you like your eggs over easy? I use fresh ingredients from the locals. Farm-to-home is a term I employed before it became trendy."

"Scrambled eggs are my favorite, but I'm already enjoying a salad and cookie, remember?

"Indulge me."

Sally wasn't up to disputing with him. Besides, she was still hungry, and it was hard to resist the intoxicating aromas of fresh coffee, grilled hamburgers, and butter-topped biscuits. She took a swallow of water. "I like my eggs with toast. I love toast."

"Wheat or white bread?"

"Do you have rye bread?"

"Of course." An enigmatic lazy smile crossed his lips while he scanned her features. She had the surprising notion that he was delighted she was sitting and talking with him, a notion that was highlighted when he lifted a loaf of rye bread in the form of a salute. "May I say, Sally, that you look lovely when your blond curls frame your face."

Her pulse fluttered. She'd never been complimented by a man waving a loaf of rye bread, but somehow his comment meant a great deal.

Somehow, she knew his compliment was heartfelt.

Wait. She set down her glass. Her curls framed her face? That meant her hair was a mass of oversized, wiry waves. She yanked at a curl near her cheek and watched it spring back into place. She really needed to look into purchasing a hair straightener.

"Well, okay, thank you," she said softly, then dug into her salad.

"Can you give me a minute before I cook your eggs?" he asked.

"Absolutely. I need more than a minute to digest."

Oliver started toward the dining room with a pot of coffee, refilling cups and talking with the customers. There were only a handful, Joe and Emily and the newlyweds, but he treated each person as if they were the most important one in the room, stopping to listen, nodding and optimistically commenting.

"You don't employ anyone else, Oliver?" Sally asked when he came back behind the counter. As he poured coffee for himself, then set the pot on the burner, she noticed the way his white T-shirt fit across his broad shoulders. He was strong and muscular, as if he routinely exercised each day.

"I have a dishwasher, hostess, and several local waitresses," he replied. "Because those raindrops were getting as big as hailstones, I sent everyone home early."

Five minutes later, he set a plateful of steaming scrambled eggs, two slices of buttered rye toast, and a mug of coffee next to her salad. She eyed the mug, and he smiled. "I assumed you may want coffee, because it might be a long night."

"Thanks."

"Cream and sugar?"

"Black is fine."

"Me too." He rolled his coffee mug between his palms. "Joe and I chatted a while before you arrived. He told me you own a candy store, and he was on his way to deliver wholesale chocolate to you."

"Then you know my story."

"Yes, I expect I do, but I'm always interested in learning more."

About her?

She fell silent, sipping her coffee, and evaded questioning why he might be so interested. Perhaps he simply craved conversation. Long hours in a diner might cause him to become lonely and disconnected. Sometimes in her candy shop, a sense of isolation would sweep over her, prompting her to phone one of her siblings. She wondered if Oliver felt the same.

"There isn't much else to say," she replied.

He splashed more coffee into her mug. "I didn't mean about your business. I meant about you."

She gave a little laugh and decided to talk about her business again. "When Joe's truck broke down, he phoned my brother Ben. I drove here to pick up the chocolate for my special infusion candy, because I couldn't wait another day for the delivery."

Oliver popped two more slices of toast into the toaster, then regarded her. "Ironic, because the tree fell unexpectedly and you're delayed, anyway."

There was something about the matter-of-fact way he described her situation, something about his easy manner and intoxicating grin that triggered a sudden, irrepressible, and, considering the turn of events, curious response from Sally. She began chuckling. And then she began laughing so hard, tears coursed down her cheeks. Her ribs still hurt from laughing when Oliver walked over carrying another plate of buttered rye toast.

A minute later, he seated himself on a stool next to her with a second mug of coffee, joking with her because she couldn't choose between a slice of coconut layered cake or cherry pie for dessert.

"Try both." He swallowed some coffee and put the mug aside.

Deliberately, she turned to gaze at him. "Honestly, Oliver, you believe in feeding your customers extraordinarily well."

His gaze never left hers. "That's my saying, remember?" She smiled at his contagious good nature and attempted to match his humor. "One of your many sayings," she reminded.

He stood to clear away her dishes. "By the way, being that

you seem to want to focus only on business, what is infusion candy?"

She laughed and dismissed his inquiry with a wave. "Never mind. Let's just say it's a fancy specialty candy."

With the plates in his hands, he paused to consider her—from the top of her wavy hair which surely resembled a lion's mane by now, to the toes of her rain boots.

Another bewildering tingle went through her. She shook her head, mystified at her reaction to this man.

"You own Bloomingfield's Candy Shop," he said.

"Yes. I assumed you knew that from your conversation with Joe."

"I didn't piece everything together until now. Your picture and an article were featured in the newspaper at Christmastime. I thought I recognized you from some-where." Across the two feet between them, their gazes held, the silence punctuated by the newlyweds giggling and smooching, Joe and Emily chatting quietly, and Patsy Cline singing from the juke box about falling to pieces. "In any event, we're both in the food service industry, so we can commiserate about the long hours. And speaking of which, I'd better put more coffee on."

Sally smiled as he stepped behind the counter, and she stood to wander to the window. Through the rain-streaked glass, she located the large tree, the lifeless limbs lying across the road. Fortunately, the Department of Transportation, truck lights flashing a dull yellow, had arrived.

After a few moments, Oliver walked over to join her.

"How long does it take to remove a tree?" she asked.

"First, the DOT will check to be sure the tree hasn't hit any power lines," he said. "We have power, so the electric company won't be called in."

"How long?" she repeated.

"Are you in a hurry?"

"You know I have a candy shop to run. More important, my seven-year-old daughter is at home. My brother and his fiancée are watching her tonight."

"You didn't mention you had a daughter. What's her name?"

"Clarissa." Sally pulled her cellphone from her pocket and scrolled through the pictures, opening a recent one where Clarissa, pink-cheeked and giggling, was sliding down a slide in the town park. Her hands were raised in utter delight. She'd skinned her knee that day, and Sally had held and comforted her in a steady grip, never wanting to let go.

"She's adorable." Oliver peered over her shoulder as she pointed to the photo. "As an aside, I thought you were a *miss*."

"I am." Sally slipped the cellphone back into her pocket. "I'm divorced."

"Me too. No kids for me, unfortunately."

Unfortunately? This tall, handsome man liked children? She couldn't stop from voicing her inquiry aloud.

"Of course. Who doesn't like children?" His expression gentled. "I wanted kids desperately. My ex-wife, however, had other plans, which included running off with my best friend."

"I'm sorry. Were you married long?"

"Two years. You?"

"I married my high school sweetheart." She sighed. "We were young, and when Clarissa came along … It's complicated."

"That's life. In the end, it's all about living life and appreciating every moment."

This was the time for her to utter something profound and witty, but all she did was nod in agreement.

"Even if life is chaotic and unpredictable?" she asked.

"It's the journey that matters," he said softly.

She stared out the window at the rain streaming down

the glass, the blinking yellow truck lights as crewmen moved debris to the grassy shoulder.

"At any rate," Oliver continued, "the DOT will cut the tree into pieces and stack it on the side of the road, which will be challenging, because this road isn't very wide. To answer your question, plan on a two-or three-hour wait, depending on how quickly the work progresses. The police must have directed traffic off the last exit."

Frustrated, she expelled an impatient breath.

"Can I get you more coffee?" He headed toward the counter.

"Thank you." She trailed him and reclaimed a stool.

He replenished her mug, then again carried the coffee pot from customer to customer, refilling their mugs, chatting, offering food. His manner was jovial and inviting. He focused his attention outward, on his customers, ensuring they were satisfied.

"Still hungry?" he asked, when he returned to Sally. "Can I get you anything else? I'm used to preparing a lot of orders quickly, but apparently not tonight."

"Honestly, I'm stuffed." She raised her mug in a toast. "My sincere compliments. Oliver. Everything you served is delicious."

"My world-famous vegetable soup will be done in a few hours. You can have a bowl then."

"World-famous?" she teased.

"Well, in this town, anyway."

"I'd love some, but I expect I'll be long gone by the time it's finished." She peered at her watch. "I meant to ask you earlier—no meat loaf and mashed potatoes on your menu?"

"Of course." He grinned. "It's not on the menu because customers know I have it."

"Telepathy?"

"Something like that." He laughed out loud, full and hearty. "I can heat a plateful, if you'd like."

She chuckled and patted her stomach. "Perhaps another day."

"I'll prepare any meal, if I have the ingredients on hand. That's my saying."

"I thought your saying was 'Calm and deliberate wins the race'?"

He shrugged.

Comically, she raised her eyebrows. "How about your other saying that a well-fed, contented customer will return?"

He seemed to be trying to keep his features straight. "I suppose I have three sayings, then."

She chuckled. "What's in your soup?"

"You name the vegetable—"

"Onions, celery …" she began.

"And my homemade beef broth, potatoes and carrots." Lightly, he touched her arm before pointing to the kitchen. It was friendly and casual, yet her pulse fired into a tailspin. "Can you guess the best thing about my soup?"

"Oliver, I'm not good at guessing."

"Tonight, the soup is on the house." His grin was boyish for such a confident, compelling man. "In fact, everything I've provided is on the house."

"Absolutely not. I can pay for my own food."

"I insist."

"Why?"

"Because you're the prettiest woman I've seen all day." He dragged up a stool to perch closer to her. "Correction. You're the most beautiful woman I've ever met."

"And you're staring at me because—"

"I told you why."

Self-consciously, she patted her hair. Sure enough, it had

frizzed. "Thank you," she murmured, although she suspected she'd never looked worse.

"Tell me again why you're so eager to get back to Bloomingfield?" he asked.

"My daughter Clarissa is reason number one."

However, contemplating the hundreds of jobs awaiting her made Sally anxious. She chewed her bottom lip and took in the diner's coziness, the patrons sipping coffee and speaking quietly among themselves. The unhurried pace was quiet and relaxing.

"From what I understand," Oliver said, "your daughter is safe with your brother and his date. So again, what's your hurry to travel on these unsafe roads?"

"My candy shop's orders have exploded since the December newspaper article, and I've publicized a unique new product, which is why I came here tonight. Joe's truck—"

Oliver's quick nod interrupted her. "I was delighted to hear his story."

He was a good listener. Not many men possessed that quality. Not many *folks* possessed that quality. Most wanted to talk only about themselves. But with Oliver, she felt like she could chat with him for hours.

"In summary, I have hundreds of orders." She stared at him, stared down at her coffee. She hadn't intended to talk about her shop, but the shop was always on her mind.

"Therefore, it's a bad thing to have all this new business and the subsequent profits that go along with it?"

"No, of course not." She grabbed a napkin from the dispenser and dabbed at her mouth. "You're an entrepreneur. You of all people should understand."

"Aren't you thrilled to earn a living doing what you love?"

"I'm extremely grateful. It's just that so many rely on me

—my employees, my customers, and everyone else along the supply chain. It's an enormous responsibility."

He scrubbed a hand over his face. "Your candy shop sounds tremendously successful."

She paused, realizing her unintended implication—that because his diner was modest, he didn't have the same pressures she did.

"Oliver, I apologize," she said.

He eased the awkward moment with a smile, then answered the cellphone buzzing in his jean pocket. After an abrupt conversation, he clicked off the phone.

"Excuse me. I need to pull together an order for takeout."

"Go ahead. I'll attend to the customers."

"Thanks, Sally." Oliver excused himself and hastened into the kitchen.

CHAPTER 3

$\mathcal{E}$mily, who had been sitting with Joe, stood. She flattened the creases in her tailored slacks, and her booted heels assertively clicked on the tile floor as she made her way to Sally. Joe grabbed a newspaper and sank back into the booth.

"I'm Emily Varon, as you probably know." She accompanied her introduction with a vibrant smile and direct eye contact. Something about her understated beauty, the cream-colored wool cardigan contrasting with her dark skin, her friendly mannerisms and overall interest, made Sally feel at home.

"I'm Sally Elliot."

"It's lovely to formally meet you, Sally."

In view of Emily's gracious greeting, Sally extended a smile in return. "I admired your outfit when I walked in," she said. "You are stunning and entirely put together."

With a toss of perfectly coiffed platinum-silver hair, Emily chuckled and sat straight and proper on the stool next to Sally, her hands clasped neatly on her lap. "You mean for a woman of a certain age."

"What I meant was … you carry an aura of self-confidence."

"At seventy years old, I'm finally content with myself. Along the way, I've learned that women are beautiful no matter their age." Emily motioned toward the honeymooners cuddling and kissing, whispering and laughing. Once in a while, they paused to take a selfie. "Earlier, those two told me they've been together from the time they were in high school. They'll share many joys and sorrows." Wistfully, she exhaled. "There's something magical about a first love."

Sally flinched. For her, the couple was a painful reminder of her own marriage gone wrong, and the emptiness that had followed her for years. Not once since the final evening when Leon left had she wept, but in turn, a massive weight of sadness and heartache had accumulated inside her.

"My experience with first love didn't work out," she said quietly.

"You were married?" Emily inquired.

"And divorced. I took my maiden surname. I'm an Elliot again."

"It's your last love who truly matters." Emily's blue-eyed gaze fixed on Sally, as if she were seeking something. "He's the man to treasure."

Sitting on the sidelines of love, Sally attempted a serene smile.

"I overheard some of your conversation with Oliver. I wanted to come over earlier, but you two were so intent on each other, I didn't want to interrupt."

Sally rolled her eyes, an attempt at dismissing any attraction she might feel for Oliver. "I wouldn't say that."

"I would." Emily flicked a glance toward the kitchen. "At my age, I don't apologize for eavesdropping. Perhaps you should get to know a person before deciding who they are."

"I agree." Sally pinched the bridge of her nose and briefly

closed her eyes. "My comments to him about my candy shop being so busy were thoughtless."

In all honesty, his remarks to her were insightful—about being grateful and connecting with men and women and families. He stirred her to reflect on where she put her energy these days. Orders were at an all-time high. So why was she stressed and unhappy?

An older couple wandered into the diner, and Sally stood, excusing herself from Emily and taking it upon herself to greet the couple. The man, she noted, walked with a shuffle and used a cane.

"Hello, and welcome to Olive's Diner. Please sit anywhere." Sally gestured to an empty booth near the juke box.

"We were stopped by the fallen tree." The woman shrugged off her tan-colored raincoat and draped it on the seat beside her. "We came off a side road, and the police refused to wave us any farther."

"Can I get you anything?" Sally asked. "Coffee? Food?"

"I'm starved." The man's spotted, aged hands splayed across his chest. "We drove quite a while."

"Harold, we were on the road ten minutes. We've been married over thirty years and rarely agree on anything." His wife snorted with dismissive amusement, then leaned back and pulled her thin mouth into a scowl. "I'll just have coffee."

There was no similarity between them, Sally thought, as sometimes happened when men and women were married a long time. The wife was thin, gray-haired, and under five feet tall, whereas her husband was a solid foot taller and at least one hundred pounds heavier.

"What do you have to eat?" the man asked.

"You've eaten too much today already," came his wife's reply.

He set his cane beside him and removed his cap, revealing

the polished brilliance of his bald head. "You call that bowl of cereal this morning a meal?"

"You're forgetting you ate a massive lunch."

"Let me see what the owner recommends." Sally held up the couple's bickering with a smile. "I'll return shortly."

When Sally stepped into the spotless kitchen, the mouthwatering aroma of vegetable soup flooded her nostrils. On a large stainless steel table, Oliver was arranging a dozen sandwiches, some with meat and cheese, others peanut butter and jelly, as well as apple slices and shortbread cookies. On the side were twelve bottles of water.

"That's quite a takeout order," she said.

"Cora, the friend who phoned, runs a daycare center not far from here," he replied. "She's in a frenzy because of the storm. I wanted to prepare food that appealed to everyone."

"Wow, I'm impressed at how quickly you worked."

"Thanks. That's why I'm called a short-order cook." A lazy smile swept over his face. "Everything under control out there?"

"Two more customers arrived. Can you suggest what I can serve? They can't decide."

"How about a couple of deli sandwiches and two slices of cherry pie?"

"I'll check." Sally scurried to the couple, got their drink orders and served them, then rushed back into the kitchen.

"They actually agreed," she joked. Quickly, she made up the two plates.

Meanwhile, Oliver, without rushing, deftly finished the sandwich preparation and began wrapping each in brown paper bags.

With a businesslike tenor in her voice, Sally asked, "Are you always this efficient?"

"Like everyone, I try my best."

This was Oliver, believing the good in everyone. She

studied him surreptitiously as she plated the couple's sand-wiches, then sliced two pieces of cherry pie.

Their mood of quiet camaraderie as they worked together, along with his heart-stopping grin and relaxed bantering, left her oddly unwilling to leave the confines of the kitchen. She was drawn to him, more and more for every minute they spent together. She knew he was thoughtful and considerate, his actions compassionate and kind-hearted. Beyond his handsome physique was an innate quality—a genuine caring about people.

Reluctantly, she placed the sandwich plates and slices of pie on a tray and headed for the dining room.

"I'll be in as soon as these sandwiches are wrapped," Oliver said. "Thanks for taking care of the orders for me."

"Absolutely."

A car pulled into the parking lot, stopping in front of the door. A thirty-something woman rushed inside as Oliver appeared with an armload of brown bags.

"I'm almost done, Cora. Give me a couple more minutes." He gestured to Sally. "But first, let me introduce you."

"I know Cora and I'll take it from here." Emily slid from her stool and walked over to Cora and Sally as Oliver returned to the kitchen. "Cora runs the daycare in town, and all the children love her. My neighbor's kids are always thrilled when they're dropped off there."

Cora raked a hand through her glossy brown hair, the short pixie cut accentuating her vivid amber eyes and creamy complexion. "I love watching these kids, they're like family to me. Some of them were a little frightened when the storm hit, but most are excited."

"Where are they now?" Sally asked.

"With my brother at the daycare. He helps me out sometimes."

"I have a daughter. Her name is Clarissa," Sally said. "She's not afraid of anything, except fireworks on the Fourth of July. Then she cries and puts her hands over her ears."

"What do you do to calm her down?"

"I give her a piece of fudge and tell her that it has a magical ingredient which will make her happy."

"Does it work?" Emily inquired.

"Most of the time. If anything, the candy distracts her," Sally said. "You see, I own a candy shop, thus a supply of chocolate fudge is usually in a box on my kitchen counter. Don't worry, Clarissa brushes her teeth afterward."

From the corner of her eye, Sally noted that a smiling Oliver had surfaced from the kitchen.

"Oliver, thank you," Cora said as he slipped the takeout containers into several bags. "The kids can't return home yet since their parents are trapped on the other side of that downed tree."

"Glad I can help. I'll carry these to the car for you."

"I'm fine, but thanks for your support." Cora drew a wallet from her purse. "How much do I owe you?"

"Nothing. My treat and my pleasure." As she left, his lips curved upward into a dazzling smile that he directed toward Sally. That smile—honest and sincere, with exactly the right touch of straightforwardness—prompted a warmth in the pit of her stomach. She was getting it: he had his community too. Moreover, his heart was generous and empathetic.

She returned his thoughtfulness with her own twinkling smile.

Emily swiveled to face Sally. "Explain what is so vitally important about this chocolate of yours that you had to come fetch it yourself."

"I'm creating an infusion candy which requires a certain type of bittersweet chocolate."

"What's infusion candy?" Emily crossed her arms. "Some sort of millennial fad?"

"No, it's not a fad. The process is somewhat complex, but the design is important. However, I'm not sure I'll get back to my store in time to produce all the candy."

"How about a trade?" Oliver still stood by the doorway with them. "You can use my kitchen to create your candy. Afterwards, you can try my soup, which I guarantee is the most delicious taste in the world."

"Better than my signature fudge?"

"Yup."

She shook her head. "I doubt you have everything I need for my specialty chocolates."

"How about regular candy?" He grinned. "Specialty is overrated."

"We like peanut butter cups," the honeymooners chimed from their booth. Apparently the patrons were delighted to listen to each other's conversations, Sally mused.

"I stock jars of peanut butter," Oliver said. "And I have a recipe from my sister that calls for margarine and graham crackers and semisweet chocolate chips."

"I'm a candymaker."

"Peanut butter cups are candy," Emily pointed out.

"But my infusion candy uses high-quality bittersweet chocolate."

"Yes, yes, so we've heard." Emily looked so determined that Sally peered at her with a mixture of laughter and surrender.

"I prefer store-bought chocolate chips, of which I have plenty," Oliver broke in. Gently, he touched Sally's cheek, guiding her to gaze at him. "Sally Elliot, I challenge you to prepare a batch of peanut butter cups in my kitchen. In fact, I predict our candy will be better than your infusion … whatever."

"*Our* candy?"

"A blending of two magnificent cooks' expertise."

His blunt response made her laugh. Her spirit crazily soared. Despite the exhausting workdays, he'd thrown down a gauntlet she couldn't resist picking up.

Tamping down her smile, she quickly texted her brother, telling him she would be late. She looked up at Oliver. "In that case, I accept your challenge."

This was a decisive decision for her, and she could feel herself poised on the threshold of an unforgettable evening. Granted, she wouldn't be making specialty chocolate, but she was creating something better. Memories.

Since Leon, she'd held men at a distance, but with Oliver she felt safe. She enjoyed being near him—the way he put others before himself, his selfless manner, his witty responses. And the way he looked, as if he'd materialized from a Hollywood magazine with his effortlessly attractive features.

"Good. I'll help you." Oliver's mouth quirked in a smile. "We can enhance the semisweet with a few pieces of your fancy bittersweet candy if you'd like."

"And I'll pour our little group of diners more coffee while Joe gets your chocolate," Emily said.

Joe returned with a pound of chocolate and handed it to Sally, but Emily stopped him from continuing on into the kitchen by grabbing his hand and leading him to a booth. "You two go ahead," she directed Sally and Oliver. "We'll be your taste testers when you're done."

"Shall we?" Oliver affectionately rumpled Sally's hair, then showed her the kitchen. The effect of his strong hand on her arm sparked sudden tears, and she swallowed the surge of grateful emotion in her throat.

Here in Evanville, this tiny diner and everyone in it had welcomed her, and she felt happier than she'd been in ages.

A few minutes later, she tugged her hair back with a

ponytail holder, rolled up her sleeves, and faced him at the sink while they washed their hands.

"I can't wait to watch you doing what you do best." He handed her a clean apron. "I never imagined the most prominent candymaker in Bloomingfield would be in my diner."

As she tied the apron about her waist, she quipped, "Be prepared to taste the finest candy Evanville has ever experienced. But only if you promise to help me with cleanup afterward."

He chuckled. "It's a deal."

CHAPTER 4

*C*ooking with Sally in his cozy diner proved strangely intimate, Oliver thought.

Hyper focused, Sally concentrated on melting and stirring chips and margarine, while Oliver spread thick chocolate into mini-muffin tins. He seldom spoke, allowing his cooking companion to work with no interruptions.

He attempted to concentrate, but in the comfortable ambiance of his kitchen, he was more absorbed in pondering the remarkable turn of fate that had caused Sally Elliot to wind up at his diner. For many reasons, beginning with his failed marriage, his first consideration was that it would have been better if Sally hadn't been stranded at his diner, because of his instant attraction to her.

However, after the last few hours establishing a friendship, she was compelling him to acknowledge and contemplate everything he'd missed since his divorce, and the fact that he'd hidden behind the familiar confines of his small-town diner.

A safe refuge. Not that there was anything wrong with that.

He gave himself a firm mental shake.

Nonetheless, he wanted to experience life again. And all this reflection had begun with a beautiful, vivacious, and intelligent woman who was busily creating candy across from him. She stopped in the process of stirring chocolate and raised her gaze to his, the color of her soft eyes reminding him of colorful blue cornflowers. Shiny, golden highlights around her face accentuated her ivory skin. Her lips were full, the perfect shade of pink.

"You're not spreading," she reminded.

"Sorry." He laughed. "By the way, do you want to sit down?"

"I'm okay." She hesitated, but remained doggedly standing. "Thank you for asking, though."

They exchanged cheerful nods and went quietly back to their tasks.

Deep in contemplation, he studied her.

What if she'd entered his diner two years ago, when his divorce was still raw? Would he have noticed her then, or would he have been wallowing in the hurt and disappointment, the mistrust of his once-wife leaving him for his best friend?

Would he have admired her high cheekbones and soft lips, her slim figure and gorgeous, thick hair?

He blew out a silent sigh. Yes, he concluded, he would have admired her charm, her straightforwardness, her work ethic. However, he wouldn't have taken the relationship any further.

Absently, he grinned at her offhand remark that if he chose to cook, he was also slated for cleanup duty. This woman drove a hard bargain.

She slanted him a teasing smile, gazing at him with those incredibly striking eyes. "Cat got your tongue, Mr. Oliver?"

He was so lost in his reflections, he jumped at her question.

"Some people like more chocolate, some less," he advised, waving his wooden spoon jokingly in the air.

"Shouldn't you use a measuring cup so that all the candy is even?"

He raised an eyebrow. "Nope."

"Well we're about out of semisweet chips." Sally plunked her hands on her hips. "What should we do with the leftover peanut butter mixture?"

"That's where your specialty chocolate comes in." He opened the box of bittersweet chocolate and spooned a modest amount into the semisweet chips. Deftly, he stirred, then heated the remainder.

"Innovation is the mother of—" he began.

"The saying is, 'Necessity is the mother of invention,'" she corrected, a smile flickering across her face. "However, you are an impressive innovator."

"A trait learned from my father. We were poor, so he learned to make do with what we had—simple, wholesome food. Although, observing and listening to you inspires me to want to pursue more formal chef training."

She beamed, the sort of beam that begins from within and cannot be contained. "You're an expert in your own right, Oliver."

She stood by his side while they continued to portion and bake. Continuously distracted by her, he admired the easy, natural way she handled herself in the kitchen—a pinch of this, a shake of that, then meticulously measuring the key ingredients. As he did his own mixing, he reminisced about his boyhood in Evanville and the happy-go-lucky days of his youth before his mother got sick, then his father, leaving him at an inexperienced age to raise a twelve-year-old sister.

Sally chatted about her daughter and touched on the piercing defeat of losing her husband when she'd needed him most, and Oliver's heart squeezed.

"Ben came to my rescue." Tears welled in her eyes, and she wiped them away with the back of her hand. "I'm sorry for getting so emotional."

"Please don't apologize," he said.

"All these years I've numbed my emotions and immersed myself in work."

"I completely understand," he commiserated. "Much the same happened to me." He was silent for a beat before setting down his spoon and tipping up her chin. "I imagine being a single mother isn't easy, but I bet you're the best mother in the world."

"Clarissa is my greatest reward." Sally's flawless complexion fairly glowed whenever she mentioned her daughter. Without hesitation, she continued, "Oliver, I was thinking."

"Forever dangerous where women are concerned." At her frown, he prodded, "Thinking about what?"

"When I leave here tonight, who will shower me with compliments?"

"Compliments will definitely be forthcoming." His heartbeat doubled as he shifted closer. For a moment, he debated. Should he kiss her? Was it too soon? They'd only met a few hours earlier.

He did kiss her, but opted for a sweet brush of his lips on her forehead.

"Hey, you two lovebirds! It's not Valentine's Day yet!" Emily burst into the kitchen with the others in tow. "How long does it take to make a few peanut butter cups?"

"The first batch is ready," Sally said.

Emily snatched one up. "Delicious," she declared, and the

newlyweds agreed as they shared bites. Joe grabbed two, stating that he deserved more than the others because he'd delivered the chocolate.

"Not quite all the way to my shop," Sally reminded him.

"Close enough," came his response.

"Too sweet," the older woman proclaimed, refusing to eat another bite.

"Not sweet enough," her husband declared, devouring an entire peanut butter cup and then seizing the rest of hers.

Oliver split a peanut butter cup with Sally. They stood closer together, his arm brushing against hers, the air between them fairly charged with an electrical current. He knew she recognized the change in their relationship from when she'd first scurried into the diner. He knew that as surely as he knew that he wanted to see her again, *planned* on seeing her again.

He wanted to appreciate the contagious ring of her laughter, their easy-going banter. He hoped to meet her adorable daughter.

And he wanted to feel her lips pressed against his.

Closing hour at the Bloomingfield Candy Shop couldn't arrive soon enough, Sally mused three days later. The last of the customers had picked up their orders, and there was scarcely a piece of candy left in the store.

Valentine's Day sales were a success.

Bone tired, she bent to arrange two red lollipops that had toppled over on the white display case. The chocolate coffee fudge had won out over her infusion salted caramel candies as the store's bestselling Valentine candy.

Her thoughts drifted to Olive's Diner, the night she'd been stranded.

Initially, she'd intended to bring home the peanut butter cups she'd prepared, but the candy hadn't made it out of the diner. The newlyweds, Emily, and Joe had waxed poetic about the flavor with every bite. The older couple, not so much.

She grinned. The wonderful people she'd met were the ideal antidote to her crazy work life. Since then, she decided she wanted other people's opinions of her products, that is, people who weren't in her business—her staff and candymakers.

She'd brought up the idea of monthly taste-testings to Ben, who, as she'd anticipated, had scolded her for taking on additional work. Nonetheless, she intended to go ahead with her new idea.

"*Spontaneous people have more fun,*" Oliver had said.

Still, planning was important if a person wished to get things accomplished.

Oliver. She had to put him out of her mind, but even while she told herself that, her musings returned to the diner.

By the time the tree in the middle of the road had been cleared, she hadn't arrived home until after midnight, with a case full of specialty chocolate, minus one pound.

She gathered a deep breath. Oliver hadn't texted her since she left Evanville, although he'd requested her phone number. Perhaps she'd return to his diner with Clarissa and order the meat loaf and mashed potatoes that wasn't on his menu.

"*It's not on the menu because customers know I have it,*" he'd said.

Truly the man needed someone to advise him on how to run a profitable business. And if he didn't contact her by the end of the week, she'd contact him.

No, no, she couldn't do that, a desperate attempt at a relationship with a man who might not be interested. She'd done that once already, and her marriage to Leon had almost destroyed her self-esteem.

She paused, her thoughts circling back to Oliver, as they often did. In the midst of an impromptu candy-making session, she'd found something she'd searched for her entire life.

Contentment. Joy in a simple project.

And maybe, just maybe, a good, sincere man.

"I'M LEAVING," Ben said. "Congratulations on a remarkably successful holiday." He grabbed his jacket. "Maise and I are dining out tonight."

"Is it one of her food critic jobs?" Sally asked.

"No. Although she does it for work, she loves going out for pleasure. Please join us."

"I can't." Sally declined with an apologetic sigh. "I'm committed to mac and cheese with Clarissa."

"Valentine's Day is over."

"I know, but barely."

"We're going to Julie's restaurant, and you love her home-made fettuccini."

"Some other night. Soon. I promise."

"That's what you always say," he reminded.

As he walked out the door, Sally called after him, "We'll take a raincheck."

Five minutes later, as she was rearranging a display that had little candy left, the bell on the door jingled, indicating one more customer. She stifled a groan. Hadn't Ben posted the closed sign?

"Sally?" The deep male voice made her pause.

She hesitated for a second before she spun. Her heart beat double time, taking in his strong, athletic features, his wonderful smile. "Oliver?"

"Your hair looks ... different. Wonderful."

There was no mistaking the huskiness in his tone. She couldn't free her stare from his intent gaze. "I used a hair straightener." She fingered a strand that had come loose from her ponytail. "Do you like it?"

"You look gorgeous, whether your hair is curly or straight." He strode to her, bearing a foil-covered plate. "I brought you something for Valentine's Day."

She stepped over to him, peering at the plate as he uncovered it. Peanut butter cups, unevenly spaced, some thicker than others.

"I've been trying these out for the past two days, incorporating some ideas you suggested about working with chocolate." He offered that boyish grin. "I'm not claiming these peanut butter cups are better than your fancy infusion candies, but ..."

As he chatted, she plucked up a candy and took a bite. "Oliver, this is amazing." She closed her eyes, allowing the flavors of peanut butter and chocolate to melt on her tongue.

"I used more sugar."

"Excellent." She grinned. "Perhaps we can start selling your peanut butter cups in my shop."

"Are they as delicious as my vegetable soup?"

"I don't know. I never had the opportunity to try your soup."

"I'll make it again." He set the candy aside, took her in his arms and brushed a kiss on her mouth. "Just for you."

Just for her. His words swirled around in her mind. His voice lowered, his gaze loving, his lips tasting of chocolate.

She drew a quiet, steadying inhale, shaking her head at

her resolutions to avoid love. With Oliver, there was no need for false pride and relationship games.

Because the truth was, in the short time she'd known him, she had begun to fall in love with him. And by his affectionate gaze, the romantic way he stroked her cheek, he felt the same about her.

"Happy Valentine's Day, Sally," he said. "And thank you."

She cleared her throat to prevent her voice from shaking. "Whatever for?"

"For coming into my diner. For looking beautiful and never missing a single step, no matter the obstacles. And for creating the most delectable candy in the world for me and my customers."

"Not as tasty as your diner food."

"Because diner food is the best." He laughed and linked his fingers through hers. "Miss Sally Elliot, about all that planning you do …"

She tipped back her head, smiling at him with wide-eyed innocence. "Me?"

"I'm available if you can squeeze me into your calendar." His tone was firm. He wouldn't allow otherwise. "And I'd love to meet your daughter."

"How about tonight?"

His gaze searched hers, glinting with amusement. "You're being spontaneous?"

"Absolutely. I'm picking Clarissa up at the sitter's in a few minutes." Quickly, Sally adjusted her plans. "How would you like to go to dinner with us at my sister's restaurant?"

"The Pasta Junction?"

"Everyone will be there. Ben and Maise, and Lorenzo, the TV weatherman. He and Julie are dating."

"Count me in." His deep voice had a precarious effect on her heart beat. "Sounds like the perfect Valentine's Day celebration."

She eyed his handsome features, his poignant smile, the look in his eyes—warm and inviting. He was her Valentine. Now and always.

Because, she realized, it's your last love who truly matters.

THE END

RECIPE FOR AMY'S PEANUT BUTTER CUPS

Bottom layer:

  2 sticks margarine melted

  1 18-ounce jar peanut butter

  2 sleeves graham crackers, crushed

  1 pound powdered sugar

Mix until well blended

Top layer

1 12-ounce bag semisweet chocolate chips

1 stick margarine

Melt together in the microwave for about 90 seconds, stirring halfway through.

Place bottom layer in the prepared tins and pour the top layer over it.

Prepare in mini muffin or regular sized tins. The thickness of the chocolate can be varied according to your preferences.

Can also be done in a 9x13 dish and cut into squares.

A NOTE FROM JOSIE

Dear Friends,

Thank you for reading *A Chocolate-Box Valentine*.

I wanted to write a Valentine romance centering around chocolate, which continues the story of my other *Chocolate-Box* books.

If you loved this romance as much as I loved writing it, please help other people find *A Chocolate-Box Valentine* by posting your review.

A Chocolate-Box Valentine is available in ebook, paperback, Large Print paperback, Hardcover, and Audiobook.

My Spotify Play List for A Chocolate-Box Valentine is here.

Want more of the Chocolate-Box Series?
Click here.

ACKNOWLEDGMENTS

An appreciative thank you to my patient husband, Dave, and our three wonderful children.

ACKNOWLEDGMENTS

An appreciative thank you to my patient husband, Dave, and our three wonderful children.

ABOUT THE AUTHOR

Josie Riviera is a *USA TODAY* bestselling author of contemporary, inspirational, and historical sweet romances that read like Hallmark movies. She lives in the Charlotte, NC, area with her wonderfully supportive husband. They share their home with an adorable shih tzu, who constantly needs grooming, and live in an old house forever needing renovations.

To receive my Newsletter and your free sweet romance novella ebook as a thank you gift, sign up HERE.

Become a member of my
   Read and Review VIP Facebook
   group for exclusive giveaways and FREE ARC's.

josieriviera.com/

josieriviera@aol.com

ALSO BY JOSIE RIVIERA

Seeking Patience

Seeking Catherine (always Free!)

Seeking Fortune

Seeking Charity

Seeking Rachel

The Seeking Series

Oh Danny Boy

I Love You More

A Snowy White Christmas

A Portuguese Christmas

Holiday Hearts Book Bundle Volume One

Holiday Hearts Book Bundle Volume Two

Holiday Hearts Book Bundle Volume Three

Holiday Hearts Book Bundle Volume Four

Candleglow and Mistletoe

Maeve (Perfect Match)

A Love Song To Cherish

A Christmas To Cherish

A Valentine To Cherish

A Christmas Puppy To Cherish

A Homecoming To Cherish

A Summer To Cherish

Romance Stories To Cherish

Romance Stories To Cherish Volume Two

Cherished Hearts Six Book Volume

Aloha To Love

Sweet Peppermint Kisses

Valentine Hearts Boxed Set

1-800-CUPID

1-800-CHRISTMAS

1-800-IRELAND

1-800-SUMMER

1-800-NEW YEAR

The 1-800-Series Sweet Contemporary Romance Bundle

Irish Hearts Sweet Romance Bundle

Holly's Gift

A Chocolate-Box Christmas

A Chocolate-Box New Years

A Chocolate-Box Valentine

A Chocolate-Box Summer Breeze

A Chocolate-Box Christmas Wish

A Chocolate-Box Irish Wedding

Chocolate-Box Hearts

Chocolate-Box Hearts Volume Two

Chocolate-Box Double Hearts

Recipes From The Heart

Leading Hearts

New Year Hearts

SENIOR HEARTS

Summer Hearts

Christmas in the Air (1-800-Book)

A Very Christian Christmas

Most books are available in ebook, audiobook, paperback, Large Print paperback and Hardcover.

Many are FREE on Kindle Unlimited!

www.ingramcontent.com/pod-product-compliance
Lightning Source LLC
Chambersburg PA
CBHW070805030726
47504CB00003B/701